PENGUIN BOOKS

THE BLUFFS

Kyle Perry is a drug and alcohol counsellor based in Hobart, Tasmania. He has grown up around the Tasmanian bush and seas, with the landscape a key feature of his writing and his spare time. He loves the sea, and his entire leg is covered in ocean tattoos.

His debut novel, *The Bluffs*, has been translated into five languages. It was shortlisted for the Dymocks Book of the Year, the Indie's Debut Fiction Book of the Year and Best First Novel at the International Thriller Writers Awards, and was longlisted for the Australian Book Industry Awards' General Fiction Book of the Year.

T0363029

THE BLUFFS

KYLE PERRY

PENGUIN BOOKS

PENGUIN BOOKS

UK | USA | Canada | Ireland | Australia
India | New Zealand | South Africa | China

Penguin Books is part of the Penguin Random House group of companies,
whose addresses can be found at global.penguinrandomhouse.com.

Penguin
Random House
Australia

First published by Michael Joseph, 2020
This edition published by Penguin Books, 2021

Cover design by Adam Laszczuk © Penguin Random House Australia Pty Ltd
Cover image courtesy Getty Images
Author photo by James Brewer

Typeset in Sabon by Midland Typesetters, Australia
Printed and bound in Australia by Griffin Press, an accredited
ISO AS/NZS 14001 Environmental Management Systems printer

A catalogue record for this
book is available from the
National Library of Australia

ISBN 978 1 76104 189 1

penguin.com.au

Firstly, to my family

I pay my respects to the Traditional Custodians of country, the Pallitore of the North tribe, who are the custodians of the Meander region. I pay my respects to the Elders past, present and emerging, to whom Kooparoona Niara – Mountain of Spirits – is of cultural significance.

I acknowledge today's Aboriginal community on all Lutruwita, who are the custodians of this island, and I recognise their continuing connection to land, waters, and culture.

Today I thought I saw him. He was at the tree line, watching the school. I think he saw me, and then he was gone.
Rose said I'm not the only one who's seen him.
I'm never leaving the house again.

From the diary of Victoria Compton, sixteen years old, one of the five girls taken during the 1985 abductions in the Great Western Tiers.

Up in the hills, he hides and kills.
Down in the caves, he hides and waits.
The Hungry Man, who likes little girls,
with their pretty faces and pretty curls.
Don't believe what the grown-ups say,
the Hungry Man will find a way.
So I won't walk alone by the mountain trees,
or the Hungry Man will come for me.

Schoolyard rhyme, found written on the wall of a girls bathroom, Limestone Creek District School, 1985.

PROLOGUE

ELIZA
Present day, the Great Western Tiers, Tasmania

The rain woke her.

She needs you.

Eliza opened her eyes. She was facedown in the gravel of the hiking track, the smell of wet earth in her nose.

You have to get up.

She sucked a breath through her teeth. Everything ached. The back of her head stung. Her glasses dug into her temple, the left lens cracked. Her puffer jacket and hiking tights were soaked through to the skin.

The icy mountain rain grew heavy, slapping against the gum leaves with the wind. A yellow wattlebird called off in the bush: the sound like a cork pulled from a bottle.

Get up. She needs you.

At the edge of the track grew a native laurel, peppered with white flowers. She leaned on it, dragging herself to her feet, spiky leaves cutting her palm, the crushed flowers releasing their sweet wild scent.

Her hiking boots were gone, her socks were gone, her feet numb and tinged blue in the alpine cold.

She spun, scanning the fog. The motion caused her skull to throb. She put her hand to the back of her head and it came away red.

She realised her honey hair was stuck to her cheeks by something sticky-brown. She pinched it away from her cheek, confused.

A human voice – distant, but growing closer.

Eliza froze. All her half-thoughts snapped into one decision. She lifted a white gum branch off the track: thick and smooth. She stepped into the ferns at the edge of the path, her clothes catching on the laurel. Was there a place she could hide? Did she really want to leave the track?

The sound of breaking branches behind her. 'Miss Ellis!'

Eliza shouted, spun, and swung her stick.

The figure – a teenage girl – scrambled back with a yelp.

'Jasmine!' Eliza could have cried with relief. 'No . . . Carmen?'

'You tried to hit me!' Carmen backed away, her long dark hair slick against her face. 'What the hell is wrong with you?'

The stick fell from Eliza's frozen fingers. 'I'm sorry.' She grabbed Carmen's wrist and pulled her closer, into the cover beneath the trees.

'You're freezing, Miss Ellis.'

The rain stopped, like a tap turned off. The bush was suddenly fog-quiet, save for gentle dripping. Waiting.

'Where are the others?' whispered Eliza.

'Everyone's at the bus, but they can't find Jasmine, Cierra, Bree or Georgia. Mr North says we need to call off the hike because of the storm. He's already called the bus.' Carmen seemed unaware her own voice had grown hushed. 'You weren't answering your phone. He sent me and Mr Michaels to find you.'

'No one has seen those girls?'

'Aren't they with you? Is it true there was a fight?' Carmen peered closer. 'Is that blood on your face?'

'Where's Mr Michaels?'

Carmen was looking at the blood, at the bruise on Eliza's face, at her cracked glasses. Realisation dawned.

'*Carmen*. Where is Jack – where is Mr Michaels?'

'We split up, he took another track. We've been looking for you for ages,' said Carmen. 'What's happened? *What's happened?*'

'You were on this path *alone*?' shouted Eliza, and Carmen scurried another step back, panicked.

Eliza's world lurched and she steadied herself against a gum tree.

Her phone buzzed in her pocket – maybe it had been buzzing the whole time and she hadn't noticed. She had to see to Carmen's safety first.

'Where's your phone, Carmen?'

'We left them at school,' said Carmen, voice shaking. 'We handed them to Mr North before we left. Oh, God. Don't you remember? Oh God, help . . . w-what happened to you? *Where are the others?*'

'Carmen, I need you to listen carefully . . . in just a moment, I need you to run back to Mr Michaels. *Run.* Don't stop for anything.' She picked up the stick she had dropped and handed it to Carmen. 'If you see anyone you don't know . . .'

'Miss Ellis?'

'If you can't find Mr Michaels, just run back to the bus. Stay away from *anyone* else. *Do you understand me?*'

'Wh-what's going on?' Carmen whimpered.

'Just wait there a moment.' Eliza answered her phone. 'Tom?' she said. 'Are all the girls back?'

'Eliza! Finally! Where the hell are you?'

'The *girls*, Tom.'

'We're still missing Georgia, Bree, Jasmine and Cierra. I sent Carmen and Jack to find you. Are they with you?'

'I'm sending Carmen to find Jack, and then back to you. If she's not there in the next fifteen minutes, lock the other girls in the bus and come looking. I don't know where we are right now.'

'We're j-just off the Lake Nameless trail,' stammered Carmen. 'W-west of it.'

Suddenly the rain started again, this time with ice in the water. Eliza's skin stung in the sleet.

'Carmen's coming from the western track of the Lake Nameless trail. And call the police. *Now*.'

'What the hell's going on? Where are the others?' said Tom.

'I'll find them,' said Eliza. 'Just call the police, Tom.'

'Eliza, you shouldn't —'

'Tom. Call the police.' She ended the call and looked at Carmen. '*Go.*'

Carmen hesitated, then crashed through the branches and sprinted off down the track. Eliza watched her disappear around a corner, then stepped back out onto the track.

Lightning flashed overhead and three seconds later it was followed by a long, echoing boom, pressing down on her eardrums, startling the yellow wattlebird into another cry.

The sleet grew heavier, making the bushland feel threatening in the cloud-gloom wet. This was a bad place to be in a storm: it was said anything could happen in the Great Western Tiers. Kooparoona Niara in language, or 'Mountain of Spirits', they were the stark bluffs that bordered the Central Plateau. They were dense, claustrophobic, and dangerous. You could walk in circles for days and never see a path right beneath you, you could freeze to death in the snowstorms that came from nowhere, you could fall off a fog-hidden cliff or into one of countless ravines and never be found.

Warmth and feeling slowly re-entered her bare feet, stinging against the sharp gravel and icy water. She'd walked barely a minute when she heard the sound of a different bird – a yellow-throated honeyeater – far up ahead, a harsh raspy call that keeps other birds away from its territory. Or warns about the presence of people.

Eliza stopped and shivered.

This is your fault. You deserve this.

She tried to shut out memories of the old rhyme, the one they'd banned students from saying, the one even she and her sister used to whisper at night, giggling with the thrill of fear. The town of Limestone Creek, nestled at the base of the Tiers, had only ever known one monster; the bodies of those girls had never been found.

She stepped off the path again, into a copse of mountain needle-bush that scratched her skin, and walked beside the trail, creeping low to the ground. Her feet stung. Her jacket snagged and tore. She'd lost an earring – now a golden hoop dangled from only her left ear.

And then, a minute later, she heard heavy footsteps in the scrub, matching her every step.

She didn't stop. She kept creeping.

'Just your imagination,' she whispered.

The scrunch-thud of footsteps, the scratch of ferns and branches. She didn't look.

If she didn't look, she would be okay.

The legend said that if you didn't see his face, he wouldn't take you.

CHAPTER 1

MURPHY
The morning before

Murphy sighed. 'We are not having this conversation again.' He was shirtless, sitting at their rickety dining table, speaking loudly over the thumping Jon Bellion song playing from the bluetooth speaker in the corner. 'Camping is *good* for you.'

'I can help out at home,' wheedled his 16-year-old daughter, Jasmine. She was leaning on the table, their chubby black-and-white cat Myrtle squirming in her arms. 'I can mow the lawns. I can clean the windows —'

'School. *Get.*' Murphy lifted a clump of the sweet, sticky marijuana that covered the table and placed it on the electric scales.

The kitchen was falling apart, the cupboard doors loose and the fittings cracked, the wallpaper and the brown lino floor both peeling. Feline-safe houseplants covered most surfaces – devils ivy crawled above the cupboards, where the cats couldn't reach. They were Jasmine's additions, her latest attempt to purify the air of cigarettes and weed.

'I can —'

'*Get,*' said Murphy again.

Jasmine was short and lithe like her late mother, her clear blue eyes smudged with shadow and dark liner. Her hair was pulled back in a ponytail: once ginger like her mum's, it was now dyed raven black.

Murphy, by comparison, was tall, bearded, and built like a lumberjack. Celtic tattoos covered a solid chest, big arms, thick legs. He was clad only in the crumpled Calvin Klein boxer-briefs he had slept in.

The cat mewled and leapt out of Jasmine's arms. Named Myrtle after the Harry Potter character, the cat walked a few feet away, fell onto her side, and appeared to fall immediately asleep.

'Look, Dad, I don't think you understand what I'm offering here . . .'

'I know exactly what you're offering, sweetheart.'

'But it's *hiking*, Dad!'

'And it won't kill you.'

'You don't know that —'

'She *could* stay and clean her room, lad,' offered her uncle, Butch. He was in the kitchen with them, cooking breakfast, bopping along to the music, a joint in one hand and a pan frying bacon in the other. As always, he wore a navy singlet and dirty footy shorts.

'Don't,' warned Murphy, focused on his task. He added more weed to the scale, until it was exactly an ounce.

The family resemblance between Butch and his younger brother Murphy was obvious, but Butch was much rounder in the cheeks and body. He also had daggers and a Mexican sugar skull tattooed on his neck. Butch had earnt his nickname in high school for his size, but both of them were an identical six-foot-three. No one called them by their first names unless they wanted a fight.

'Uncle Butch, can I stay home?' Jasmine skipped to his side, light as a feather. 'Please? Can I?'

'Sure thing, Jaz,' said Butch, taking a drag from his joint. 'Arty-pay at the Urphys-may.'

'Your teacher called me *specifically* to check you'd be there,' Murphy said. He put the ounce into a ziplock bag and sealed it with a vacuum tool, his movements careful and deliberate. 'You've wagged too many days this year already. So you *are* going to school, and you *are* going on the camp, *and you are going to like it*.'

'Yeah, Jaz, if *Miss Ellis* says so . . .' said Butch.

'That's the only reason he's making me go,' said Jasmine in disgust. 'He just wants to get in her pants.'

Murphy turned back to his work, taking the sealed ziplock bag and slapping a sticker onto it – one of the 'THE CAPTAIN' stickers they'd bought in bulk online at The Mad Hueys – that now identified it as the best bush bud in Northern Tasmania. Even though identifying their product was risky, it had the added benefit of shoving it in the face of Sergeant Doble, their rival and constant pain in the arse, who seized as much of their product out on the streets as he could.

'What makes you think I'm not in her pants already?' said Murphy.

'Dad, gross.'

'Ayyy, Murphy, I had dibs,' said Butch, winking at Jasmine.

'And don't think that if you miss the bus I'll let you off,' Murphy continued loudly. 'I'll still drive you up.' He flashed a white smile with crooked teeth. 'Just in my undies. I'll even hop out to kiss you goodbye in front of all your little girlfriends.'

'You're such a creep. Please, Dad, it won't matter if you tell them I'm sick or something . . .'

Murphy glanced her way, pausing. Her pale face, mouth a little too tight; up on her toes like she was about to fly out the window. 'Jasmine,' he said finally. 'It's only one night. Nothing's going to happen to me. I'll still be right here when you get back.'

'Dad, I'm not —'

'Sweetheart, I'm not going anywhere. I promise.'

Jasmine's sadness turned to something else, cold and resigned. 'Fine.' She lifted one of the bags out of the box, pinched between two fingers. 'Then I'm taking one of these.'

He took it from her hand. 'Nice try.'

'Hypocrite. Uncle Butch said you took weed to all *your* school camps.'

'Shhh,' said Butch in a loud stage whisper.

'If you come back with even a *whiff* of it, you are grounded until you're thirty-eight,' said Murphy, glaring at Butch. 'Your uncle should keep his mouth shut.'

'Maybe I exaggerated, Jaz,' said Butch. 'As I remember, he wasn't always smoking: sometimes his lips were attached to one of the Lindsay girls, and not always her —'

'*Ew!*' Jasmine squealed. 'I'm going!'

She pulled her camping pack over her shoulders. She picked up Myrtle from the floor and rubbed her face against the cat's, singing a few lines from James Blunt's 'Goodbye My Lover'. Myrtle meowed, and Jasmine squeezed her once more before she let her back onto the ground.

'Just so you know, Dad, I don't think Miss Ellis is your type. *Love you!*' Jasmine slammed the door behind her: not out of anger, but because slamming it was the only way to get the dicky door fully closed.

'She gets that from you, dickhead,' said Murphy after a moment. He weighed out the next ounce.

'You mean her sticky fingers?' said Butch. 'I barely saw her lift that bag and stuff it up her sleeve.'

'No, I meant her — *what*?'

'Nothing,' said Butch, his smile growing wider.

'Shit!' Murphy ran to the door, knocking over his chair, leaping over a hissing Myrtle, stumbling out onto the street. The ever-present valley breeze of Limestone Creek brought the country town smell of diesel, smoke and gumtree.

Up the end of the street, Jasmine was already climbing into the bus. It was a good fifty metres – she must have run the whole way to get so far ahead of him. She scampered up inside.

Murphy sprinted towards the bus, dodging over broken pavers, a Jack Russell running to a nearby fence and yapping at him.

The bus pulled away. A magpie called from a gumtree above as he slowed, bare feet aching from the hard pavement.

Across the street were two young women in matching Adidas jogging gear. They giggled. Peggie and Darcy, the housemates from down the road. He knew them, of course: he knew nearly everyone who lived around here. They had their phones out, the cameras pointed his way.

He realised he was still in his undies.

He hurried back home.

The door was shut.

He pushed it.

Locked.

'Butch, don't be a knob.' He pounded on the door with his fist, glancing back at Peggie and Darcy, who were waving at him.

The window beside the door opened and Butch's face appeared. 'Hey, everyone!' he shouted. 'Murph is outside in his undies!'

'I'm gonna punch you in the balls.'

'*There's a man who is starkers outside! Someone call the cops!* Hey, how you going, ladies? Murphy's looking a bit cold, hey?'

Peggie and Darcy laughed, a kookaburra took up the call, and the Jack Russell kept barking.

'You're dead, Butch,' said Murphy. He stalked around the side of the house and pulled himself over the peeling white fence.

Their backyard was a tangle of weeds, long grass and scraggly bush. There was a chicken coop in the far corner, a shed in the other, and a rusty Hills Hoist stood in the middle. There was no back fence, the yard backing onto a line of blackberry bushes and white gums. Their property here in the outskirts of Limestone Creek bordered the Western Tiers National Park. One and a half kilometres away, hidden in all that scrub and bush, was his and Butch's marijuana crop, the route leading there rigged up with homemade booby traps.

Beyond that rose the Great Western Tiers, steep inclines of blue-grey streaked with columns of rock. Away to the west was Devils Gullet: a rugged prehistoric gorge, with a lookout on the cliffs that offered views of the misty mountains of Tasmania. That lookout was to be one of the locations on Jasmine's school hike, even though she had been there countless times before. Murphy had even taken her camping to the same spot on Western Bluff where they'd be sleeping tonight: it was only a twenty-minute trip if you had a dirt-bike and knew the forestry roads. That was back when Jasmine's mum, Sara, was alive.

Murphy stomped in through the back door and into the kitchen.

Butch wolf-whistled at the sight of him, arms folded across his singlet, joint between his fingers. 'Why the *hell* are you single?'

'Dickhead. I'll get you back for that.' Murphy shot his hand out to try and whack Butch in the groin, who dodged just in time. 'The Hilux keys.' Murphy patted the wall where they usually hung. 'Where'd you put them?'

'It's fine, Murph, she's a smart kid, she won't get caught.'

'Where are the bloody keys?'

Butch laughed. 'Mate. Calm *down*. You think you're gonna keep Jasmine away from the bud forever when it's her old man's job to *grow it*? She's sixteen, it's school camp, she's had a tough year: let her loosen up a bit.'

'Where are the *fucking keys*, Butch?'

Butch sighed as he went back to cooking the eggs and bacon. 'Don't worry about it, lad. I was only joking.'

'What?'

'She didn't take anything . . . should've seen your face though.' He cackled. 'I should've filmed you out there.'

'You're a fucking goose, mate.' He punched Butch in the shoulder, hard. Their other cat, Gus the Muss, skittered away, knocking over a large potted sword fern, scattering potting mix.

Butch winced, nearly dropping his plate, but the grin crept back onto his face. 'Skinner is comin' round tonight and we've got a bloody *truckload* of bud to bag.' He shoved the joint into his mouth and then pressed the other plate into Murphy's hands. 'Get your strength up, lad.'

CHAPTER 2

JASMINE

Jasmine hurried down the aisle of the bus, her heart pounding. Sure enough, Dad had come after her – Butch must've seen her take that second bag, the snitch, but she was sure neither of them had seen her swipe the first one.

As long as Dad didn't drive up to the school . . .

She groaned. That's probably exactly what he'd do.

A sudden flutter of relief: maybe she'd get suspended and kicked off the camp. The others wouldn't think any less of her . . .

No.

She had to do it. It was up to her to make this happen. She just had to make it through the day without backing out.

Hopefully Dad *didn't* come up to the school . . .

She felt strangely on display in her Billabong jacket as she walked down the aisle, with most of the other students in their grey-and-green school uniforms. Only the Year 10 girls were permitted to be in casual clothes, as they were leaving for the camp after Homegroup.

On the back seat were Georgia and the twins, Cierra and

Madison – Jasmine's best friends, her squad, the other three members of their Fab Four.

'Your dad is so hot?' sighed Cierra, watching Jasmine's dad through the back window. Cierra had a habit of speaking as though everything was a question, even though Jasmine had tried repeatedly to make her break it. She wore a cobalt-blue wig, cut to a bob just above her ears, even though she was gorgeous in that naturally tanned beach-model way, with freckles and winged eyeliner. Jasmine didn't know why Cierra felt she needed the wig – Cierra probably didn't even know herself.

'He's really not,' said Jasmine. She slid her backpack into the aisle, manoeuvring the bags of weed, one from each sleeve, into her bag and shoving them down to the bottom. She sat between Cierra and Madison, her identical twin.

'Hey, bitch,' said Madison, slipping an arm through Jasmine's. In her other hand – permanently attached – was the latest iPhone and its many cameras. Madison filmed her entire life for her thousands of followers, wearing the most expensive brands, bought and paid for by either ad revenue or her 'influencer collaborations'. Her natural red hair was styled in long curls that fell around her face, she had the same winged eyeliner as Cierra, and a luxe Tommy Hilfiger puffer jacket over denim cut-offs.

Her phone case was lined with LED lights to illuminate her subject, and she trained the camera on Jasmine's face. 'So, what do *you* have to say about this cruel and unusual punishment? A school camp?' Jasmine saw the mischief in her eyes, the smirk in her volcano-red lips. 'A hike, and *camping*, up there in the Suicide Woods. How *Wolf Creek*.'

'If it doesn't at least get hot enough for Mr Michaels to take his shirt off, the whole thing will be a waste of time,' said Jasmine to the camera.

'It'll probably snow,' said Georgia from the other side of Madison, matter-of-fact.

'Maybe he'll need someone to cuddle him, then,' said Jasmine.

Madison laughed. 'That's definitely going online, Jaz.' She turned the camera on herself. 'Hello, Mr Michaels.' She winked.

Madison's YouTube channel, MMMMadisonMason, had over 700 000 subscribers. Jasmine knew for a fact that their teacher's assistant, Jack Michaels, was one of them.

'*Don't* call it the Suicide Woods.' Georgia Lenah had thick-rimmed glasses on a round face, with bright coral lipstick between dimpled cheeks – she might not have been as stunning as Madison or Cierra, but more boys asked her out on dates than any of the other members of the Fab Four. Her Aboriginal heritage gave her a perspective that Jasmine felt was very healthy for the twins: Jasmine and Georgia both tried to act as a counterbalance to the Mason girls' privileged view of the world.

'Why not? We'll be walking right by the Hanging Tree,' said Madison, turning her camera on Georgia. 'We could call it the *Hungry Woods* instead.'

'Don't, Madison,' called Cierra with a shudder. 'Not today?'

'You're scared of the Hungry Man?' said Madison, camera now on her sister. '*Up in the hills, he hides and kills, down in the caves, he hides and waits . . .*'

'Stop it!' Cierra squealed, and Madison chuckled.

Jasmine could already imagine Madison's video for the day. It'd start with the four of them on the back seat, then footage from the hike, and then some snatches from the campfire. Jasmine was grateful she'd bought a new jacket for this camping trip, because it'd look good on camera: Madison had helped her choose it. It was handy, having an internet-famous friend, someone who was good with angles, make-up and clothes.

The bus made another stop and one of the Year 12 girls – Yani Hugh, the pastor's daughter – stepped up into the bus.

Madison made a noise, pursing her red lips.

Jasmine's smile became fixed. *Oh, here we go . . .*

Yani walked down the aisle, her skirt flicking, short hair stiff with product, and sat with her Year 12 friends near the middle of the bus. Those girls once thought they'd had a right to the back seat – that was before the Fab Four came along.

'Hey, does anyone smell carrots?' called Madison over the chatter.

The bus went quiet. The back of Yani's neck turned pink.

The bus driver was half-deaf: he never heard these exchanges. Jasmine wished he would.

'Leave her alone, Madison,' said Jasmine quietly.

'Ease up, bitch, I'll be right back,' said Madison with a smile, heading down the aisle, moving with the sway of the bus, her phone in her hand.

It was Yani's fault, Jasmine tried to reassure herself. But that had been months ago. Madison was *relentless*.

Madison sat down across the aisle from Yani and her friends, brandishing her phone.

Yani sunk lower into her seat as Madison insulted her – her looks, her sex life – drawing chuckles from some of the other students. 'Mmm . . . yep, I can smell carrots,' finished Madison nastily. Yani didn't respond: if Madison had her camera trained on you, anything you said could be used against you online. Plus, Madison had other ammunition.

Madison made her way back to the back seat. Her face was flushed, a wide smirk for the girls.

'You're such a bitch, Madison,' said Georgia.

'Yani is *literally* a whore. We hate her, Georgia,' said Madison. She snuggled in beside Jasmine and her. 'For all our new viewers, tell us again what your people call the Great Western Tiers?'

Georgia sat up straighter, brushing her ringlets back as she slipped into her activist voice. 'The traditional name for the Tiers is *Kooparoona Niara*,' she began. 'Meaning "Mountain of Spirits".

It was a significant meeting place for three separate mobs. They'd come for ceremonies, to exchange news, and to trade for the sacred ochre – hang on, why are you giving me that look? No! You're just gonna make this about those bloody portals you think are up there!'

'C'mon, Georgia —' said Madison.

'*No way.* They are *not* part of Aboriginal story. I won't help you appropriate my culture to —'

'Appropriate *your* culture?' said Madison. 'What about *Avengers*? You love Thor, who is *literally* a god for some people.'

'That's completely different and you know it!' Georgia's voice was growing heated. 'There are no magical spirit portals in the mountains! There is no mystical Aboriginal-afterlife vortex sucking people in!'

'That sounds suspiciously like something someone would say if they were trying to hide the fact there *are* portals in the mountains —'

Jasmine, who had heard all this before, turned away, looking past Cierra – who was scrolling on her phone – and out the window.

She pretended she didn't see Yani's shoulders shaking with quiet sobs as her friends tried to comfort her. The whole thing felt particularly wrong because anti-bullying was one of MMMMadisonMason's biggest themes. But then, a lot of things Madison did in real life went against what MMMMadisonMason said online.

Don't worry about it . . . for the greater good . . .

The houses of Limestone Creek rolled past. Most were run down: fibro joints and dirty brick houses, a community that had risen and fallen with the local mining industry, and then again with the timber industry. These days, Limestone Creek was a mongrel town, part tourism, part ageing population. Rusting cars in overgrown yards, goats on nature strips, houses that doubled as antique-dealers, with colourful flags flying out the front to attract the tourists on their way along the Meander Valley Scenic Route, which led into the pristine, misty wilderness of Tasmania's highlands.

Jasmine knew what Limestone Creek was really like. You heard a lot of things about your town when your dad sold weed. Especially in a town that had a population of less than 6000.

The house they just passed – the mother worked in a clothes shop and the father as a mechanic, and Jasmine knew that they fought, violently. They had a little girl, who got caught up in it once, over a year ago; the father, drunk, smacked her so hard across the face with a bottle she suffered a brain injury. They told everyone she slipped and hit her head in the playground, and even tried to sue the school. When the mother told a friend how it really happened, it got around town, and Dad found out. He told the cops, but as far as they were concerned there was no proof, and they didn't look any closer.

A house a little further along belonged to a lawyer. His son ran a woodcraft workshop from the garage, with 'OPEN' and 'SALE ON NOW' flags out the front. The lawyer was married, but he had still flown in an 'au pair' from Vietnam, who was actually his mistress. A girl in Year 11 at Jasmine's school – Julie Jacobson – was technically his son's girlfriend, but she also got 'private tutoring' from the lawyer.

How many other stories like that did she know? Riddling the town like cavities in a tooth. Abuse, corruption, sex, drugs . . . Jasmine was going to get out of there *as soon as she could*.

That was one of the few secrets she hadn't told the girls yet. They didn't understand: they liked being in Limestone Creek, where everything was easy and simple and Madison was a celebrity and everyone rode in her shadow. When you didn't know about the underbelly, she supposed it was quite a nice place. And Madison was convinced they were all going to live here together forever, probably in a mansion she'd build with her internet income, and that they'd start some sort of saucy Instagram reality series.

The other girls didn't understand how much Jasmine needed to leave, needed to get Dad out of here, too. That she was the only one who could get Dad out of here.

And then she could also be as far as possible from Madison. Because this was another secret Jasmine had: she *hated* Madison Mason. Hated her guts, her soul, hated her right down to the cells that made up her marrow, her stupid red hair, her stupid voice, her stupid red smirk.

Jasmine felt Madison squeeze her arm affectionately, and she turned with a smile, patted Madison's leg, snuggled closer. *I hate you so much, bitch,* she thought.

They were driving through the middle of town now, over the wide stone bridge across the namesake river of Limestone Creek. Built by convicts, the bridge was said to be haunted. One of Jasmine's ex-boyfriends swore black and blue he'd seen the ghost before, a man wearing a straw hat.

There were many reported hauntings in Limestone Creek, most of them in the convict-era buildings in the town centre. In the summer there was a ghost tour that ran every weekend, but even now it was on every fortnight, for the tourists who flocked to Limestone Creek in unpredictable patterns. Theirs was 'the third-most haunted town in Australia'.

It was all bullshit, as far as Jasmine was concerned. Mr Carswell, Jasmine's Science teacher, a staunch sceptic, had shown their class a TED Talk about how certain frequencies of sound gave people 'the creeps' and caused them to see blurred figures out of the corner of their eyes. Mr Carswell then explained how the wind blowing through the rocks of the Tiers sometimes makes a heavy thrumming noise, which could be contributing to the dubious history of 'hauntings'.

They were supposed to design an experiment to test this, but no one really put much effort into it: Mr Carswell was a pushover. And, as Madison pointed out whenever he brought it up, it didn't explain the Min Min lights that used to be seen up on the Tiers. Mr Carswell would demand photographic evidence of the lights, and then run into a tangent on swamp gas and limestone methane, which Jasmine had googled and had to admit probably wasn't a real thing.

But Madison believed in all that sort of stuff: one of the reasons her YouTube channel had grown so big, besides the fact she was drop-dead gorgeous, was that she uploaded her own ghost tours around town, as well as seances and overnight stakeouts. While Jasmine didn't believe in that stuff, there was no denying that Madison's ghost stories got views.

And what earned her the most views were videos on the Hungry Man Abductions – the mystery of the five girls who disappeared in 1985 and were never found. In Limestone Creek, those disappearances were never far from anyone's mind.

Madison was a genius when it came to creating consumable content. When you combined her looks with her varied content: make-up and fashion tips, social issues, hauntings and ghost tours and Dark Tourism, it was no surprise her channel had grown so popular. But it was the Hungry Man stories and theories that had taken her to another level; all of Tasmania, all of Australia, was still hung up on that story.

But God help anyone who mentioned the Hungry Man or the 1985 disappearances at school. Kids had been suspended for just singing the rhyme in the corridor. The whole town shied away from the topic. Old ladies at the coffee shop would give you dirty looks if you joked about it to the barista.

The school bus began its ascent towards the expansive school grounds, which were nestled halfway up the escarpment. Jasmine rode the rest of the way in silence, looking out at the bushland that crowded the road, dense and thick, white gum and dogwood and ferns and scrub, a cliff on one side and a steep drop on the other.

Her dad had once made a joke about this road, how the bush in that gully was so thick you could just chuck a body from the side of the road and no one would ever find it: it could sit mere metres from the asphalt and never be seen again, especially since the scavenger Tasmanian devils with their wicked strong jaws would make short work of the body. Mum had hit Dad in the arm after that comment, made a scathing remark about how the girls from 1985 still hadn't been found and reminding him that his own daughter was in the car, listening to his every word.

Of course years later, when Mum was dead and Dad was significantly more prone to getting drunk, he had rambled on about a guy he used to kick around with who had been desperate for money and so had taken on a hit from one of the gangs. It was only $3000, but he did it anyway. He brought the mark – a dog from a drug case – up here from Hobart, killed him, and rolled his body into the bush somewhere on this road. That was years ago, and as far as she knew, no one had ever found the body.

They came around the corner and the grassy grounds of the school opened up. The bus rolled down the school driveway, the sun disappearing behind the leafy branches of the conker trees that lined the way. Jasmine noticed that Yani was one of the first to leave the bus, fleeing across the car park before Madison could reach her.

The walk to Homegroup seemed to take no time at all. The four of them stuck together, Madison interviewing them about the coming trip, twirling her hair with one finger.

They passed the Year 7 area, and a few boys who worshipped Madison called out to her; they passed the Home Economics block, which smelled of concrete dust and mildew, closed off for renovations that had been happening for years; passed the weird alternative kids who sat out the front, hiding the cigarettes they were obviously smoking.

When they passed the library, and the staffroom beside it,

Jasmine slowed. She caught the eye of Mr Michaels, one of the teacher's assistants. He was only twenty-one, with a bit of scruff on a cinderblock jaw and dazed-looking brown eyes.

Those eyes were watching her as they passed, as she knew they would be. She returned his smile. He bared his crooked teeth, his joy infectious, his happiness at seeing her so genuine. The problem wasn't that he was dopier than a sheep, it was that she'd recently found out he'd done wrong by her dad. It didn't matter that he was hot and authentic and treated her right – she was loyal to her dad first. She had to break up with him. The thought made her sad, but she liked the buzz of vengeance.

When the Fab Four sat down in home group there was excitement in the air. The mountain camp was part of the compulsory Outdoor Education curriculum of Year 10 PE, although these days they split up the boys and girls as it had been too difficult to keep them out of each other's tents. The boys had gone last week, so now they were sitting on the girls' desks and telling them about the strange noises they'd heard in the dark up there.

'Like a demon. Low, rasping. It whispered things to me . . .' Tyler Cabot flicked back his hair.

'Oh, really?' said Cierra, eyebrows disappearing up into her blue fringe. 'And what did it tell you?'

'It said, "Cierra thinks you're hot, and she's thinking of you right now . . . in her bed . . . her lights off . . ."'

'Ah, I get it, you were dreaming,' said Cierra. 'Did you wake up with something sticky in your Spider-Man undies?'

The boys hooted like monkeys. Tyler grinned. 'Why don't you check?' He pulled out the front of his shorts.

'Ewwww,' Cierra squealed. Georgia dry-retched, hiding her face in Madison's shoulder.

'Nah, I'll tell you what I heard,' said Jye Calloway, his school shirt unbuttoned to bare his singlet. 'Coming from Mr Michaels' tent . . . it was Miss Ellis's voice.' He thudded his palm against Jasmine's desk and started groaning. *'Oh, Jack! Oh . . . JACK!'*

The boys fell about laughing again.

Jasmine didn't think it was *that* funny.

It was lucky none of the teachers had heard. Mr North, the PE teacher, was sitting with the footy boys, chatting, and Miss Ellis was marking attendance on her computer at the front of the room. As well as Homegroup, she took Literacy and History, although a district school had to make do with what it had and she taught other things too when called upon. She wore her hair in a stylish ponytail with a red ribbon and large hoop earrings – which were not at all practical for a bushwalk, but she almost always wore them. She'd once given the Fab Four a little lesson on 'Big Hoop Energy', and after that Cierra had gone for months only wearing hoop earrings.

Miss Ellis was full of those little tips and tricks. She was open with all her students about her own mental health; her grief at the loss of her niece, Denni King, but also her turbulent upbringing, her dad dying from drink-driving and her mum OD'ing and orphaning Miss Ellis and her two sisters.

Miss Ellis had a glowing face, with freckles across her nose that made her look both sun-kissed and yet kind of like a British model. She was fit – always into bushwalking, or jogging, or boxing. Most teachers treated the cool kids or good-looking kids differently: with that half-desperate 'please, let me be cool too' kind of attitude that even adults seemed to have, which Jasmine found a bit depressing. But not Miss Ellis. She treated everyone the same. Even if she talked to you like she'd seen all your secret Snapchats. All of the girls at Limestone District were fiercely protective of her – especially since the tragedy. Denni King had been one of their own, after all.

Jasmine caught more than a few of the boys checking out Miss Ellis's bum as she turned to wipe something off the board, including

Mr North, who unfortunately would be coming with them on the camp. Jasmine had it on good authority that he took steroids, which not only made him big as a brick shithouse but also made him want to root like a rabbit. *All* of the girls knew that, and some of them loved it and used it, while some others were quite rightfully creeped out by it, including Jasmine.

Joining Miss Ellis and Mr North on the camp was Mr Michaels – Jack – her sweet, secret, ditzy, soon-to-be-ex-boyfriend. Supervising thirty hormone-ravaged teenage girls. They were heroes, really.

'Alright, ladies,' shouted Mr North above the noise. 'Grab your things and we'll head out to the oval. Hand in your phones and don't whinge. You all agreed to it. This is a *wilderness experience* not a *spend all day on your phone experience*, and *yes*, I will give them back so you can take photos when we reach the lookout, *tomorrow*.'

Madison, of course, only handed over a fake phone: an old iPhone she hadn't used since last year. Her real phone was hidden in her bra, even though, as Georgia pointed out, Mr North would happily search there.

Jasmine followed along with the group as they headed out onto the oval, from where they would hike directly to the campsite.

The October skies above were blue and cloudless. The track was rough: thin, lined with gravel and roots and rocks, edged by mountain needlebush and native laurel that snagged on socks and shorts, and scratched bare legs. The air was heady with eucalypt. Bird noises filled the air, loudest from the flock of yellow-tailed black cockatoos flying overhead, their harsh caws sounding through the trees.

'A storm is coming,' commented a girl behind Jasmine. 'When they all fly somewhere like that, they're looking for shelter from a storm.'

'Bullshit,' said her friend. 'Forecast says we're good.'

'I'm telling you, the birds know better.'

'Alright, bird-whisperer.'

Jasmine focused on where she was placing her feet, the ascent already growing steep, the pack heavy against her back. She was one of the smallest in the class, but she'd push through. She'd carry this damn pack all the way.

Dimly, she hoped there wasn't a storm coming. They'd been enjoying the warm weather they'd had the last few days. *Indian summer*, came Dad's voice in her mind. *Warm weather that will last a week and then we'll get another month of storms . . .*

She shivered. Something *did* feel a bit weird in the air.

The trees and scrub beside them soon gave way to a burbling creek of yellow-brown silt, smelling loamy. One girl had stopped to fill up her empty bottle, even though they were barely five minutes into the hike, and another was trying to convince her there was wallaby poo in the water.

Five minutes later, the creek wended away from the path and they reached the first real milestone of the trip: the Hanging Tree. Jasmine could tell when they were drawing close, because all the laughter stopped.

It was a crooked King Billy Pine, with spreading branches and wide roots. A freak of nature, it had three trunks instead of one; the two smaller, stunted trunks twisted away from the central one like tortured arms. It stood in a rocky clearing all of its own.

Nestled in its roots and the blanket of pine needles were ribbons and bouquets of flowers – some fresh, some old and plastic – as well as framed photographs. A large rusty sign on a post read: LIFELINE – NEED SUPPORT? – WE WILL LISTEN – 13 11 14.

Carved into the trunk was a large and messy capital A, dull red from where someone, long ago, had spray-painted the carving, keeping the bark from growing back.

It was called the Hanging Tree by the locals. Five people had hung themselves on this tree: all at separate times, none of them related. There had been two other suicide attempts. The first was found trying to climb the tree with a rope and the second was intercepted on the way up the escarpment.

The first known hanging on the tree had been the Aboriginal man Theodore Barclay. Everyone knew his name. He had been the number-one suspect in the 1985 Hungry Man disappearances. He killed himself before a trial could be held, after his house had been burned down and he'd been bashed to within an inch of his life by vigilantes.

Then, over the years, three other hangings, right up until last year: Denni King. She had gone to the school's farewell dinner, then come up here that same night to kill herself. It rocked the community to the core, and changed Jasmine's life.

She stood watching the tree, suddenly aware she was holding her breath. She let it go.

Scarlett Watkinson, the straight-backed and big-boobed year-level captain, laid a bouquet at the base of the tree. They were beautiful roses, in pink paper. They looked like they should've been a bride's bouquet. The thought made Jasmine feel sick.

Miss Ellis was crying. Jasmine's heart went out to her. She didn't deserve any of this.

Mr North blinked a lot, too, fighting back the tears. He was married to Miss Ellis's sister, Monica, and so he had been Denni's uncle. Jasmine's heart didn't go out to him, though. Bum-chin, steroid-munching fuck.

Madison was crying now as well, smudging her make-up. Jasmine, Cierra and Georgia huddled around her, drawing comfort from one another. Madison had been the one who'd found Denni's body. She'd been filming at the time, live-streaming a ghost hunt. The plan had been for her and Denni to film it together, so Denni had told Madison to meet at the Hanging Tree right after the fare-well dinner. That way, they both would look amazing on camera, up in the creepy bush in their beautiful dresses.

Clearly Denni had wanted Madison to be the one to find her body, and for the whole discovery to be live-streamed. A white dress, her tattoos visible on her bare arms, her brown braid piled up on top of her head with a golden hairnet . . . hanging by the neck.

The incident made Madison's subscriber numbers skyrocket, but of course it was horrible. Jasmine still had nightmares about Denni's body – she had been watching live. Aside from her mother dying, it was the worst thing that she'd ever experienced. The video had done the rounds afterwards, before all the images were taken down. Georgia had told Jasmine that if you googled it, you could still find some of those stills of Denni's body on foreign blogs.

Jasmine rubbed Madison's back through her jacket. A separate knot of girls kept glancing their way, whispering to each other. Some people believed Madison had been in on it, had known what Denni was planning and went along with it for the views. Jasmine scowled at the girls and they looked away.

The wind grew stronger, and the branches of the Hanging Tree groaned and creaked. An eerie chill ran down Jasmine's back, and she knew she wasn't the only one who felt it. One girl nearby jumped, as though the tree itself had spoken. It seemed a good cue to continue: girls started getting ready, pulling their backpacks on.

But not Bree Wilkins. She stood all alone, on a flat rock that was raised like a stage. Her scowl could've been felt a mile away. Angsty Bree.

She looked Jasmine's way. Jasmine held those angry pale eyes for a moment, until Bree's lips curled back in a sneer and Jasmine turned away in what she hoped was a dignified fashion.

They all continued on, Miss Ellis taking off her glasses to wipe her eyes. Mr North was comforting her, his massive hand low on her back.

And so, on they went, deeper into the bush, towards the bluffs, the wind howling up the escarpment.

I will not back out, I will not back out, I will not back out.

An hour later, they came to a small clearing ringed by sassafras trees, with soft grass, a bench carved into a log. A sign detailed the three hiking tracks that split here: a short hike to the Devils Gullet lookout, a five-and-a-half hour loop along the top of the Tiers, and the three-hour walk they would be doing, to the Western Bluff lookout. As well as the incredible view, there was a campsite there, by the historic Trapper's Hut from the 1900s. Jasmine had seen it before. It was built out of bark and logs. You were allowed to camp in it, but it was scary as hell.

The whole group stopped to drink and eat and complain, and someone shrieked when they found a tiger snake curled up nearby. 'I know it's an early riser for the season but calm down, girls, it's more scared of you than you are of it. Just keep your eyes open. This is their home, not yours,' said Mr North.

They split into two groups before continuing on: Miss Ellis took the smaller, faster group ahead, and Mr North and Jack would hang back with the slower group. The Fab Four stayed with the slower group.

An hour down the path Jasmine's pack was digging into her shoulders, sweat making her back prickly. Pollen burned her nose; her feet were hot and aching. She didn't complain: she was very aware of how close Jack was walking behind her. She didn't want him to think she couldn't do it.

She glanced back at him. He was watching her closely. 'Are you okay? Pack isn't too heavy?'

'No.' She faced the front again. He was *still* worried about her. She felt guilty.

The bush was less dense in this area at the cloud base: an open forest of alpine cider gum and snow peppermint, the smell Christmas-like. A few metres off the path was the cliff edge, with a very long drop. A constant breeze rolled up over it.

A thump off in the trees made her flinch, and she saw the back of a large Forester kangaroo bounding away. She tried to disguise her flinch as a cough. *Why* was she so unsettled?

At a chirping call she glanced up and saw a dusky woodswallow, perched on the edge of a branch up ahead, out near the cliff edge, returned from the mainland for the spring.

It was weird. They usually flew away at the approach of humans. But this one watched her, and so she watched it back. Her breath grew heavier until it was the only sound in her ears. The pine smell was thick in her lungs, it was choking her . . .

'Jasmine!' yelled Jack, grabbing her pack and pulling her backwards. 'What are you *doing*?'

She shook her head, dizzy. The woodswallow was gone, and she realised she was several paces off the track. 'What . . .?'

'Didn't you hear me calling? You're about to go off the cliff!'

Her friends had gathered behind, along with some other curious girls, while the rest took the opportunity to walk ahead.

Jasmine felt uneasy. 'I'm fine,' she said, pulling away from Jack.

'Calm down, Mr Michaels,' said Madison wryly.

'I reckon she's just hungry,' said Georgia, concerned behind her glasses, pushing a muesli bar into Jasmine's hand.

'You really didn't hear us, Jaz?' said Cierra quietly.

'Everything alright back there?' called Mr North from up ahead.

'Yeah, Northo, we're good,' said Jasmine. She began walking and the others followed behind, Jack muttering under his breath.

Jasmine did her best to hide her trembling hands as she unwrapped the muesli bar. She picked up her pace.

I'm just stressed, she thought. *I'm just very fucking stressed. What the hell are we doing?*

She thought of her dad. She straightened her back.

I will not back out.

Standing up ahead was Mr North, at the side of the path with his arms folded across his chest, his mouth moving as he counted the girls going past.

'How much further?' moaned Cierra.

'We're over halfway, girls,' said Mr North.

As they continued, they heard someone yelling for Mr North from further up the track. A moment later Carmen, the fittest girl in class, came jogging back down the trail. 'Mr North,' she said, barely out of breath. 'We think Missy has broken her ankle.'

Mr North cursed, and together they went running up the track.

A few minutes later Jasmine and the rest of the group caught up. Missy Carswell was on the ground, sitting up against a fallen tree, crying while Mr North tested her ankle's movement.

'It's not broken, just twisted,' whispered Carmen to Jasmine and the others. 'She just doesn't want to walk anymore. Plus she landed right in a jack jumper nest.'

'Ouch,' winced Jasmine.

'Yes, how *Hunger Games*,' said Madison, rolling her eyes.

Mr North took charge, but didn't even attempt to show sympathy. 'Mr Michaels, Miss Ellis, take the girls on to the campsite.' The frustration was clear in his voice. 'I'll help little Miss Carswell back to the road. We'll call someone to pick her up.'

The rest of them made their way to the campsite as one big group. There were no more incidents except someone saw a wood scorpion and freaked out – 'I didn't even know we *had* scorpions here! Are they venomous? Will they be at the campsite?' – and a few girls got sunburnt, Jasmine included.

Once they arrived, Jasmine, Cierra and Madison hurried to find the most private camping spot they could. They wanted to sleep as far as possible from the creepy Trapper's Hut in the centre of the clearing: a one-room hut made of dark, rotting timber that creaked in the wind, windows boarded up and the cracked door swinging wide.

They found a spot of soft grass between two dolomite boulders and a fallen cider gum, on the very edge of the cleared camping area, almost bordering the cliff itself. Miss Ellis had decided the sleeping arrangements. Madison and Cierra would share a tent and Jasmine would be sharing with Bree, in a tent she'd pitched right beside theirs, snug against a boulder. Georgia was sleeping in with Carmen, who had already set up her tent near the Trapper's Hut.

Jasmine was midway through erecting her tent, sweating in the muggy spring air, swatting away bristle flies and one stubborn spider wasp.

'Didn't think to ask me whether I wanted the tent here?' came Bree's harsh voice from behind her.

Jasmine turned to see her blotchy red face, tight with fury. 'Sorry. Thought this was a good spot.'

'I just thought you might've asked me where *I* wanted to sleep tonight. You know, *considering*.'

'Sorry. But look, it's already half up.'

Bree clenched her fists and spat, *'Bitch.'* She stomped off.

Madison laughed. 'Notice how she didn't offer to help?'

'Alright over here, girls?' said Jack, appearing at Jasmine's side. 'What's wrong?'

'Nothing, Mr Michaels. Jasmine just needs a bit of help setting up her tent,' said Madison. 'Aren't you hot in that shirt?'

'Let me help you with that,' said Jack, taking the tent pegs from Jasmine's hands.

She stood back and let him finish it, brushing the wasp off his back when it landed there: a large black wasp with orange wings and antennae. It moved away with its weird jumping motion.

'At least there won't be any huntsmen around our tents tonight,' she mused.

Cierra shuddered. Jasmine knew she hated spiders: especially the thick, palm-sized huntsmen that bred around the mountains.

'I reckon this spider wasp has a nest in this fallen tree,' said Jasmine.

Cierra squealed. 'What the *fuck* is a *spider wasp?*'

'Relax, it's not a wasp crossed with a spider. It *eats* spiders, especially huntsmen. Drags them along the ground, sometimes it bites their legs off to make them easier to handle.'

'That is *messed up*.' Cierra shuddered.

Madison snorted. 'How do you know this, bug woman?'

'Dad told me. I saw one at our house once, with a huntsman. Dad told me it had paralysed it and was going to plant its eggs inside, that the larvae would eat it from the inside out, leaving the vital organs until last so it would live as long as possible . . .' She laughed. 'It freaked me out. I cried for hours. Mum went ape at him. Told him it was a stupid thing to tell me.'

'He was right,' said Jack. He had finished setting up the tent. 'Stupid thing to tell a little girl.'

Jasmine hit him playfully, but a little harder than necessary. 'Luckily it didn't scar me too badly.'

Bree came stalking back, still furious. She saw the tent was up and she shouldered past to get inside, then zipped the flap shut behind her.

Jasmine rolled her eyes. 'It's going to be a long six months,' she whispered to the girls. They nodded and sighed, and Madison just smirked. Together they headed towards the middle of the camp-site, carefully moving across the occasional patch of mossy rocks. The campfire was already going and some girls had gathered a pile of dead wood.

Miss Ellis was nearby, supervising the construction of a commu-nal gazebo tent, which had been left behind for them by the boys the weekend before. Jack rushed to help. 'You can go find some more firewood if you like,' she said to Jasmine and her friends, taking off her glasses to wipe away the sweaty condensation that had gathered on the lenses.

The four girls turned, grumbling, and headed for the edge of the clearing.

'Remember,' Miss Ellis called after them as she put her glasses back on, '*stick to the tracks.*'

'Like we're gonna find any firewood on the track,' muttered Madison. As soon as they were out of sight of the camp, she pulled her phone out of her pocket.

'She's suspicious,' said Georgia. 'I can tell.'

'You can't tell,' said Madison.

'She's looking at us differently.'

'Don't worry,' said Madison sagely. 'I'll take care of it.' She looked around. 'We'll split up, we'll find more wood that way.'

She and her sister broke away from Jasmine and Georgia, moving off the path and through a patch of needlebush, Madison tapping away at her phone. 'Reception is *literally* shit.'

Jasmine and Georgia walked a little way by themselves, leaving the track and gathering sticks, checking for insects before picking them up. Jasmine couldn't stop thinking about the twins. It wasn't good for them to be keeping secrets, not right now. After a few more moments, she dropped her bundle of sticks on the ground.

'Madison is up to something.'

Georgia sighed. 'Yeah, duh. We all are.'

'That's not what I mean. I'm gonna go listen . . .'

'Jasmine!' said Georgia, but she was already moving off through the bush.

She walked softly on the ground, avoiding branches and shrubs: she'd had practice sneaking through the bush, following her dad and uncle when they visited their secret marijuana crop. Soon she heard Madison and Cierra's voices, and she stopped and crouched lower.

'. . . three new players,' Madison was saying.

'Where are they from?' said Cierra.

'One from Surfers Paradise, one from Geelong, and one from Hobart,' said Madison. 'Ew. Hobart.'

'Any guys this time?'

'Two.' Madison chuckled. 'Look at this one. Hot as a Hemsworth. Jackpot.'

'Hopefully they all send their nudes by tonight . . .' Cierra's voice was sombre. A moment later, she started sniffling.

'Don't cry – hey, we talked about this,' said Madison softly.

Jasmine backed away, worried they were going to start moving again and stumble across her in the bushes. She returned to the trail, but Georgia had gone already. She retrieved her own pile of wood and headed back to the campsite.

Once she'd added to the growing firewood pile, she spotted Bree sitting by the fire. Jasmine took a breath. It was probably now or never. Time to see if she had an ally.

She walked over and sat beside her.

'What do you want?' snapped Bree.

'I heard Madison mention the game again, and nudes,' said Jasmine softly. 'I think you're right: it's something like Honcho Dori.'

Bree gave a great heave of sarcasm. 'That's what I *told* you.' She glanced across, angry again. 'You can drop the act, bitch. I know you're spying for her.'

'No, I'm not, *bitch*.'

'Spare me,' said Bree. 'Just keep your end of the deal and I'll keep mine.'

Jasmine watched her stalk off. She was frustrated, but it was alright, she'd have time to talk to Bree in their tent tonight. Jasmine could be convincing when she needed to be.

Georgia returned to the campsite, her hair full of little twigs, and delivered her armful of wood to the pile. She stopped by the gazebo, where there was a box of squashed fruit from someone's pack, and then sat down next to Jasmine, handing her a banana. 'We can't afford to fight right now, Jaz,' she said. 'We have to stick together.' She unpeeled her own banana, watching Jack, who was helping some girls still struggling to set up their tent.

Madison and Cierra returned, still arm in arm.

'I know,' said Jasmine. 'I just don't think there should be secrets.' She threw the banana skin onto the fire.

Georgia laughed. 'Not knowing each other's secrets is the only reason we can all be friends.'

After a dinner of pork sausages cooked on the smoky camp-fire and salad, all of the campers sat in loose knots. The Fab Four and Carmen sat in a semi-circle, on a straw mat that had been left behind in the Trapper's Hut. On the other side of the fire, Scarlett, the year-level captain, had set up a portable speaker and her Triple J playlist beat against the sound of crackling fire and conversation. She was the only student who'd been allowed to bring her phone, although she'd be sharing a tent with Miss Ellis tonight, right beside the Trapper's Hut, so the privilege kind of cancelled out.

Without their phones, the rest of the girls chatted about nor-mal things – the girls from school, the boys from school, the boys from town, the girls from town. Jasmine ignored a few not-so-subtle remarks about her and Jack, who they all noticed kept glancing across at her. Carmen seemed especially miffed by it. Jasmine knew she had a crush on him, but she didn't even have the energy to feel pleased about that. All she felt now was nervous. The first chance she had, she was going to sneak away and smoke some of her dad's weed. Tonight, of all nights, she had earned it.

As the evening drew on, most girls were content to stay up and chat. Miss Ellis went to bed not long after the first group of girls did, telling the rest, 'Remember, we have a long walk tomorrow,' but in the sort of resigned voice of a teacher who knew the girls would do whatever they wanted.

Mr North had finally made it to camp a little before dinner, having seen Missy Carswell safely home. He chatted to Jack and a smaller group of the football girls. He, too, eventually stood up, warned the girls to get their rest before the long hike tomorrow, and headed off to his tent.

Jasmine watched him all the way, just to make sure he didn't try to sneak into anyone else's tent. Cierra and Madison's, for example.

Jack stayed where he was, at the other end of the communal area, staring into the fire. He seemed to be trying his hardest not to glance at Jasmine. If she was a good person, she'd break up with him tonight. But she knew that she wouldn't.

'Looks like Mum and Dad have gone to bed,' said Madison. She huddled closer to the girls and pulled her phone from her pocket.

'Madison,' hissed Carmen. '*How* did you smuggle that in? You'll get suspended.'

Madison passed her phone to Cierra. 'Who wants a story?'

'Mr Michaels is still over there,' said Georgia. 'He'll catch you.'

'Not if Jasmine flashes her boobs.'

Cierra began filming.

'We're here, at the Western Bluff campsite,' said Madison to the camera. 'This is the only place any trace was found of the girls who went missing in 1985. Both of Rose Cahil's shoes, laces neatly tied, sitting side by side at the edge of the cliff just behind us . . . and a torn scrap of her jeans inside the Trapper's Hut. They say her ghost still haunts the hut.' Cierra swung the camera around towards it. 'Everyone knows to *never go inside at night*.'

Carmen shuddered. 'I would like to be able to sleep tonight, Maddy. My tent is right next to it.'

'The Hungry Man Abductions. Five girls, all disappearing within two months of each other,' continued Madison. 'Mallory Andrew, fourteen, last seen walking along the school track. Yolanda Swift, sixteen, taken while walking through Devils Gullet: her parents were only metres away but didn't see a thing. Victoria Compton, sixteen, while —'

'Stop,' squealed Carmen, hands over her ears.

Madison continued listing the details of each disappearance, finishing with, 'And, one survivor . . . little Dorrie Dossett, fourteen years old. Who told us all about him, the bushman who took them.' She paused. 'The Hungry Man.'

'What's happening over here, girls?' said Jack, approaching from the other side of the fire.

'We're just telling ghost stories, Mr Michaels,' said Jasmine.

Cierra had quickly hidden the phone in the front of her jacket, but the camera was still visible, and still recording.

'The Hungry Man is tall: freakishly tall,' said Madison, ignoring Jack.

'Hey, Madison, you know you're not supposed to talk about that stuff,' he said.

'He wears a bushman's hat, and his face is long and ghostly white. He hides in the bush beside you and, if you listen carefully, you can hear his footsteps matching pace with yours. If you call out, he won't reply: but you'll hear his breathing. If you make eye contact with him . . .'

'Alright, that's enough, Madison.'

'What's wrong, Mr Michaels?' said Cierra, surreptitiously training the camera on him. 'Scared of a ghost story?'

'Even before 1985, there had been rumours for years that a hermit bushman lived in these woods,' continued Madison, pursing her lips seriously, her hair creating a dramatic frame for her face. 'Sometimes you could see the smoke of his campfire. Sometimes you heard gunshots as he hunted game. And once . . . they found the bones of a woman, who he'd eaten clean, and her shoes, the laces neatly tied.'

'That never happened.'

'Then who took those girls, Mr Michaels?' said Madison. 'What happened to them? Little Dorrie Dossett saw the Hungry Man. He kidnapped her from her own backyard.'

'Dorrie Dossett had Down's syndrome.'

'Doesn't mean she's a liar,' countered Madison.

'Theodore Barclay was —'

'Ted Barclay *literally* had the IQ of a ten-year-old. There was no way he took all those girls without a trace. And then he *killed* himself?' said Madison.

'He only got blamed because he was Aboriginal,' added Georgia.

'Alright, everyone go to bed.' Mr Michaels clapped his hands. 'Now. Or I'll get Mr North.'

Slowly the girls stood up, with some dark mutters. He kicked some of the coals back into the centre of the fire, then continued to shoo the girls along. Madison took her phone from Cierra, slipping it quietly into her pocket.

When Jasmine unzipped the flap of her tent, she saw Bree lying on top of the sleeping bag, still awake, staring at the tent's ceiling. She rolled onto her side, facing away. Jasmine grabbed her toothbrush, water bottle and the cloth toiletries bag that now held one of the bags of weed, a cigarette lighter and a pipe.

She walked off into the trees and sat on a rock, taking out the weed and the pipe. A moment later, Cierra joined her. Jasmine packed the pipe, lit it, and then handed it to Cierra.

'How you doing?' said Cierra, before taking a drag.

'We're really doing this, aren't we,' said Jasmine.

'After tomorrow, everything's going to change,' said Cierra. She handed the pipe back.

Jasmine took a heavy drag and coughed. 'Are we doing the right thing?'

Cierra took a drag. 'We are. Madison knows what she's doing.'

They sat there smoking, neither speaking. Jasmine watched the trees. Finally she said, 'What is the game?'

Cierra went perfectly still.

'The game,' said Jasmine. 'I've heard you and Madison talking. Players, nudes.'

'I don't know what —'

'Tell me or I swear I'm going to tell Miss Ellis everything. *Everything*.'

'Don't be a bitch,' snapped Cierra.

'I'm not going into this if you and Madison are keeping secrets.'

Cierra looked like she was about to reply, then hesitated. She took another drag of the pipe. 'Alright, I'll tell you . . . tomorrow. This time tomorrow. Alright?'

Jasmine watched Cierra. 'You don't have to be afraid of Madison, you know,' she said. 'We would protect you.'

Cierra laughed. 'I'm not afraid of her. You don't know what you're talking about.'

'Alright, Cierra. If you say so. But just remember, me and Georgia are here for you.'

They turned back to the trees, and that's when Jasmine saw it. A chill ran down her back, the hairs rose on her arms.

'Cierra,' she hissed. 'Keep very still, and look to that group of trees, a little to the left.'

'What is it?' Cierra whispered back.

'It looks like someone's standing there. Watching us.'

Cierra shook her head. 'It's just a tree, Jaz.'

Jasmine kept watching. After a while, her breathing slowed down. 'Just a tree,' she said. She chuckled and tapped out the remaining weed. 'Gotta be careful with this stuff, it'll make you paranoid.'

Cierra laughed too, and they both stood up. She gave Jasmine a quick kiss on the cheek. 'You're my best friend, Jaz. Thank you for doing this.'

They walked back to the tents, shoulder to shoulder.

A branch cracked behind them.

'Just a wallaby?' said Cierra, even more high-pitched than normal.

The two of them walked faster, faster again, until they were running.

CHAPTER 3

MURPHY

It was well after nightfall when there was a knock on the door. Butch, rubbing the crick from his neck, went to answer it.

Murphy pushed himself away from the table and gently nudged Gus the Muss off his lap so he could stand, a headache sitting at the base of his skull. He stretched his back. The day had been long.

'G'day, lads,' drawled Skinner. He wore servo sunglasses, had long stringy hair, and tribal tattoos up both his wiry arms. He hugged Butch first, then Murphy. Murphy automatically turned to the side to avoid Skinner's bad breath – drugs had ruined his digestion. 'I brought a little gift tonight, to thank you for all your hard work.'

Butch's eyes lit up. 'What have you got?'

Skinner slipped a white spray bottle out of his pocket. 'Angel dust, my angels. And the best shit of its kind I've *ever tried*. Who wants fries with that?'

'I might sit this one out, mate,' said Murphy, eyeing the bottle. A fry was the street term for a joint sprayed with angel dust. Murphy had tried a fry only once, and it had been a very bad experience.

Besides, he avoided hard drugs like angel dust whenever possible. He was a father, after all.

'Don't be chicken shit, you're trying it,' said Skinner.

'Murphy is in, or I'll call the school and tell them Jasmine brought something a little *extra* to camp,' said Butch.

'She didn't bring anything,' said Murphy quickly.

'Murphy is in,' said Butch.

'Good man,' said Skinner. He tugged Murphy's beard as he walked towards the back door.

Their shed was decked out with plush couches, a loud sound-system, a fully stocked beer fridge, and a rusty wood stove.

Murphy sat smoking the fry he had reluctantly lit, watching the flames in the stove. Gus the Muss was on his lap again, purring. Skinner and Butch were debating something about politics – Skinner always got political when he was high.

Sara's face appeared in his mind. Ginger hair, brown eyes, wide smile, perfect teeth. Something twinged in his chest. Sara had always won political debates with the boys. It helped that she was always sober – she'd never even smoked weed. Still, she hadn't minded rubbing shoulders with Skinner. She was good like that. She didn't judge any of them for their business. She'd been a lawyer; she'd seen all kinds. Was fiercely smart.

He missed her so much. He'd do anything to have her back again. To have been there to keep her safe, somehow, from the illness that took her life.

A fierce fear ripped through him and he sat up suddenly. *Jasmine . . .*

The world lurched, the couch seemed like it was swallowing him. The PCP was setting in, waves flushing through his body – except not his body anymore, it felt like he was floating away from it. The fear seemed both childish and feverishly important.

He glanced out the cracked window, into the inky blackness of the Tiers at night. As the crow flew, the girls weren't really that far from where Murphy sat right now. *Jasmine. I can't lose you too . . .*

That was strange. His face was hot. He felt good. He felt scared.

The couch laughed, its stomach growling as it swallowed him deeper. He lifted up Gus the Muss, the cat looking at him, full of alien intelligence. It was beaming thoughts into his head. White lights flitted across his vision. A pleasant buzzing echoed in his ears, in his belly, in his groin . . . his heart pounded as he watched tears running down his own hairy cheeks.

He had two thoughts: *Take that fry out of your mouth before you pass out or you'll singe your beard* and *Sara . . . I can't lose you again.*

'Murph. Shit, man, wake up.'

Murphy stirred. Strobe lights pulsed under his eyelids, and when he opened them he saw it was morning. He was lying under a cabbage gum at the edge of the yard, protected from the rain. He had his big hunting jacket on but he was still freezing cold, and aching, and he was covered in scratches and scrapes. Even under the cover of the big tree, it felt like every stitch of his clothing was drenched.

He rolled onto his side and retched. Nothing came out; he could barely spit.

Butch patted his back. 'Clean yourself up, a bloody cop's here. She's inside. Wants to talk to you.'

'What?' His mouth felt as dry as cotton wool. Twigs stuck to his clothes, and thorns were caught in his hands. Had he been rolling around in the bush? How high had he *been*?

He put his hand to his head – his whole arm felt light as a feather. Scratch that: he was *still* high.

'Cops?' came Skinner's voice. He poked his head out of the shed. He looked to be naked.

'Nothing to do with you, Skin,' said Butch. 'Something's happened on Jasmine's school trip —'

'*What?*' said Murphy.

'I said, something's happened —'

But Murphy was already stumbling through the rain, into the house. He lurched from side to side, one leg feeling bigger than the other. The lights were still stuck to his vision.

A blonde policewoman stood in the dining room. 'Murphy. Remember me? Constable Cavanagh.'

Of course he remembered her, he knew all the local cops. 'Where's Jaz? What's happened?' He rested a hand against the table as the world tipped away from him.

When she spoke the words seemed to come from far away, as though deadened by strong wind. He shook his head, trying to dislodge whatever was in his ears. He had heard wrong.

'I think you better come with me,' said Cavanagh slowly.

'. . . but she wouldn't have *left* the track,' repeated Murphy over the sound of the siren and the wiper blades. He was hunched in the front of the police car, a Kia Stinger, gripping the handle. He was sobering up, but too slowly. Adrenaline and shock were making him shake. The car smelled of bloody *lavender*, and it was doing his head in.

'I believe you, Mr Murphy,' said Cavanagh.

Murphy understood he'd probably already told her all of this, but he couldn't remember how many times he'd said it. The world kept spinning around like he was on a show ride. And his mouth was *so bloody dry*. The rain on the outside of the windscreen, getting swished to the side, was enough to make him pant.

'We'll find them. But think, *are* there any other places she might have gone?'

'I'm telling you, she'd have come home first. And she's not stupid: there's no way she'd walk off in weather like this!' he shouted.

Cavanagh winced. 'Can you try not to yell? You're hurting my ears.'

A minute later, they turned a corner and pulled into the gravel car park of the hiking track.

Murphy was out and stumbling along before the car had even stopped.

Above them loomed the Tiers – misty, impenetrable. People were swarming everywhere in the sassafras clearing of the car park. Murphy was soaked with rain again. He tried to cup it in his palms to drink.

The largest assembly of people were huddled around the school bus, where he could make out a group of teenage girls dressed in hiking gear. None of them was Jasmine. Among them were two men he recognised, Thomas North and Jack Michaels.

Murphy felt a surge of anger at the sight of Jack, but pushed it to the side.

Everywhere were journalists – rough ones rugged up in jackets, dainty women with make-up and high heels who had assistants holding umbrellas over their heads, even a couple with big remote controls in their hands, flying camera drones overhead.

Watery flashing lights came from three ambulances and five police cars. One of the Limestone Creek rural fire trucks was also parked to the side, with equipment being unloaded. A few more dirtbikes were being unloaded from utes and even a couple horses in fluoro horse coats were interspersed in the crowds.

'Stop, mate.' A burly blond man in a suit stood in Murphy's way. He had the face of a boxer: crooked nose, scar on his eyebrow, looking slightly punch-drunk, with a stupid blond moustache. 'Where are you going?'

Murphy pulled out of the man's grip. 'Piss off.'

'He's with me, Detective Coops,' said Cavanagh, jogging up to them. 'His daughter is one of the missing.'

'There's a tent set up for families over there, there's soup and coffee —'

'Like hell,' said Murphy.

'— or if you want to help the search, go to the orange SES tent,' said Detective Coops. 'Join a search party, don't just run like a maniac through the kind of bush that'll kill you before you've gone fifty metres.'

'Want me to cuff him, Coops?' said a voice from behind.

Murphy spun, hands curling into fists.

Don't punch him, they'll lock you up, you have to find Jasmine . . . The voice of reason was stronger, but it took a physical effort not to square up to the man who approached.

Fleshy-faced with wobbly jowls like a basset hound. Police uniform stretched tight across a beer belly. Sergeant Doble.

'Heard your daughter is one of the missing, mate. You alright?' Doble's voice showed concern, but Murphy knew better.

'I'm going up there, Doble,' he said through clenched teeth.

'You've gotta follow rules, Murphy.'

'Sergeant Doble —' began Cavanagh.

'Thanks, constable. Leave him with me,' said Doble, then turned to the detective. 'I know this one, Coops,' he said in a loud whisper. 'Good job stopping him. Who knows what damage he might've caused up there.'

The detective looked Murphy up and down one last time, then continued on his way.

Murphy's skin felt like fire: the rage was building.

'Speaking of: where were you early this morning, Murphy? We aren't gonna find any sweet little girls in your basement, are we?' said Doble.

Murphy began to raise himself to his fullest height, ready to punch this fat prick —

'Everything alright here?' came a deep voice, a broad Australian accent with the faintest burring lisp.

'We're fine, Badenhorst,' said Doble. 'This is Jordan Murphy. The one I was telling you about – I bet you have some questions for him.'

'Ah. Good to meet you, mate.' The newcomer held out his hand to shake; the burr came from the way he spoke out of the side of his mouth. 'I'm Con Badenhorst.'

'*Senior Sergeant Detective* Con Badenhorst,' muttered Doble for Murphy's ears. 'Running lead on this.'

Badenhorst was a good-looking man with light sun-streaked hair, rain-swept to the side, and a jaw roughened with five o'clock shadow. He was lithe and athletic, but Murphy thought he could beat him in a fight. He looked like a surfer from the Gold Coast – distinctly out of place in Limestone Creek.

Badenhorst still had his hand held out, all the time in the world. His blue eyes studied Murphy, unaffected by his stiff refusal to shake his hand. He glanced away, over the crowd, taking in everything else, before swinging back around to Murphy. Arm still outstretched. Calm and assured.

There was a bustle of movement at a nearby tent, then a group jogged towards the head of the trail, guided by men and women in orange SES overalls.

Ignoring Badenhorst, Murphy ran after them, shaking his head to clear the last of the dizziness.

An SES officer stopped him at the entrance to the trail. 'Who are you?' she snapped.

'My daughter is up there.' He tried to push past her, but she moved in front of him.

'Then go to the tent. You can join the next party.'

'I don't need your *fucking permission* to search for *my* daughter!' Murphy shouted.

'Everything alright here?' said a large bearded man, one of the other SES officers.

'He wants to join the search, but doesn't want to join a team.'

'Then tell him to piss off.'

Murphy lunged for the trail, past them both, but the giant man grabbed him from behind. Murphy roared, twisting the man's pinkie finger back on itself until it popped, and the man howled.

Murphy ran three more metres before two SES workers tackled him to the ground, shouting, burying his face into the gravel.

Murphy went wild.

Minutes later, he was being muscled into the back of a police van, a bruise already forming on his cheek, a small trail of bruised searchers and bloodied noses behind him. He roared insults at the officers as he strained against the handcuffs, veins popping in his neck, his beard flecked with saliva, blood dripping from his nose. Cameras flashed, even as lightning streaked through the clouds and thunder boomed.

CHAPTER 4

CON

Detective Con Badenhorst watched the police van pull out of the car park, with Jordan Murphy still raging inside. His eyes lingered on the road even after the van had disappeared around the corner.

Bit of a loose unit, he finally decided.

'I'll go down to the station and have a chat with Murphy now, Badenhorst,' said Sergeant Doble, appearing at his side.

'Thanks, mate, but I need you here.'

'Nah, I'm telling you, if anyone in this town has something to do with this, it'll be Murphy. You saw him.' He spoke half to himself. 'Someone needs to find out why he was so keen to get onto that track, and if this blows up any more than it already has —'

'It's alright, mate. Thanks for the offer,' said Con again, eyes roving the car park.

'Look, Badenhorst —' began Doble.

'Detective, a few words?' came a voice from nearby. It was a newswoman, closing in fast.

Her approach identified him to the gaggle of media huddled under a shell of umbrellas. They came swarming like seagulls to a chip.

'Of course,' he said, forcing a smile.

Once word had got out about four teenage girls going missing, media from all over Australia had gathered to this nowhere country town with inhuman speed. Con had transferred to Tasmania from his native Sydney over a year ago, but even there he'd rarely seen so much media assemble so fast.

Commander Normandy should have been dealing with them. Which, of course, meant Con would be dealing with them. *It's all part of the job,* he reminded himself. But damn, he wanted this case solved as quickly as possible.

'Are you expecting to find the girls safe and unharmed?' asked one journalist.

'We are hoping for the best, of course, but preparing for any eventuality.'

'But the Tiers are dangerous, especially this area,' prompted another. 'What safety precautions are the SES taking?'

'They're trained for situations exactly like this.'

The media swarm shuffled, jostling for position.

'Could the girls have just run away?'

'Considering the conditions, it's not likely,' said Con.

'Is there an assumed connection to the 1985 disappearances in the Meander Valley area? Teenage girls, taken from bushland?' The journalist paused for effect. 'Is the Hungry Man active again?'

The swarm pressed closer.

'We have four teenage girls missing on a hiking track in a storm,' said Con. 'So it would be helpful not to make it bigger than it is. It's not something we haven't dealt with before, we know where the girls are – they're up there *somewhere,*' he waved his hand in the direction of the looming bluffs, 'and the SES will get to them.'

'So why are the CIB here?'

'Standard procedure,' said Con with a toothy grin.

'So there is no assumption that the 1985 killings are related . . .?'

'No. The 1985 killer was found,' said Con.

Now the questions came hard and fast.

'Could there be a copycat killer?' shouted one newswoman.

'The family of Theodore Barclay still claim his innocence,' shouted another. 'And the bodies were never found.'

'Should the teenage girls of Limestone Creek be taking extra security measures?'

'A man was just taken away,' said another. 'Jordan Murphy. He's the father of one of the missing. Is it true he assaulted a search volunteer? Is he considered a person of interest?'

'Well, yes, but we can't discuss our suspects yet,' said Doble loudly.

'Sergeant, leave this to me,' said Con firmly.

'Of course, if anyone has information, please come forward,' continued Doble, shouting over the top of Con. 'You can call Crime Stoppers on 1800 333 000, or come down to the Limestone Creek station. We promise you – your safety is our concern. We do not condone intimidation of any kind, and you don't need to be afraid of men like Jordan Murphy.'

'*Enough*, mate,' said Con.

Doble looked pleased with himself: the damage was done. He muttered under his breath, 'Out-of-towner dipshit . . .'

Just what Con needed: local police with attitude.

Over the heads of the media, he could see his partner, Detective Sergeant Gabriella Pakinga. She was leading one of the uniformed officers over to the media pack. She shoved him in front of the cameras and shouted, in a husky Kiwi accent, 'This is Constable Darren Cahil. He's a local and he knows these mountains, so he's going to be coordinating the search. Any questions?'

As the cameras and reporters descended on the sharp-eyed Constable Darren, Gabriella pulled Con away, holding her umbrella above them both.

Doble was still alongside him, and Con grabbed his arm. 'I've changed my mind. Head down to the station. You can write a report for me on everything that's happened so far. I can send it through to the commander.'

Doble looked down at where Con held his arm. 'You wanna let go of me? I'm not your secretary.'

'Remember, nice big words in the report. Think you can manage that?' Con let go and Doble stalked off towards his patrol car.

Gabriella stepped in beside Con with the umbrella. 'We don't like him?'

'Just your usual dickhead. Thinks I'm an arrogant out-of-towner.'

'You *are* an arrogant out-of-towner.' Gabriella's whole body shook when she laughed.

He sighed and led the way to the command centre tent. 'What have you got for me, Gabby?'

'Don't call me Gabby,' she said. 'They're going to have to go slower with the search. There's sleet in that rain, it might even start snowing soon. The fog is only getting thicker. The last thing we need is to lose a couple of volunteer searchers over a cliff, and in these conditions they're just as likely to ruin the girls' tracks as find them.'

'Surely it's not cold enough to snow,' said Con, distracted. 'Can the dogs scent anything?'

'They just sit down. It's like they don't want to search.'

'That's no good,' said Con. 'Dock their pay.'

She snorted. 'I don't get it either.' Then she shivered. 'First the legends, now the dogs. This whole place is giving me the willies. How do four girls just disappear? Those stories from 1985 . . .'

'Four girls *don't* just disappear,' he said sternly. 'Don't start getting weird on me.' He pointed up towards the mountains, hidden by the weather. 'We know that they're up there somewhere. We'll find them and then we can go home. And after that you can burn your sage and cleanse your chakras.'

'Don't joke about it,' she said, slapping the back of his head. 'What about Eliza Ellis and her head wounds?'

Con went silent, footsteps crunching in the wet gravel. 'Maybe she tripped?'

'Ah, of course, poor helpless woman just tripped over in the big scary bush,' said Gabriella scathingly. 'So, what next?'

'We wait for the ambos to finish with Eliza and, when they say she's ready to speak, we question her and then head to where the girls were last seen. Anything we find out in the meantime is a bonus.'

Suddenly it grew cold. Icily cold. White flecks filled the air in a flurry.

Con held out his hand, catching a flake. 'What?'

'I hear the cool kids are calling it "snow",' said Gabriella with false sincerity. 'The SES say the Tiers are like an even shittier version of Melbourne: four seasons in one day. Also, that means it could get worse.'

The flurry of snow swirled around them, and just as fast it was replaced by cold rain again.

Gabriella shivered. 'Creepy.'

In that moment one of the local constables came bustling into the command tent.

'They've found something,' she said, voice trembling.

'Oh good,' said Gabriella.

'Ah shit,' said Con.

CHAPTER 5

MURPHY

He'd been there at least three hours – it had to be mid-afternoon by now. Murphy beat his fists against the table of the interview room, the metal cuffs stoking his fury. No amount of shouting brought anyone to the room. He was cold, wet, thirsty, and blood from his nose had congealed in his beard.

Jasmine . . . Please, God, let her be okay.

Bang.

Let her be okay. I swear I'll do better. I'll stop dealing weed.

Bang bang bang.

I'll stop being a dickhead of a dad . . .

The door opened and Sergeant Doble walked in with a folder of documents and a digital recorder.

Murphy stood, the chain around his cuffs catching on the table and holding his big frame hunched. 'Have they found her?'

'You've done it now,' said Doble. He put the recorder on the table and clicked it on. 'Where were you this morning, Mr Murphy?'

'Answer my question.'

'No alibi?'

He sat back down. Murphy wasn't an idiot. He knew what Doble was angling for. 'With Butch. Playing video games.'

'Yep, of course. That's always your answer, isn't it, Murphy? "Playing *GTA* and shooting up cops."'

'Ask Butch.'

'It's serious this time, Murphy.' He flicked the file he'd brought. 'Your alibi is always the same thing.'

'I want my lawyer,' said Murphy. This was driving him crazy, but you couldn't show weakness around cops.

Doble watched him a moment, a faint smile turning his lips. He switched off the recorder. 'You're in over your head this time, aren't you?'

Murphy refused to look away. He bared his teeth, knowing they were smeared with blood.

'You know . . . I could help you out of this,' said Doble.

There was a knock at the door.

'I'm busy in here,' shouted Doble. He hastily switched the recorder back on.

The door opened and Detective Con Badenhorst entered, the top two buttons of his wet shirt undone. 'Wrap up your questions please. Pakinga and I need a chat with Mr Murphy.' His face gave away nothing that Murphy could read.

A Maori woman walked in behind him. She immediately sized up Murphy, and he did the same. She was huge, and she looked hard.

For a moment Murphy thought Doble would argue, but he gave a sickening smile and gestured for Badenhorst to take the empty chair beside him. 'I'm not sure how much good it will do. Mr Murphy has demanded legal representation.'

'Have you found Jasmine?' said Murphy.

'We don't have any more info than what Sergeant Doble has already told you,' said Con.

'They haven't found nothing at all?'

'Sergeant Doble *didn't* tell you?' said Con.

'I didn't get the chance to,' said Doble. 'He was being unco-operative.'

'You found something?' Murphy hated the desperation in his voice.

'On the trail. A bag of marijuana, with a sticker that says THE CAPTAIN, and a bit further up a water bottle with blood on it.' Con's voice changed, grew a bit softer. 'The bottle has Jasmine's name on it. We need your permission to grab some DNA off her toothbrush to confirm it's Jasmine's blood —'

Jasmine's blood . . .

Something roared in Murphy's ears. He wrenched against the cuffs on the table, shouting profanity. He was barely aware of the words leaving his mouth as he kicked the chair over behind him, kicked against the metal legs of the table. 'Let me go right this fucking second or I'll rip out your throats!'

It took a few moments before he came back to himself. He stood panting and sweaty, his wrists bleeding, his temple pounding, his throat raw.

The woman righted the chair for him, looking for all the world like she'd enjoyed the show. He sat down heavily.

'Not such a big man now, are you?' murmured Doble.

'Sergeant, give us the room,' said Con. His eyes were trained on Murphy.

'I think I'll stay here,' said Doble. 'He's a dangerous man.'

'Mr Murphy is chained to the table,' said Con, voice dry.

'This is my station. I'm staying right here,' said Doble.

The door slammed open. 'It's alright, Murphy, mate. I'm here now.'

Murphy felt a swell of relief in his chest. Dave Llewellyn, his dad's old lawyer, from back when Dad ran the business. In his mid-fifties and always somewhat toadlike, today he looked particularly pale and unwell.

'Get me out of here, Dave,' Murphy croaked.

'Sorry I'm so late. Butch called me this morning, but I had to come all the way from Hobart. Lots of bloody corners between here and there.' Dave wiped his sleeve across his face and sat beside Murphy. He glanced up at Detective Badenhorst, took in his wet shirt, his tousled hair.

Badenhorst introduced himself and his partner – Detective Sergeant Gabriella Pakinga – before starting his questioning. 'I know this is a difficult time, Mr Murphy. Please remember these are just standard questions, okay?'

Murphy only scowled.

'Does your daughter have any enemies, that you know of?'

Murphy glanced at Dave, who nodded. 'I think you better answer their questions. Go ahead.'

'No,' said Murphy. 'No enemies.'

'Do *you* have any enemies?'

Murphy looked straight at Doble. 'None.'

'Do we have permission to grab Jasmine's DNA from her toothbrush? And release a photo of her to the media?'

'Yeah,' said Murphy.

'And can you think of *any* reason someone might want to kidnap your daughter? Maybe because of some sort of . . . product you provide?' said Con.

'Don't answer that,' said Dave.

'I don't know what you're talking about,' said Murphy.

'Listen, my client is bleeding,' said Dave. 'Are the cuffs *really* necessary, Detective?'

Con sighed. 'Sergeant Doble, remove the cuffs.'

'You can't be serious,' said Doble. 'He assaulted two policemen up at the search. He just went bloody apeshit right in this room. No.'

'Bloody hell, Murph,' muttered Dave. 'Again?'

'Sergeant Doble, the cuffs, *please*,' said Con.

'No, I won't,' snapped Doble.

'Very well,' said Dave, swelling up like a bullfrog. 'Then I'm taking my client out of here. He hasn't been charged with anything and he needs to go to the hospital to have his injuries attended to.'

'Alright. Fair enough,' Con said, sounding tired.

'What?' said Doble. He looked between Dave and Con. 'Like hell he's leaving.'

'If you'd listened to me before, we wouldn't be in this mess.' Con stood up. 'As the superior officer in this room for this case, I asked you to remove the cuffs. You refused. Under the police brutality laws, Mr Murphy is now free to leave.'

Doble's mouth widened and closed. 'Bullshit,' he finally said.

'Sergeant Doble, if you don't unlock those cuffs right now, I'm going to have to take this to the commander,' said Con.

Doble's jowls flushed pink, rising up into his cheeks until they burned red. He unlocked Murphy's cuffs.

Murphy stood, feeling his bleeding wrists to judge the damage.

Con reached his hand across the desk, a peace offering. 'Let's try this again. I'm Detective Con Badenhorst.'

After a moment, surprising even himself, Murphy took Con's hand and shook it, blood running down his palm. He had questions, but he knew to keep them to himself in a police interview room.

'Here's our card, it has both our numbers on it,' said Gabriella, handing business cards to both Dave and Murphy. 'If you think of anything that might be useful, give one of us a yell. Come on, Con. And *don't* touch me,' she said, shuddering as Con held open the hand smeared with Murphy's blood.

The two detectives left the room, leaving the door wide open behind them.

'Are those two for real?' muttered Dave. 'How did *they* make it to detective?'

Murphy turned to Doble. 'You're gonna spend the rest of your life eating through a —'

'Enough, Murphy,' snapped Dave. Doble just glared at them. 'Let's go.'

They headed out through the tiled and whitewashed station corridors. It was a path Murphy knew well.

'Well, that was a lucky throw. Those must be the two thickest detectives I've ever met. I was just trying to bluff our way out of there – you looked like you were about to explode – but I had no idea about that police brutality law. Or maybe I did, subconsciously? You know, I took an IQ test once, and I'm not saying I'm a genius, *but . . .*'

Murphy wasn't listening. *Don't think about Jasmine's drink bottle. You have to stay strong for her. But why* would *there be blood on her bottle? And a bag of our weed – oh God, please don't let anything happen to her . . .*

They turned the corner into the lobby and there were the detectives, standing at a coffee machine.

'I'm not *that* thick, Mr Llewellyn,' said Badenhorst, cleaning his hands from one of the hand sanitisers on the wall. 'The law doesn't work like that, but Doble wouldn't know.'

Dave stopped short, looking between Badenhorst and Pakinga. 'What?'

'Mr Murphy, I know you don't have anything to do with the girls going missing,' said Badenhorst. 'Your brother stopped in earlier, corroborating your alibi. So look, Gabby and I are on our way to the hospital. Want to come with us? We'll have the sirens on.'

'I don't need the hospital.'

'Well, here's some reasons you might want to come. Number one: Eliza Ellis is awake and ready to talk to us. I'm sure you're as keen to know what happened up there as we are. Two: honestly, going by the blood still coming out of your wrists, you probably *do* need to go to the hospital. Three: if we find Jasmine, she'll be taken straight to emergency. It would be good if you were there.'

Con shrugged, hands in his pockets now.

'Four . . . it means you don't go trying to climb that mountain again by yourself, and Doble doesn't give you any more grief. Just saves *me* a headache.' He grinned, trying to make the last statement a joke.

Pakinga handed Badenhorst a takeaway cup. When she tasted her own, she grimaced and threw the entire thing in the bin.

Badenhorst turned to the door, sipping his coffee. 'Your choice, but we're leaving now.' He kept walking, Gabriella walking behind.

Murphy hesitated. Truthfully, he wanted to be up there in the mountains searching . . . but would he learn more by speaking to Eliza?

The mountains or the hospital. He stood there until Con and Gabriella were out of sight. Finally, reason won out.

'Dave, I need to be there when they question Eliza. But stay in town for a bit. I don't think Doble's done with me. Butch will make sure you're paid.'

He jogged after the detectives.

He didn't trust them as far as he could throw them, but Jasmine came first.

CHAPTER 6

CON

Con drove the squad car with the heaters on, his pants and shirt saturated. Launceston Hospital was almost an hour's drive from Limestone Creek, but a lot faster in a police car. The red and blue lights of the Kia Stinger flashed off the guideposts as they sped through the rain and gathering gloom of the Tasmanian countryside. A glance in the side mirror showed the shrouded Great Western Tiers disappearing into the distance.

I'm gonna use every trick in the book to solve this is as quick as possible, he thought, tapping his fingers against the steering wheel.

Murphy leaned against the back-seat window, his wrists messily bandaged by Gabriella from the car's first-aid kit, nursing the bottle of water they'd given him. Even though Con was blasting the warm air and Murphy was in a thick jacket, the big man was shivering: it could have been his wet clothes, it could have been shock, it could have been plain fatigue.

Con felt a nudge of unease when he thought of the man's outbursts, up at the search area and then again at the station. Murphy had been like an animal, more beast than man. Con had worked youth cases for almost his whole police career, so he knew quite a bit about childhood trauma – how it looked, how it worked, what triggered it. Based on a look at Murphy's police file earlier, which boasted violence, risk-taking behaviour and alleged drug dealing, Con thought there were decent odds there was trauma in that man's past, which would help to explain the explosive anger. He'd need to tread lightly to get him to cooperate.

In the passenger seat beside him, Gabriella was on her laptop, also studying Murphy's file. Neither of them believed Murphy's alibi for a second, but Con still wanted him with them at the hospital.

Con knew that he needed to get Murphy somewhere more comfortable before he'd talk, and more importantly, away from Doble. It didn't hurt that the lawyer hadn't come along either, although the man didn't seem like he'd have been much of an obstacle if he had.

Most of all, Con wanted Murphy to talk to Eliza. When they'd first arrived at the scene, the teacher had been in an ambulance and was unable to say anything that made sense. They needed to send someone else in before they spoke to her. A familiar face – a worried parent – would be perfect to draw some sense out of Eliza Ellis, because if she was *this* concussed, then detectives, no matter how nice they were, would make her anxious and forgetful. He didn't love the idea of putting a potential suspect in the room with her, but considering the girls had already been missing for hours, it was an acceptable gamble.

'How are you going back there, mate?' said Con. 'Anyone you want us to call?'

Murphy shook his head, watching the window.

'Warm enough back there?' Murphy didn't respond. Finally, Con said softly, 'What does your gut say?'

Murphy glanced up at him through the rear-view mirror. 'What?'

'Your daughter. What does your gut say has happened?'

Murphy's eyes narrowed, looking for a trap. Then he said, 'She's too smart to go off the trail. If she got lost, she'd stay where she was. She's really protective, so if one of her friends was hurt, she'd probably jump off a cliff to save her. Otherwise, the only way she'd leave that track is if she was taken or if she was tricked.' He shook his head once, like brushing off a fly. 'How far away are we?'

'That bad?' said Gabriella. 'We might have some painkillers.'

'I'm bloody fine,' he said, 'but no one has told me anything about what happened up there. Was Eliza the only one there?'

'You know her, do you?' said Gabriella.

Con approved of her avoiding his question. They'd agreed to keep Murphy in the dark as much as possible, in case he offered details about the case he shouldn't know.

'I know most people in this town. Plus she's Jasmine's teacher.'

'But it's not just that school connection, right?' said Con. It was important if he knew Eliza well – it made him an even better choice for drawing sense out of her.

'I've seen her at the pub a lot of times. Even had a few drinks together, back in the day. But not since she became Jasmine's teacher. Why?' he said, gruff, those piercing blue eyes narrowed again.

'Just wondering what she's like,' said Con. 'Haven't properly met her yet. The ambulance took her almost as soon as we got there. We didn't get a chance to ask too many questions. She was a bit . . . would you say "delirious", Gab?'

'"Delirious" is a good descriptor,' said Gabriella. She had closed the file on Murphy and was reading the emails being sent their way – Detective Stuart Coops, also assigned to this case, was currently interviewing the teachers, the school social worker, the parents, going through school reports and police records.

'Yeah, well . . .' said Murphy, sounding defensive. 'Eliza's good with the kids. Best Literacy teacher Jasmine's ever had. The girls all love her. She went through the ringer last year when her niece killed herself, so this is going to really mess her up.'

'Her niece?' That caught Gabriella's attention and she began typing into her computer to look up the details.

They entered the outskirts of Deloraine, the closest large-ish town – not that any towns in Tasmania were particularly large; the whole island had a lower population than the district of Geelong. Con navigated the streets, all the traffic pulling aside for his lights and siren, until they merged onto the Bass Highway. Now he could really stretch the Stinger's legs, and they sped towards Launceston.

'Do you mind if I ask another question?' said Con. 'Do you know why Sergeant Doble has a grudge against you?'

'Yeah, I slept with his wife,' said Murphy sarcastically.

Gabriella chuckled without looking up from her laptop. 'Delicious. I love a little country-bogan scandal.'

'Laugh at me again and see what happens.'

'Threaten my partner again and I'll bury you in the ground,' said Con, his voice sudden ice.

'Stop it, boys, you're both pretty,' said Gabriella, hitting Con on the leg.

The men had a brief staring contest, until Con had to look away to focus on the road. 'Whatever, mate,' muttered Murphy, leaning against the window.

Gabriella turned on the radio, so she and Con could talk without being overheard. He glanced back at Murphy and saw his eyes closed.

'What's wrong with you, Badenhorst?' said Gabriella. 'Getting a bit testy there? Those poor girls going missing a bit of an inconvenience for you?'

'Keep your voice down, he's still awake,' whispered Con.

Gabriella glanced behind her. 'No he isn't.'

'He's pretending,' said Con, watching him in the rear-view.

'I don't reckon he had anything to do with the girls disappearing,' said Gabriella.

'You're just a sucker for a lumberjack,' said Con. 'Listen, I have an idea.' He leaned across, watching the road even as he spoke low into Gabriella's ear. Whispering, he explained that he wanted to send Murphy in to coax information out of Eliza, but he needed to find some way to get his voice recorder into the room to capture their conversation.

Gabriella shook her head. 'Sounds unnecessarily complicated.'

'I don't want to take risks, but time is important here. You know what these country folk are like: probably more likely to open up to one of their own.'

'Con, even after a year down here, I think the only thing you know about country folk is what you've read in books.'

They drove in silence for some time, Gabriella tapping at the computer. 'Eliza's niece was named Denni King. Her suicide was a messy affair . . . and it involved Madison Mason, Cierra's sister. She's some kind of YouTube celebrity. This is interesting.'

'Jasmine . . .' Murphy croaked, pulling at his seatbelt as he woke up. He cast around, eyes bloodshot and wide. When he realised Con was watching him, he looked away with a scowl. He covered his face with his forearm, resting against the car door. Though he tried to hide it, his shoulders shook in silent sobs, tears rolling down from behind his arm.

Con shifted in his seat. *Still a suspect,* he thought.

The Launceston General Hospital was a grey and sprawling complex, the traffic in its avenues and car parks moving slowly in the rain. They pulled into a loading zone near the emergency department.

Murphy jumped out of the car before it had stopped moving.

The three of them headed straight into emergency. Con showed his badge to the nurse at the desk, asking about Eliza.

'Transferred to the medical ward,' said the nurse without looking up from her computer.

Con nudged Murphy forward. 'Well, here's where we leave you. You'd better get your wrists sorted.'

'Like hell,' said Murphy. 'I'm coming with you.' He set off in search of the medical ward, and Con and Gabriella jogged to catch up with him. When they found it, the nurse at the desk pointed the way to Eliza's room.

'Ah, damn,' said Con, pausing. 'We need to call the commander first.'

'What?' said Murphy.

'It's fine . . . you go ahead,' said Gabriella. 'We'll be right in behind you.'

'Gabby, I dunno if we should let him in without us —'

'It's fine, he deserves to see her,' she said. 'Go, Mr Murphy. We'll follow once we've made all the right calls.'

Murphy glanced between them, then loped off into the ward.

'Good job,' said Con quietly.

'Call me Gabby one more time and I'll blind you,' she muttered, flicking her hair back.

Con flashed his badge again and asked someone on the staff to bring them Eliza's current medical file. Then he and Gabriella stepped into an empty room that smelled of antiseptic and urine, and sat on a crisp-linen bed. Con pulled out his phone and AirPods, passing one to Gabriella. He pulled open the app that was synced to his live voice recorder.

'Slipped it in his pocket when I nudged him at the intake desk.'

'You sly fox. Ignoring the fact this is illegal, of course.'

She went silent as a burly male nurse entered, holding the

requested folder with all of Eliza's details, including photos of her injuries. Gabriella winked at the nurse, who winked back.

'Plus, given he's Jasmine's dad, if she takes the chance to apologise to him and ease some of that guilt she's carrying, *we* should be able to get to the point much quicker when we go in.'

'Your compassion is overwhelming,' said Gabriella, her finger to her ear.

CHAPTER 7

MURPHY

Murphy stepped into Eliza's room.

Eliza was upright in bed, propped up by pillows. Her head was wrapped in bandages, her honey hair falling around her face. She wore a thick white bathrobe, the blankets pulled up to her waist, and she was speaking with a plump, grey-haired nurse who sat beside her.

'Who're you?' demanded the nurse, standing up. 'If you're another journalist, I swear to the Lord Jesus that I'll —'

'Murphy!' said Eliza, leaning forward. 'Have they found them?' Her voice was hoarse. 'Tell me they've found them.'

Murphy shook his head.

Eliza swayed, putting one hand to her head. 'No . . . Murphy. It's . . . it's all my fault.'

'You know this man?' said the nurse. 'Is he family?'

'He's the father of one of the girls.'

The nurse's face softened. 'Oh, you poor thing,' she said to him, changing her attitude instantly. 'If there's anything I can . . .' She saw the blood on his bandaged wrists.

'It's fine,' said Murphy.

Undeterred, the nurse quickly snapped on some gloves, lifted his hands and began unravelling the bandages.

'Who wrapped this, a child? This is woeful . . .' She hissed at the cuff wounds once they were exposed, still oozing blood.

'Are you okay, Murphy?' said Eliza. 'You must want to kill me . . .'

'What happened up there? They're not telling me anything.' He ignored the nurse as she rummaged in a trolley, returning to spray sharp-smelling antiseptic onto his wounds.

'It . . . it's hazy, Murphy. I think I took a blow to the head. But . . . I was with the four of them. Cierra, Georgia, Bree, Jasmine. We were trailing behind the main group.'

'Why weren't you with everyone else?'

'I held them back. *I* did. This morning . . . there was a fight. I thought it would be better to keep them separate.'

'A fight?'

'Between Madison and Jasmine.'

Murphy's stomach lurched, even as he recognised it was an irrational thing to be concerned about, considering she was missing. 'Was Jaz alright?'

'Madison ended up with a black eye, and Jasmine had a cut lip. Tom and Jack had already left with all the other girls. I still had Madison and Jasmine, as well as Georgia, Cierra, and Bree Wilkins. Do you remember Bree?'

'She was friends with your Denni.'

'Yes,' said Eliza. 'Friends with my Denni. And now I've lost four more girls . . .' Her voice wavered.

'Don't say that. It wasn't your fault,' said Murphy. 'Not Denni, not these girls. But what were they fighting about?'

'I don't know, Murphy! I think it was about a boy. The five of them were lagging behind everyone else at the campsite. I thought they were just being lazy, and I knew better than to let Tom or Jack try to hurry them up. You know what those girls are like.

'But before I knew it they were pushing and shoving and shouting. Madison punched Jasmine and Jasmine hit her back, then it was just chaos. I broke it up, with the help of the other girls. Madison was still fuming, and I was sure they would start up again, so I sent her on ahead to catch up with Tom and Jack.' Eliza spoke quickly. 'I know that was a mistake, but they hadn't gone that far ahead . . . I thought it was best . . .'

'But Jasmine was okay?' said Murphy. The nurse had finished treating his wrists and led him to the chair beside Eliza's bed.

'She seemed fine. You know that she's strong, Murphy. I tried to find out what had happened, but the girls were all tight-lipped. I made the rest walk with me . . . slowly, so we wouldn't catch up with Madison. Cierra was crying and Georgia looked like she was going to vomit. Bree was blaming Jasmine, but Jasmine was fine, just kept chewing on her drink bottle.' She paused. Her lip trembled for a moment, but she brought it back under control, seeming irritated at her weakness. 'If I hadn't made them walk so slow —'

'Then what?' Murphy hated himself for rushing her, but he was desperate.

'We walked together, I don't know, maybe thirty minutes? I was at the front and Georgia was talking to me, but the other three kept dragging their feet – Bree especially – and everyone was getting spread out and . . .' Eliza made a conscious effort to slow down. 'It took me too long to realise we had become separated from Jasmine, Cierra and Bree. I told Georgia we needed to go back and find them, but she sat down on the ground and said she was too tired, she was going to wait for me. And . . . and . . . I went back, and . . .' She took another breath. 'This is where my memory goes . . . funny. It's almost like it's a dream. Does that make sense, Murphy?'

Murphy put a hand on her wrist. Eliza was shaking like a leaf, and her skin was hot to the touch.

'Murphy,' she said, 'things went *strange*.'

'What do you mean?' Murphy moved closer, now sitting on the bed beside her. He ignored the nurse, who was still hovering, keenly listening in.

'It's crazy to say it now, but it was like walking into a bubble . . . All the noise stopped. The birds, the wind. I couldn't hear anything except my own footsteps, and they were so *loud* . . .' She took a shaky breath. 'I got scared. I've never felt so scared in my life. It wasn't even normal, I was running – it was like I was running for my life.' She grunted, tears now running down her cheeks. 'It sounds so *stupid!*'

'Eliza, what *happened*?'

'I don't know! I don't know! I kept walking, shouting, until – something hit me on the head? I remember waking up in bare feet – one of the other girls, Carmen, she was the one who found me. I told her to run back to safety, but she came back with Jack. They found me under a flower bush further down the track, I was curled up and vomiting. I don't remember how I got there, but I remember them finding me. The doctors say I was vomiting because I was concussed. They brought me back to the bus, and that's when they called . . . everyone. It feels like . . . I can't explain it, but things just went so weird up there . . .'

Murphy felt a pain in his hands. He looked down to see his knuckles were white from clenching so tight. 'Who hit you? Did you see them?' he asked.

'No,' said Eliza, her voice full of pain. 'I didn't see a thing.'

CHAPTER 8

CON

In the room next door, scratching his stubble and listening to every word, Con glanced at Gabriella.

'The sounds on the mountain went quiet . . .?' he said.

Gabriella looked excited. 'You go in,' she said. 'I want to google something real quick.'

'Google what?'

'Just go, Con.'

He stood up, leaving his phone and the earphones with her.

When he walked into Eliza's room, all eyes turned to him. 'G'day, everyone,' he said pleasantly. He flashed his badge, then nodded to Eliza. 'Sorry I'm late. Had to sort a few things out. My name is Detective Con Badenhorst, but you can call me Con. Murphy, can you give us the room please?' He smiled at the nurse. 'I'm sure the hospital can find you something to eat.'

He felt Murphy's jacket, reaching into the pocket with one hand as he gripped the collar with his other. 'This is still soaked. Want me to find a heater and dry it off?'

'Get off me!' Murphy pushed his hands away and Con pocketed

the voice recorder. The nurse took hold of Murphy, leading him out of the room.

'Hey, we're *not* done,' protested Murphy, even as the door clicked shut behind them.

Con sat down in the chair beside Eliza's bed.

'Have they found them?' she begged, her bloodshot eyes searching his. 'Anything at all?'

'The weather has been hampering the search. But they did find Jasmine's drink bottle, with blood on it.'

'She had a cut lip,' said Eliza. 'From the fight.'

She let her head fall back on the pillow. Con stayed silent. He pulled out his notebook and waited. She glanced at him, down at his notebook, up to his face. He kept an expression of deepest interest, but didn't say a word.

'You want to know what happened up there,' she said.

Con smiled and clicked his pen.

She waited a moment, then began to recount the same tale he'd heard her tell Murphy. The fight, and sending Madison ahead. How Eliza realised the other girls were missing and went back to find them. Things going strange. The silence, the disorientation, the storm.

Con stayed silent throughout the whole thing, jotting down notes occasionally, but keeping his eyes on her. He'd been told his deep blue eyes could be unnerving – he had this trick where he didn't blink, didn't waver, just stared, writing notes without looking at the page.

When she'd finished, she fell silent and watched him. 'Does that all sound mad?' she finally said.

Con didn't reply. He let the silence build further. People often provided more information than necessary in order to fill silence.

'Are you okay, detective?' She was watching him curiously.

'Anything else?' he said, irritated. Neither his eye trick nor the silence was working.

'Well . . . I think . . .' she began. 'It just sounds so stupid, and I honestly think Georgia might've been making it up.'

'What's that?' he said, leaning forward.

'On the path, before the girls disappeared . . . Georgia told me that she thought she saw a figure watching us.'

'She saw someone? Why haven't you told anyone?'

'I thought she was seeing things,' she said. 'Even *she* didn't tell me right away because *she* didn't believe it. But when we walked through one of the patches of swamp, where the trees are clearer, she said she'd seen someone at the top of one of the ridges, one that looks like a fish fin.'

'Did she say what they looked like?' said Con.

'Georgia said that . . . well, like a . . . huge . . .' Her voice trailed off in frustration.

'Like a what?'

'A bear-man.' She sighed. 'See? This is why I didn't tell anyone. Georgia thought she saw a bear in the bush.'

'A . . . bear.' Con had a mad urge to laugh, which he quickly quelled. 'But you didn't see it?'

'Like I said, she didn't point it out at the time. She said she didn't want to scare any of the other girls, or let them make fun of her.'

'Did Georgia say *anything* else?'

'Just that, whatever it was, once she had seen it, it ducked behind a tree. It didn't want to be seen. Georgia said it looked like it was carrying something on its back.'

The door opened and an elderly doctor entered. He looked angry. 'Sorry, detective, I'm not sure who told you you could be in here. Miss Ellis needs to rest. She's in no state to answer questions.'

Gabriella stepped in beside the doctor. She shrugged at Con, sipping a coffee she must have weaselled out of the hospital staff. 'I told him you needed more time, but he insisted.'

Con felt another flash of irritation, but he hid it. 'Sorry, mate, but this is important,' he said to the doctor. 'Lives might be at stake.'

'Don't call me mate, it's crass,' said the doctor, but he softened. 'How much longer?'

'Eliza, this other figure – however weird, it might be our only lead. Is there anything else? Could you take us back to that location?'

'Maybe? Right now, in this state, I'm not sure.' She pointed angrily at her own head, indignant at her weakness. 'But I've told you everything I remember. The girls were there, and then they weren't.' She put her hands over her face. 'This has to be a nightmare. I have to help find them.'

The doctor coughed meaningfully at Con and gestured towards the door.

'Thanks for talking to me, Eliza. It's been very helpful,' said Con. 'Focus on getting better first, but let us know if you remember *anything* else. That's how you can help find the girls.'

He nodded at the doctor and stepped out into the corridor, where Gabriella was waiting for him.

'I spoke to that doctor, but he wouldn't budge,' she said. 'He told me we're obviously dealing with a concussion, and that doesn't just mess with your memory, it can affect your personality too – confusion, mood swings, paranoia. It's not just that she doesn't remember, she might not be entirely herself, and who knows how long that will last. We need to take everything she says with a grain of salt.'

'Yeah, I gathered that. Just how hard *did* she hit her head?'

Gabriella showed him one of the photos from Eliza's file: it was Eliza's forehead, showing a big gash surrounded by a purple bruise. 'She hit her forehead on the ground – but the wound on the back of her head . . .' She showed him another photo: the back of Eliza's head, her blonde hair pulled aside to reveal a bloody lump. 'Blunt force. They found pieces of bark in there.' Gabriella showed him a third photo. 'The soles of her feet. Look how scratched up they are: she was walking around barefoot for hours, probably.' Her face was flushed. 'Isn't this *weird*?'

'You just missed the best part.' He loaded up the recording on his phone and played it back.

When it was done, Gabriella let out a breath. 'Georgia saw someone?'

'Georgia thought she saw a bear,' clarified Con.

'Or a yowie. Could it have been one of the girls on its back?'

'The girls were all still with Eliza at that stage.'

'Maybe it was someone in a costume? Or just in a thick jacket?' She sounded excited. *'Or a yowie.'*

'Or the ravings of someone who's just been hit over the head with a tree branch and then traumatised by the shock of losing girls in her care,' said Con. 'What does she mean, "everything went silent"? That part makes no sense either.'

'Yes, it does, Con. It's called the Oz effect,' said Gabriella, bouncing on her heels and speaking quickly. 'It's a real phenomenon, there's heaps of accounts. It usually begins with a sense of fear. Time seems to lose meaning. You feel isolation. And *everything goes silent*.'

'And when do people feel this, exactly?'

'Well, usually it's associated with UFO encounters.'

Con was silent for five full seconds. He closed his eyes. 'Please tell me you're joking.'

'That's not all,' she said, only gaining speed. 'Sometimes it's experienced during Bigfoot sightings.'

'Come on, Gabby —'

'And in Australia, those are called yowies.'

'I thought we finally got you off all of this conspiracy junk.'

'Just because it freaks you out doesn't mean we have to ignore it,' said Gabriella, her Kiwi accent heavier as she took offence.

'We are *not* having this conversation,' said Con.

'Just take your cynic hat off for one second of your life —'

'Wait,' said Con, stopping short. 'Where's Murphy?'

'His brother came to take him home. The lawyer tipped him off. The brother was mad to find him alone with us. Probably just as well: poor bloke was a mess. Murphy started to break down after talking to Eliza – I'm not sure that was good for him.' Gabriella's voice was frosty, but it was better than having to hear her conspiracy theories. 'Should I have stopped him from going home?'

'Probably, but you'll learn. We'll make a detective out of you yet.'

She punched him in the ribs.

Con and Gabriella agreed the case was not going to be solved before nightfall, so before leaving Launceston they stopped by their homes to pick up enough gear to stay a few days in Limestone Creek. As well as packing several suitcases, Con grabbed the go bag from his personal car, which included a swiss army knife, lock picks, zip ties, parachute cord and a few other things that might come in handy.

Every trick in the book.

After that, without the sirens, it was a long drive back to Limestone Creek. Gabriella continued researching on her laptop, making the occasional comment, hoping to draw Con into speaking.

'Oh, that's right, the dogs didn't want to search, did they? I wonder what they were scared of?'

'Hmm, a history of Min Min lights in the Tiers. That's interesting . . . did you know they still can't explain what causes those lights . . .'

'Third-most haunted town in Australia . . . *how interesting.*'

The sun had well and truly set by the time they reached the Limestone Creek station. They swapped the squad car for an unmarked police car, a silver BMW sedan, then finally pulled into the Western Tiers Country Inn.

The rain was torrential. Globular garden lights lit the driveway gold, right to the massive building itself, historic grey brick lit up by watery floodlights. He rolled their sedan under an ivy arch strung with white fairy lights and switched his wipers off.

The moment he stepped out of the car he was drenched again. He pulled the three large suitcases out of the boot, stacking and rolling them towards the main entrance with practised ease. Gabriella walked beside him with her own, much smaller suitcase, her shoulders hunched against the rain.

An elderly gentleman, having dinner in the Inn's restaurant and in view of the door, leapt to his feet to open it for Con, helping him lift the suitcases over the doorstep.

'Horrible weather, isn't it?' said the man once they were inside. He looked sadly towards the mountains.

'Too right, mate,' said Con.

The smell of food from the Inn's restaurant made his stomach rumble, but the noise coming from the dining room was very subdued.

'Feels like a funeral in here,' Gabriella commented to Con.

Those four girls up there in this weather, at night, must have been in most people's minds that night, not just here in Limestone Creek but all over Australia.

The woman behind the reception desk put down her magazine and eyed Con's luggage up and down. 'Another journo? Do you have a reservation?'

'Not a journo, I'm a detective. And yes, surname Badenhorst.'

She tapped at her computer. 'You're late.' She looked down at all his luggage. 'And the reservation is for one.'

'That's a relief, because I only booked for one.'

She cocked an eyebrow. 'Lot of suitcases for one person. Do you have ID?'

Gabriella appeared beside him, putting her arm in his. 'Isn't he a sweetheart, helping me with my bags?'

Con showed the receptionist his police ID and was given the key to his room.

'Sorry for being stroppy,' the receptionist said, not sounding sorry at all. 'We've just had a lot of stickybeaks today. Some of them even pretended to be cops.' She glanced towards the window and the rain that beat against it. 'Poor girls. You lot will find them, right?'

'Probably,' said Con.

Gabriella hit him. 'Yes, ma'am, we will definitely find them.'

Con waited as Gabriella checked in, and then they both rolled their luggage down the hallway towards their rooms.

'Meet back in there for dinner?' said Gabriella.

'I think I'll order room service and get an early night,' said Con.

'No worries,' she said. She left him at his door.

Once he had closed the door behind him, he breathed a long sigh.

The room was sturdy, open, with elements of country homestead: brick veneer on one wall, a gas fire in a cosmetic fireplace, a line of wicker boxes that were surplus to use. It also had modern comforts, like a coffee machine, bar fridge, and a folding window into the adjoining bathroom, allowing someone taking a bath to watch the flat-screen TV across from the bed. The bed was king size, the carpet plush, the lamps golden soft.

It was part of Con's self-care plan that he always stayed in the best hotel rooms.

His therapist was the one who'd suggested it. Con had never been the self-care type, not until the Jaguar case. Cheap rooms and surf clothes and basic essentials. Things were different now – a lot of changes had been made.

He lifted each of his three suitcases up onto the bed and unzipped them. For the first time all day, the tension in his shoulders eased.

First, he plugged in his faithful old radio, sitting it on the bedhead. The soft sound of a news broadcast.

'. . . *have begun a petition to instate a curfew for all young women in the Limestone Creek and Meander Valley area. The petition has received over 5000 signatures already, most of them from outside of the town itself, which has led to mixed responses from the community. Local MP Alejandro Tully has described the petition as both alarmist and sexist, but a small committee of concerned mothers . . .*'

He lined up his medication bottles beside the radio. Sertraline, 200 mg. Temazepam, 15 mg. Mag phos, as required. Nexium, 10 mg.

He walked to the windows and lifted the curtain rod down off the hooks. Sliding the heavy grey curtains off the rod and folding them carefully, he pulled his own navy curtains from a suitcase and replaced them. Setting the rod back in place, he stepped back.

'. . . *meanwhile, the search has officially ended for the night due to bad weather. But dedicated individuals from the community – including extended family members and friends of the missing girls – have refused to stop their search. They will continue throughout the night with spotlights and wet-weather gear, against the strong advice of emergency services . . .*'

The framed photographs on the walls – Australian forests and aerial shots of the Great Western Tiers – Con stowed in the wardrobe. In their place he put up a framed photo of his parents, a photo of his cohort from the academy, and a group shot of him and his Sydney mates. He stacked a few books he'd been reading on the dressing table, although he knew he wouldn't get to them.

He placed his laptop in the middle of the oak desk, beside the coffee machine, and his own bright LED desk lamp replaced those trendy golden lamps. When he switched on the TV it showed a re-run of *House Rules*; Con left it, the volume turned low, adding to the background noise of the radio.

His pistol he placed on the bedside table and he slipped a cricket bat under the other side of the bed. Finally, he took his much-lighter suitcases off the bed and replaced the bedcover and sheets with his own – navy, the same colour as the curtains.

When he was done, to his immense shame, his throat itched and his eyes began to leak. He rubbed them. It sometimes happened at the end of a long day. He ordered room service – a chicken parmi – that arrived in record time. He chewed it thoughtfully, mind on the case, then rinsed the plate in the bathroom sink before leaving it neatly outside the door.

He checked the thermostat and stripped naked. He left his damp clothes beside the bed and then walked into the open shower. As the water fell down onto the back of his neck, steam billowing around him, he unwrapped the complimentary soap and began to think.

Schoolgirls lost in the bush . . . schoolgirls taken *from the bush? A string of disappearances decades earlier . . . a resurgence . . . a copycat?*

His mind went back to the blood on the drink bottle, and Eliza's testimony.

Eliza's head injuries . . . Eliza's shoes . . . the Oz effect . . .

He hadn't wanted this case. The commander had told him that morning that it was probably just girls lost in the bush, that he'd most likely be sleeping in his own bed back in Launceston that night.

Of course he had been assigned to this case. He always got the cases involving teenagers or kids. Because he was good at them. When he transferred from Sydney, he'd just solved one of the biggest cases involving . . . well, he'd been too late to save anyone, but still, he *had* solved it . . .

The theories would come. They always did.

A transfer to Tasmania. Not even to the busy part of Tasmania – if the word "busy" could ever be applied to Tasmania. He needed the break, but he wasn't going to give up his job. He was good at it. Even the commander thought so. She was the one who advocated for him to come here. Not a leave of absence. He wouldn't leave. When he was doing something, it felt good.

Alright. Focus, Cornelius. What are the interesting points about this case? Jasmine is the daughter of a possible drug dealer. Jasmine fought with Madison and had a cut lip. Cierra and Madison are twins: is that important? Madison has some YouTube channel, and she'd split from the rest of the group before they disappeared. Tomorrow, I'll need to make time to talk to her. And Georgia saw a bear-man . . .?

He began to consider the suspects.

In the safety of his own mind, he used the alignment system from *Dungeons & Dragons*, a system from his childhood and one that he'd always used since joining the force, but one he would never, *ever* admit to. It was a matrix used to categorise ethical and moral perspectives: good versus evil, lawful versus chaotic, and neutral right in the middle.

Good and evil were self-explanatory. But lawful and chaotic . . . that was the category that had always fascinated Con.

'Lawful' implied someone adhered to a system, some code or set of rules. 'Neutral' meant they had no qualms about hurting people, but they wouldn't go out of their way to do so for no reason. And 'chaotic': no governing logic to their behaviour except their own desires.

Slowly, using the system, he worked through the possibilities. He stepped out of the shower, dried with a towel, and typed up his current list of suspects on his laptop.

1. Eliza Ellis (& accomplice?) – Neutral Evil?
2. Jordan Murphy – Lawful Evil

3. Unknown Drug Agent – Lawful Evil
4. Unknown Sexual Predator – Chaotic Evil
5. Mentally-Ill Psychopath (?) – Chaotic Evil
6. Bear-Man – Who the hell knows

Con hesitated before adding a final suspect:

7. The Hungry Man of 1985 – ? Evil

He snorted softly and deleted the final line.

He saved the file, closed the laptop and slipped into bed.

A second later, he returned to the laptop. He opened the file and quickly added the Hungry Man again.

He went back to bed, swallowed his medications, flicked the lamp off. Outside, the rain howled and beat against his windows.

When he finally slipped into sleep, the girls from his last case in Sydney – the Jaguar's victims – strolled into his mind. Their beaten faces and bloody limbs. They were screaming for his help. But he was, as always, too late to save them.

CHAPTER 9

ELIZA

It was morning at the hospital.

Eliza stood in the bathroom attached to her ward, naked, looking at herself in the mirror, heart beating fast. Slightly dizzy – slightly nauseated. But she'd had a shower and was beginning to regain some sense of self.

Lungs tight, stomach clenched, eyes on the brink of tears.

It's my fault.

Her twin sister, Monica, had brought her a bag of clothes, as well as toiletries and make-up and jewellery. Monica was waiting, right now, out on Eliza's bed. It had been easy to pack Eliza a bag – most of Eliza's things were at Monica's house already. Ever since Denni had killed herself, Eliza had been living with Monica and her husband, Tom.

Eliza dried herself slowly, looking over her scrapes and bruises. She dressed. Underwear, make-up, clothes, jewellery.

She stood before herself, feeling a little renewed. She wore her spare glasses – round-wire rims, big and retro. She wore a grey knit sweater, blue jeans, flats. Gold hoop earrings. The nurse still wanted to re-dress the wound on the back of her head, but she felt a little more normal. Just in so much pain.

No matter what anyone says, it's all my fault.

She examined the cut over her brow, a butterfly stitch holding it in place. She dabbed more foundation over the bruise on her cheek. She wanted to hide what had happened to her – she didn't deserve the sympathy.

She thought of Wren – Monica's little girl. Then she thought of her and Monica's older sister Kiera, who was Denni's mother. Denni, with her underage tattoos and her sense of humour and her long brown side-braid.

Denni, who had killed herself on the Hanging Tree almost a year ago, the discovery of her body streamed live on the internet.

Denni, who had been like a daughter to Eliza.

Guilt. Indecision. What should she tell them?

Use your tools, Eliza, she thought. The tools the therapist had given her, to help her work through the insurmountable grief of losing Denni. *Use your permission slips.*

She had a small hospital notebook that the nurse had procured for her. She wrote:

I give permission for Eliza Ellis to be strong today, to not feel guilty, and to work her hardest to find the missing girls.
Signed, E. Ellis

She ripped it out and tucked it into the frame of the mirror. A token to leave behind. Signing a permission slip for herself was an intention-setting exercise she now swore by, a technique that had worked well for her this past year.

A knock on the bathroom door. 'You okay in there, Eliza?' It was Monica.

'You have permission to be strong,' she told herself in the mirror. 'You *will* find the girls. You'll fix this.'

She opened the door. Her identical twin sister, with the shorter haircut and the unbruised face and the watering eyes. Monica hugged her tight. She smelled like cinnamon and roses. 'Shhh, it's okay . . . we'll find them . . .'

The familiar nurse walked into the room. When she was done re-bandaging Eliza's head, she pulled a leopard-print headscarf out of her pocket.

'I brought this in from home this morning, poor love. It'll cover both this bandage and the butterfly stitch.'

Eliza let the nurse tie the headscarf around her head with a large bow by her temple. It covered everything neatly.

Monica and Eliza walked out through the long corridors of the hospital, Monica clutching Eliza's arm as though worried she would fall over.

All the while, Eliza's mind kept returning to the trail.

When they stepped outside, the sounds of Launceston rushed through the air around them. The rain hadn't stopped overnight but a pair of hopeful journalists was loitering outside, waiting for her release, and Monica cursed them out loudly as they pushed past to her car.

'Just a quick word! How are you feeling, Eliza?' shouted one. 'Do you know what happened?'

Eliza grimaced, silent as she climbed into the car, holding back all the apologies she wanted to make.

Then they were on their way back. Back to Limestone Creek.

Eliza watched the clouds as they faded and thinned, the storm finally easing. Monica held her hand, rubbing the back of it with her thumb.

I'm so selfish, she thought suddenly. 'How's Tom?'

Monica's husband had been on the hike too. He would likely

feel as responsible as Eliza did, even though he and Jack'd had all the other girls to take care of at the time.

'He's waiting at home. He was going to help with the search, but he had to look after Wren while I came and got you.'

More guilt. 'I'm sorry.'

'Don't you dare say sorry, Eliza,' said Monica firmly. 'Not after what you've been through.'

Eliza felt like she wanted to cry, but she couldn't. She felt herself slowly retreating back into herself and cut it short. *No. You will feel every shred of this. You don't get the easy way out.*

The tears formed. Soon she was sobbing hysterically.

'Shhh . . . it's okay, Eliza . . .'

The foggy line of the Great Western Tiers was cutting in and out of view as the rain started and stopped. They left the highway and soon drove through the winding roads of the Meander Valley, bordered by clumps of pine trees, sodden paddocks, lonely convict-era graveyards. An hour after they left Launceston, they pulled up at Monica and Tom's house, on the outskirts of Limestone Creek, bordered at the back by paddocks and poplar trees.

The house was double-storey, federation architecture of red brick, with a verandah, a big rambling cottage garden of wattle trees and rose bushes and lavender, and two vehicles in the gravel driveway: Eliza's Corolla and Tom's Landcruiser.

Eliza, now all cried out, walked up the gravel footpath to the front door – it wasn't locked – and went inside. Family photos hung in the entryway. Eliza looked instantly at Denni's portrait; she did it every time.

Tom came rushing out of the kitchen to meet them, bumping into the walls as he did. He hugged Monica first, then swept Eliza up into his crushing, muscular arms. He wore a singlet and track pants. He smelled of whisky. 'I'm so sorry, Eliza. I —'

Eliza put her finger on his lips and he went quiet, but he didn't let go of her. 'I'm not hearing another apology from anyone today,' she said croakily. She pressed harder on his lips, the stubble on his cleft chin scratchy against her finger. He released her, but didn't pull away from her finger, so she pulled it away herself.

'The police called. They're going to come around later to ask some more questions,' he said.

'What have they told you? What's happened? Tom, I haven't seen you since yesterday . . .'

'Aunty Leesey!' said seven-year-old Wren, running up to her. She had cornflower-blue eyes like Tom but honey-blonde hair like Monica and Eliza, plus a mouth full of missing teeth.

Eliza swept Wren up into a fierce hug. 'Hello, sweetheart,' she said into her hair. She felt love and tenderness rush through her. She didn't want to let go.

'I told the police what I could,' said Tom. 'They had a million questions about the four girls, about the others on the trip, the timing of things, whether the girls had seemed strange yesterday . . . whether *you* had seemed strange.'

'Me?' said Eliza, putting the squirming Wren down. 'What did they want to know?'

'I'll make some lunch,' said Monica hurriedly.

Tom raised a hand. 'I've already started making sandwiches. You ladies go sit down.' Monica hesitated, but Tom grabbed her shoulders and steered her towards the big lounge room, where a charcoal-grey couch swept around the corner, facing a huge TV. 'Please.' He planted a kiss on all three of their cheeks – Monica, Wren, Eliza – and walked back to the kitchen.

Sarge, Tom's Boxer-cross-Rottweiler, came out of the corridor, claws clacking on the tiles. Speckled with dry mud, he rested up against Eliza's side, looking up at her lovingly.

'Come watch *Piebald Rangers* with me,' said Wren, tugging at Eliza's hand.

'No, sweetheart,' said Monica, 'we need to keep an eye on the news.' She turned to Eliza. '*Sunrise* are doing a special with live coverage from the search, all day. Remember when they did that for the miners at Beaconsfield?'

'I think *Piebald Rangers* is exactly what I need right now.' Eliza patted Sarge's head and then let Wren lead her into the lounge and onto the couch beside her. 'I don't think I can handle hearing about the teacher who lost four girls on a school hike.'

'Nobody is saying that!' said Monica. She settled on Wren's other side, holding her hand in her lap, clutching tighter when Wren tried to pull away. 'Mummy is a bit sad this morning. Can I hold your hand?' Wren, grumbling, acquiesced.

Sarge jumped up beside Eliza, resting his head in her lap and pressing his weight against her. He was snoring before long.

Together, they watched the cartoon heroes on their talking horses save the town from an earthquake. The bright TV and the flashing animations hurt Eliza's eyes. The doctor had said this might happen – the effects of her concussion. If the symptoms grew worse, she was supposed to go back in for observation, but there was no way that was going to happen. She would stay right here, with her family. She closed her eyes and enjoyed their presence.

After a while, Tom joined them, carrying four plates of cut ham-and-lettuce sandwiches. 'Wren, we need to put the news on, sweetheart,' he began, seeing the cartoon credits on the screen.

'Not yet,' said Eliza, before Wren could even protest. 'Can we watch another episode?'

Tom snuggled in behind Wren, holding her in his lap and coaxing her to eat her sandwich. Eliza felt his leg pressing hard against hers.

Sarge snuffled, woke up, yawned, and climbed down, heading for his doggy-door into the backyard.

Eliza listened blissfully as the Piebald Rangers successfully navigated the conflicts of friendship, and then another episode was over.

Without another word – just a glance in Eliza's direction – Tom let the next episode auto-play. The four of them finished their meal and sat, silent, watching the Piebald Rangers yet again save the town. Eliza's mind was far, far away.

The doorbell rang and Sarge came sprinting through from outside, straight to the door.

'It's alright, it's just Tom's mum,' said Monica. 'I asked her to come take Wren for a while . . . if the police are coming, I . . .' She broke off into sniffles.

'No, no, *get down, you stupid mongrel*,' came the voice of Mrs North in the hallway. 'Good boy.' She bustled into the lounge room. 'Eliza, you *poor thing*!'

Eliza rose and let Tom's mum hug her.

'How are you? Are you okay? How *dreadful*. Anything you need. Anything at all.'

Wren, not understanding the sudden emotion, began crying. Mrs North quickly scooped the girl up into her arms. 'Don't you worry, baby. It's fine. You're okay. Quick, say goodbye to Mummy and Daddy and Aunt Leesey.' Mrs North let them all kiss Wren, before she took the screaming girl away.

'Can I . . .?' said Monica, teary, reaching for the remote.

Eliza nodded.

Immediately footage of Cierra, Jasmine and Georgia filled the screen. It was from the morning of the hike, on the school bus. It must have been footage from Madison's YouTube channel. No Bree. She wasn't in the girls' self-dubbed 'Fab Four'.

Eliza watched the footage, wiping her tears away, annoyed. Jasmine, slight but so fierce. Cierra, looking nervous in her blue wig. Georgia and her intelligent eyes.

Tom made them each a whisky and Coke, pressing one into each woman's hands. He settled in between them again, pulling them both tight. Eliza pulled away. Sarge tried to climb up, but Tom pointed towards the door and said, 'Outside.' The dog obeyed, tail wagging feebly.

Tom looked back to the TV.

They watched footage of the search efforts, the reporters under umbrellas informing the viewers it was now over twenty-four hours since the girls first went missing. The broadcast changed to aerial shots of the Tiers, zooming in on the cliffs and the impenetrable summits.

Tom muted the TV. 'If anyone's to blame, it's me,' he said. 'I should've been back there with them.'

'Neither of you is to blame,' said Monica. 'Don't be stupid . . .'

'But if I had been back there . . .' began Tom. He breathed heavily, staring at Eliza, putting his hand on her thigh.

Even *now*? He was insatiable. He'd never made a secret of his attraction to Eliza, not even in front of Monica, admitting that the idea of twins excited him. She couldn't believe that he would try to make a move right now, with all that was going on, and after she had rejected his forthright advances so many times. She supposed maybe the trauma was messing with him just like it was messing with her.

She stood up and excused herself. Monica sent her a look of sympathy, but Eliza couldn't look at her in that moment – she went to the bathroom and locked the door. Monica had no right to show pity. Eliza loved her, would always love her, but she had to take responsibility eventually. When Tom had expressed a desire to sleep with her, not that long after Wren was born, Monica had given him permission: she always let Tom have what he wanted.

When Eliza had refused him, he was disappointed, but took it in his stride. It wasn't long before he turned his eyes to the older girls at school. He was not so confident that he flirted with them right in front of Eliza, but it was clear enough what was going on. She knew she should intervene – she understood that it was the right thing to do, and her obligation as a teacher – but she was too protective of Monica, of Wren. She didn't feel good about it, but it was a moral compromise. Staying silent was selfish, but she had experienced the suffering a broken family could cause and, for Wren's sake, she could not bring herself to do anything that might jeopardise Tom's job or reputation.

Of course, Tom paid particular attention to girls who returned his interest. As Denni had.

Locked in Monica's bathroom, her mind was back there, now. That first day, the winter of two years ago. Their oldest sister, Kiera, had shown up at Eliza's house in one of her rare moments of sobriety. She'd had Denni in tow and begged Eliza to take care of her daughter. Kiera loved Denni, but she knew she was a bad mother to her – it was *because* she loved her that she wanted Eliza to raise her. Denni had stomped past Eliza and into the spare room, which in time would become her room, swearing and screaming at Kiera.

Eliza couldn't refuse. Poor Kiera had suffered the most from their parents' neglect and abuse. She was a bad mother. And Eliza . . . to be a mother was all she'd ever wanted.

She spent the time with Denni. Slowly, gently, calming her. Comforting her. Listening to her, validating her, giving her permission to be strong, to be kind, to be present. Eliza read all the books, wanting to learn all the ways a daughter should be treated in order to grow up strong. Something that Eliza and Monica and Kiera's parents had never been able to do. But Eliza and Monica had always had each other, while Kiera had borne the full brunt.

Kiera. Now she was somewhere on the mainland, shacked up with a drug dealer, numb and oblivious to the world outside her own addiction, trying to bury the pain of her daughter's suicide. It'd been months since Eliza had heard from her, although that wasn't unusual. She and Monica had both resigned themselves to the fact it was only a matter of time before they got a call, from the cops or a hospital, saying Kiera was dead.

But back in the memory, months after Denni's arrival, the edgy and rebellious but only half-healed teenager had begun reeling in Tom. Little comments and touches and looks full of meaning. And Tom, horny and hungry as always, had *responded*.

Eliza had tried everything to make Denni stop, to make Tom stop, but nothing had worked – reasoning, threatening to report Tom to the school, bribing Denni with gifts. Once she'd given her the ultimatum that, if they didn't stop, Eliza would move the two of them to another town entirely. That hadn't worked – Denni just said she'd move in with Tom and Monica instead.

Monica . . . sweet, infatuated Monica, with all of her own childhood trauma and fear of abandonment, had never stood up to Tom. Even now, Eliza could hardly bring herself to look at him, even though they shared a house. He was big, strong – scary when angry. He was a man's man, in a man's world, in a country town where men were still the ruling class.

But, just like that, his relationship with Denni stopped. Eliza could never explain it; after all she had done, it seemed almost overnight Denni called it all off herself.

But it seemed as though no time at all passed before Eliza realised he held affection for another girl at school. Cierra Mason. She thought for a while that maybe that's what had made Denni give up her relationship with Tom, but it seemed to be a new development; she would have noticed earlier otherwise. Just one look between Tom and Cierra told her everything she needed to know. She knew that glimmer in his eye all too well – she had been its object before, as had Denni.

If Eliza knew about Tom and Cierra, it was only a matter of time before Madison found out. And after all, she knew Tom wouldn't settle for just one of the Mason twins. She couldn't let that happen – Madison would tell the whole world. Wren couldn't lose her father to the law – or worse. Eliza simply couldn't allow it, not after she'd already lost one niece. She needed forgiveness, she needed something. She had been *her* Denni, the most valuable thing in her whole world – and she had killed herself, on Eliza's watch.

Eliza *had* a plan to end Cierra and Tom's relationship, but now Cierra was missing – if it came out now that Tom had been sleeping with her, he would be lynched in the street. And poor, sweet Wren would be . . .

Eliza had grown up without a father. She'd hated it, she still felt broken hearted whenever she thought of it. She wanted Wren to grow up healthy and happy. Not just with a father, but a father she could respect.

It had felt like she'd had to choose: Wren or Cierra.

It always came back to Eliza, somehow. Everything was always her responsibility. Or her fault.

No. *That's an old tool,* she told herself. *That's your deadbeat mother talking. Nothing is your fault. It's not your fault Tom takes whatever he wants. It's not your fault he went after Cierra.*

Eliza rubbed her forehead. She thought of her nieces. Both Wren and Denni. *You have permission to be strong.*

She walked into the shower, ripping off the bandages and dressings on her head.

I, Eliza Ellis, give you permission to be strong . . .

. . . even if this is *all your fault.*

Right?

Strangely, unbidden, the rhyme came into her head.

Up in the hills, he hides and kills.

Down in the caves, he hides and waits.

She gently tapped her forehead against the shower tiles, trying to force it out of her brain, but all she did was beat it staccato into her consciousness. A half-memory of footsteps . . . footsteps in the scrub . . .

I won't walk alone by the mountain trees,

or the Hungry Man will come for me.

CHAPTER 10

MURPHY

Murphy dreamed he was falling down the side of a cliff.

The ground rushed towards him, rocks and jagged edges. Wind ripped through his clothes, pressing against his face, eucalypt and fresh, loud in his ears.

I can't die! I have to find Jasmine!

And then he hit the ground. And woke. He found himself on the couch at home, beer cans scattered around him, and wind blowing through the open window.

It was late morning. The girls had been missing for twenty-four hours.

Half an hour later, Murphy sat at his dining-room table, a breakfast can of beer in his hand, eyes on the open window and the heavy rain beyond. Sweet weed smoke from Butch's joint hung in the air.

Murphy's chest ached. He wanted nothing more than to go join the search in the mountains, which had resumed at daybreak. But

Dave had texted him to say the SES had sought a restraining order against Murphy's participation.

I shouldn't have broken that bloke's finger . . .

Butch hadn't stopped speaking since Murphy woke up: complaining about the SES, the school, the teachers, the police, the media, the search, how cold the night had been, how they weren't doing enough, the search-and-rescue horses that had been spooked by the thunder and bucked their riders, the bloody helicopters that should just brave the bloody rain and get up into the bloody sky and start bloody helping, or else get their bloody drones to get some useful bloody pictures, where was the infrared, what the hell were they even doing?

Murphy put the beer can to his forehead and closed his eyes, trying to block Butch out. The live coverage was playing on the TV. He should be up there. Fuck the restraining order – he'd risk the jail time.

But Dave had also said that if he was a suspect, to be seen up there would cast even more suspicion on him. The restraining order made things so much more complicated. And if he ended up in custody, what help would he be to Jasmine?

Yeah, and what help am I right now?

He decided he'd give it until noon, then he was going to join the search, whether they wanted him there or not. They'd have to chain him to the ground to keep him from scouring that mountain range, all alone if he had to.

But he'd try to be sensible first. Try to be rational. That's what Sara would do. Heaven knew it would've been better if she were here right now and Murphy was the one dead.

It wasn't fair.

He tried not to think about the dense bush, how you could walk right past a body up there and not have a clue. That you could get lost without even leaving the path, walking in circles on tracks that all looked the same, until you stumbled off a cliff.

His lips trembled. He pushed them tight together. That stopped the tears from flowing. He wasn't gonna cry any more. He was stronger than that.

The TV chattered in the background: '. . . *to the district mayor, Meredith Phythian, who has lived in Limestone Creek her whole life. Miss Phythian, many people are convinced these disappearances can be attributed to the same person responsible for murders of 1985 – that the supposed "Hungry Man" is still alive and, now, active. Do you think the public has reason to fear?'*

'No. The worst *thing we can do is panic. These girls need us to stick together and work to find them. The monster responsible for 1985 is dead. Limestone Creek has* always *banded together in times of hardship, be that bushfires or floods or the GFC, and this is no exception —'*

There was a knock on the door.

Murphy fell out of the chair in his rush to open it.

A short woman with a lined face and a platinum blonde bob stood on the step. She wore an expensive black coat, pearl earrings, high-heeled shoes. She was out of place at the Murphys' house. And she was crying.

Murphy frowned. 'Nelly?'

'Please, Murphy,' said Nelly Mason, mother of Cierra and Madison. Her mascara was running. She held up a photo: it was a school photo of Cierra. 'Please bring her back.'

Murphy stepped away from her. 'What?'

'Please, Murphy. *Please.*' She followed him inside the house.

It took him a few moments to understand what she was asking. 'Hang on – I didn't take them!'

'Liar,' she shouted. She brandished the photo like a weapon. 'I know you were in her room!'

'Are you fucking *serious*, Nelly?' Butch stepped in beside his brother.

'*Where are they?*'

'I wish I knew!' Murphy backed away further as she tried to dodge around Butch. 'Jasmine is missing too!'

'Your own daughter! How could you?'

'Alright, lady, time for you to go.' Butch hoisted the diminutive woman up over his shoulder and marched her out of the house.

'*We know it was you, Murphy!*' she screeched, pounding her tiny fists against Butch's back. '*We all know!*'

Butch put her down on the other side of the door, then slammed it shut.

'Bring them back!' She beat against the door. '*Bring them back!*'

Murphy backed into the table. 'I didn't take them,' he said. 'I didn't.'

'Don't listen to her, lad,' said Butch.

Murphy's heart pounded as Nelly Mason kept beating at the door. 'I have to talk to her.'

'Stop,' said Butch, grabbing him by the shoulders and forcing him into a seat. He fixed a joint up and lit it. 'Don't listen to her.'

Butch handed him the lit joint and Murphy put it to his mouth. The beating on the door stopped. 'Please . . . please . . .' Each word felt like a gunshot. He took the joint away and handed it back to Butch, without taking a drag. He wiped the sweat from his forehead.

'You can't let her —' began Butch.

'She thinks I did it,' said Murphy. '*Listen to her.*'

Murphy returned to the couch and turned up the volume on the TV, trying to drown out Nelly's sobs.

He knew Doble would try to pin it on him, but it never occurred to him the rest of the town would think that too . . .

He hadn't forgotten Theodore Barclay, the school groundsman who'd been blamed for the 1985 disappearances; first they burned down his house, then he'd been chased through the streets and bashed black and blue. After he was locked up, he'd killed himself the moment he had bail. Out here, in the wilds of Tasmania, people tended to take justice into their own hands, and they usually got away with it.

All that pain out there . . . and people think I'm the cause . . .

These people had grown up with him, or seen him grow up. They were there when he lost Sara, lost his business, his house – nearly lost his mind. How could they think he'd do this? Jasmine was all he had.

But in the back of his mind . . .

It's because I'm a drug dealer.

Exhaustion dragged at his bones, and he lurched up the corridor and into his bedroom. Maybe it'd be better if he didn't leave the house for a while. He didn't want to be bashed to death just yet. Not until after he'd found Jasmine.

Blessedly, he couldn't hear Nelly Mason's crying from his bed. Gus the Muss jumped up beside him, curling against his back, purring. Murphy absently rubbed his hands through Gus's fur, one question rolling through his head: *But why would she think that I've been in Cierra's room?*

CHAPTER 11

CON

Con woke to the sound of banging on his door. He leapt out of bed, reaching for his cricket bat, his teeth bared —

He froze. He remembered where he was. He dropped the bat, kicking it back under the bed. He pulled a fresh towel from the wardrobe and wrapped it around his waist, then opened the door.

Gabriella walked in, fully dressed, carrying her computer in one hand and a takeaway coffee from the Inn's restaurant in the other. She sat on his bed, patting for him to sit down beside her, coffee on her breath. 'You slept in. It's nearly 8 am.' She paused. 'You alright?'

It had been a fitful night, full of vivid nightmares. 'You were just trying to catch me in the nude, admit it,' said Con, leaving a space between them, one hand on his towel. 'What is it?'

'Madison Mason. The sister of Cierra. Yesterday, I told you she was a YouTuber. Detective Coops reported that the school social worker said she wielded it like a weapon. Well, she's uploaded a video this morning, and . . .' She sipped her coffee, wiggling her eyebrows.

'Not good?' said Con.

'Good intentions, I'm sure,' she said, opening her computer. 'But this whole damn town is about to blow up.'

'Are you serious?'

Instead of answering, she hit play.

Madison's red hair was artfully tousled, her face heavy with make-up, except where a purple bruise surrounded her left eye, gaudy in high-definition. She sat on a lush bed, speaking straight to the camera. Tears glistened in her eyes as she gave her account of events.

'We fought, Jasmine and me, but the others got involved too. Even Bree Wilkins. I want to tell you what the fight was about but it's not fair, because Jasmine isn't here to defend herself. But it got . . . pretty bad.' She touched the bruise around her eye. 'Miss Ellis made me leave the group, made me go ahead and join the rest of the class. I was still so angry with her, with Jasmine, and even Georgia and Cierra. I . . . I told Jasmine I hated her, and then I walked away, and that was . . . that was the last I saw of them . . . I caught up with the main group, and it started to rain and thunder and Mr North made us hurry up. They'd called for a bus to pick us up at the Lake Nameless car park. But that's . . . that's when we realised Miss Ellis and the four girls hadn't been seen . . .

'And now . . . the people that you know and love from my channel, my best friend, Jasmine, is missing. My sister, Cierra, is missing. The woman I call my surrogate sister, Georgia, is missing. And a woman I once considered one of my best friends, Bree Wilkins . . . once Denni's best friend . . . missing. Up in the bluffs. Time is . . .' She put her head in her hands.

'Please . . .' She looked back up the camera, doe eyes imploring the viewer. 'If anyone out there can help, please come join the search efforts. I know my sister is still out there – I know she is. I can feel it in my . . . There's just so much ground to cover . . . no matter where you are in Australia, or in the world —'

'Look how many views she's had already,' said Gabriella over the top of Madison's voice. 'Over a million. It's only been up for an hour! I got a call from Constable Darren Cahil, the search controller, saying there's been carloads of people showing up at the lookout track. It's a nightmare. They need to preserve the tracks in case there's evidence that's been missed, but a lot of them are going vigilante. In this weather, it'll be a miracle if we don't lose any searchers.'

The video had continued, showing some footage of three of the girls – Georgia, Cierra and Jasmine – from the back seat of their school bus, apparently on the first morning of the camp, Madison introducing each of them through voiceover. The music was quite stirring.

'Why did these girls fight?' muttered Con. 'What was it about?'

The video cut back to Madison in her bedroom. 'I only have a little bit of footage of Bree – we were good friends last year, but things changed after Denni . . . But we did film a project together at the start of last year, for Health. I'll upload it tonight. Please, keep all four of them in your prayers, and if anyone is able: please please please come to Limestone Creek. Join the search . . . bring our girls home . . .

'I know that some of you don't believe in . . . in the Hungry Man. But, once upon a time, five girls went missing in these same mountains, and they were never heard or seen again. I can't . . .' Her voice broke and she needed a few seconds to calm herself. 'I believe he's real. I think the Hungry Man is back. Don't let the Hungry Man take four new victims. Not only for these girls, but the girls of the past. We'll take back the bone of the bone man. We need to stop the Hungry Man.'

And then the video was over.

After several long moments, Gabriella said, 'Thoughts?'

'Too many to list,' murmured Con.

'My vote is the Hungry Man is back.'

'What did she mean about the bone man? Is that another name for the Hungry Man?' Con was scrolling through Madison's channel. 'Damn. She really has over a million subscribers.'

'And it was only 700 000 just yesterday. It's only going to grow. Especially as the Hungry Man stories start to get around again. The notes from the station this morning said there were reports of some families with young girls who are packing up and leaving the area entirely.'

Con clicked on one of the videos at random and scrolled through the frames. It showed Cierra and Madison, sitting on the same bed, doing each other's make-up. They were scantily clad in silk pyjamas.

'They're very pretty girls . . .' commented Gabriella.

'Pretty enough to take?' wondered Con, an uneasy feeling growing in his stomach. His mind slipped back to Sydney and the Jaguar case.

I should've known it wouldn't be so simple as girls lost in the bush.

The thought made him unbearably sad.

'We'll have a chat with Miss Madison Mason,' said Con. 'I'll meet you in the lobby in fifteen.'

He opened the wardrobe and pulled out some of the clothes he'd hung there the night before – a white linen shirt, grey suit trousers, his underwear. He realised Gabriella hadn't moved, and when he turned back he saw her watching him, a smirk on her lips and iPhone in her hand.

'Don't stop on my account,' she said, her phone camera pointed his way.

'This is sexual objectification,' he said.

'Yep . . .' Her whole chest moved as she laughed and danced out of the room.

Gabriella whistled at the sight of the Masons' house, taking her sunglasses off to get a clearer look. 'Damn.'

The two-storey house was rendered with white and gold finishes, turrets and bay windows emerging from between jacaranda trees, the air heady with their scent and buzzing with bees. The path from the driveway to the verandah was a line of marble stepping stones set in a meticulous lawn.

'I feel like I'm walking towards a rich person's house. Do you think that's the effect they were going for?' said Gabriella in a stage whisper.

Con knocked on the door. A moment later there was a squeak of metal from the peephole opening, and then a familiar girl's voice from just behind the door. 'Who are you?'

Con held up his police badge for the peephole. 'Madison? I'm Detective Badenhorst and this is Detective Pakinga. Are your parents home?'

The door unlocked with clinking chains. Madison was as she'd appeared in the video. She held a shivering grey whippet dog to her chest.

'Dad's up at the search,' said Madison. 'Mum's at the school, with my younger brother.'

'There's no school today,' said Gabriella.

'They've brought in counsellors,' said Madison, a little waspishly. 'Especially for the kids affected. Like my little brother. Shouldn't you know that?'

'We're a little focused on other things, Madison,' said Con, smiling, but voice hard.

'Sorry, I don't mean to sound rude,' she said. 'Come in.'

She guided them to a sparkling clean and massive dining room, where they took a seat at the Tasmanian oak dining table. She placed the whippet on the ground. 'This is Mr Bruiser. He won't hurt you.' As if to prove her point, the dog scampered out of the room.

'Do you want anything? A drink? Something to eat?'

'We just wondered if we could have a chat,' said Gabriella. 'Particularly about something you said in your video this morning.'

Madison's red lips curled into a wry smile. She leaned back against the table, folding her arms across her chest. 'You saw that? What do you want to know?'

'We need to wait for your parents —' started Con.

'I don't know when they'll be back. And honestly, detectives, I have quite a bit to do. Can we just get to the point?' She sighed. 'Sorry, that was rude again. I don't have the energy to be polite right now. Can you just ask what you want to know?'

'So long as you understand that these are not formal questions. You don't have to talk to us without your parents.'

Madison nodded impatiently.

'You and Jasmine had a fight. Can you tell us what you were fighting over?' said Gabriella.

'No.'

Gabriella gave a weird sound that was half grunt, half indignant snort.

'Madison, this is important,' said Con.

'I can't tell you.'

'I don't think you understand —'

Madison interrupted him. 'How would you feel knowing that you'd hit one of your friends, told them you hated them, and then a few hours later they were *missing*? I don't want to talk about it. You said I didn't have to answer your questions.'

'Alright,' said Con. 'Just a few more *casual* questions. How long did it take you to catch up with the other group when Miss Ellis sent you ahead?'

'I don't know, fifteen minutes? I was dragging my feet – I kept trying to decide whether I should go back and apologise, or go back and punch Jasmine again.' Tears appeared in her eyes. 'Maybe it would've been better if I had. Maybe I could've stopped whatever happened . . .' She wiped her nose with her knuckle.

'Or you could've been caught up in it too, remember. Whatever *it* is,' said Con. 'Did you see anything, when you left the others? Anything weird on the trail, anything out of place? No matter how small.' He thought of the bear that Georgia had thought she'd seen. 'Or big.'

'No. Nothing at all. Not even the sound of footsteps.'

'What do you mean by that?' said Gabriella.

'It's part of the Hungry Man legend. They say you hear his footsteps in the bush beside you, and that if you look at him . . . he takes you.'

'*Interesting,*' said Gabriella.

'But you heard nothing, saw no one,' said Con.

'No one,' agreed Madison. 'But we know *someone* else was up there, right? Someone hit Miss Ellis. What has she been saying?'

'Were any of the four girls acting strangely?' said Con.

'We were all pretty heated . . . and then Bree lost it, of course.' She took the time to wipe her nose properly with a tissue, then realised Con and Gabriella were waiting for her to keep speaking. 'What?'

'Why was *Bree* angry?' said Gabriella.

'Don't you have files on this stuff? Denni King, Miss Ellis's niece, was Bree's best friend. Ever since Denni died, she gets angry – *really* angry. They told her it's post-traumatic stress. I don't know how many times she's been suspended since Denni died.'

Con and Gabriella glanced at each other.

'You *did* know that, right?' said Madison slowly.

Con shrugged, not liking how this girl kept him on the back foot. 'We're still reviewing information.'

It might've been in the files Coops sent, but he couldn't remember reading it. Surely the social worker would have mentioned it.

'You didn't *know* about Bree's PTS?' Anger crept into Madison's voice. 'Have you done *any* research? It's not a secret: Bree tells anyone who will listen.'

'You mentioned in your video that you had footage of Bree,' said Gabriella quickly. 'Could we see that before you upload it?'

'If you have to,' she said, her voice still heated. 'I was midway through editing it when you arrived. All I can do is these videos. You know, something that actually *helps*?'

'Well, actually —' began Con, but Gabriella kicked him. He had been thinking of the chaos her last video had caused up at the track.

They followed Madison to her bedroom: a bright and open space, tidy and clean, boasting a king-sized bed with plush birds lined up along the pillow. A large computer screen stood on a desk against the wall, video-editing software open.

Madison sat down at the desk. 'We filmed this last year . . . a lot has changed since then.'

She played the video. Bree sat in front of a black backdrop. She wore no make-up, her blonde hair was scruffy and loose around her face, and her pale eyes were full of anger.

'My name is Bree Wilkins . . . and this is my spoken word.'

A steady drum beat played in the background. The video cut to another angle: Bree's face blurred, then sharpened back into focus. The production was artsy and sleek. A guitar riff began, and so did Bree's performance:

'Some days it's like I'll feel only one of three things:
hollow or lifeless or like I'm covered in stings
from the clothes I have to wear,
the smile on my face that won't compare
with the smile on the screen
from an Instagram Queen.
I can't pretend I don't feel bad about my waist,

but maybe there's more than how much food is on my plate
to make me feel like I'm not beneath the Queen Bee,
maybe I can be Queen Bree without needing to kill me —'

Gabriella glanced at Con, eyebrows raised. He kept watching the screen.

'If people get near me, they'll be infected too:
then they'll hate me as much as I do —'

Abruptly, the video ended in a black screen.

Madison shook her head. 'Since Denni, she's been struggling with suicidal thoughts, too,' she said. 'But that's all that I've done so far. There's so much footage, but we never finished it. Bree freaked out after we filmed it and made me swear never to share it.'

'Freaked out?' said Gabriella.

'Got angry. Got upset. Told me she thought the whole project was a waste of time and she'd sue me if the footage ever came out. Or hit me. Or kill me. I forget the details.'

'So you're going to share it now?' said Con, a little more accusatory than he intended.

'Do you know how many people my video has brought to the search?' said Madison, suddenly defensive again, voice rising. 'You didn't even *know* Bree had PTS! Don't you even profile the missing? I can't sit here and do nothing. You don't know what those girls mean to me! My twin sister. My *best friends*!'

'I thought you didn't get on with Bree,' said Con.

Gabriella kicked him again and this time he gave her a look. Madison was putting on a good act, but he was starting to feel an act was all it was. *What the hell does she know that she's not telling us?*

Madison gave him a withering look. She turned back to the screen. 'I need to finish this video. You can find your own way out.'

Being dismissed by a 16-year-old was not an experience Con enjoyed, but Gabriella grabbed his arm and he let her drag him outside. His mind was turning, carefully putting observations and facts into boxes, listing options and priorities and questions he needed answered.

They were in the car before Gabriella spoke, ignoring a foreign journalist nearby, in make-up and high heels standing in front of a camera, the Masons' house in the background. 'Madison was all by herself on that same trail, but she wasn't taken. I mean, she's the one with the massive profile – did someone take Cierra by mistake?'

'Madison is hiding something,' said Con.

'Oh? Maybe you should go back in and you can do some more of your delicate questioning?'

'Surely she would tell us anything she thought would help find the girls.'

'Back to my question then, Badenhorst – could someone have taken Cierra by mistake?'

'Cierra was wearing a bright blue wig, which makes it hard to confuse the pair,' said Con. 'But could *Bree* have had something to do with it? Madison said she got angry —'

'Eliza is right: I bet it's a boy,' Gabriella interrupted.

'What?'

'The reason for the fight. It must be about a boy.'

'How could you possibly know —'

'If *you* get to have your special detective intuition, so do I,' Gabriella said.

'I agree that there's more here. Call Coops and ask him to send us *everything* he's got from talking with the teachers and friends.'

'Coops is a good detective but *we* should be out there, interviewing everyone —'

'We can't be everywhere.'

'— finding out who is dating who, who cheated on who. All teenage girls care about are boys, or girls if they prefer, and the only way we're going to —'

'Getting bogged down sorting through the quagmire of teenage relationships is a slow way to start a case,' he said.

'You don't think it's important?' she demanded.

'Yes, it is. But it will take a long time, and it's just one item on the list of inferences we're dealing with – it's a big list. Was there foul play or are they just lost? What about Eliza's head wound? What about the "bear" in the trees? If it's foul play, any one of the girls could be the target – and the others could be *in* on it, or taken out as witnesses. Then there's the historic disappearances – we don't really know if Ted Barclay was guilty of those or not. One of the fathers is a drug dealer. A YouTube celebrity is friends with all the missing girls.'

'So the case is full of mysteries! Let's cross one off the list.' She pulled out her phone and began scrolling. 'I'm calling the hospital. I want to know why Eliza Ellis thinks the fight was about a boy.'

Con opened his mouth to argue – they still didn't have the doctor's all-clear – but Gabriella was already speaking on the phone. He huffed, then started the BMW in what he hoped was an angry sort of manner.

'Fantastic,' said Gabriella when she hung up. 'Eliza was released from hospital this morning. Apparently they left a message with the station, but no one told us.'

'These country police stations,' said Con, a burst of frustration rolling through him. 'They don't know their inbox from their elbow.'

'They said she's gone to stay with her sister. I've got her address.'

'Well, hopefully Eliza's mind is a lot clearer today.'

'Maybe she's remembered something else . . . *paranormal*.'

'I bloody hope not.'

Tom and Monica North's house was on the outskirts of Limestone
Creek, where the nature strips were lined with tall poplar trees –
full of water, they were a natural firebreak that the early settlers
had planted against the dreaded bushfires. The rain brought out the
smell of lawns and fertiliser.

Con rang the doorbell. A dog's booming bark came from inside.

'Down, Sarge – no, outside! Go! Outside!' came Eliza's voice.
When she opened the door, she looked different: her hair was shorter,
she wasn't wearing glasses, and her face wasn't cut and bruised. She
was still just as pretty, with the same smattering of freckles across
the nose. She kept a hold of the door handle.

'Hello again, Eliza,' said Con, a little uncertainly.

'I'm Monica,' she said coldly, her amber eyes narrowed. 'I'm
Eliza's sister. And you are?'

Gabriella showed Monica her badge. 'Sorry, Monica. Eliza
didn't tell us you were twins.'

Two sets of twins . . . thought Con. *Is that just a coincidence?*

Monica relaxed. 'Thought you were journalists. They've already
tried to speak with her twice.' She opened the door wide. 'Please, come
in. Eliza is in bed, or maybe she's in the shower by now: I'll go get her.'

They followed Monica into the kitchen – black marble with
bone-white flourishes – and sat at the counter. Monica headed down
the corridor, short hair bouncing.

'Two sets of identical twins in one town,' said Con. 'Is that
unusual?'

'Limestone Creek isn't *that* small,' said Gabriella. 'It's not necessarily *ab*normal.'

A few moments later Monica returned, Eliza following behind.

The bruising on Eliza's face had worsened, but she wore a pink
dressing gown, hoop earrings and a leopard-print scarf around her
head. 'Hi again, Detective Badenhorst.' She held out her hand to
Gabriella. 'I'm not sure we've met, Detective . . .?'

'This is Detective Pakinga, but just calling us Con and Gabriella is fine,' said Con. 'How are you feeling this morning?'

'Physically? Much better.' Her smile didn't reach her eyes. 'Apart from that . . . what am I supposed to say? That this feels like a nightmare and I'm barely holding on? That I keep reliving that morning over and over?'

'Yesterday . . . you said you couldn't quite remember . . .'

'I don't remember anything more than I've already told you,' she said. 'The last thing I remember is leaving Georgia to find the girls, everything going all weird, then waking up on the ground.'

'Did you hear footsteps?' said Gabriella suddenly.

'Ah . . . so the Hungry Man is a suspect now, is that right?' said Eliza, a little uneasily. 'Look . . . when I woke up, I thought maybe I did. My memory is hazy, part of the concussion, the doctor said. I don't remember half of what I said to Carmen, I don't remember walking down the trail as far as I did before they found me, and I have a vague memory of . . . Maybe I did hear footsteps? I *do* keep getting that stupid rhyme in my head, so it's hard to tell.'

'What rhyme?' said Gabriella.

'You haven't heard it yet? It's legend up here – does the rounds every generation . . .

Up in the hills, he hides and kills.
Down in the caves, he hides and waits.
The Hungry Man, who likes little girls,
with their pretty faces and pretty curls.
Don't believe what the grown-ups say,
the Hungry Man will find a way.
So I won't walk alone by the mountain trees,
or the Hungry Man will come for me.'

Gabriella shuddered. 'That's horrifying.'

'Tell me about it. Denni used to write it on her walls – she was obsessed with the Hungry Man.'

'I have nieces of my own . . .' said Gabriella. 'I'm so sorry about what happened.'

'And now I've lost another four girls.' Eliza covered her face with her hands. 'Teacher of the year.'

'It wasn't your fault —' began Gabriella.

'I know, I know,' Eliza said, although she sounded thankful. She dropped her hands, her eyes fresh with tears. 'Everyone keeps telling me. In my head, I *know* that. But in my heart . . .'

'Can I ask about the fight the girls had?' said Con. 'You definitely don't know what caused it?'

'They wouldn't tell me.'

'You have an idea, though, don't you?' said Gabriella.

'Honestly? I think it was about boys. What else would it be?'

Gabriella nodded, a smirk in Con's direction. 'I think you're right.'

'Madison always has approximately fifty thousand boys on the go,' said Eliza. 'Jasmine never seems interested in anyone for more than a day, but there's been rumours she's dating someone. It must have been serious, though, for the fight to go the way it did. Neither of them is the type to go to blows over some crush.'

'Something serious,' said Gabriella. 'A relationship . . . I wonder if anyone else knew about Jasmine's supposed boyfriend.' She turned away from the conversation and began typing on her phone – Con knew she would be texting Detective Coops.

'Yesterday you told me that Georgia had seen a . . . bear,' said Con. 'Now that you've had a chance to rest and recover – do you think she could've been making that up?'

'Georgia isn't that kind of girl . . . But when you're up in those mountains, detective, it *is* easy to see things. The whole place is eerie. And, I mean, for her especially, all that blood in the soil.'

'You mean from 1985?'

'I mean the Black War,' said Eliza. When Con and Gabriella looked at her blankly, she continued. 'Aboriginal history was never a strong point of our generation's schooling, was it? The Black War was one of the first recorded genocides in human history. The European settlers declared all-out war on Tasmania's Aboriginal people, killing almost all of them. And it began here, at the Great Western Tiers. *Kooparoona Niara*, the local mob call it. Mountain of Spirits.'

'Mountain of *Spirits*,' said Gabriella with something akin to glee.

'Okay, so the mountains can be unnerving,' said Con, not liking the interest appearing on Gabriella's face, her text message to Coops unsent. 'Helped, I'm sure, by the legend of the Hungry Man.'

'There are many who think the Hungry Man is not just a legend, detective.'

'Do you?' said Con.

'It's all I can think about. When you're up there in the bush, among the trees and the cliffs, it's hard not to believe there's someone out there, watching you. And, well, the one thing that was never explained in 1985 was little Dorrie Dossett. She was the only witness, she's the source of the Hungry Man stories.'

'From what I understand, she had Down's syndrome,' said Con.

'That doesn't make you see things that aren't there, Con,' said Gabriella.

'Dorrie said that a tall, thin, bearded bushman took her from her backyard,' said Eliza. 'He took her up the mountain and down into a cave. She said she saw Rose Cahil there, still alive. She said Rose was missing fingers and toes. She said the man, the Hungry Man, had eaten them. Then Dorrie escaped when he was sleeping and found her way back.'

'Again, I'm sorry, but Down's syndrome doesn't lend itself to daring escapes from deranged serial killers,' said Con.

'But you're not the only one who thinks that way,' said Gabriella. 'Maybe he was complacent around her, maybe he didn't tie her up.'

'Dorrie was never taken seriously, she was an inconvenience,' said Eliza. 'The police had their man – Ted Barclay – but he was in custody at the time Dorrie Dossett was taken. They weren't happy about it, but Ted was granted bail after that, and you know what happened then.

'A lot of people disregarded Dorrie's testimony. Ted was the groundsman at the school and there were rumours that she knew him, that they were friends and she made up a story to protect him.'

Footsteps came down the hall and then a shirtless Tom North appeared, hesitating at the sight of Con and Gabriella. 'Ah,' said Tom. 'Sorry.' He spun on his heel and headed back up the corridor.

'No, please,' said Con, rising. 'We need to chat with you, too.'

Tom hesitated, then returned. Con and Gabriella had spoken to him briefly in the car park by the trail, together with Jack Michaels, but he looked different now in just track pants. His jaw looked too big for his face – 'Juice Jaw', they called it. When he'd turned, Con had seen the acne on his back. Tom North was definitely on steroids. He filed that away in his mind.

'Not sure what else I can tell you,' said Tom.

'I have some new questions. Take a seat,' said Con. 'Tell me about the girls – let's start with Jasmine Murphy.'

'She's a good egg,' said Tom. He sat down at the kitchen counter. 'I only had her for PE. She'd get in and have a go. Little thing, had a bit of a reputation for being a bad girl. The guys just flocked to her. I'm not sure how she did it.'

Eliza nodded. 'Her and Georgia weren't as stunning as the twins, but they still drew the boys. They were more down to earth. Or maybe less . . . untouchable.'

'So did Jasmine have a boyfriend?' said Con, looking between the two of them.

Tom spoke first. 'She told all the boys at school that she did, but she wouldn't say who it was,' he said. 'It drove them *wild*. I'm telling you, if you think girls are gossips, just come along to the locker room before footy training.' He chuckled. 'Or not. It gets pretty dirty sometimes. Jasmine has this temper – the boys go wild for it. Like her dad, in that way.'

'You know Jordan Murphy?'

'Sure,' said Tom. Monica appeared and pushed a shirt into Tom's hands, which he hastily pulled on, prompting a quiet sigh of disappointment from Gabriella. 'We were in the same year, growing up here. We didn't mix in the same circles, though, if you know what I mean.'

'Let's pretend that I don't,' said Con, with a smile.

'Ah. Well. Murphy . . . he didn't show up at school much. And when he did, he spent half the day smoking by the basketball courts and the other half in the principal's office. His dad was our dealer. Best bush bud around. Then he dropped out and followed in Daddy's footsteps . . .'

Eliza hit him on the side.

'What?' said Tom. 'As if they don't already know.' He leaned towards Con. '*He's* the one you should be interrogating.'

'Didn't realise this was an interrogation,' said Con.

'Just having a joke, mate,' said Tom.

'Tell us about Cierra Mason,' said Gabriella.

Monica had lingered in the kitchen, washing dishes, and at this question Con heard her pause, just for a second.

'I don't have too much to do with her,' said Tom. 'Whenever she shows up to PE, she doesn't do much. I called home about it a few times but nothing ever happened: you'd think the sun shone out of those two girls' backsides, the way their parents talk about them.' He shrugged. 'Eliza would know more.'

'Cierra isn't much into Literacy or History or Indigenous Studies or . . . anything, really,' said Eliza, a small catch in her voice, a half-glance in Tom's direction. 'To be honest, she's a pain in the classroom:

whenever she finally opens up her books, which usually takes half the lesson, she just complains it's too hard. You have to be helping her one-on-one all the time. Polar opposite of her sister.'

'Was Cierra seeing anyone?' said Gabriella.

'Oh yeah. She had someone on the go all the time,' interjected Tom. 'Tyler Cabot? Or is it Jye Calloway now?' Tom stood up, long legs unfolding. 'I better dry some of these dishes for Monica. I'm afraid I don't know much more about the other two girls, either.'

'Stick around, mate, I'm not finished yet,' said Con. 'Up in the mountains, when you first realised the girls and Eliza were missing, did you see anything unusual?'

'Nothing at all, mate. Same as I told you yesterday. Those storm clouds came in a lot quicker than we expected, but you get that in the Tiers – sometimes we'll get thunder on a calm blue day. You just can't pick it.'

'What can you tell us about Madison?' said Gabriella. 'What we're picking up is she's a bit of a local celebrity . . . was she a bully as well?'

Both Tom and Eliza nodded.

'Who were her main victims? We should talk to them,' said Gabriella.

'Good luck,' said Eliza. 'The last person to come forward was Yani Hugh, the pastor's daughter. As much as we tried to protect her, the backlash she received outside of school was pretty bad.'

'Like what?' said Gabriella.

'Online harassment from a bunch of strangers,' said Eliza. 'All of whom just happened to be followers of Madison's accounts. But since it wasn't Madison herself, there was nothing we could do.'

'Yani had come to us saying Madison was collecting nude photos of girls at school,' said Tom. 'But after the online abuse, Yani took all that back. She claimed she'd made it up, that it was a lie.'

'Except it may well be true.' Eliza sighed heavily. 'After she came forward, a picture of Yani was circulated online . . . thankfully everything but her face was blurred, but it was clearly a warning.'

'Madison sounds like a sociopath,' said Gabriella frankly. 'She was *collecting* nudes?'

Con's phone buzzed. The commander was calling. 'Excuse me a moment . . .' He walked into the hallway, the phone to his ear.

'Cornelius,' came the cool, refined voice of Commander Agatha Normandy.

'Hello, commander. Everything all good?'

'I'm sorry, but I'm afraid I miscalculated.' Con closed his eyes: he knew what was coming. 'There would have been questions if I didn't assign this case to you, given your expertise. But all the same, there are some who doubt you're up to it, if you've recovered from the Sydney case. I thought this was just a case of some girls lost in the bush. I thought it'd help you get some runs on the board . . . Forgive an old woman her mistakes . . .'

'Ah, shit . . .'

'Yes, I'm afraid so. The helicopters have found a body.'

There was a faint whine in Con's head. The commander was still speaking, but he couldn't quite catch it. He forced his breathing to slow. *Get it together, mate.*

'. . . Cornelius, did you hear what I said?'

'Sorry, I think we've got a bad line,' he said, a touch too late.

'Very convincing. Are you okay to go see the body? You can say no.'

Con took another deep breath. 'No. It's fine. I'll go.'

'I'm relying on you to know your limits,' she said. 'But I pulled some strings, and I've managed to get Detective Tran onto the task-force, from Hobart. Out of her long service leave early. I'm sending her along too.'

'Melinda Tran?' said Con. 'Good. Good idea.' He hadn't met her, but knew her by reputation, a detective from Hobart who was great with cases in the bush.

They ended the call and he wiped the sweat off his forehead and went back down the hall, catching Gabriella's eye. 'I'm sorry, but Detective Pakinga and I need to go. Thank you for your time. We'll be in touch if we have any more questions.'

Con saw himself out, Gabriella close behind.

'What is it?' she asked once they were in the car. 'You look sick.'

'They've found a body,' said Con.

'*What?* Whose?'

'They don't know yet,' said Con. 'They've spotted it from the chopper, but the bush is too dense to land: they're sending a crew in overland. The commander asked if I wanted to go down there —'

'Want me to go?' she said instantly. 'I'll go instead. You stay and chat with these two, see what else you can find out.'

'No,' he said. 'I'll be alright.'

She watched him a moment, then shrugged. 'Okay, then I'm driving.' She nudged him out of the door, climbing across the console to take the driver's seat.

Con walked around the front of the car and took a seat on the passenger side. A second later, he pounded the dash. '*Shit.*'

'You don't owe this job anything, you can quit whenever you want to,' said Gabriella. 'Just remember that. You know if the wound was outside and not inside, you'd be a lot kinder to yourself.'

He didn't respond. He focused on his breathing, tried not to think about what seeing the body of a dead teenage girl would bring up for him.

So much for solving this case before anyone got hurt.

CHAPTER 12

CON

The chopper circled above the cliffs of Devils Gullet, a deep basalt canyon just off the western end of the Tiers. It swung back around for another pass and Con peered down through the window. The old SES pilot, Dicky, sat beside him and over the headset intercom he spoke to him about the search so far.

'All these volunteers, they're more a curse than a blessing. Will you shut down that video that girl posted?' said Dicky. 'Feels like all of Australia's showed up to the search site.'

'It's not that easy to get a video taken down,' said Con. 'These huge companies are a nightmare. The video is on lots of different platforms now anyway.'

'Crazy, mate, it's bloody crazy. The world's gone mad.'

The chopper dipped even lower, skirting the edge of a cliff, the tops of the gum trees swinging in the downdraft. 'You see it now?'

The body was just visible through the trees, stark against the cliffside. It looked like a dummy had been thrown over the side, tumbling right to the base, where it lay facedown in scrub.

Big breath in, slow breath out. He scanned the surrounding bush. 'Looks like a trek to get there.'

'We're going to land over to our left, in that clearing near the river,' said Dicky. Con saw utes and motorbikes assembled there. 'There's a team of Forensics and SES already there, waiting for you. They drove up the river track, takes bloody forever. Do you want us to touch down, or do you need to see anything else from up here?'

'Swing by the body again. Show me the top of the cliff.'

'Roger.'

They drew closer again. The rocky precipice was edged by the mottled trunks of snow gums, the bark shedding in strips of brown-red and light grey.

'Dicky, any paths to the cliff through those trees?'

'There's something fluoro . . . do you see it? Just perched on the end.'

Following Dicky's pointing, Con could see a speck of yellow colour. He'd taken it for a shrub, but saw now that it was too brightly coloured.

'How close can we get?' said Con.

'Not much closer,' he said. 'But there are binoculars in the seat pocket.'

Con found the binoculars, adapted to the pitch of the chopper and focused in on the object.

'What do you see?' said Dicky.

'I can't be certain, but I think they're shoes . . . side by side.' Con pressed the binoculars harder against his face, but the pitch of the helicopter was too much to see anything more than a glimpse. 'We need Forensics up there to check them out. It's very important no one else touches them.' He put the binoculars on the seat and rested his forehead against the window, eyes on the tiny speck of colour. He brought out his phone and called Constable Darren, the search controller, preparing to explain the details of what he'd seen.

The chopper touched down in the empty area beside a rocky, beer-coloured river at the bottom of the gorge. Con climbed down while dirt was still drifting through the air from their landing. People were milling nervously about – some of the forensics team, a group of local and imported police officers, and the SES workers, wielding chainsaws and slash-hooks.

And Detective Melinda Tran. She was short, and wore a leather jacket, jeans, and well-worn hiking boots. She had a hiking pole.

'Detective Badenhorst,' she said. 'Great to finally meet you. I've heard a lot about you.'

Con shook her outstretched hand. 'Likewise. Welcome to the team – it's a relief to have someone with your expertise. Let me tell you something, real quick.'

He spoke quietly into her ear, explaining what they'd seen on top of the cliff. He didn't want it getting out, not with so many people up on the mountains who could disturb the evidence. And because of the hysteria it might bring – in 1985 they had found the shoes of one of the victims, Rose, neatly tied on the edge of a cliff.

He glanced at the group of people milling about them, looking their way curiously, waiting for Con's order to move, perhaps wondering what he was whispering to Tran about. Their nervousness and excitement palpable.

A woman in an orange vest and baseball cap approached them. 'Welcome, Detective. I'm Anaya, I'm with the SES.' She pointed at her uniform, perhaps unnecessarily. 'Constable Darren was going to be here, but he's trying to sort out the nightmare at the start of the track.'

'That's okay, Anaya, I just got off the phone with him,' said Con.

Con and Detective Tran followed Anaya into the bush, picking their way over the trail of debris the SES workers were
leaving in their wake, the sound of their chainsaws startling some
kookaburras into flight.

*On our way to the first dead body of the case. Please, God, let it
be the last.*

'What did Constable Darren have to say about the search?
Any updates?' asked Tran. 'I've only spoken with him briefly – I'm
surprised you even have reception down here.'

'Officially they called the search off when the sun set last night,
but there were still people out there, all night,' said Con. 'We've
been lucky: plenty of sprained ankles and at least one broken leg,
but nothing worse. We've had drones and two choppers searching
the area all today, but the canopy is too thick for them to see much,
although one of them found this body. On the ground, the SES is
leading teams of searchers, with Darren coordinating, but that's a
mess now that Madison Mason brought the entire population of
YouTube to the mountain.'

'I'll work closely with Darren to get that sorted, don't worry.
And then I'll filter anything important from the search through to
you, so you can keep focusing on your investigation,' said Tran.
'Again, just wanted to say good job on the Jaguar case. I remember
that when it was all over the news.'

'Thanks,' said Con. He was used to the congratulations. He
accepted them on autopilot.

She caught his tone. 'I get it,' she said. 'Didn't feel much like
a victory.'

He gave a wry smile. 'Something like that. But as everyone keeps
telling me —'

'*It's not your fault they died*,' finished Tran. 'I get it.'

She turned her attention to Anaya, asking questions about the
terrain and the weather. The bush was interspersed with rocks and

holes, and the dogwood and musk understory was thick enough to make heavy work for the chainsaws and slash-hooks.

Con watched the approach of the cliff above them through the gaps in the trees. Belatedly he realised he was holding his breath. He was not a superstitious man. He definitely didn't buy into any of Gabriella's theories. But the rocky escarpment, dotted with clinging plants and clods of soil and bird nests, it emanated something . . . menacing.

He dug his fingernails into his palms, taking steadying breaths, trying to bring himself back to the present. He knew it wasn't something evil in the cliffs that was making him nervous, it was just the thought of seeing the girl's body.

You're not in Sydney . . . these are not the same girls . . . keep it together, Cornelius . . . it's not your fault she died.

Detective Tran caught his elbow. 'Are you alright, Badenhorst? Are you listening?'

'Sorry,' he said, catching his feet again. 'I was distracted.'

Con wondered, briefly, if his mum and dad had seen him on TV, watching yesterday's impromptu press conference in the lounge of their expensive retirement-village home. He wondered if they'd tried to call him, asking if this was finally enough action for him in sleepy Launceston. His dad, especially, felt Con had been exiled – 'poor repayment for the man who single-handedly solved the Jaguar case'.

Mum would probably call him the moment she found out there had been a dead body involved. She'd try to make him quit. She wanted him to move back to Sydney and find a new career.

Con shook his shoulders and cricked his neck.

Head in the game, Badenhorst.

He still hadn't heard a word Tran had said to him.

Suddenly they were there, at the base of the cliff. The sound of flies like a beacon.

Head. In. The. Game.

He saw her.

Con wasn't prepared for how pathetic the body looked. He felt a fresh surge of nausea. Dicky swore, Anaya made a noise in her throat, and Detective Tran began taking photos.

The girl's clothes were ripped almost to shreds, and puddles of congealed blood sat in dips in the rocks. Flesh had been torn off her legs, right down to the pink bone in places.

'That's where Tassie devils have been at her, poor thing,' said Anaya.

'The devils are nocturnal, so she's been there through the night,' observed Tran. 'But where are her shoes?' She nudged Con.

Con's gaze zeroed in on her bare feet.

So those shoes on the cliff . . . just like Rose Cahil's shoes, neatly tied, in 1985 . . .

Eliza had been found barefoot the day before – perhaps the shoes on the cliff were hers? He hoped Constable Darren managed to get to the shoes soon.

Four forensics officers hovered around the body, placing markers and taking their own photos. When they were done, it was time for their gloved hands to turn the body over to see the face.

Con dug his fingers deeper into his palms. Gently, almost reverently, a forensics officer tilted her face.

It was battered and bloody, but the features were clear.

'Georgia Lenah,' said Con, although his voice seemed to come from far, far away. 'Prep the stretcher: we need to get her back for autopsy ASAP. I'll call it in.'

He was just ending the call when a forensics officer called for his attention. She reached out for his arm; he was dimly aware that he was propped up against the cliff, sweaty, his head light, his knees weak as piss.

'Detective, are you alright?' she said. 'Did you trip?'

'Yeah, bloody rocks,' he said, composing himself.

'You need to see this.'

Reluctantly, Con turned back to the body. Another woman from the forensics team had pulled something out of the pocket of Georgia's trousers.

It was a small plastic bag, half-full of marijuana. A sticker on the front said 'THE CAPTAIN'.

CHAPTER 13

MURPHY

Murphy was in the same dream. He fell down the cliff, the wind whipping his clothes. He was too scared to scream.

I have to find her. I can't die. I'm the only one who can find her.

And then he hit the ground.

He jerked awake. The clock beside his bed said 2.12 pm. After Nelly's outburst he had fallen asleep on his bed, fully clothed, emotionally spent.

It was time to go join the search. To hell with the SES and to hell with the cops. To hell with the town. So what if they bashed him to death? He'd fight them all off and make it to the mountain on bloody foot.

He opened his wardrobe, pulling out sturdy work trousers and a thick shirt. His eyes moved to the crayon drawing sticky-taped to the wardrobe door: a stick figure holding a rounded glass vial, obviously a bong. Jasmine had drawn it in Year 1, and told everyone it was her Uncle Butch.

Murphy had thought it was hilarious. Sara had been furious at first, but then eventually saw the funny side. Sara knew when to laugh. When she'd died and Murphy had moved in with Butch, this picture was one of the few things he'd brought from the old house.

What would Sara say now, if she could see Murphy raising Jasmine in Butch's home? Worse, that Murphy himself was *working* for Butch, in Dad's trade, which he'd always sworn to Sara he'd never have anything to do with? That he'd let his landscaping business go, lost all his clients, now spent all his talents growing weed?

What had he been *doing*? He'd let his grief drive him over the edge.

You've done this to Jasmine. You cockhead. You've done this to Sara's memory.

Once he got Jasmine back, he'd make some changes. He'd build his business back up, move out, buy another house. He wouldn't leave Limestone Creek, though. Jasmine loved it here, and Butch was still family, and besides . . . Murphy had never lived anywhere else.

Moaning Myrtle waddled into the room, meowing in indignation. Of course. Jasmine hadn't been there to feed her.

She moved on top of his big hunting jacket, scratching at it with her claws. It was crumpled on the ground; he'd been wearing it yesterday when he'd woken up at the edge of the yard. It was still full of twigs and thorns, with a large muddy patch from where he'd been tackled to the ground up at the car park, when he'd broken that SES officer's fingers and punched the cops.

He pushed Myrtle off, then paused, running his fingers down the sleeve of the jacket. There was a rip, from the elbow to the wrist. He felt the edge of the tear. Where had that come from?

From the front of the house came the sudden sound of glass smashing, followed by Butch swearing. Murphy ran down the corridor, Myrtle following behind, still meowing at him.

A brick sat on the dining-room floor, amidst chips of glass from the smashed window. Outside, raised voices.

'You can't prove nothing, Butch,' shouted a big voice.

Murphy ran out the front door. Four men stood on the nature strip. The biggest man was arguing with Butch, waving his arms, garden gloves on his hands. A red beard perfectly kept and a heavy gold chain around his neck: Kevin Mason, Nelly's husband. Cierra and Madison's father.

Kevin's eyes landed on Murphy. 'There he is, the pedo,' he roared.

'You're gonna piss off from my property, Mason,' replied Butch.

'What are you gonna do, call the cops? We know you won't do that.' Kevin slipped the gloves off his hands and shoved them into his back pocket. 'No fingerprints, so you can't prove nothing. But if you don't bring the girls back by the end of today, I'm gonna burn this house to the ground – with you still in it.'

Heat had started building in Murphy's chest. He stepped down off the front steps, flexing his fingers as he walked towards Kevin. 'Want to say that again, Mason?'

'Don't, bro,' said Butch, moving between them, one hand on Murphy's chest. Dimly, Murphy was aware of one of Kevin's mates pulling out his phone, pointing the camera Murphy's way. 'Don't. There's journos over there.'

Murphy glanced in the direction Butch pointed. Two journalists were snapping pictures, and another was clearly filming.

'You took her,' said Kevin. He turned to the small crowd of neighbours that had gathered on the street. 'This pedo bastard was fooling around with my daughter.' Kevin pulled a small plastic bag of marijuana from his jacket pocket, a THE CAPTAIN sticker on the front. 'I found this in her room. Your weed, Murphy.' He pointed at Murphy. 'You've always been too friendly with my girls!'

Murphy saw there were also three wrapped condoms inside the bag. 'We don't sell weed to minors,' he growled.

'Shut up, lad,' said Butch.

The man filming on his phone nodded to Mason. 'I got it: "We don't sell weed to minors."'

Murphy glanced at the journalists. *Shit*. They would have recorded it, too.

A BMW pulled into the street, lights flashing up in the corners of the windshield. Murphy bent to grab the packet of weed from Kevin Mason, but he snatched it away.

The BMW pulled over outside their house, and out stepped Detective Badenhorst, his shirt untucked and sleeves rolled up to his elbows.

Someone *had* called the cops. Murphy guessed it was someone in the crowd.

'What's that?' Badenhorst pointed to Kevin's hand. Kevin immediately made to hand the bag over, but the detective first fished some latex gloves out of his pocket.

'I found it in Cierra's room. I'm her father – remember when we met up at the trail?' said Kevin. He pointed at Murphy. 'This weed is his. You can tell by the sticker.'

'You fucking liar —' began Murphy. Butch pulled him back.

Con pulled an evidence bag out of another pocket and dropped the weed packet inside. 'And you came here to confront him rather than coming to us, Mr Mason?'

'No, I was just out for a stroll, detective,' said Kevin. 'This is all just a coincidence.'

Before Badenhorst could say anything more, a police Stinger sped around the corner, lights flashing and siren blaring. It screeched to a halt and out leapt Constable Cavanagh and Sergeant Doble.

Murphy saw Badenhorst grimace.

'Well, look at what we have here, Murphy,' said Doble, seeing the bag in Badenhorst's hand. 'THE CAPTAIN . . . a bit of your product, hey?'

'Sergeant Doble,' said Con, 'can you and Constable Cavanagh

see to these men while myself and Mr Murphy have a chat inside? The rest of you – perhaps there's somewhere else you can be?' he added wryly to the gathered audience.

'No. I think I'll come with you,' said Doble.

'I promise you, you can arrest him soon. I just need to chat with him first,' said Con evenly. 'Inside, Mr Murphy.'

Murphy had a mind to disagree, but Butch pushed him towards the front door. 'Go. This looks bad for both of us,' he muttered.

Murphy stalked inside, hearing Butch unloading on Cavanagh and Doble with the story of the brick and the smashed window, while Kevin Mason and his mates began denying it just as loudly. It showed how worried Butch was, or how scared – usually he wouldn't be caught dead trying to talk to the cops, least of all Doble. The nearby journalists walked over to add their part to the narrative, backing up Butch's story.

Badenhorst followed Murphy into the lounge room and sat down. Gus the Muss jumped up into his lap, and the detective absently pushed him to the side. He held up the bag, the sticker visible. 'Is this your product?'

'I don't know what you're talking about.'

'Mate, we're going to find out sooner or later.'

'I'm not your mate.'

Con pulled out his phone and showed Murphy a photo: it showed another THE CAPTAIN bag of marijuana, on rocky ground with a yellow evidence tag beside it. 'Is this your product too?'

'No,' said Murphy.

'You didn't sell any to Georgia Lenah?' said Con.

'No,' said Murphy. 'Why?'

'Because we just found her body. And this was in her pocket.'

Murphy felt a swooping sensation, deep in his stomach. 'What?' he said. 'Georgia's dead?' A whine began in the back of his mind. His vision grew bright.

'We just found the body of Georgia Lenah. No sign of the others.' Badenhorst watched his face closely, but Murphy couldn't care less. The whine in his head grew louder. 'We found this in her pocket and now it seems a similar bag was found in Cierra's room.'

Everything was too bright. Too loud. Murphy's throat was tight. He couldn't breathe. 'Was there any sign of Jasmine?'

'Just Georgia.'

'She could be dead. I have to get up there,' said Murphy. 'Where did you find Georgia? What happened to her body? Show me.'

'You're not going anywhere. Jordan Murphy, you're under arrest for cultivating and selling a controlled plant.'

'Like hell.' Murphy didn't remember standing up, or stepping so close to Badenhorst. 'You think I did it?'

Badenhorst pulled his jacket away from his hip holster, unclipping the retention on his firearm, unfolding himself from the chair slowly. His eyes flicked back and forth between Murphy's. 'Prove me wrong,' said Badenhorst, voice level. 'Come to the station.'

'I'm not going anywhere!' Murphy shouted, feeling the floodgates of his anger start to release.

'Calm down, Murphy.'

But Murphy was too far gone now: he shoved the detective. '*No one* is gonna stop me from going up there and searching for my —'

The blow to Murphy's solar plexus was so fast he didn't even see it. He bent over, wheezing, and Badenhorst's leg swept his own from under him. He fell to his knees with a heavy thump, and then the detective was across his back, pulling his arms up behind him and into the cuffs.

'You're not making this easy for yourself, you know that, right?' said Badenhorst. He wrenched Murphy to his feet. 'Not that you care, but I'm not having a great day myself.' He dragged him towards the door.

By the time the handcuffed Murphy was led roughly from the house, red and angry, the crowd on the footpath had grown. Kevin's friend was still recording the whole thing. So were the journalists.

In minutes, the footage was uploaded to Facebook. And then broadcast on the news. In half an hour, the whole town knew that the body of Georgia Lenah had been found, that she'd had a bag of marijuana in her pocket potentially linked to Murphy's weed business, an operation he'd basically admitted to on camera, and that after that he'd been arrested by police.

Within an hour, the first death threat arrived in the Murphys' mailbox. Only Butch was there to receive it.

CHAPTER 14

ELIZA

Eliza sat on the couch as Monica rubbed her back. She kept repeating Detective Pakinga's phone call in her head: 'I'm sorry, Eliza, but we have news . . . We've found Georgia's body. It looks like she fell from a cliff . . .'

'Eliza . . . talk to me . . . How can I help?' said Monica, her own voice raspy from tears.

'I have to go back,' Eliza said woodenly.

'Where?' said Monica. 'The hospital?'

'I have to find a way to remember.'

I have to tell them about the fight, part of her screamed, but it was a very distant part, almost like someone else's voice. *I have to tell them about Tom and Cierra. This changes everything!* She pushed that thought away. She had to do what was best for Wren. *I have permission to be strong.*

'Eliza, you *can't* go back up there. It's dangerous. Let the searchers do their job . . .'

'I need to go to Georgia's family. I have to explain. I have to . . .

I have to apologise.' Suddenly that was all that mattered, the most
vital thing in the world.

'It's not your fault!'

'I left Georgia alone!' she shouted, turning on Monica. 'When I
went back to search for the others, I left her all alone!'

Monica didn't flinch. 'You had to search for the others,' she said.
'Stop blaming yourself! Eliza, you can't save *everyone*!'

'Me, my fault, *my own fault*!'

'Not if she fell off a cliff —'

'You really think that's what happened?'

'Of course! Wh-what do you think happened?'

The flare of anger had faded. New emotions pressed on Eliza's
skin, external and distant. Memories, thoughts, things she didn't
want to remember. Grief.

'Up in the hills, he hides and kills . . .' she said.

'No. Impossible.'

The memories made her feel dizzy now. 'Terror. I was so scared,
I would've jumped off a cliff to escape. And I ran, I ran so fast . . . I
can't remember . . . it all feels so close to the surface . . . I think
there were footsteps . . . but . . . Will you take me to Georgia's
house?'

'Are you *sure* that's a good —'

'Monica. *Please*.'

'I'll grab our jackets.'

The Lenahs' home was a rundown fibro house that backed onto the
bushland of the mountain's escarpment, sassafras and wattle trees
encroaching over the fence. It sat at the end of a long gravel driveway lined with waratahs, and a white picket fence ran around a
yard, overgrown and full of squat native laurel.

It had started to rain when Monica pulled up behind a police car parked out the front. On a short flagpole in the front yard hung an Aboriginal flag, limp in the rain.

'Want me to come in with you?' said Monica.

'I'll be fine,' said Eliza, hugging herself. She was familiar with this house: she had come a few times before, to help Georgia with her museum project. She felt another sharp pang in her gut as she realised that would never happen again.

When she opened the car door, she could hear wailing from inside the house. A sudden grip of nausea rolled through her, and she had to hold on to the edge of the little gate at the side of the footpath. It was the sound of a woman in pain.

She heard the car door open behind her. 'Eliza?' called Monica. 'Are you okay?'

Eliza nodded. The air smelled clean and full of waratah. She pushed through the gate and knocked on the door. A man answered it. He was tall, with blonde hair, a blonde moustache, a crooked nose. He looked dazed.

'Are you family?' he said, not unkindly.

'No, I'm Eliza Ellis. The teacher who . . .'

'Miss Ellis. Sorry, we haven't met yet.' He opened the door. 'I'm Detective Stuart Coops. I've been working closely with the social worker at the school. We're just waiting for Rosie's family to arrive, but it's good you're here. Rosie might be glad to see a familiar face.'

'I'm here to apologise to her.'

But Detective Coops had already walked off deeper into the house. 'Pakinga? Eliza Ellis is here.'

Gabriella Pakinga appeared at the end of the corridor. She smiled at the sight of Eliza. 'Come in. It's good you're here: Rosie needs someone she can hug, and she's not too keen on police.' She leaned in close to whisper in her ear. 'Do you know about Sorry Business?'

'I teach some of the Indigenous Studies curriculum at the school,' said Eliza. 'And Georgia taught me a lot.' Her voice broke. 'I shouldn't say the name of the dead.'

'Then you're further ahead than Coops,' Gabriella said darkly. 'Alright, come on through.'

They entered the dining room, where Rosie Lenah was sprawled across the table, her back heaving with grief. She had grey in her dark hair and wore a big floral dress.

At the sight of her anguish, Eliza's own guilt nearly made her retch. 'Rosie?' she said. 'I'm so . . . so sorry . . .'

Rosie turned and in one movement swept Eliza up into her arms, her words incoherent. All Eliza could do was hold her, letting her own tears fall. Rosie smelled of perfume and baking. Eliza's mind returned to Denni, to the moment she'd heard of her death, and her own grief was amplified in Rosie.

Finally she heard Rosie speaking through the crying. 'The mountain *needed* my girl,' she sobbed. 'We *needed* her . . . Why did it take her . . .?'

Over Rosie's shoulder, Eliza saw Gabriella and Coops glance at each other. Confusion was clear on Coops' face, but Gabriella only looked strangely excited, her eyes sparkling.

There came loud knocking from the door. Coops went to answer, and returned with two elderly women. The family resemblance was clear, and the way Rosie threw herself into their arms confirmed it. Together the three women howled their grief, and Rosie was bundled away into the tiny lounge room and onto the threadbare couch.

Gabriella grabbed Eliza by the shoulder and steered her into the corridor. 'Can you show us her bedroom?' she whispered. 'We just want to have a look around, and time may be of the essence. Rosie already gave us permission. Or at least, I think she nodded when we asked. It's not until today that they've even let any cops inside to look. We were working on getting a warrant . . .'

'What do you hope to find?' whispered Eliza.

'We're not sure yet,' said Gabriella. 'But do you know what Rosie meant, about the mountain needing G—' She caught herself, looking around the walls of the house. 'Needing the girl?'

'Yes. You'll see . . .' It was a small bedroom already, but the large table taking up the centre dominated the space.

'What's this?' said Gabriella, stepping immediately up to the table.

Upon it sat a scale model of a wide, sweeping building, with a large flagpole rising from the centre peak, waving a miniature Aboriginal flag.

'This was her dream. The Kooparoona Niara Aboriginal Heritage Museum,' said Eliza. The display was a mixture of architectural and trainset models. Georgia had even included tiny people, lazing in the picnic area, walking through the outdoor gallery, lining up at the coffee stand. 'She wanted to build an Aboriginal history museum, right here in Limestone Creek. And she would've done it, too. She had what it took.'

Gabriella examined the contents of a folder. 'Permit applications . . .' She picked up a large hardcover book. 'A book about property law.'

Coops read out the titles of the books scattered on the floor. '*The Aboriginal Tasmanians, The Black War, Whitewash . . .*'

One of the papers that littered the floor caught Eliza's eye, because it had her own handwriting across the bottom: giving feedback on an essay. With another pang, she picked it up. As the detectives rummaged through the rest of the room, speculating aloud to each other on whether the museum might give someone the motive to kill Georgia, Eliza wiped her eyes and began to read.

The Mountain of the Spirits, by Georgia Lenah

At the bottom of the world, there is an island.

It has the purest air in the world, the purest water. It is a land of rugged wilderness, of ice and snow, blistering heat, the oldest trees on earth, deep lakes of which no man nor machine has found the bottom. A fifth of the island is protected, where no business can exploit nor industrialise, and precious little can be reached by road. They say extinct tigers still roam there. They say other things roam, too. Strange lights haunt the night sky and unearthly howls the bushland.

It is the location of one of the earliest recorded genocides, cannibals and convicts, the introduction of psychological torture of inmates, Australia's biggest massacre. Its name once brought fear to people's hearts; it is said the soil still cries from the blood of its First Peoples, and that their bones curse the land.

If you believe in such things.

Near the top of the island, in the centre, at the edge of the Central Plateau, is a rocky mountain range. These days it is called the Great Western Tiers. But always it was called Kooparoona Niara. It was a sacred place, a meeting ground, and a pass. They say it is the gate to Tasmania's heart.

It is a place of changing weather, silence, brooding and looming menace, secret caves and urban legends and murderers who once made it their stalking ground.

It is a mountain that, they say, takes care of itself.

If you believe in such things.

Eliza shuddered. She put the paper down beside her.

'What is this?' said Gabriella, picking it up and raising her eyebrows as she began to read.

'Maybe this will help,' said Coops. He was lying beside the bed, holding up a purple book he'd pulled from under it. 'I think it's her diary.'

'Perfect,' said Gabriella, taking it out of his hands.

'Put that down – it's none of your fucking business,' said a gruff male voice from the doorway. 'Why are you pigs in my sister's room?' A short young man stood there, in a muddy t-shirt and football shorts, dark brows narrowed. Tears ran down his cheeks, but he seemed unaware of them. 'Get out.'

'Calm down, Carl,' said Eliza. 'They're the police.'

'I know who they are. I want them out of her room.'

'I'm sorry, I know this is hard,' said Gabriella. 'But a diary is important, it could help us build a picture of what might have happened.'

'Get out,' Carl snarled. He lunged for the diary.

'Don't hurt him,' shouted Coops, as Gabriella deftly caught the boy's wrist and pulled it back on itself. Carl let out a howl and Gabriella let him go, but kept her eye on him.

Carl balled his fists. 'Give it back or I'll kill you.'

'I'm really sorry. Carl, is it?' said Coops. 'It's important for us to use everything we can to try to find out what happened to your sister, to bring back the other girls.'

'Like you give a fuck about my sister, pig.'

'Carl, please,' said Eliza. 'Mum needs you right now.' Carl glared at Eliza for a moment. They could still hear Rosie's anguish at the other end of the house. 'She really, really needs you . . .'

He stalked out of the room.

Gabriella looked back down at Georgia's diary. 'Good job, Eliza.'

Suddenly one of Rosie's relatives rushed into the room. A red mark was across her cheek. 'I'm sorry, I'm sorry, he's going to your car!'

Cursing, Gabriella ran out the door.

Coops approached the woman slowly. 'Your cheek – are you alright?'

'It's fine. I hit myself on the door.' Tears welled and spilled over. 'He's not himself right now.'

A moment later his radio crackled. 'I've got him, Coops,' said Gabriella. 'He started scratching a lovely message into the car. K-U-N . . .'

Coops sighed through his nose, ruffling his moustache. 'Can't even spell . . .' Eliza followed him outside.

There was now a small crowd of Rosie's family in the driveway – more had arrived – and they were clustered around the police car, getting drenched in the rain. Eliza and Coops pushed through the people to find Gabriella, nursing her forearm and a red bite mark, swearing profusely. Carl was nowhere to be seen.

'He *bit* me,' said Gabriella. 'The little feral.'

Her words invoked a reaction from the crowd, who began buzzing dangerously. Coops immediately put his radio to his mouth. 'This is Detective Coops, requesting back-up. Young male on the run; needed for questioning and assault of a police officer. Carl Lenah. He's just taken off on a dirtbike – brown helmet, orange bike.'

'No!' screamed Rosie, leaning against another man for support. 'Please, not again! Don't take him back to the station!'

'Please, sir, have a heart –' said someone. 'Mate, he didn't mean it,' said someone else.

'I'm sorry, Mrs Lenah, but he has assaulted an officer,' said Stuart. 'We should have explained to him how important Georgia's diary could be.'

The crowd of people muttered angrily.

'Don't say her name!' hissed Gabriella.

'Shit! I'm sorry!' said Coops.

Rosie surged forward, her bulky hips swinging, her floral dress catching in a sudden breeze. 'Give me her diary.'

'Sir, please give her the diary —' 'Have a heart, mate, it's her daughter's diary —'

The group pressed closer. One man swiped for the book in Gabriella's hand.

'Eliza,' said Monica, appearing at her side. 'Let's go.' She steered Eliza away from the group and into the car. 'It looks like it could get ugly.'

They pulled out of the driveway.

'We should have stayed and helped calm everyone down,' said Eliza.

'It's going to be like this until the girls are found . . .' began Monica. 'Look, do you still want to go back up the mountain?'

Reading Georgia's essay had made her feel sick. And the rhyme was back again:

I won't walk alone by the mountain trees . . .

'I'll need to get changed. Take me back home. I'm going to join the search. But I won't go alone.'

Or the Hungry Man will come for me.

CHAPTER 15

CON

Con paced the corridor outside the station's interview room, speaking to Commander Normandy on the phone. Inside the interview room Murphy and his lawyer, Dave, were waiting alone.

He heard the sound of another incoming call and checked the screen briefly. Unknown number. It would have to wait.

In the corridor with him was Detective Melinda Tran, crouched against the wall, scrolling through her phone as she waited for Con to finish his call.

'Yes, commander,' said Con, speaking slowly. 'I reviewed the autopsy report. No obvious signs of a struggle – no skin under her nails, at least . . . No, but her head was too damaged to see if she'd been hit. No sign of her backpack, so we have to assume she wasn't wearing it or someone took it . . . Yes, I agree that's most likely . . . They got up on the cliff and confirmed they were her shoes . . . No, he confirmed they had their laces tied up, and he really felt as though they'd been carefully placed there. If you look at the photos you can . . . No, just *her* DNA so far, but there was a lot of rain overnight.

'Pakinga is at Georgia's house now, with Detective Coops . . . Because I heard over the radio there was an altercation at the Murphys' house . . . Call it a hunch, ma'am. They've got no evidence, even though they've searched for his crop a half dozen times. Everyone local seems to know Murphy and his brother run the weed trade here . . . I'm about to speak with – well, I wouldn't call it a mob exactly . . . I did hear they wanted to kill him on my way into the station, yes . . . I hate small country towns, ma'am . . . No, I'll take him out by a back door . . . Well, it could be that the missing girls are hidden wherever his crop is . . . Of course. I'll do my best to get something out of him, ma'am. I'll keep you up to date.'

He ended the call. After a moment he said to Tran, 'Catch all that?'

'The guys down in Hobart call her "the Hellcat",' said Tran.

'There are *many* names that would suit that woman,' he said with fondness. 'Do you want to watch from inside or on the cameras?'

'Cameras. He might let his guard down if it's just you.' She stood up. 'We really think he's involved? His own daughter?'

Con hesitated. 'There's a lot of coincidences. Keep an eye on him and let me know what you make of him after.'

At that moment, a text message came through, from the same number as the missed call:

Hello, detective. This is Pastor Hugh. Can you please call me back on this number?

Con glanced at it, then stepped inside the interview room. Murphy and his lawyer sat across from him. He slipped the phone into his pocket. 'Okay, Murphy,' said Con. 'Shall we begin?'

Murphy was pale and dark rings lay under his eyes, but with his heavy brow and beard this only made him look more fearsome. 'You need to let me out of here. I have to join the search.'

'You must have more pressing concerns right now, detective,' said Dave. 'You're bringing petty charges against my client regarding *weed*. Shouldn't you be examining a crime scene?'

'We're giving you a chance to come clean, Murphy,' said Con, ignoring Dave. 'The signs don't look good.'

'Your "signs" do not constitute evidence,' interjected Dave.

Con pulled four photographs from his folder and placed them down on the table, leaving the last face down. The first three each showed a bag of marijuana with the THE CAPTAIN sticker. The one found on the trail, one from Georgia's pocket and the bag with the three condoms that Kevin Mason had brandished in Murphy's face barely an hour before.

'Are these your product?' said Con.

'No,' said Dave.

'No,' said Murphy.

'This one was found on the trail,' said Con.

'Any of the girls could've dropped it,' said Dave. 'Hell, one of the teachers could've dropped it, or some other hiker.'

'This one, as we know,' Con tapped on the photo, 'was found in Cierra Mason's room. With condoms inside.'

'Allegedly,' said Dave.

Con tapped another photo, watching Murphy's face. 'This one was found in Georgia Lenah's pocket.'

No reaction. Murphy wasn't even looking at the photos, his eyes were piercingly focused on Con.

'And these . . .' Con turned over the final photograph. It showed a pair of running shoes, fluoro yellow, sitting on a rock. The laces were neatly tied up, a pair of damp socks balled up beside them. 'These are Georgia's shoes, found at the top of the cliff from which she fell.'

That got Murphy's attention. He looked down at the photo.

Silence filled the room.

'And what does this have to do with Murphy?' said Dave belatedly.

Con didn't reply. He scanned Murphy's face for any spark of recognition.

'Why are they just sitting there . . .?' Murphy picked up the photo. 'Why are they tied up?' His hands shook. 'What else did you find?'

'Where have you hidden your crop?' said Con.

'I don't know what you're talking about,' said Murphy, eyes still on the photo. 'Did you find anything else up there? Why are they bloody *tied* like that? I thought you said she fell? Did she jump? *Was she pushed?*'

'Your marijuana crop. Where is it, Murphy? Your drying room? Your storage?'

'Ah, so as we expected, you have no actual evidence for the charges you're bringing?' said Dave. 'I imagine my client is free to leave, in that case?'

'I need to know, mate,' said Con, ignoring Dave. 'Forensics have proven that all the marijuana came from the same plant strain, as if the common sticker wasn't enough. If it's yours, Murphy, I need to know *now*.' He leaned forward. 'If I'm forced to find out another way, it'll look even worse for you.'

'Like you haven't set him up to take the fall either way,' said Dave scathingly. 'We are *very* familiar with the way "justice" works around here.'

'It's not my weed, and I don't know what you're talking about,' said Murphy. He put the photo down. Now those eyes were back on Con, sharp with fury. 'You've searched my property, right? While you left me waiting in this room, while my daughter is out there, while a body has already been found, you got a bunch of cops to search my house instead. Even though I've had my property searched *six times*. They never find anything, and you didn't find anything this time either. So why don't you go out there and *do your job* and find my *daughter*, and get the *fuck out of my way!*' He was standing by the end, roaring into Con's face.

Con slowly stood. He stared back, not blinking, turning his eye trick to full power. He let the silence build.

It took some time, and he grumbled about it, but Murphy eventually sat back down. He even mumbled, 'Sorry.'

That's more like it, thought Con.

'What I want to hear from you, Detective Badenhorst,' said Dave, 'is what has happened to those thugs who threw a brick through my client's window. Have *any* charges been laid against them? Or is everyone else in this witch-hunt of an investigation above the law?'

'Murphy, were you sleeping with Cierra Mason?' said Con.

'*What?*' exploded Murphy, shooting to his feet again.

'You *dare* —' began Dave.

'Answer the question,' said Con.

Murphy leaned forward over the table. He was quivering with rage again, his face contorted in disgust. 'No, I have not slept with Cierra Mason. Nor any other underage girl.' He tried to spit on the table, but he was in such a state it barely dribbled out. 'She's the same age as my daughter, for fuck's sake!' He wiped his chin with a sharp movement.

Con leaned back. Murphy's eyebrows had pulled down, his nose had wrinkled. The 'disgust face' was the body's way of protecting itself – the eyes squinted to shield themselves from damage, the nasal passages closed to protect from dangerous fumes, leaving the lips loose. Murphy's disgust was real. He was telling the truth.

'Alright, Murphy,' said Con, his suspicion draining away. He focused on setting his own body language to something that would put Murphy at ease, relaxing his shoulders, raising his eyebrows. He pitched his voice so it sounded reasonable, and concerned, not accusatory. 'But whoever supplied your bag to Cierra also supplied it to Georgia.'

'You've never had daughters, have you, detective?' said Dave suddenly.

Con glanced his way for the first time. 'Excuse me?' Even
Murphy seemed caught off guard by Dave's question.

'Teenage girls *share*,' said Dave. 'If Cierra had a bag of weed in
her room, then odds are she gave some to her friends.'

'I'm well aware of the habits of teenage girls, but we need to
know where it came from —'

'What the hell do marijuana and condoms have to do with their
disappearance?' Dave leaned forward now. 'Check the rooms of
half the girls in this town and you'll find the same. Out here, you
can get marijuana one of two ways – you can grow it yourself, but
it's reasonably priced and way less risky to buy it from the supplier
who works at this very station. Not that your lot care one whit
about that.'

This station? thought Con, falling silent for a moment.

'You don't know that Sergeant Doble is a weed dealer,' said
Murphy flatly. 'Oh this is just fucking perfect.'

'I'm not here to talk about anyone else,' said Con, thrown off
balance. 'We're talking about you.'

'How about we talk about you?' said Dave. 'I've done some
research. You did a good job with the Jaguar case in Sydney, no
one's denying that, but in Tasmania the rules are different. And in
the meantime, I've had an interesting text message come through
from Butch. You *have* sent police to check the property for this
supposed crop, haven't you?'

Con didn't reply. Truthfully, he hadn't: he didn't expect to find
anything more than the other searches had, and besides, he didn't
like the stir it would cause. Murphy already attracted a crowd outside the station that wanted to beat him to death, it wouldn't help to
have uniformed officers scouring his property.

'I'd appreciate it if you kept your phone switched off while in
this room, Mr Llewellyn.'

'Because Butch reported a break-in.'

'What?' said Murphy. 'Is he alright?'

'Which surely wouldn't have happened if you'd had your offic-ers there.' Dave stood up. 'So you didn't search it, *nor* did you think to send officers to guard the house? Considering the mob that's outside this place?'

'What mob?' said Murphy.

'You're just as bloody useless as the rest, aren't you, detective? Let's go, Murphy. Someone's broken into your house, and your brother needs you.'

'You're sure you have nothing else to tell us, Murphy?' said Con.

'Does "fuck you" count?' said Murphy.

Con made a dismissive gesture, but they were almost to the door when he said, 'Use the western exit. You don't want to leave through the front door. Exit code is 9779.'

He heard Murphy hesitate, then the door shut behind him.

Immediately Con was on the phone, calling Gabriella.

'Hey, how did you go at —'

He didn't even finish his question before he got an explosive run-down from Gabriella about everything that had happened at the Lenahs' house. 'They haven't tracked down Carl yet – I hope they do, I've already got a bruise where he bit me.'

'And the diary?' said Con.

'There's not a whole lot in there that's useful to us: just ideas and plans about her museum. I've left the diary with Coops, he's going to scan it and email it to us.'

'Okay. Do we think Georgia was targeted because of the museum?'

'It's possible. I called the mayor, Meredith Phythian, and had a very interesting chat about it all,' said Gabriella. 'I'll tell you in person: we're nearly at the station.'

'Good, you can pick me up. We'll leave Coops in charge of track-ing down Carl and we'll have lunch somewhere. Hopefully things will have calmed down by then – I want to head to the Masons' and talk to them. I'll give you the rundown on my chat with Murphy.'

'I still can't believe that Kevin dickhead moved the bag he found in Cierra's room,' said Gabriella. 'No way are we getting any prints off that.'

Melinda Tran stepped into the room. Her face was pale. 'Talk to you in a minute, Gab,' Con said, hanging up the phone. 'What is it?'

'You better get outside,' said Melinda. 'Your weed dealer is getting the shit beat out of him.'

CHAPTER 16

MURPHY

Murphy and Dave used the side exit, Badenhorst's code proving true.

A lonely prowler waited for them, sitting cross-legged on the ground, a painted cardboard sign beside him that read *BRING THEM HOME*. He was a young man with spiky black hair and a smartphone. 'He's here,' he screeched, leaping to his feet and pointing the camera at Murphy. 'Where are the girls? What have you done with them?'

Fists balling up, Murphy walked towards the prowler, who backed away, his phone still recording.

Cursing, Dave ran ahead to his car, parked further down the street.

'What the fuck did you say to me?' said Murphy.

A group of people and journalists appeared around the corner, excitement loud in their voices.

Cameras flashed. People yelled. Murphy kept advancing on the young man, his anger pulsing in his temple.

A journalist shoved a microphone towards Murphy's mouth. 'What do you have to say about —'

Murphy's fist connected with the journalist's nose. The man fell, his microphone clattering to the ground beside him. Murphy rounded on the next journalist, his shoulders hunched like a beast.

Soon he was surrounded by bulky men, flexing their knuckles. 'You know what we do to pedos around here?' said the closest, a man with a flat nose, black eyes, and long hair.

Two of them grabbed Murphy from behind, and a third swung his fist into his belly, then his face. Murphy felt blood spurting down across his mouth and beard: he tasted the iron. He tore himself free, but three more grappled with him, dragging him to the ground. They started stamping on his shoulders, his head, his ribs. Pain and adrenaline filled him with heat.

Murphy had taken a lot of beatings in his life; he was hardier than most. He found his way to his feet and before he knew it blood was on his knuckles, and two of his assailants were on the ground.

People were screaming, sirens were ringing, and then Dave was there, shoving people away, pulling Murphy from the crowd. Murphy, wild with fury, threw Dave off. Uniformed police officers appeared, moving between Murphy and the vigilantes.

'Your brother needs you, Murphy. *Go*,' came Badenhorst's voice from right beside him. Murphy turned to see him spreading his arms to hold people back.

Dave tried to wrench Murphy towards his waiting car. *'I'm going to sue all of you bastards! I'll see you in court!'* He tugged on Murphy. '*Move*, for fuck's sake!'

Murphy saw that Badenhorst was now supervising the arrest of the vigilantes. He let himself be pushed into Dave's car, even as a group of teenagers started clambering on top of it, jumping up and down, calling him a paedophile, shouting threats.

'*Mad-i-son! Mad-i-son!*' they began to chant.

The teenagers leapt off, screaming and laughing, as Dave put the car into gear and sped off.

Blood in his mouth and dripping into his eye, Murphy nearly started swinging again when Dave pushed a box of tissues from the centre console into Murphy's hand.

'We should take you to hospital.'

'I'm gonna kill them.'

'Who?' said Dave.

'Anyone.'

Dave didn't reply. He drove towards Butch's house, not speaking as Murphy swore and raged, punching the door.

'I didn't give her weed,' Murphy finally said. 'Any of them. You know I didn't.'

'If *you* don't supply Cierra or Georgia, then someone you *do* supply must have . . . maybe *they* were having sex with Cierra.'

'We have a middle-man,' said Murphy. 'His name is Skinner. I don't know everyone he sells to: he has this rule where he won't tell his suppliers who he sells to. Keeps a buffer between things. But I *know* he doesn't sell to minors.'

'You need to talk to him. Do some investigating yourself. If you won't tell the cops that the weed really did come from you —'

'You told me not to!'

'And I stand by that,' said Dave. 'But Cierra had a bag, and Georgia had a bag, so —'

'And Jasmine had one,' said Murphy.

'What?'

'She stole a bag of weed on her way out the door, before the camp. Butch knew, but he lied to me about it.'

Dave was silent for a moment. 'So . . .' he began gently. 'We do know that *someone* who smokes your weed was in Cierra's room. It's not much to go off, but you need to sort this out, mate . . . because if Jasmine had a target on her . . .'

Murphy felt like a bullet ripped through his chest. 'What?' His voice rose. 'What did you just —'

'No, you don't get to start raging on me. You're a *drug dealer*. A *criminal*. You have enemies in this town – powerful enemies. The bloody station sergeant for one! If Jasmine was taken by someone, for ransom or . . . something else . . .'

Murphy's shoulders tensed up and he thought he might just start swinging anyway. Then he slumped against the car door. An aching fire ran up his side, and his nose and face truly began to pound.

He began to cry.

'Hey, mate, it's okay . . . Shh, it's okay,' said Dave.

'What do I do, Dave?' sobbed Murphy. 'What the fuck do I do?'

'You gotta ask Skinner who he sells to.'

'He won't tell me!'

'Convince him.' They pulled up outside the Murphy's house. Three journalists were standing on the footpath.

'I dunno how.'

Dave sighed. He switched the engine off. 'Look . . . your old man was always a good mate to me.' He raised his hands. 'I know, I know. He was a mongrel to his own sons, and he was generous with his fists with you. But . . . I've always seen you boys like nephews. Did you know that? Well, I think if your Dad was alive, he'd be okay with me giving you this – keep an eye on those jokers outside for a sec.'

'What are you . . .?' said Murphy.

Dave flipped open the glovebox and reached inside. 'Just keep an eye on them.' From behind a hidden flap, he pulled out a pistol. It was a 9-millimetre Glock, the same used by Tasmania Police.

'Holy shit, Dave.'

'Consider it a gift. Now, I'm not telling you to use it, but if you need to convince Skinner . . . well, if it's to get Jasmine back, all bets are off, right?' Dave chewed his lip as he handed it to him. 'You're not stupid enough to get caught with this, are you?'

Murphy held it between his hands. It was heavy and cold. Something stirred inside of him. 'I've never shot a handgun before.'

'Just remember to hold it in both hands and breathe evenly,' said Dave. 'Here's an extra magazine, and here's how you load it . . .'

Minutes later, Murphy headed towards his front door, the gun shoved into the back of his belt and under his shirt. The bystanders flinched when he glanced at them, and he knew he must look fearsome: his face bruised, mouth oozing blood.

He shoved the door open.

Something hissed near his feet, and he leapt back with a yell.

'Murph! Stay back!' called Butch from inside, his voice high-pitched.

Murphy took another backwards step. A long tiger snake, at least a metre and half in length, reared up on the doormat and barked like a dog. It had a black-scaled back and yellow tiger-stripes ran up from its belly.

'The bastards dropped them in through the broken window,' shouted Butch.

'Are you alright?' He feinted at the snake, and it flattened and slithered away.

'They haven't bit me yet, if that's what you mean.' His voice wavered.

Murphy found his big brother curled up in the middle of the dining-room table. Butch was terrified of snakes.

'How many?' said Murphy.

'They're *venomous* as *fuck*!' shouted Butch, starting to lose it. '*One is too many!*'

'Alright, alright. I'll deal with it, Butch.'

He went around the side of the house, leaving the front door wide open to encourage the snakes' escape, and jumped over the fence into his own backyard, ignoring the looks from those journalists still waiting out the front. He went into the shed, retrieving a broom, gumboots and heavy gloves.

He paused, then hid the Glock in one of the holes in the back of the couch, under one of the timber slats. He noticed something on the couch cushions: a spray bottle. It was Skinner's angel dust. He picked it up, shaking it – there was still half the bottle left. It was lucky the cops *hadn't* searched . . .

He put the bottle in the same hiding place as the Glock, left the shed and entered through the back door of the house, flicking on the lights.

A tiger snake coiled itself tighter in the corner, right next to the doorframe. The black-and-yellow stripes evoked a primal fear in Murphy he had to fight to quench. All children who grew up in the Tasmanian bush knew to fear the tiger snake, they were everywhere on the island.

Using the broom, he brushed it towards the door. It reared, barking like a dog, but eventually it slithered away.

Next was his bedroom. He flicked on the light, carefully stepping around the carpet, poking the broom into corners and under the desk. Finally, he poked it under his bed.

It hit something soft that set the broom twitching.

Grunting, Murphy pulled the broom back, and it came back with a snake wrapped around it, the black arrow-shape of its head looking at Murphy.

It launched at him.

With reflexes sharpened by adrenaline, Murphy's gloved hands grabbed it behind the head. It struggled in his fists and instinctively he twisted as hard as he could. A few moments later it stopped thrashing, hanging limp like a hose.

He opened the window and hurled it out, feeling a touch sad. They were a protected species, after all.

In the dining room, walking around Butch and his table, Murphy found three more snakes. He swept them out the front door, even as they hissed and reared and struck at his boots, eventually slithering away.

The journalists, still standing there on the footpath, screamed and ran into their cars.

Finally, brushing two more snakes out of the kitchen, Murphy systematically searched the rest of the house. He found one more snake, already dead, hanging through the broken window. Around its crushed head was a note attached by a piece of baling twine: *BRING OUR GIRLS BACK PEDO SNAKE OR YOU'LL BE NEXT.*

He looked out the broken window, where two teenagers were now filming Murphy's house. Running to the front door, he wrenched it open and hurled the dead snake at them.

Satisfied by their squeals and the way they sprinted away, he finally returned to Butch and gave him the all clear. The big man climbed down off the table, trying to hide a wet patch on the front of his trousers.

'I pissed myself . . .' he muttered, avoiding Murphy's eyes. He gave a double-take. 'What the fuck happened to your face?'

'I'm fine,' said Murphy. 'Go get yourself cleaned up.'

Murphy's phone rang while he waited for Butch to shower. It was Dave calling. He answered it. 'Have they found them?' said Murphy.

'No, I'm back at the station . . . that journo you punched, he wants to press charges.'

Murphy slumped into a chair.

'Don't worry, I'm sorting it out. I've argued for reasonable self-defence, and Badenhorst is backing me up, surprisingly. I honestly can't work him out. But he did give me a message for you: if you want to stay out of custody, and stay alive, don't leave the house until he tells you to. He's gonna organise for a regular patrol to go past your place as protection.'

Murphy stayed silent.

Dave's voice went quieter. 'That might make it harder to get this Skinner to come to your place . . .'

'I'll work it out. I'm not keen on running into another mob.'

Dave ended the call, and Murphy rested his head on the table.

'Was that Dave?' said Butch, coming out of the shower naked. 'Do they have news on Jasmine? Did you tell him about the snakes?'

'I'm gonna call Skinner around tonight. Is that an issue for you?' said Murphy without lifting his head.

'You want to sell some weed *now*?' said Butch.

'No. I need to know who he sells our weed to.'

'You know he won't tell us, lad.'

'He will if we get him high enough. We'll take him out to the shed – we still have some of his angel dust,' said Murphy.

'You want to dose him with angel dust? Shit.' Butch headed down the hallway towards his bedroom to get dressed. 'Let me know when he's on his way.'

CHAPTER 17

ELIZA

Eliza stood in the doorway of the Limestone Creek Community Hall, now converted into the search command centre.

In her hand, crinkled tight, was a permission slip:

I give Eliza Ellis permission to join the search and not feel guilty.
Signed, E. Ellis

She stole another glance behind her. The SES officer there had let her in the door when she'd explained who she was, and now found herself in a debate with another young woman, who was also demanding to join the search.

'You just let that woman in, why can't you let me in?' she said. 'We're here to help!'

There was a whole crowd of wannabe search volunteers, camped in tents around the paddock that bordered the community hall, which had once been an old church, complete with ramshackle cemetery. It had begun snowing, out of what had previously been a clear blue sky, and some people had started campfires. It was becoming a miniature festival, complete with coffee and toastie vans, and music pumping from somewhere.

Eliza shook the slush off her hiking jacket and walked towards the end of the timber-floored hall. A group of men and women stood around a table on the small stage, framed by red curtains and dusty plaques and trophies on the walls. The room was loud and echoing with voices, and even though the old radiators were firing from the walls, Eliza's breath still misted, her glasses fogging up.

As she walked up the steps, she brushed her hair from the leopard-print scarf, still tied around her head, and she studied the people around the table. There was a man standing at the head of the table, pointing at the map, trailing his finger along a path. The others were all angled towards him, leaning in, so it had to be Constable Darren Cahil, the search controller. He was in his mid-forties, dark full hair swept back, a Geelong Cats scarf loose around his neck, trailing down either side of his jacket.

Eliza drew closer until she could hear what he was saying.

'. . . even if just one person stays overnight in each hut, you never know when they might stumble into —' He looked up. His eyes were alert. 'Miss Ellis,' he said.

The others around the table looked her way. She caught glimpses of curiosity and pity on their faces. She could imagine what they were thinking. *This is the teacher who was there when the girls went missing. She's the whole reason we're in this mess. Who does she think she is, coming here?*

You're being paranoid, she chided herself, gripping her permission slip tighter.

'You've come to help with the search,' said Darren matter-of-factly.

'I want to join a team,' she said.

A woman in SES overalls picked at her nails and an important-looking man in police uniform turned to Darren. 'I know exactly where we could take Miss Ellis to —'

'Let me go for a walk with Miss Ellis,' said Darren quickly, giving the others a warm smile. 'Make sure we get someone stationed in all the remaining mountain huts, and give each of them a satellite phone.'

He stepped out from behind the table before they could argue and grabbed Eliza's elbow, steering her towards a makeshift café that was serving espresso coffee, the barista lining the takeaway cups up on the table. A group of farmers mingled there, dressed in Akubras and hi-vis, filling the air with strained and overloud laughter.

'The barista only makes cappuccinos, I'm afraid,' said Darren, passing one of the cups into Eliza's hands. 'I prefer a flat white, myself.' Eliza noticed the plain wedding ring on his finger, the dirt under his nails. 'Drink. Get warm. It'll be cold up there. Unless it's not – who knows with the Tiers.'

Eliza let the cup warm her hands, as Darren gestured towards a door that led out to the hall's enclosed yard.

'Thank you for coming. Thanks to you, I'll have an excuse to get up there and join the search myself.'

'Can't you just assign yourself to a team?' said Eliza. 'I thought you were in charge?'

He laughed. 'Apparently I'm more useful down here, even if it's just so people can see me gesturing at maps.' His eyes pinned hers. 'If I'm being honest, I was hoping you'd arrive. You're the most valuable asset we have, Miss Ellis. I want to go exactly where they found you and search there.' He looked her up and down and nodded, approving her attire. 'They told me you were an experienced hiker. Are you ready now?'

'You want to go to the Lake Nameless trail.'

'The others in your group have helped us locate where they

found you, but I'd like to see what you make of it. Does that sound like a plan, Miss Ellis?'

She fingered her headscarf, the memory of the queasy ache still fresh. 'You can call me Eliza.'

He inclined his head. 'Miss Ellis.' Wannabe searchers glanced their way, calling out, but Darren ignored them. 'I hope you don't mind, we'll take my Yamaha. I'll just find you a helmet, and I'll grab some hiking packs from the SES and a few others to help us.'

They stepped out of the community centre, into sunshine and light wind.

Eliza and Darren walked up the steep muddy hiking trail. In the low branches of an alpine cider gum was a Bassian thrush, its flute-like song trilling around them. Eliza shivered. These birds only came out at twilight or, like now, when it was so overcast it felt like twilight. It seemed a bad omen.

She had been grateful when they parked their bike a little earlier, when the trail became too steep – the bumpy ride had made her queasy and dizzy, but she couldn't let the concussion stop her from what she had to do. Three other motorbikes had already been parked there, with two SES volunteers and a farmer now trailing behind her and Darren. Each of those three was looking in a different direction: ahead, left or right.

'I had no idea there were so many dirtbike trails through the bush here,' said Eliza. 'You got us here so quickly . . .'

'Don't thank me yet,' said Darren. 'It's still a bit of a walk to the Lake Nameless trail.'

The clouds broke overhead, sun bursting down over them like a wave. The Bassian thrush's song ended in a high-pitched 'seet', but other birds took up the call. Sudden insects buzzed around her, tiny flies with metallic blue bodies.

'We'll have to cross a waterfall up ahead,' commented Darren, brushing at the flies.

Listening now, Eliza heard the rushing up ahead. Her heart lifted: waterfalls in this area were beautiful. 'Lucky my boots are waterproof,' she said. Silence built between them, until she said, 'So you're a constable, right?'

'Yes, ma'am.'

'Can I ask: how did you become search controller?'

'You mean as a lowly constable?' said Darren, chuckling. 'Generally you want someone practical, knowledgeable . . . feet firmly on the ground, if you know what I mean. Characters like that are usually happy to stay where they are, even if they've been a constable for longer than their sergeant has been in the force. Not that that's the situation in my case,' he said, tapping his thumb to his chest wryly. 'I'm just lucky enough to be a local. Grew up on a farm in Meander — my parents still own it. I've hiked these mountains many, many times. I know this place better than probably any other copper in Tasmania. That's the reason they put me in charge of the search. It's not my first search-and-rescue in the Tiers.'

'You'll find the girls, then,' said Eliza.

Darren was silent as he walked, boots swishing in the muddy gravel of the track. By the time he spoke again, the rushing of the waterfall had grown so loud it almost masked his words: 'The Tiers don't like to let go of things, Miss Ellis . . . but we'll do our best.'

They arrived at a shallow tributary, falling down a jagged dolomite rockface into a deeper stream below. They had approached the falls from the top, and Eliza saw the thick galvanised wire across the span, designed to be held as they crossed. 'I've been here before,' she said with surprise.

'Could be,' said Darren. 'But there are many like this all over the Tiers, and they all look similar. Although in winter, the streams sometimes change their paths completely . . .'

One of the SES workers – a woman with grey hair – overtook him and walked right to the edge of the falls, peering down. Despite herself, Eliza stepped up onto a slippery rock beside her. The water below was amber brown and rolling with foam and waves, beautiful in the sunlight, treacherous among jutting rocks.

'Could they be down there?' she found herself asking the woman, nausea rolling through her belly at the thought.

'Possibly,' said the SES volunteer with a heavy sigh. 'Should we have some divers come check?' she shouted to Darren above the sound of the falls.

Darren's feet were steady as he looked down into the base of the waterfall, even as the water rushed over his hiking boots. 'We can't search every pool we pass,' he said, 'but . . . maybe we can try this one.'

Eliza listened as he called it in, following Darren as he walked to the other side. He was matter-of-fact, detailing the co-ordinates of the waterfall, the route there, his request for divers.

The cable bit into her palm as she crossed, while her mind returned to the rolling, boiling water. *We can't search every pool . . .*

The rest of their party followed behind, their eyes on their respective directions, their mouths shut, faces grim.

After half an hour's walk, they stopped, the sky overcast again and a chill wind starting to blow. 'Now, I believe this is where Mr Jack Michaels eventually found you, once he'd met up with Miss Carmen,' said Darren.

A large daisy bush reached over the edge of the trail here, its hundreds of beautiful white flowers early for the season. The smell was sharp and spicy, and the air droned with bees.

Somewhere, we joined the Lake Nameless trail, she thought in surprise. *I didn't even notice.*

She felt completely lost.

But she had a pang of memory as she crouched down, pressing a hand to the soft flowers of the bush. She remembered lying here, in the mud and wet. The aroma was wilder than other flowers.

'This is where they found you.' said Darren. 'Any details come back to you?'

'I think I remember stopping here.' She looked over to the bush. It was taller than her, taller than Darren, so big it felt otherworldly: like someone had taken it from a suburban garden and sprinkled magic powder on it, making it grow wild and ferocious. 'I don't know why, but it felt like the right place to stop.'

'Probably the flowers,' remarked the grizzled farmer from their party, scratching behind his knee. 'Girls like flowers.'

Eliza pinched off one of the flowers, cradling it in her hand. The wild bees buzzed.

This daisy bush protected me from the person who was following me. The thought came to her from nowhere, and then a wild and irrational fear rushed through her. She spun around, staring into the forest, groping for Darren's hand. Her breath came in heaving pants, her chest tight and throat dry. 'There was someone else . . . footsteps, I know it . . . *someone was hunting me!*'

'Relax, Miss Ellis,' said Darren. 'Just breathe. You're fine. You're okay.'

'He followed me here. I remember his footsteps! *I do!*' She gasped.

'Should we call someone? She can't breathe,' said the farmer.

'No, it's fine,' said Darren. 'She's fine. Aren't you, Miss Ellis?' He rubbed her back. 'It's okay for you to have a panic attack, you've been under a lot of stress. Try to breathe, but take your time – we'll still be here, ready when you are. Just take your time.'

Slowly, with Darren's encouragement, Eliza's breathing began to slow, until she could spit out angrily, 'I'm not . . . having . . . a panic . . . attack.'

'Either way, you're doing a good job,' he said. 'There, that's better. You're okay.'

'I'm really not,' said Eliza, when she could finally speak again. 'I'm falling apart.'

It had begun to rain, the water icy cold. The other searchers all took off their packs, pulling out raincoats, but Darren let it run down his hair and face. 'So . . . you *do* remember something?'

'Someone was following me here.'

'What do you remember about them?'

'Just footsteps . . .' The back of her head begun to ache. She remembered the terror of being followed, the urgency in her chest to reach the girls, the urgency not to lead this hunter to the girls . . .

'Just think, Miss Ellis. You can do this.'

'I *can't.*'

'Please. You . . . Can you try?'

'I'm not remembering —'

'Eliza,' he said, cutting her off. 'I . . . have a confession to make.'

Eliza looked at him. His face was striking now that his hair was wet in the lashing rain.

'My sister was one of the girls taken in 1985.'

'*What?*'

'Rose. Rose Cahil.'

'Oh, Darren. I'm so sorry.'

'No one in my family ever believed Ted Barclay was responsible. And if the Hungry Man is active again . . . I want to stop him. I want to find him. I have to *stop him.*' He gripped her shoulders. 'I need you to think. Really think. Do you remember where you were when you woke up? When you first realised you were being hunted?'

Eliza looked up and down the trail. She pulled herself out of his grip. 'I don't think I could even find my way back to the motorbikes, let alone back to where I woke up, where Carmen first found me.'

'You might be the only one who can help us. We have to find the other girls. If they're still alive.'

'Darren . . .' said the grey-haired SES officer.

'Yeah, I know,' said Darren, throwing up his hands. He walked a few steps down the track before coming back. 'I'm sorry. I just thought it was worth a try.'

He pulled his own raincoat out and handed it to Eliza to slip over her hiking jacket. She slid her pack off, her heart beating fast from the remembered terror. She turned her back and let him help her into the raincoat. She looked into the bush, the heavy raindrops setting the leaves dancing. 'We'll come back another time. I'll try harder. I promise.'

'That's all we can ask,' murmured Darren. Thunder crackled in the distance. He looked towards where it had boomed, raising his free hand to test the wind. 'Alright, people, time to get off this mountain. And in the meantime, I'll call Detective Badenhorst and let him know what you've remembered.'

CHAPTER 18

CON

Con and Gabriella sat in a café off the main street of Limestone Creek, next to a bay window. The sun was shining, the street outside was wet with rain and slushy snow, and people walked around in T-shirts. Con supposed these locals were used to the changing weather. Or perhaps the drama was exciting enough to get them out of their houses.

Con and Gabriella had been discussing the phone call from Constable Darren.

'Someone else was up there. We knew that from the head wound. The question is, who?' said Con.

'Maybe we just need to wait until Eliza remembers more?' said Gabriella.

'I hate waiting,' said Con. 'And this diary is less than useless.'

Spread across the table, between their coffees and Gabriella's second bowl of nachos, were the photocopied pages of Georgia Lenah's diary.

'Don't be petty. What were we expecting? That she'd write out the name of her killer?' Gabriella picked up another page.

'It's not even a diary,' said Con. 'It's just a notebook of ideas for her bloody museum.'

'The museum *was* her life,' said Gabriella.

Con put aside another sheet, which showed plans for an art gallery for Tasmanian artists. 'Was this really going to happen? Did they have funding?'

'Not all of it, but it was under way. When I talked to the mayor, she said that Georgia had supporters all around Tasmania and even on the mainland.'

'Well, that's impressive I suppose,' said Con.

'The thing is, here in Limestone Creek . . . Well, it's a bit of a sore spot, these mountains, right? *Kooparoona Niara* – Mountain of Spirits. This whole area was significant, but the local industries don't want to remind people of that. Georgia had to deal with opposition from the timber industry and the mining industry – both have interests in this area, and both of them have very smart business-people who recognise that a museum about the area's Aboriginal history could lead to bad news for them.'

'Was this a big enough threat that they would kill her?'

'Out here in the middle of nowhere, who knows?' said Gabriella. 'But here, look at this one.' She slid a page across to Con.

Con scanned the page. 'I've read it.'

'Well then read it again. Properly.'

Con picked up the page and read aloud: 'I found some more of the surviving descendants of the local mobs today. They live down in Hobart now, but they had stories about Kooparoona Niara. They do have some mythology about these mountains, but nothing like what Madison was blabbing on about, soul traps and whatever, the stupid bitch. Love her though.'

He looked up at Gabriella. 'I hate how teenagers talk.'

'*Soul traps*,' she said. 'Like portals, Con. You know what happens around portals? *The Oz effect*.'

Con read the rest of the page, ignoring her. 'This is interesting.' He read aloud: 'Madison is obsessed with these stories. Like,
actual obsessed: I've never seen her this excited. She wants to interview these people for a video, but they don't want to, and I'm not
going to put her in contact with them. She asked if I'd talk about it.
When I told her I'd need to research it more, she said it'd be alright if
I made a bit of it up. I refuse to be part of a video where she makes
up fantasies about our stories. So of course, she went ahead and
filmed a video where she made them up herself. She thinks she can
get through by bluffing, but she doesn't know a thing about our
culture, she just wants to warp it so she can get more views . . . but
her videos are getting me attention and exposure for the museum,
so I think I have to put up with a bit of it. Hopefully no one in the
community hates me for it.'

Con opened his laptop, bringing up a new browser tab and heading to Madison's YouTube account. It didn't take him long to find
a recent video that looked promising: *DID I JUST FIND SPIRIT
PORTALS IN THE MOUNTAINS?!!'*

He played the video, turning the screen so Gabriella could see.

It was up in the Tiers, on the edge of a rocky cliff, the Tasmanian
mountains rolling into the distance. Snow gums clung to the precipice. The camera panned around to Madison and Cierra, standing
by three motorbikes. Madison in perfect make-up – green lipstick
this time – and Cierra wearing a pink wig.

'Hi guys,' said Madison. 'Today we're exploring a very special
place up in the Great Western Tiers, that we were told about by our
very own Georgia, who as some of you would know is the driving
force behind the Kooparoona Niara Aboriginal Heritage Museum.
Today, however, we're joined by the Babe of the Year, Jasmine.'

The camera spun around so Jasmine could wave – she was the
one filming – and then it returned to Madison and Cierra as they
walked to the edge of a cliff. It was a spectacular view. Jasmine

showed the escarpment of the cliff itself: rugged ridges of rocks and eucalypts that stretched towards mountains in the distance, and then the camera panned up to show a beautiful sky, pastel blue and streaked with hazy clouds.

'Tell us what we've learned, Madison,' said Cierra.

'Well, this cliffside is said to hold one of the gateways to the spirit world. Like a portal. Young men and women used to come here to test their courage, and try to speak to their ancestors on the other side.'

'How?' said Cierra. Jasmine pointed the camera over the edge again.

'Well, apparently there were several ways: one was to hang over the edge of the cliff by your hands – a test of strength. But it was said that one young man who did this disappeared, and then when he returned some time later, he thought it was the same day: he'd fallen through *time*.'

'No way!' squealed Cierra.

'There were other ways. Other rituals. It depended on what the spirits said, what time you were here.'

'The spirits spoke to them? And it was this cliff only?'

'No, but this cliff was special . . .'

The twins continued to speak, Madison chatting about the other portals, about the stories that the local people could tell, followed by the inevitable link back to the Hungry Man disappearances.

'This is fascinating,' said Gabriella.

'It's completely made up, Gabby,' said Con. 'None of those stories are real.'

'Don't call me Gabby, Cornelius.'

But then there was a hard cut in the video. It was night time, and Cierra and Madison were alone. Madison wore a fluffy white beanie and white lipstick, and Cierra a white curly wig.

'We're here, back at what we're calling Sacred Cliff,' said

Madison. 'We're camping up here tonight. We're going to try and commune with the spirits . . .'

Gabriella leaned forward with a melodramatic gasp. The girls sat in their tent and squealed at noises, telling ghost stories and legends of people encountering spirits in the mountains. Suddenly there was a strange light outside of the tent, the girls screamed, and the camera went dark.

Con snorted. 'Notice how Cierra wasn't in the shot when the light hit the side of the tent?'

'Shhhh,' said Gabriella.

Now the video moved to Madison and Cierra, lying in sleeping bags. Daylight streamed in through the open tent flap.

'Guys, we saw something up here last night,' said Madison, face pale, cheeks drawn. Her make-up was smudged. 'We think that the spirits actually spoke to us – we think we have a way to reach the spirit world . . . but we aren't allowed to talk about it yet.'

'Don't sound so dramatic,' said Cierra, nudging Madison in the side, her voice shaking. 'We don't even know if it was the spirits.'

'It's just a coincidence that we both had the same dream?' said Madison, pushing her back.

'This is crazy . . .' said Cierra. Her fear, if feigned, was perfect.

'We need to think about how to share it, and who to share it with.' Madison eyed the camera. 'We better go. See you soon.'

Con paused it just before the end. 'Look there, there's something written on the outside of the sleeping bag. In white lipstick.'

'The word is kundela,' read Gabriella. 'What's that mean?'

A quick Google search returned their answer. 'In Australian Aboriginal culture, it's a bone used to curse people,' said Con.

There was silence.

'This is the best case we've ever had,' whispered Gabriella.

Con closed the laptop. 'Enough of that bullshit. Let's go see her.'

CHAPTER 19

ELIZA

It was five o'clock in the evening. Eliza and Tom sat on the couch, both watching the video on their phones. Sarge was on the other side of Eliza, sandwiching her between the hulking dog and the hulking man, the smell of dog and Tom's sweat mixed with his David Beckham cologne heavy in her nose.

She kept trying to think about anything other than her memories.

How close was I to . . .?

The video they were watching had been posted by a public Facebook page called 'Justice for the Limestone Four'. It had been shared by thousands.

The video was a splice of the Facebook Live video of Kevin Mason confronting Murphy outside his house, including Murphy's damning confession – 'We don't sell weed to minors' – followed by new footage of Murphy leaving the police station, punching a journalist, and being set upon by a mob. The end of the video displayed Murphy's home address and a photo of his house.

'I always thought Murphy was sketchy,' Tom muttered.

'Don't,' said Eliza. 'Don't you *dare*.' She scrolled through the comments. 'This is horrible . . .'

I have to tell someone, she thought, still shaky from the trip to the mountains. *Before this gets even further out of hand . . .*

'Madison has posted her own video in response,' said Tom. Eliza watched on his screen:

'I know Jasmine's dad, Mr Murphy, and I can promise you, he would never have taken the girls. Yes, I know that was my dad in the first video, making accusations against him, but he's wrong: Mr Murphy is not that kind of man. He would not have done this! Please stop accusing an innocent man. For the sake of my friend – whose name we can't say anymore – for the sake of her memory, we can't waste time chasing the wrong people. If you want to confront Murphy, then come confront me first. My address is 23 Wirrawee Way, Limestone Creek.'

'She just put her *own* address up on her video? Is she *insane*?' said Tom.

The front door opened: Monica was back from visiting Wren at Tom's mother's house. She was in tears again, her make-up smudged, her hair in disarray.

While Monica came and kissed Tom, Eliza left the lounge room, heading into her bedroom, arguing with herself. Jack and Jasmine. It was time for her tell the police.

Did she have a right to? Was it truly even her decision?

She took a post-it note from her desk and quickly scribbled on it.

I give permission for Eliza Ellis to do what's right.
Signed, E. Ellis

So that was that.

Con Badenhorst had left her his business card. He picked up on the fourth ring.

'Detective? It's Eliza Ellis.'

'Everything alright?'

'Yes . . . I mean, no. Not really. There's something I should've told you. But you have to promise me, no one can know it was me who told you.'

'What is it, Eliza?'

'I *do* know who Jasmine was dating. But he couldn't have been involved . . . he has an alibi, so I didn't think I needed to tell you . . . He's a good man, and —'

'Who is it, Eliza?'

'The teacher's assistant . . . Jack Michaels.'

CHAPTER 20

CON

'Thank you, Eliza. Let me know if you think of anything else.'

Con ended the call, resting his shoulder against the Masons' front door, having just stepped outside to take the call.

Jack Michaels was dating Jasmine Murphy. Why didn't I interview him sooner? Stupid, stupid, stupid . . .

But seriously, what the hell is wrong with this town?

Gabriella and Con had arrived at the Masons' house only ten minutes earlier, and only then heard about Madison's video giving out her address. Mrs Nelly Mason was in hysterics, terrified someone was going to kidnap Madison.

'That *stupid* channel,' she'd kept wailing.

Con re-joined Gabriella at the kitchen counter. It smelled of detergent and red wine. He sipped the coffee Nelly Mason had handed him, which had a faint soapy taste. Mr Bruiser, the trembling little whippet, was adding his own incessant yipping to the mix.

Jack Michaels, he thought again. *Surely Detective Coops interviewed him. Did I miss the report?*

He vaguely remembered someone at the car park mentioning Jack Michaels that first morning. Was it a parent? A search volunteer? Or Tom North himself?

When the girls were walking back from the camp, Jack had been at the front of the group and far from the action, but he still should have talked to him. Would he even have known what questions to ask? There was just so much going on, so much material coming into his inbox, and there were only so many leads Con could follow. Had he made a bad mistake?

I'm an idiot, he thought angrily. *Jack Michaels was the one who found Eliza!*

He wondered how he could tell Gabriella without Nelly or Madison hearing.

'I'm sure Kevin will be back any minute,' Nelly Mason was saying, fluttering around the kitchen, her platinum bob flicking as she cleaned things that already looked clean to Con. 'I know you have so much else to do, but I *will* feel safer once Kevin's home.' It was the fifth time she'd told Con and Gabriella that. She glanced out the window. 'Do you want tea or coffee?' She saw the cups in front of them and gave a hysterical chuckle. Mr Bruiser kept yipping.

'Could you take a seat, please?' said Con, setting aside the coffee.

'Of course,' she said, sitting down beside him, a saucepan still in her hands.

'Can you think of anyone other than Mr Murphy who those condoms might belong to?' said Gabriella.

'No one,' she replied instantly. 'My Cierra wasn't seeing anyone. I knew she always had bit of a soft spot for . . . Jasmine's dad . . . but I would never have guessed —'

'Is there anyone else she might've told who she was sleeping with? Or anyone who might know?' said Gabriella.

'No one,' said Nelly.

'Gee, thanks, Mum,' came Madison's cold voice. She was in the lounge, just off the kitchen, on her laptop. She had told them she was editing a memorial video for Georgia and didn't have time to talk to them. She wore a luxurious purple dressing gown and her hair was wet. 'I've already told you: Mr Murphy wasn't banging Cierra.'

'Don't say that!' Nelly shrieked, slamming the saucepan on the counter. 'He was always too friendly with you girls! And . . . *how could you give our address to the whole world?*' She sobbed and ran to another part of the house.

Mr Bruiser yipped and raced after her, leaving a puddle of urine on the floor.

There was a moment of ringing silence.

'The condoms don't belong to Murphy,' said Madison again. 'He's a good man.'

'Then whose are they?' asked Con. Of course, the whole point of their visit had been to speak to Madison again, but they'd tried to be subtle about it.

'Why do they have to belong to anyone except Cierra? Why does everyone freak out about the idea of Cierra having sex?' said Madison. 'She's sixteen. If they were found in a teenage *boy's* room, you wouldn't even blink.'

'Your parents seem concerned about it,' said Gabriella, arching her eyebrow.

'And again, if she was a *boy*, they wouldn't care. Dad would be *proud*. I'm telling you: it's not important. And Murphy has nothing to do with it.'

'If you know something, you should tell us,' said Con.

'Because you're doing such a great job with the info you've already been given,' said Madison, flicking her wet hair back and fixing them with a stare. 'Georgia is *dead* and you're chasing up condoms and weed.'

'Who did they belong to?' said Con. He could hear Nelly's sobs from next door. It meant she was in earshot – it was shaky grounds, but he was gonna run with that counting as her being present. 'If it's not important, why won't you tell us?'

'The person Cierra was sleeping with didn't take her.'

'How can you be so sure?' said Con.

'A rock-solid alibi.' The face she made, just for an instant, confirmed it.

Time to take a risk.

'She is sleeping with Jack Michaels,' said Con. 'And so is Jasmine.'

Madison's face went slack. 'What did you say?'

'I just asked if —'

'Who told you?' She stood up, her hands balled into fists. 'Who told you about Jasmine and Jack?'

'It's true, then?' said Con, avoiding Gabriella's curious eyes: he hadn't had time to fill her in.

'Jack was up with Mr North when they disappeared,' said Madison. 'There are plenty of witnesses.' She bared her perfect white teeth. 'You will *not* pin this on him.'

'The condoms *didn't* belong to Jack Michaels?' said Con.

'For the last time: the condoms belong to *Cierra*.' She sat back down. 'Dad might be a while: he's up there on the mountain, actually *helping*, unlike you two. You should head off and, I don't know, contribute to the investigation, maybe?'

'Is that what the fight was about, up at the campsite?' said Gabriella quietly. 'Was it about Jack? Did one of the other girls threaten to expose him? Did someone else like him?'

Madison pulled out her phone. She ran her hands through her brushed hair, so it looked like she'd only just got out of the shower. A few seconds later she spoke to the front-facing camera.

'Hello, Instagram Live, Facebook Live, or whatever platform you're watching this on. I want to thank everyone for their support today. It has been . . .' Her voice caught. 'Knowing that our friend is gone . . . knowing that Cierra and Jasmine are still out there, and even Bree . . .' Perfect little tears rolled down her cheeks. 'Thank you to all the brave volunteers who are out there searching. I wish there was more that all of us could do, except hope . . .'

Con glanced at Gabriella, sensing danger. He stood up to leave, but Gabriella remained, leaning back and crossing her arms.

'How could she not tell us about this?' she hissed at Con. 'This is major.'

'I want to thank everyone for their kind words about Cierra . . . and yes, I'll talk about it again: a video has gone viral, showing my dad at Jasmine Murphy's house. He was accusing Jasmine's dad of sleeping with my sister. As I've already told you all, that is *unequivocally untrue*. My sister's sex life is no one else's business, and has nothing to do with her going missing, but blaming Jasmine's dad . . .' She shook her head. 'How do you think Jasmine would feel, hearing that her own father was being blamed for taking her? Please, share your messages of support for Murphy, using the hashtag "#JusticeForMurphy".'

Con grabbed Gabriella's shoulder, trying to pull her out of her seat, but she knocked his hand away.

'We should go,' said Con.

'I'm not gonna be bullied,' said Gabriella. 'Besides, you're the one who said she's hiding something. I bet she's hiding more.'

'I'm streaming this live because I have something else to share . . . you see, since the discovery of those condoms in my sister's room, we've seen police resources used to falsely arrest an innocent man and, what's more, the detectives responsible for *finding our girls* have come here, to *my house*, to ask about those condoms *again*. As though having sex is some dirty thing, and that's the reason for Cierra going missing. *We are women: we own our bodies. It is normal for us to have sex!*'

She tapped the screen, switching to the back camera, angling her phone towards Con and Gabriella. 'Say hello to Detective Badenhorst and Detective Pakinga. My sister has been missing for thirty-six hours and they're chasing up *condoms*. If anyone out there knows how to lodge complaints against dodgy police, please let me know in the comments.'

'We know Madison is hiding something from us,' called Gabriella suddenly, addressing the camera. 'Someone out there knows what it is. We need to know what Madison isn't telling us. Don't be afraid: come forward and let us know. Help us find the girls.'

Madison gasped, furious, and switched the camera back onto herself. 'See? They want to turn us against each other. Just tonight I've heard them accuse our teacher's assistant, Mr Jack Michaels, of being involved. There are thirty eye witnesses to vouch that he didn't take them. He was the one who actually *found* Miss Ellis, wounded on the trail. Don't let them make up another suspect. Justice for Murphy! Justice for Jack! *Bring our girls home!*'

Con pulled Gabriella away and down the hall, before she could say anything more. 'Why the hell did you do that?' he demanded as they left the house, desperate to get out of there.

'She's not telling us something. We both know it.' Gabriella stalked along the paving stones, bristling like a cat. 'The little bitch. She wants to try and paint us as the villains – she wants to play the victim? Oh, she'll see what we're capable of, just you wait . . . Did you see the way she loosened the dressing gown and then pulled the camera back, so everyone could see she was barely wearing anything underneath? It made it look like we'd just dragged her out of bed, or from the bath, or . . . something equally creepy.'

'We need to speak to Jack Michaels,' said Con.

'Yeah, and he'll know we're coming now.'

'We can use that,' said Con. 'We might just need to bend a couple rules.'

'Done. I don't care, as long as we find out what Madison is up to.' Gabriella pulled the driver's side door open.

A text message came through on Con's phone: *Hello, this is Pastor Hugh again. Please call me when you can. It is a matter of some urgency.*

Con quickly texted his reply: *Sorry, will call soon. Can you text what this is regarding?*

Ignoring the journalists trying to get their attention, Con climbed into the passenger side and they sped off. It began to rain again.

CHAPTER 21

MURPHY

Murphy, Butch and Skinner sat in the cushy couches around the fireplace in the shed. The other two were taking long drags from their joints and relaxing. Skinner didn't know, but the one they'd given him had been painted in angel dust. Once they'd pumped Skinner full of the stuff they planned to interrogate him. Or it could go terribly wrong and he'd try and kill them. They had to wait for it to kick in and see.

Murphy scrolled through the comments on the video posted by the Justice for the Limestone Four Facebook page. It was surprising how many people he'd known his whole life wanted him dead. His mind went to the Glock hidden in the back of the couch he was sitting on; maybe he should keep it with him from now on.

Catching MMMMadisonMason's comment, he clicked on her page, and saw she was streaming a live video.

'Knowing that our friend is gone . . . knowing that Cierra and Jasmine are still out there, and even Bree . . .'

Jasmine, where are you? I'm coming for you, I promise.

Butch and Skinner had gone quiet, listening in. They both

cheered when Madison declared Murphy's innocence. At the mention of Jack Michaels, Murphy felt a flash of anger. Butch spat on the floor, and Skinner looked sheepish.

When Madison flipped the camera to show the detectives, and Detective Pakinga called for someone to come forward about whatever Madison was hiding, Butch roared. 'How dare those pigs say that about the poor girl!'

'Shut up, dopey,' said Skinner, punching his shoulder. 'We're listening.'

Madison again declared Murphy and Jack's innocence, and then the stream ended. The sound of the fire crackling and Butch taking deep draws on his joint filled the silence.

'Well,' said Skinner, 'someone is on your side. Her support should go a long way. But I wonder why someone is trying to pin it on Michaels?'

'One of the only men in this town who couldn't have done it,' muttered Murphy. 'Vouched for by all the little schoolgirls. But I wouldn't argue with someone who wanted to set that mob onto him.'

'You're still sore about the seeds, are you?' said Skinner, overly casual.

'Of course we bloody are,' said Butch, glaring fiercely. 'You know how long it took Dad to breed our strain? There's a reason you can sell for so much – because it's bloody good. Jack bloody well stole our seeds and you bloody let him!'

'I didn't know he would, did I! In his defence, he got rid of them all – he's always asking to buy more weed,' said Skinner. He held up his hands to cut off the protest he knew was coming. 'I know, I know – I haven't sold him any, have I? But he'll just get it off someone else. Tom North and him are good mates, and Tom buys more than enough from me.'

'Then stop selling it to Tom,' said Murphy.

Skinner laughed, but it was forced. 'You wanna lose that much income? Honestly, Jack made a mistake – a stupid mistake – but he's good now.'

'We welcomed him into our house. We treated him like a little brother,' said Butch. 'And how did he repay us?' He stood up, staggered, sat back down. He swiped at something in front of him.

'Everyone goes a little crazy over money, Butch, and we all know he was struggling for it.' He eyed Butch uneasily. 'Mate, you're burning yourself.'

Butch stood again, chest puffed up. 'What's that got to do with anything?'

'Bloody hell, mate. What have you got in that thing?' Skinner snatched the joint away from Butch's finger and licked it. 'You put angel dust on this thing. How much?'

'No, I didn't,' said Butch, scowling at the wall. 'Although . . . that would explain the freaky shit I'm seeing.'

'I think you've had enough.' Skinner opened the fireplace and tossed it in.

'Hey,' roared Butch.

'I told you the other night not to go to heavy on the stuff: even that tiny bit made you aggro.'

'Come off it. Weed *never* makes me aggressive,' said Butch, standing over Skinner.

'But *angel dust* does a bunch of crazy shit.' Skinner glanced at Murphy. 'Murphy, help me calm him down, would you? Shit, you haven't had some too? You were bloody scary the other night.'

'Butch, take a seat,' said Murphy.

Butch sat back down, 'Where's my phone? I'm calling someone over.'

'What do you mean by that?' said Murphy to Skinner, ignoring Butch. 'All I did was fall asleep.'

'Fell asleep.' Skinner laughed. Butch was on his feet again and lumbering around the shed, muttering to himself and scowling at the walls. 'You went apeshit, bro. Started talking about your dead wife and Jasmine.'

'What?' said Murphy. 'I don't remember any of that.'

'*Amnesia,* mate. It's part of the package with angel dust. We thought you'd gone to bed, or maybe you were off somewhere still chatting with your dead wife. Didn't Butch find you on the ground? You probably passed out. You weren't naked, were you?'

Murphy's mind spun back. Waking up to Butch's voice, freezing and wet on the ground, wrapped up in his hunting jacket.

Butch yelled at something invisible. 'I can't breathe, I need water.' He smashed the line of empty beer bottles they'd built over the course of the night.

'Butch, mate. It's alright,' said Murphy.

'I'll go get some water,' said Skinner, ducking out of the shed.

'There's bloody tiger snakes climbing up the walls again,' said Butch, tears forming in his eyes. 'I bloody *hate* the bloody snakes, mate. Where's Jasmine gone? I can't lose her . . .'

Butch slumped into Murphy's arms and began blubbering into his shoulder. 'I gotta tell her I'm sorry. I'm so *sorry* . . .' His hands gripped Murphy's back. 'There's a bloody demon hanging from the ceiling. He's showing me his ass. I'm gonna kill him.' He pushed Murphy aside and groped for something that wasn't there.

The door flew open and Skinner pushed a bottle of water into Butch's hand.

'Potion . . .' moaned Butch. He began drinking the water, then nestled into the couch, still seeing things that weren't there.

Murphy glanced at Skinner. He looked a little guilty – Murphy didn't know if it was from remembering the incident with Jack or because of the angel dust, but one way or the other, Skinner was off balance. Murphy grabbed his arm and dragged him outside. It was now or never.

'I need the list,' Murphy said, without preamble. 'Everyone around here you sell our weed to.'

'You know I can't do that,' he said. 'Goes against my code. Distance keeps politics out of it, stops people from going to the cops if things go south. You've got enough heat on you with that corrupt copper watching your every move. And everyone knows it. No one would buy your product if it wasn't for me in the middle.'

'Someone you sell to was in Cierra's room —' began Murphy.

'I watch the news too, mate. She was taken from a mountain, not her bedroom,' said Skinner. 'Mate, your bush bud is the best around, so there's a *lot* of people on my lists.'

Butch howled inside the shed and something else smashed. Murphy dug his toes into his shoes, fighting the urge to run back to his brother. *Drugs haven't killed him yet* . . . 'If I was able to convince you, you could show me the list right now?'

'Yeah, I've got it all on my phone. Encrypted obviously, so don't try anything funny, but . . . mate, I'd need more than weed and condoms in a teenage girl's room. There are *rules,* man.'

'I've got proof,' said Murphy. 'In the dry room.'

Skinner's eyes went wide. 'You're gonna show me your dry room? I'm honoured.'

'I just need to get something first.' Murphy stepped inside the shed, seeing Butch curled up on his side. He crouched down behind the couch and pulled the Glock out of its hiding place. He tucked it into the back of his belt, then grabbed a key off the hook beside the door.

'Really, I'm honoured, mate,' said Skinner when he came back outside. 'Truly honoured —'

'Just have the list ready,' said Murphy. He wondered if Butch was going to lose his shit if he found out Murphy was showing someone else where their dry room was: it was almost as bad as showing him their crop, it gave Skinner too much power over them, but he couldn't see any other way.

At the end of a concrete path down from the house, lit by the porch light, was a Hills Hoist, empty save a line of rusting pegs. Murphy cranked the handle until the arms of the clothes line were vertical.

'What are you . . .?' said Skinner.

Murphy lifted up the edge of some fake turf, revealing a latch and a large padlock. He used the key from the shed to unlock it.

'No bloody way,' breathed Skinner.

Murphy grabbed the clothes line with two hands and levered it to the ground, the metal groaning as the whole concrete base hinged open, revealing a rectangular hatch.

'It's right here in your backyard? That's ballsy . . .'

Murphy climbed down the metal ladder, into darkness. The air was heady – sweet and warm and full of life. He felt for a light switch on the end of a cable and flicked it on. Fluorescent lights lit a long metal room with corrugated walls.

'It's a shipping container,' said Skinner, stepping off the ladder behind him. He knocked away the dangling basket that hung beside the ladder. 'You buried a bloody shipping container in your backyard.'

Drying marijuana plants were draped from long lines of wire, like clothes on a rack. A digital thermometer and humidity indicator hung on the side wall, and a thick air-conditioning pipe unit ran along the ceiling, curling around on itself, both ends burrowing through the ceiling into the earth.

'I thought the cops brought dogs here?' said Skinner. 'How'd they not smell the ventilation?'

'Goes up into the chicken coop – looks like a stilt above ground. All the dogs smell is chicken shit.'

'This is unreal, mate. Absolutely unreal. You set this up?'

'Dad buried the container. Had it brought in during New Year's Eve, when the parties were all going on and no one heard the sound of the truck or the excavator. Butch and me have made some improvements since.'

'I can't believe Doble hasn't found this. He'd be spewing if he knew, the fat fuck. Doesn't the power show up on your bill?'

'Siphon it from an old mate down the road – we've got a line buried under the fence. He had a deal with Dad.' Murphy shrugged. 'You've got your list?'

'You know, I bet this is where you were the other night.'

'What?'

'Well, you weren't in your bed. I came inside to find food, dropped by your room to see how you were doing, but you weren't there. I looked all through the house – had me a bit worried, mate – but I guess you were here. You aren't hiding one of them girls down here, are you?' Skinner chuckled.

Murphy, his hand behind his back, holding the grip of the Glock, paused. 'I couldn't have been in here,' he said, 'there's only one key and it was hanging up in the shed just then.'

'Ah, don't worry about it, mate. Angel dust is some crazy shit. You could burn your own house down and have no memory of it.' Skinner looked at him quizzically. 'What are you doing back there?'

Murphy squeezed the grip of the gun.

This was it.

What was he willing to do?

How far was he willing to go?

Skinner is still a mate, I can't threaten him with a gun . . . can I? What else can I do?

He let go of the gun, his hand swinging back to his side.

'I really need to see that list.'

'I told you, I can't. Unless you can prove it was one of my clients who took your girl, I can't.'

Murphy hesitated, then slowly kneeled. 'Mate . . . my daughter . . . I've got to try. I'm *begging* you.'

In this world, the Murphys' reputation was one of the most important things they possessed. That's why they put THE CAPTAIN on their product: *they* were in charge. They didn't have many weapons in their arsenal – threats and intimidation could be the difference between them being players and losing everything.

And now here he was, kneeling on the ground like a grub.

He could get bashed for less. He could get rolled for less.

'Get off the ground, Murph,' said Skinner uneasily.

Murphy put his forehead on the old stained carpet that covered the floor. 'I'll do anything. Anything.' His throat felt tight. Tears broke through. 'Just name it.'

'Mate . . . you don't understand. It's not even up to me. All of us would be out of a job – my boss wouldn't be happy. Don't start crying . . . if you start crying, mate, I'm gonna start crying. I can't handle this emotional shit.'

'Please. I'll do anything. I'll tell you where our crop is. I'll *give* you our crop. I'll give you our *seeds* —'

'Murph . . .' Skinner crouched down. 'Get up. Look at me. You gotta snap out of this. I'm not taking your seeds: I dunno how to grow shit. It's alright, mate. You'll find her. Someone will find her. It'll be alright.'

Murphy's pocket buzzed. Someone was calling. He ignored it. 'Your list is the only direction I know to go . . .'

Skinner's lip was wobbling. 'Ah, shit, you're getting me fucked up. I can't give you the list. I *can't*. Stop asking me. Please. Want me to call some of my boys, get them to rough some people up or something?'

Murphy's phone buzzed. Whoever it was, they were calling again.

'I wanna help, mate, I really do,' said Skinner. 'I just can't throw away my livelihood. I know I'm a coward —'

Murphy pulled himself to his feet. He was very aware of the gun pressing against his back.

He'd shown weakness, made himself vulnerable, and that hadn't worked. Now the gun was his only option.

But first he needed to focus – the buzzing in his pocket was distracting him.

He pulled his phone out to switch it off. The caller name read Eliza Ellis. That stopped him cold.

'We're cool, right?' said Skinner. 'You've let me into your inner sanctum – I respect that. You know I don't believe that shit they're saying —'

'Eliza?' Murphy said, bringing the phone to his ear, his whole body suddenly awake. 'What's wrong? *Did you remember something?*'

'No, I . . . It's something else. I thought I'd better tell you myself before you heard it from someone else.' Her voice was flat and tired. 'I should've told you sooner, but I only found out the day before, and, well, he's a friend . . .'

'Eliza, what is it?'

'Jasmine was sleeping with someone.'

Murphy heard his pulse thudding in his ears. He stood up straighter. 'Who?'

'Don't freak out —'

'*Who is it?*' he shouted.

'Jack Michaels.'

Murphy stood in silence, then headed for the ladder.

'What's wrong?' said Skinner.

He hung up the phone. 'Take care of Butch,' he said, then climbed out of the hatch, stalking towards the house, his mind already on the road to Jack's house.

The gun was in his hand.

CHAPTER 22

CON

Con and Gabriella parked the squad car. They were a block away from Jack's house. They walked down the footpath huddled together under a shared umbrella, looking like a couple on an evening stroll. Con ignored the phone buzzing in his coat pocket: the commander had called twice on the drive over, and both times he'd ignored it.

He knew she would be furious, but at the moment it was more important they get to Jack. Knowing police were on their way should make Jack act erratic or careless, and that meant his behaviour could be very telling.

He lived in a small unit beneath towering golden elms and fenced in by rotten palings, dark but for the streetlight across the street. Gabriella squeezed Con's arm. He stepped away from her, disappearing into some scrub at the front fence, squeezing between the palings into the overgrown yard.

A thrill raced down his spine and down his arms. He had missed this.

He walked around the house, peering into the windows where the lights were on but finding only drawn curtains or empty rooms.

A dirtbike was in the carport. He kept on looking around until he saw a shadow inside moving against a curtain.

He padded up to that window and pressed his ear against the glass. He could hear a voice, but couldn't make out the words.

He moved quickly to the back door but found it locked. He pulled his lock pick set out, sliding in the torsion wrench and a basic rake pick. It was louder than he would have liked, but he was counting on Jack being distracted. Finally the picks rotated fully and the lock opened.

This was breaking a few laws, but the end justified the means. A girl was dead, three more were in danger, and the man inside had probably been sleeping with at least one of them.

He crept inside, closing the door quietly behind him. The tiled floor of the laundry was strewn with boots, and shirts and trousers hung along a clothesline that stretched down the hallway.

Con could hear a man's voice further down the hall. He slipped his phone out of his coat pocket, double-checking that a blank text was ready to be sent to Gabriella, which would be the signal for her to knock on the door and draw Jack away if there was any danger of Con being caught.

Carefully stepping over the shoes and around the hanging washing, he slipped into the bedroom next to the room where Jack seemed to be pacing. The bedroom was tidy but for the unmade bed, with posters of mountain bikers and half-naked women on the walls. He listened as Jack spoke hurriedly into his phone:

'. . . of course I looked there. I've looked everywhere . . . Georgia is *dead*, of course I'm *scared*! I don't know who told them. Who even knows about me and Jasmine?' His voice grew higher and louder. 'Where are they? Who's taken them? No, no – I don't care! I'm going back tonight. Maybe they've finally made it . . . I know! But we have to —'

Thuds pounded on the front door.

What are you doing, Gabriella? Con checked his phone in case he'd sent the message by accident – he saw there was a reply from Pastor Hugh.

That's when someone kicked open the door.

'You bastard!' called a male voice. 'Where are you!'

It was Murphy. Con peered around a corner and saw his wild eyes, Gabriella running in behind him. Jack came out into the hallway, slipping his phone into his pocket, and Con took the opportunity to dash away, back down the corridor and out the back door. He sprinted around the side of the house, slipping on the wet grass, and in through the front door.

Gabriella stood between Jack and Murphy in the living room, turning from one to the other. Murphy towered over Jack, whose face was pale, cinderblock jaw clenched tight.

'Stand down, Murphy,' said Con, rushing to Gabriella's side. He put his hand on Murphy's chest, trying to hold him back.

'I'm gonna rip you in half.' Murphy advanced on Jack. 'How long were you with her?'

'Easy, Murphy, I d-didn't take them, I s-swear,' stammered Jack, looking for an escape.

'You steal our seeds. You steal my daughter. Did you sell *her* to cover your ice debts as well?'

Both Con and Gabriella were now pushing against Murphy's chest, fighting to hold him back. He was reaching around them with his long arms. Con hadn't realised just how strong the man was.

For her part, Gabriella seemed to be thoroughly enjoying herself. Like Con, she had police training in hand-to-hand, but she also had the extra training of a Brazilian jiu-jitsu black belt – she was probably looking forward to a showdown.

Jack had backed into the wall, sweat shining on his forehead. 'It's not my fault . . . Jasmine came on to *me!*'

'*She's sixteen!*' roared Murphy. He shoved Con and Gabriella aside and threw himself at Jack. The next moment he was slammed to the ground and Gabriella was straddling him, wrenching his hands behind his back and into handcuffs.

Murphy struggled, but those wild eyes were still on Jack, fighting Gabriella's iron hold.

Con's foot caught on a rug and he stumbled into Jack, reaching out to steady himself against Jack's arm. Jack just watched, horrified, as Murphy kept fighting.

Con quickly turned away to check the phone he'd just lifted from Jack's pocket – he needed to see who he'd been on the call to – but it was locked. Cursing, he handed it back to Jack. 'Here, you dropped this.'

Jack took it wordlessly, still watching Murphy.

'Jack, I'm gonna need you to come down the station,' said Con. 'You're not under arrest or anything. You can drive yourself or you can come in the car with us. Me and Murphy.' He nodded significantly at Murphy.

Jack swallowed. 'I'll meet you there . . .'

'Great. Gabriella can drive with you, then.'

Gabriella shoved herself off Murphy. 'Let's go, then.' She was flushed in the face: Murphy must have given her more resistance than she'd let on.

Con helped Murphy to his feet, feeling the man's giant bicep pushing against his fingers, ready to break loose. He pushed him harder towards the car, a little rougher than he needed to. Murphy had interrupted his plans, now they would have to interview Jack the old-fashioned way.

'What am I being charged with now, Badenhorst?' snarled Murphy.

'If you can calm yourself down for like, five minutes, then nothing, mate,' said Con. 'Are you going to do something stupid if I put you in the front seat?'

'No,' said Murphy, as Con opened the door to shove him in the front seat. Murphy, off balance with his hands cuffed, stumbled back against Con's side before he found his seat.

Con walked around the car and climbed in the driver's seat, watching as Murphy pulled his hands under his legs and back in front of him, still cuffed.

'Behave yourself,' said Con, pulling his AirPods out of the centre console. Plugging them into his phone, he dialled. 'And don't talk.'

The commander picked up on the fourth ring, answering her work phone even from her Blackstone Heights home in Launceston. 'Cornelius,' she said, her voice silky. 'How lovely of you to call an old woman on such a cold, blustery night.'

'Sorry, Agatha.'

'Oh? You're sorry? Please, what were you up to?' She chuckled. 'Preparing for another YouTube cameo?'

'I don't know what you mean,' said Con.

'Yes, you do.' All false kindness left her voice. 'Is Pakinga there?'

'She's bringing Jack Michaels in to the station. We think he's a suspect.'

'And who are you with, in that case? Please don't say Jordan Murphy.'

'Would . . . would it help if I didn't say his name?' said Con. He started the car. He saw Murphy fiddling with his handcuffs and he swatted at his hands for him to stop.

'You have Jordan Murphy.' Her voice was flat. '*And* Jack Michaels. And you're taking them both to the station, even after Madison Mason just released a video declaiming their innocence.'

'We can't let her call the shots.' Con had a growing sense that he should probably start lying.

'You may encounter some difficulty, considering the mob surrounding the station.'

'*Again?*'

'The citizens of Limestone Creek appear to be very civic minded. "Justice for Jack", "Justice for Murphy". Most of the crowd are the disgruntled would-be search volunteers who have been camping out beside the community hall, all at Madison's direction. It's amazing – a few hours ago, a mob wanted to kill Murphy. Now they want to save him. Believe me, the irony has been lost on no one.'

'What should I do, ma'am? Where else I can take them?' said Con.

'Use your initiative, but don't let it be the station.' Her voice rose. 'Calling out a sixteen-year-old girl online, on her *own* channel – what was Pakinga thinking?'

'Gabriella has a plan, commander.'

'Not anymore, Badenhorst. She's off the case.'

'I . . . no,' said Con. He slowed down to pull over. 'What? Agatha?'

'Why are we stopping —' began Murphy. Con hit in the arm to silence him.

'We are making progress, ma'am. You can't take her off the case.'

'Any progress she can pass on to her successor – Melinda Tran. And yours, too, if you don't start showing me something. Do you have any idea how much damage she caused? Now my judgement is being called into question. If I don't take Gabriella off the case, they'll keep digging, and before long someone will drag up your psych records, Con, and then I'll have even more to defend. So I'll give you one more strike, then you're out and I'm getting someone else to run point.'

Con could barely believe it. It took him a moment to find a response. 'With all due respect, commander, that could be fatal for the missing girls, not to mention a colossal waste of time.'

'You and Gabriella are all over the internet. That's a bad look for the department. I know you like to break rules when you're under pressure, and I can't take that risk. You know I've given you enough chances.'

'So it's all about *optics*?' demanded Con, outraged. 'Three girls are missing! One is *dead*!'

'Grow up, Badenhorst. Everything is about optics,' she snapped, then sighed. 'Listen, you haven't made any real progress, you have no leads, no significant evidence, and as you say: a girl is dead. You might not have to think about the funding and PR nightmare this will turn into in the long-term, but I do. Madison's online presence only makes it more difficult.' Her voice softened. 'And if someone starts digging into your past, there's going to be a lot of questions about why you weren't discharged for your own benefit, never mind assigned to this case.'

'Because I'm the best, Agatha. You know I am. It's the right thing to do by the missing girls.'

'Cornelius, the people on this island will shut you out as easily as look at you. They'll turn against you – maybe they already have. This is Tasmania's biggest case of the decade, maybe Australia's too. It's a media frenzy and you and Gabriella have just been painted as the bad guys by the town's tragic heroine, Madison Mason. If your condition comes out —'

'We're about to interview Jack Michaels. We're close.'

'There is no "we". Inform Gabriella she's off the case, on my orders. Melinda Tran will take her place as your partner.'

'Commander —'

'That's my last word, Cornelius.' She sounded tired, sad. 'Update me in the morning. An old woman needs her sleep.'

The line went dead. There were a few moments of silence as Con sat, breathing deeply.

'These things are harder to use than you'd think,' said Murphy.

Irritated, Con glanced across.

He saw his own lock picks sticking out of the keyhole in the cuffs, which were still fastened around Murphy's wrists.

Con stared for several seconds, trying to make sense of it, then checked his pockets. 'What the hell?' He launched over the centre console to snatch them back.

'You're not the only one who knows how to pick pockets,' said Murphy, leaning back in his seat. 'But I never learned how to pick locks.' He rattled his cuffs.

'Stealing from a cop. Do you *want* to go to jail?'

'Don't act righteous, Badenhorst. I saw you lift Jack's phone from his pocket.'

'That doesn't concern you.'

'Since it's my missing bloody daughter that he was screwing, I'd say it bloody does concern me,' said Murphy. 'You didn't have a warrant to search his phone, did you? Be really interesting to see what your commander says about that.'

'I don't have time for this.' Con revved the engine, then sped off the kerb. 'What did you mean when you said Jack had stolen your seeds?'

'Don't know what you're talking about,' said Murphy.

'Oh, for . . .' Con took a big breath. 'Murphy, like you just said, he was with your *missing daughter*. Will you work with us or against us?'

'I'll work against anyone who thinks I'm to blame,' said Murphy.

'You think we're going to frame you? Mate, do you think this is a bloody movie? You're some misunderstood hero? The cops aren't out to get you, Murphy.'

Murphy laughed, loud and sarcastic. 'You *really* don't know how things work around here, do you?'

I'm getting real sick of people telling me that, thought Con, gripping the steering wheel until his knuckles went white. 'Then explain it to me. If you can manage to string three words together, you *inbred country dipshit.*' He didn't mean to shout the last words.

Murphy laughed without missing a beat. 'Alright, since you're too thick to get it . . .' He chuckled again. 'Listen closely, if you can hear past the massive stick in your arse. Hypothetically, these mountains – nice and remote, not many people around, pretty interesting climate – hypothetically, they're perfect for growing really good bush weed. And I mean, *really* good. Now, imagine you're a copper, and you work around here. You see how much people are willing to pay for bush bud. You try to shut it down, but it's easy to hide it around here and you're not getting anywhere. And then you start thinking, hey, I don't get paid enough, and this is bloody Tasmania, no one checks up on us and the rest of Australia doesn't give two bloody shits. You realise, hey, if I'm in charge of my own growing operation, I can shut down everyone else out here who's trying to make an honest living and have a monopoly.'

'*An honest living?*'

'Now, since you're a cop, you have more power than the normal bloke. You can absolutely demolish anyone who gets in your way.'

'Are we talking about Doble?' said Con. 'I thought all that was because you slept with his wife.'

'Yeah, but I did that out of revenge,' said Murphy. 'Doble has a nice greenhouse on the outskirts of town. Big hydroponics setup. *That's* why he hates me, but even with all his buddies behind him, he can't stop us.'

'I thought we were talking about hypotheticals,' said Con, as they approached the station. He'd been driving on autopilot – and he still hadn't told Pakinga not to take Jack to the station.

From a block away, he saw the mob outside. They were in a marked police car and not their unmarked BMW, which was still parked at the station.

He pulled over – he needed to call Pakinga.

Murphy shifted uneasily. 'The crowd is still here,' he said. 'Do you think they've built a gallows yet?' Con glanced at him.

Murphy didn't know these people were now protesting *for* him, not against him.

Some members of the mob had spotted the squad car and were creeping closer, filming with their phones.

'I think that's Jordan Murphy in the front seat,' shouted the closest. 'Madison was right!'

Con did a U-turn in a screech of wheels. They sped off.

'Didn't realised you were so concerned about my safety,' said Murphy, gripping the handle.

'Of course,' said Con. He unlocked his phone and handed it to Murphy. 'Call Gabriella – uh, she's in there as Gabby. Tell her not to go to the station. You pick somewhere for us to meet, somewhere discreet.'

'You want *me* to choose?'

'You know your stupid town better than I do,' spat Con.

Murphy tapped at the phone

'Hello? Yeah, no, it's Murphy . . . Cornelius?' He turned to Con. 'Your name is *Cornelius*?' Back into the phone, he said, 'No, he's fine, just busy driving . . . Why are you . . . What's happened?' Murphy sat up straight. 'I *knew it*.' He turned to Con. 'Jack has done a runner. Gave her the slip and took off on his dirtbike. She followed him in his own car, but he headed down one of the trails. Wait, detective: the one just around the corner from his place? . . . I know where that leads.'

'What?' said Con. 'Where is he going, Murphy? What did Gabriella say? Where does that trail lead?'

'It leads to Lake Mackenzie.'

CHAPTER 23

ELIZA

'I'm not sure this is a good idea,' said Tom. He steered his white flat-bed Landcruiser over the potholes and fallen gum branches on the Lake Mackenzie four-wheel-drive track.

'Why didn't you tell me Jack knew about this place?' said Eliza.

'Why didn't you tell me Jasmine was dating Jack?' said Tom.

'If Jack knew about this place, maybe he told Jasmine. She might be hiding there, and Cierra and Bree, too.'

'Then we should tell the cops,' said Tom.

'And what if what happened to Georgia was an accident? They might be scared. They'd think they're in trouble. They might not *want* to be found. We bring the cops, they might bolt.'

'Or whoever took them could be hiding here.'

'I know,' said Eliza. 'And that's why I brought you. And your gun.' Tom's .22 hunting rifle lay across the back seat.

The headlights bounced over the muddy track. Lake Mackenzie was invisible beside them in the thick, rainy darkness.

'You better turn the headlights off. We don't want them to know we're coming,' said Eliza.

'Well, we can walk from here. We're about 300 metres away.'

They pulled over and climbed out of the Landcruiser. The darkness – the moon hidden by the clouds – was all but complete. Eliza flicked on her torch, shining it at her feet. Puddles and wet stones sparkled in the light.

Together, they walked down the road, Tom's rifle slung across his back. The air was thick with the smell of wet, rotting leaf matter. 'They would have had to walk a *long* way to get here,' said Tom.

'If they had a compass, they could've just bashed through the bush more or less in a straight line. It's not that far, really, from where Georgia was found.'

'They would have crossed the road. Someone would have seen them,' said Tom.

'But if they didn't *want* to be found . . .'

'It's a stretch, Eliza,' said Tom. 'I think you want them to be safe so bad, you've made it all up in your head that they're just waiting in the Fisherman's Hut, safe and sound.'

'Fine,' said Eliza, speeding up her pace, footsteps squishing in the wet. 'Go back to the car then. I'll go by myself.'

'Don't be like that.' Tom jogged to catch up. 'I just don't want you getting your hopes up.'

'I know these girls, Tom. They're capable of it.'

'You think I don't? I know Cierra better than anyone else.'

That wasn't comforting in the slightest, as her mind replaced Cierra's face with Denni's. 'Why the hell did you leave your bag of weed and condoms in her room, Tom. Are you *insane*? Wren needs you around, *and* needs you to have a job. You could've thrown it all away because you were . . . careless!'

'I was *greened out*! You were there – you know I wasn't in a good way. *You* should've remembered to bring it with you.' Tom grunted angrily for a moment, footsteps squelching as he continued on, before he finally said, in a small voice, 'Sorry.' Then, like a little boy, 'What if she doesn't want to see me?'

'Cierra loves you, Tom.' She hated it, but it was true. It started to rain again. Eliza pulled her hood up over her head, but Tom left his down. 'The hell knows why . . .'

They had reached the copse of white gums that signalled the wallaby trail down to the hidden Fisherman's Hut, at the side of the lake. The torchlight glinted on the wet, dancing leaves and made motes of falling light where it hit the rain.

Eliza had first heard about the hut from Tom. Last year he had brought her, Wren and Monica here on a family date, bringing a picnic of sandwiches and wine and a mattress. They'd all watched the sun set over the lake. The hut was well hidden, overgrown, and the structure itself was partly dug into the ground. It was a perfect, secret gem.

Now she understood that it was Jack who'd shown it to Tom in the first place.

'This is it,' whispered Tom. 'Let's go see if they're here.'

'Wait,' said Eliza, pulling the hood away from her ear. 'Do you hear that? Sounds like a car.'

Even over the rain they heard the distinct sound of a car door slamming shut. Eliza and Tom froze, switching off their torches in unison. The sound had come from further down the track, the direction they were facing.

'Stay here,' said Tom, pushing the rifle into Eliza's hands and running off into the darkness.

'No, Tom!' called Eliza quietly, but he was gone. 'I hate shooting guns,' she whispered.

It was scary how quickly she felt alone. The bush rustled with the rain and wind. It seemed to close in over the top of her.

Don't freak out. Do not freak out.

There was the sound of someone stepping in a puddle.

'*Tom?*' she squeaked.

She heard a voice calling, gruff and angry. Not Tom.

She fled down the wallaby trail, towards Fisherman's Hut. She swung the rifle over her shoulder and turned her torch back on, smothering the beam with her hand, leaving enough light to show the twisting roots and erosion holes.

The trail opened onto a clearing of rocks and soil and leaf matter.

Someone was already at the hut.

Her torch beam lit up the figure, who stood in front of the hut's open door, back towards her, silhouetted in the rain. She dropped the torch from her numb fingers and it rolled on the ground, lighting up the trees, lighting up the figure. It turned and look at her.

She screamed. The figure was tall and dark as oil, with a head far, far too big for its body.

Terror flooded her. The person had no face.

A person as big as a bear . . .

She screamed again and reached for the rifle. A noise came from the figure, dark and deep and inhuman.

She backed away, levelling the rifle with shaking hands.

'*Stay away from me!*'

The figure moved towards her, raising its arms, and at the same moment footsteps crashed down the trail right behind her.

Eliza fired.

The sound was like thunder.

The figure clutched its side and dropped to the ground. Eliza spun and pointed the rifle at whoever was chasing her down the path.

'*Stay back!*'

Torchlight shone into her face, blinding her.

'Eliza!' It was Murphy's voice. 'Don't shoot!'

Her knees buckled.

He caught her around the shoulders and eased the rifle out of her grip. 'Eliza! What happened? Are you alright? Are the girls here? Tom said you thought —'

She heard muffled shouting from the hut behind her. Murphy snatched up her torch from the ground, far stronger than his phone's flashlight. She saw the figure on the ground . . . its abnormally large head . . .

It was someone in motorcycle leathers and a matte black helmet.

'Oh no,' gasped Eliza.

'Badenhorst! Down here!' roared Murphy. 'Jack's been shot.'

'*Jack?*' whispered Eliza. 'Oh no . . . oh no, oh no, oh no . . .' She slumped and Murphy held her upright.

Detective Con Badenhorst came crashing out of the wallaby trail, his own torch in hand, his white linen shirt torn. 'What happened?' he shouted. Not waiting for an answer, he ran to Jack, easing the helmet off his head.

All the overlapping torch beams made the scene shift and dance, making crazy shapes in the trees around the clearing. Eliza couldn't believe what she'd done. 'I'm so sorry, Jack. Oh no, oh no, I'm so sorry, Jack, *no* . . .'

Con clamped his phone between his shoulder and his ear. 'Gabriella, call an ambulance. Jack Michaels has been shot, down by Lake Mackenzie. We're off the road. We *cannot* afford to lose him.'

'No,' Jack groaned. 'Don't bring anyone else . . .'

Con grabbed Jack's hands and pushed them against his side. 'Keep pressure on here, mate. We need to get you out of the rain. Murphy, help me take him into the hut.'

'No,' groaned Jack. 'Don't . . .'

Murphy helped Eliza to her feet. 'Shine the torch for us.'

'I shot him!'

'Yeah, and I'll congratulate you later, but right now, we need to get him stable, so can you light the bloody way?' shouted Murphy.

Eliza took the torch from him, her whole body shaking uncontrollably. Murphy and Con lifted Jack through the hut's open door in a chair carry. Eliza followed, the rifle in one hand and the torch in the other, lighting the way for them as best she could. She saw Jack's dirtbike, resting against a tree nearby, hidden from view.

The hut was as she remembered it. Timber slats for walls, a rotten timber floor that slanted down to a rocky hollow dug out at the back. The camping mattress was still there and it brought her a strange lurch of sickening nostalgia. The men lowered Jack onto it.

Her torch beam found two large hiking backpacks propped against the wall, packed to the brim. One yellow, one pink.

'What happened, Eliza?' said Con, his hands over Jack's, keeping the wound tight.

'I . . . I saw him standing there, and in the rain, with his helmet, he looked so . . . I just . . . Murphy crashed through the bush behind me and I just lost my head.' Hot tears spilled down her cheeks. 'I'm so sorry, Jack.'

'What the hell is this?' said Murphy. He unzipped the pink backpack and pulled out girls clothes, tent pegs, protein bars and ramen noodles, a first-aid kit . . .

'Don't, Murphy,' said Con sharply. 'It's evidence. Don't touch it.'

Murphy put the pack on the floor. He turned, his hair wet, his face fierce. He raised himself to his fullest height, voice filling the hut. 'What are you doing out here, Jack? Why do you have a backpack full of girls clothes?'

'Don't, please,' said Eliza, moving to stand between him and Jack. 'Wait for the ambulance.'

'Where is *Jasmine*?' bellowed Murphy.

'Gone,' groaned Jack, shivering. 'I dunno where.'

'What *do* you know?'

'Murphy, now's not the best time,' said Con through gritted teeth, pushing down on Jack's wound as hard as he could.

'They set it up, Murphy.' Jack winced. 'Need to know . . . the girls set it up.'

Eliza held her breath. Relief rushed in through the fear and guilt.

The fight. I'll have to tell them now.

'They set up what?' said Con.

'Madison's . . . idea . . .' Every breath seemed to bring Jack agony.

'You're lying,' snarled Murphy. 'Jasmine wouldn't do anything that stupid.'

'She would . . .' said Jack. 'If she thought . . . best thing.' He gasped in pain. 'Something went wrong . . . Georgia . . . her and Bree's backpacks . . . Jasmine and Cierra's backpacks gone . . . they were supposed to . . . *they left before I got here* . . . Bree . . . girls must have been taken . . . only reason. *Someone took them.*' He dropped his head to the side and spoke no more, falling into fitful moans.

They all looked at each other.

'It's impossible,' said Murphy.

'You don't know Madison like I do,' said Eliza, feeling sick. 'She's capable. But some of it . . . it doesn't make sense.'

'Oh, you mean like *how Georgia fucking died*?' said Murphy.

'They set it up themselves,' said Con, his voice giving nothing away. 'But if they were going to wait for him . . . surely they wouldn't have left for no reason.'

'And who attacked me, up on the mountain? One of them?' said Eliza. She wiped the sweat from Jack's forehead. 'Jack, you sweet idiot, what were you thinking?'

Con was back on his phone. 'Gabriella, are you there?' He put her on speaker for the others' benefit.

'We're waiting at the top of the trail. An ambulance is on its way, but the commander has ordered a chopper from Launceston: if we lose Jack, we lose the girls. How's he doing?'

'Tell them to hurry,' said Con. 'And call in Forensics. We have evidence here, the last place the girls might've been.'

Murphy stalked out of the hut, slamming the door behind him.

'Murphy?' shouted Con. 'Gabriella, Murphy is coming your way. Keep hold of the car keys and stop him from doing anything stupid. Careful, he knows how to pick pockets.'

The sound of a motorbike engine rumbled outside the hut.

'Shit! He's taking Jack's bike. Gabriella!' shouted Con into the phone.

'On it!' came her breathless reply.

Eliza squeezed Jack's hand, but he didn't squeeze back.

I'm sorry, Jack. I need to tell them about the fight.

CHAPTER 24

MURPHY

Murphy rode Jack's dirtbike down the trail, manoeuvring around the rocks and roots, the headlight illuminating the muddy tyre tracks that showed the route Jack had arrived by.

He was approaching the end of the wallaby trail now, the sound of the engine rattling inside his helmet, the visor raised to keep from getting water-blind from the raindrops. He saw lights up ahead, coming up fast. Tom and Gabriella, standing in his way, waving him down, shouting for him to stop.

Murphy revved the engine and drove straight through.

They dodged to the side, their faces a blur in the rain and torch beams, and then Murphy was on the wider four-wheel-drive track, the bouncing headlight lighting the road and the tree limbs that spread over it, ghostly arms reaching for him.

A wallaby bounded across the trail ahead of him, joey in her pouch, pausing at the edge of the track to watch him, eyes reflecting the headlights. Murphy rode right past: he knew where he was headed.

He took old dirt tracks he knew well from a youth spent riding these same trails with Butch. He criss-crossed forestry and muddy bush routes, down the mountainside, until he came out into the out-skirts of Limestone Creek and directly onto a farm's driveway. He rode it to the road, then through paddocks and into town.

Roaring through the streets of dilapidated houses and barking dogs, it didn't take him long to reach the Masons' large double-storey house. He left the motorbike idling against the fence and stormed up to the front door, ignoring the stepping stones on the manicured lawn. He kicked open the heavy wooden door with a crash that busted the doorframe.

'Madison!' he shouted, flicking on the light in the main living area, everything sparkling clean. 'Where are you?'

Nelly Mason's scream echoed from upstairs, and seconds later the stairway light flicked on. Mr Bruiser exploded down the stairs, crouching on the final step and yapping like a guard dog. A moment later Kevin Mason ran down the steps, naked, holding a cricket bat.

Nelly was behind him, wrapped in her dressing gown.

'Murphy, you bastard, what the hell are you —' shouted Kevin.

Murphy pulled the Glock out of his belt and pointed it at his head.

Kevin fell instantly quiet, the cricket bat dropping out of his hands. Nelly fainted, her body hitting the carpeted steps with a dull thump.

'Madison. Get down here,' shouted Murphy. 'Now!'

'No,' croaked Kevin, voice strangled. 'Madison, he's got a gun!'

He heard Madison's footsteps and then she too appeared, hair messy, her phone in her hand.

'Lose the phone or I'll shoot your dad,' said Murphy.

Terror flashed across Madison's face. She dropped the phone and it cartwheeled over to Nelly's sprawled body. 'You killed Georgia? I was so sure it wasn't you . . .' she whispered. Then outrage crossed her face. 'I *defended* you.'

'Jack said you planned this,' shouted Murphy. 'You and the girls planned to go missing. For the sake of your fucking YouTube channel?'

The fear vanished from her face, replaced by a raised eyebrow. She came down the stairs and put her hands on her hips. 'That's what Jack said, is it? Did you know he's screwing your daughter?'

'Madison, go back to your room,' choked Kevin.

'Don't worry, Dad, he won't shoot – it's *Murphy*.' Madison cocked her head. 'He's just as weak as Jasmine.'

'Did you plan this, Madison? Did Jasmine agree to it?' said Murphy, shaking the gun. 'Answer me!'

'You think I told Georgia to throw herself off a cliff?' said Madison, now smirking. 'You really think I'm capable of that?'

'*Did* you set this up?' said Murphy.

'Yes,' said Madison. 'I did. I planned it all.'

'What are you saying?' said Kevin, turning towards her a fraction.

'You found the backpacks, is that it?' said Madison. 'Won't be long until it gets out then. Yes, we planned it. But something's gone wrong. They haven't made contact with me, Georgia is dead, and Bree didn't get her backpack either. I think someone has really taken them, Murphy. Or, more likely, Cierra and Jasmine are playing a game I don't know about. The little bitches.' Her eyes twinkled. 'One thing's for sure: with Georgia dead and the other three missing, maybe our story has become true. We summoned the Hungry Man.'

'What about Jasmine? Tell me,' said Murphy. 'All of it.' He shook the gun again.

'Say please,' said Madison.

He ground his teeth so hard they creaked.

'Go on,' said Madison. 'Say *please*.'

'Madison,' whispered Kevin.

'. . . please,' ground out Murphy.

'No. I'm going back to bed. I'll talk to the cops tomorrow, but I'm not talking to you while you're in such a foul mood. Goodnight, Mr Murphy. Night, Dad.'

Madison picked up her phone and walked up the stairs. Murphy watched her go.

Nelly, he saw now, was awake, but hadn't moved. Kevin was white as a sheet.

Murphy put the Glock back in his belt. 'Your daughter is out of fucking control.' He stomped out of the house, kicking over a potted plant on his way to the dirtbike.

A story was forming in Murphy's mind. Georgia's death was accidental, then Jasmine and Cierra ran – afraid of being in trouble – taking their backpacks and hiding somewhere. And for some reason Madison was calm, assured. It was agonising that she wouldn't share whatever secrets she kept behind that smug little face, but that . . . that meant whatever had happened to Jasmine, maybe it wasn't too bad.

Two emotions were warring inside him. His daughter was missing and that was like an illness, pneumonia: there was something blocking his chest and he couldn't breathe and he was burning with fever. But this other thing now inside him: a glimmer of hope.

Jasmine and Cierra's backpacks are gone, so they both made it from the Lake Nameless trail to the Fisherman's Hut at Lake Mackenzie. As he drove back home on Jack's motorbike, certainty set in. *Jasmine is alive.*

In the morning he would head to Lake Mackenzie and join the search that would surely begin there.

He left the dirtbike in the driveway, behind Butch's Hilux. He could hear music from the back shed – Butch was still out there.

Murphy walked into his room, stopping in front of Jasmine's crayon drawing. For the first time since Sara's death, he kneeled down at his bed to pray.

Sara, if you're up there – I need you now . . . bring Jasmine back and I promise, I'll never smoke weed again, I'll never . . .

He thought carefully of the things Sara didn't approve of.

I'll never smoke weed again, I'll stop swearing. I'll . . . make this right, God. Whoever I need to speak to. I will make my life right, I swear it . . . Jesus, bring her back safely and I'll take her to church every bloody Sunday, I swear it . . .

CHAPTER 25

CON

Con and Eliza sat across from each other in a waiting room at Launceston General Hospital. Gabriella lay on the carpet, her jacket bundled up into a pillow, fast asleep. Early morning sunlight shone through the skylight, revealing a blue sky.

Once Jack was safely in the ambulance chopper, Gabriella and Eliza had driven straight to the hospital, but Con had stopped past the hotel to make sure he took his meds. But despite that, the lack of sleep was dragging at his edges. He could feel himself getting jittery, the anger bubbling inside of him.

Madison Mason.

If Jack was telling the truth, then Madison had planned it all. Well, almost – certainly the disappearances. What about Georgia's death? Surely not.

Con stood and paced the room. A girl who would put her own sister in harm's way for popularity. Still, before he could speak to her . . .

His phone buzzed. The commander.

He'd left her a message when he got to the hotel, but it had been the middle of the night. It seemed she was awake now.

'I just have to make a phone call, Eliza. I'll be back soon.'

Eliza nodded, the leopard-print bow around her head slipping a little. She looked bone tired.

He headed into an adjacent room to take the call.

'Cornelius.' The commander's voice was cool as chipped ice. 'Are you okay?'

'I'm at the hospital,' replied Con. 'I'm waiting for Jack to wake up.'

Her voice turned hard. 'And you honestly believe him?'

'I . . . I did. I *do*.'

'He's trying to cover himself. He was just caught at the scene – shot at the scene. We'll have to deal with Eliza's part in that before long, but finding the girls has to be our priority. Jack claiming they arranged their own disappearance is awfully convenient.'

'To him, it was a deathbed confession,' said Con. 'He had no reason to lie.'

'You know this leaves us in a difficult situation.'

'How so?' Con was growing agitated with the way she danced around the point.

'Madison Mason anticipated this. She said in her video that the police would target first Murphy, then Michaels, and then her. With Gabriella's outburst —'

'Which turned out to be right!'

'Which was highly unprofessional. It gives any defence lawyer worth half her salt the ability to defend Madison from anything short of a smoking gun!' snapped the commander. 'That's out of our hands now. But I trust you've told Gabriella she's off the case? Don't make me do it myself. You're the lead detective.'

'Commander,' said Con, reeling – this call was not going the way he'd expected. 'I need you to reconsider.'

'I've no doubt you do,' she said. 'I'm sending Detective Tran to the Fisherman's Hut to join Forensics. You're sending Gabriella home, right now, or you'll join her.'

'Commander, I —'

'Get in there, Badenhorst, and determine if Jack is telling the truth or not. *Before* you go after Madison Mason. Oh, and Cornelius? I'm coming to Limestone Creek. It's time I was on the ground. I'll be there in a few hours. If I cross paths with Gabriella, I'll know you were too weak to follow directions.'

The line went dead.

Maybe she's not a morning person? thought Con angrily. *Well, neither am I.*

He stalked back into the waiting room. Gabriella was still sleeping, but Eliza was gone, replaced by a nurse who was scrolling through his phone. He saw Con coming and quickly put his phone away. 'Mr Michaels is awake. You can head through, if you like. Your other colleague is already in there.' He glanced at Gabriella. 'I didn't know if I should wake this one or not, but the other detective didn't seem concerned.'

Con left Gabriella asleep, stalking after the nurse towards Jack's room.

CHAPTER 26

ELIZA

Bare seconds after Con had left the room to make his phone call, Eliza looked up to see a young nurse enter the waiting room, typing on his tablet in a heavy-duty case.

The nurse looked down at Gabriella, gently snoring, and turned to Eliza. 'Detective?'

Eliza didn't hesitate. She nodded.

'Mr Michaels is conscious now, but barely. He's lost a lot of blood, and he's only just come out of surgery,' he said. 'The surgeon insists that Mr Michaels needs to rest, but we understand you need to speak to him with some urgency. He's not in a great way, but as he's just woken up from the anaesthetic and we haven't started him on the painkillers yet, this might be the only time you'll get any sense out of him.'

Eliza glanced at Gabriella, asleep on the floor, and then back to the nurse.

'Yes, we do need to talk to him,' she said.

'Okay. Well, please keep it brief, and I'll need to stay in there with you to monitor his condition.'

Eliza gestured for the nurse to lead the way. When they reached the door of Jack's room, she paused. 'I'm sorry, sir, but at this stage . . . everyone is a suspect. Police procedure. You'll need to wait outside.' She used her stern teacher's voice. 'And please don't try to listen in, okay, sir? I don't want to arrest you for obstruction. This is an active, uh, homicide investigation.'

The nurse nodded uneasily. Eliza fixed him with a stare, nodded once very professionally, and walked inside.

Jack was on the bed, a bandage around his side, an IV in his arm, a cannula in his nose. He was sweating, his eyes bloodshot, his face faintly blue.

When he tried to sit up he winced. 'Eliza . . . did they find 'em?' His words were slurred and muffled.

'I'm so sorry . . . I nearly killed you,' Eliza whispered, crouched down beside his bed. 'I'm so sorry.'

'Where are the d-detectives?' he said. His teeth chattered.

'They're on their way. Look, Jack,' Eliza said, 'you said that the girls planned the disappearance?'

'No!' he said, trying to sit up again. 'I don't! I didn't! D-don't tell anyone!'

'Jack,' said Eliza, glancing back at the door. She leaned closer to his ear. 'What does Madison have over you?'

'Wh-what are you talkin' about?' stammered Jack, breathing heavy. His eyelids fluttered and he fell back.

'Madison drew you into this, didn't she?' she said. 'She black-mailed you?'

'How . . . Wh-what did she tell you?' said Jack.

'Tell me what it is. I can help you,' insisted Eliza, hating herself for what she was doing, but knowing it was necessary. To steel herself she thought of her niece. 'Was she going to expose you and Jasmine?'

'What . . . what do you know about – *You* told Murphy?'

Eliza tapped her tongue against the back of her teeth. 'Jack —'

The door flew open and Con strode into the room. 'Michaels. You're awake. Good.' He crossed his arms. 'I need you to tell me the truth.'

'I . . . I dunno —'

'Don't bullshit me, Jack,' said Con. 'You were found with the possessions of two of the missing girls, and you were sleeping with one of them.'

'Detective, please,' said the nurse, stepping in behind him. 'Be gentle.'

'Well? Georgia's blood is on your hands. Will you help us find the others?'

Jack grimaced and writhed on the bed. 'Or are you just making it all up, to save yourself? *You* were found where we suspect the girls were last. *You* were sleeping with one of the missing. *You* were up the mountain, the day they *went* missing.'

Jack moaned. He trembled, shaking his head, tears rolling down his cheeks.

'Mr Michaels?' said the nurse, rushing to his side. He checked the digital readout of his vitals. 'Please, detectives, I need you to step outside.'

'No. I need to hear him say it. I need to hear him say he lied about their plan, that he put the girls in even more danger just to save his own skin.'

Seeing Jack's distress, Eliza realised she couldn't keep this secret. She couldn't protect Wren anymore.

She turned to Con, grabbed his arm and took him outside the door.

'Eliza, what are you —'

'It's time I told you the truth,' she said. 'But please . . . whatever you do, don't tell Madison.'

She looked around and settled on a linen closet just across the hall. Con followed her into the small nook.

'I have a confession . . . the fight between Jasmine and Madison.' Eliza had to look away from Con's eyes. 'Madison approached me a few weeks ago. She asked that Cierra and Madison share a tent on the camp, and Jasmine and Bree too.'

'That's all?' Con gave a dark laugh. He seemed rattled today. 'They wanted to sleep in each other's tents? You've blown the case wide open, thanks so much for —'

'That's not all,' interrupted Eliza. 'Madison told me that, on the second day of camp, Jasmine and her were going to have a fight. And that, afterwards, I'd have to send everyone else ahead, including Madison, and keep Jasmine, Georgia, Bree, and Cierra back with me. So it would be just us five, far at the back of the group.'

'What? And you agreed?' said Con.

'I thought they just wanted to film something! It's not that simple —'

'Why would you *agree* to that, Eliza?'

'Because Madison blackmailed me,' she said quickly.

That stopped him. He took a second to process that. 'With what? What could she possibly —'

'What I'm saying is I'm sure Jack is telling the truth. Madison made me keep the four girls behind. They were capable of staging a fight. They would be capable of staging a disappearance.'

'Why the hell didn't you tell me this sooner? Georgia is dead!'

The door to Jack's room opened and the nurse approached them. 'He needs to see you – he won't calm down. He says it's about the girls.'

Con stomped inside, Eliza trailing behind. Another nurse was helping Jack drink from a glass of water, but when he saw Con he let it fall and it spilled down his side, his face pale but for points of colour on his cheeks.

'It was Madison's idea,' said Jack. His face was still covered in sweat. 'Cierra had to be part of it, 'cause Madison's viewers know her.

Georgia . . .' Jack's voice trailed off. 'She thought it might help her museum. That in a few months, when they came out of the mountains —'

'*Months?*' said Con. 'They planned on being missing for *months?*'

Even the nurses looked shocked, both watching Jack with morbid fascination.

'Were they planning to kill Georgia?' said Con.

'Everyone *loves* Georgia!' Jack's face was pale, as the implication that he might be responsible hit home. 'The plan was to claim they'd been kidnapped . . . The only one they hated was Bree.'

'But she's part of it,' said Con.

'She's a bloody nightmare,' said Jack. 'Madison only let Bree in on it because she thought it'd help her. Bree wanted to fake her death so everyone would realise how much they miss her – Madison still blames herself for Denni's death, and that's what made Bree depressed in the first place. She thought if Bree could fake her death, she might stop being suicidal.'

Eliza's stomach lurched at the mention of Denni.

'And you thought that made sense?' said Con. 'That any of this was a good idea? You let someone who was suicidal walk into the woods *and fake their own disappearance?*'

'They were gonna do it whether I helped —'

'*They're teenage girls,*' Con roared. '*They're in your care! You should've told their parents, the school, the police, anyone!*'

'Please, detective,' said one of the nurses weakly, but the other just nodded in agreement.

Gabriella walked into the room, closing the door behind her. 'Started the party without me?' She scowled.

'Let me bring you up to speed: the girls *did* plan it,' said Con, not taking his eyes off Jack. 'Cierra wanted views for Madison's YouTube channel, Georgia wanted attention for her museum, and

Bree was desperate for people's sympathy. We're about to hear what Jasmine's reason was. Aren't we, Jack?'

'Jaz didn't tell me.'

Oh, Jack, thought Eliza. It was a lie, an obvious and complete lie.

'It didn't trouble you that the girl you were sleeping with wanted to disappear?' said Con with awful patience.

'I dunno, I didn't wanna pressure her . . .'

'But you *were* sleeping with her? And if you lie now, we're going to have problems.'

Jack hesitated. 'Yeah.'

'For how long?'

'A while.'

'*How long?*'

'Nine months . . .'

Con took a deep, calming breath through his nose. When he opened his eyes, his emotions were hidden again, a semblance of professionalism back on his face. 'So let me get this straight: you helped them with this plan, just out of your love for Jasmine?'

'Well, yeah, that . . . plus Madison said she'd tell everyone about me and Jasmine . . . and she promised me money,' he muttered.

'How much?' said Con.

'Five grand.'

'Where the hell did she get that kind of money?' said Con, glancing towards Eliza and Gabriella. 'Just how rich are her parents?'

'Kevin Mason works in real estate, has investment properties,' said Eliza, her voice small, still feeling chastised.

'Con, with her YouTube numbers, she'd make thousands in ad revenue, easy,' said Gabriella.

'And what did she ask you to do, exactly?' said Con, turning back to Jack.

'Find them somewhere to hide. Drop their bags up at Fisherman's

Hut. Gonna camp there for a while . . . pick them up and drive them to a farmhouse in Ridgley . . .'

'But they weren't there when you came,' said Con.

'Detective, I think this time he really does need to rest,' said the nurse.

Jack's eyes were closed but he continued to speak. 'Jasmine and Cierra's bags, nowhere to be seen . . . would've been on the town side, or mountain side . . . would've . . . would've found them by now . . . *someone has taken them.*'

'Two backpacks. If Georgia died before she made it, that explains her bag being there,' said Gabriella. 'If Bree didn't take her bag . . . where is she?'

'I don't know. The SES are now searching exclusively around Lake Mackenzie, and between there and Lake Nameless,' said Con, watching the nurses bustle around Jack. 'Our next step is to call Madison's parents.'

'No!' shouted Jack, lurching forward. 'She'll ruin my life! She'll ruin yours too, detective!' He started coughing and couldn't stop. Blood fell on his chest.

'Out, everyone out!' hissed the nurse, bustling them out into the corridor.

Eliza followed Con and Gabriella out. Con was already on his phone, stalking down the corridor towards an exit to a courtyard, Gabriella close behind him, shaking her head as she came to grips with the new information.

Eliza's legs grew weak and she rested against the wall.

Please be okay, Jack. Either way, it was out now. *And I'll become Public Enemy Number One. Not that I deserve any better.*

At least she could hope that, when it all played out, Madison wouldn't know that Eliza had corroborated Jack's story . . .

As though summoned by the thought, there came the sound of high heels clipping down the tiled floor.

'Hello, Miss Ellis.'

It was Madison Mason. Her hair and make-up were perfect, and she wore a green, high-end vintage jacket, starched and stiff around the collar, with an albatross brooch.

Eliza straightened. 'Madison —'

'I heard Mr Michaels was shot. I was worried. I *made* Mum drive me here. Because I had to check.' Madison's lips pursed even as her eyes moved towards the doorway of Jack's room. A doctor bustled through there, and another nurse came rushing out. 'But if you're here, now things make sense.'

'Madison, please, before you say anything —'

'Jasmine's dad came to visit me last night. We had an interesting conversation. See, the only person who could've told him we planned the disappearances is Mr Michaels. But Murphy *hates* him, so someone else must've backed up the story for him to believe it.' There was a faint twitch above Madison's left eye. 'Now, Miss Ellis, *you* didn't know about the whole plan . . . I'm guessing one of the other girls told you more? My guess is Bree – she and Denni were joined at the hip. But didn't we have a chat about what would happen if you interfered? Don't I know things about you, Miss Ellis, that would destroy you?'

'Madison, please listen to me. I didn't tell Murphy anything,' said Eliza. 'The girls are *really missing* now. Georgia is *dead —*'

'I know,' said Madison, voice harsh, a momentary crack in her mask. 'It's tragic. I loved Georgia. But . . .' She forced the pain back behind her mask. 'Georgia's dead. There's nothing we can do. I can't imagine how horrible an accident that must have been, but now the other three are scared that they'll get blamed.'

'Madison, you have to understand how serious this is!' said Eliza. 'The publicity isn't worth it!'

'*Publicity?*' said Madison incredulously, eyes wild for just a moment before she got them back under control. 'Miss Ellis, you

have *no idea* what we're doing here, what we're going to achieve . . .'
She adjusted her jacket. 'We agreed it would be too difficult if the
girls saw any media about their own disappearances, but on the off
chance Jasmine breaks the rules and has been looking at her phone
or otherwise getting news of what's happening . . . I can't have her
seeing Jack or her dad being blamed. She'd come back to protect
them. But you . . .' she said. 'You, I *don't* need to keep out of the
news. So you'll be seeing me soon, *Miss Ellis*.' She spun and walked
away down the corridor.

'Madison! Please!' Eliza rushed after her. 'Madison, you have to
call this off! Please!'

'Even if I could, I won't!' She turned on Eliza. 'You'll have
enough problems to deal with *very soon*.' She flicked her hair back.
'And just for the record, it's *your* fault that Denni killed herself.'

Hot rage, unlike anything Eliza had ever felt, rushed through
her. It took everything she had not to kick her in the mouth.

'I always love our little talks, Miss Ellis. Remember: *Big Hoop
Energy!*' she said, in a cutesy voice. *'Permission to be empowered!'*

Madison sauntered down the hall, high heels clicking.

CHAPTER 27

CON

Con stood in the hospital courtyard, free of the disinfectant smell, but the dial tone was doing his head in. For the third time, only Nelly Mason's voicemail answered.

'Call me as soon as you get this, Mrs Mason. It's very important I speak to you.' He hung up the phone as Gabriella was ending her own call. 'Did you get Tran?' he asked.

'Yeah, she was with the search controller when I called, Constable Darren Cahil.'

'Wait, why do I know that surname?' said Con.

'His sister was Rose Cahil. Taken during the 1985 abductions.'

Con rubbed at the corner of his eye. 'Coincidence?'

'He would have been ten years old,' said Gabriella pointedly. She clapped her hands. 'But I *love* this case, Con. All these little connections, and now it turns out the girls abducted themselves? *What a twist.* Thanks for not getting us kicked off the investigation just yet.'

Con felt his stomach drop.

'Follow me, I need to tell you something,' he said heavily.

Her face lit up. 'Another plot twist?'

'You're not gonna like this one.' He walked back inside, Gabriella in tow, and found a spare room. 'In here,' he said.

'Oh, detective, you scandalous man,' said Gabriella, flicking her curls back and putting a hand on her hip. 'Can't you wait until we're off the clock?'

Con grimaced. 'Gabriella.'

She caught his mood. 'Why are you using my full name? What's happened?'

'Yesterday, when you spoke on Madison's live stream —'

'You mean when I correctly predicted she was hiding something?'

'Yes, well, Commander Normandy spoke to me and . . . I think it's an overreaction – no, it *is* an overreaction – but she said that . . .' He swallowed. 'What you did, on the live stream, has made the department look bad, has turned a lot of people against us . . . has brought her, the commander, into question, and . . .' He could barely bring himself to say it. 'You're off the case.'

Gabriella blinked. *'Pardonne-moi?'*

'Effective as of yesterday. And Agatha is on her way here, so I can't even hide it.' His voice turned into a pleading whine at the end. 'I'm sorry, Gab, I have —'

She drew herself up. 'You're taking me off the case?'

'No, I'm not. The commander is. You'll have to go past the station and sign your gun in until you're reassigned. Go home, Gabriella.'

'Did you fight for me?' she demanded. 'Did you fight for the girls?'

'Of course I did,' he said, stung.

'Not very hard, obviously,' she said waspishly. 'I wonder if she'd be willing to keep *you* on if she knew what you'd been up to? The locks you picked last night, for example. Without a warrant! Oh, look at me, so noble and successful, Mr Post-Traumatic Stress But I Still Get to Keep My Job Because Everyone Ignores What a Liability I Am.'

'Hey,' said Con, face red, voice rising to match hers. 'It's not my fault you called out a teenage girl on *her own live stream*. What the hell made you think that was a good idea?'

'Instinct, Badenhorst,' she hissed, her cheeks burning, obviously ashamed for her comment but too proud to back down. 'All good detectives have it.'

'You acted like you were still in high school, and look at what it got you – kicked off a case that could've made your career,' said Con. 'Worse, it'll turn everyone against me, the professional who still has to try and solve this case.'

'Oh no, "I'm the hero of the Jaguar case, I need everyone to love me." Not everyone likes you? The *horror!*'

'Why are you getting angry at me? It's not my fault.'

'Why are you yelling at me?' she shouted.

'I'm not!' he shouted.

'You think you can solve the case without me? Fine. Good luck, *dickhead*.' She stormed out of the room.

The unfairness of it made Con bristle. It was made worse by the fact she was right – it *was* good instinct on her part.

He turned to head after her – he wanted to give her another serve, he wanted to make sure she was okay, he didn't know what he wanted – then pulled up short. He'd forgotten something.

He ran back to Jack's ward. The young man was being wheeled out of his room, unconscious and with a breathing tube down his throat. Nurses and doctors buzzed around him.

'What's going on?' said Con, even as he squeezed against the wall to allow them past.

The nurse from Jack's room spoke to him. 'He's on his way to surgery. There may be more internal damage than we thought.'

Con felt a stab of guilt that he angrily pushed aside: the harsh questioning had been necessary. Three girls' lives were hanging in the balance.

'What about the other woman? Eliza – blonde, glasses. Did you see where she went?'

The nurse shrugged, already catching up to Jack's bed. 'Haven't seen her.'

Con watched them go, then headed for his car.

Should he call Gabriella or the commander first?

He called Gabriella.

She rejected his call.

He swore and called the commander.

'Cornelius,' she said. 'What do you have to tell me?'

CHAPTER 28

ELIZA

Eliza gripped tightly to Darren's back, the search controller's jacket rough against her cheek, the seat of his dirtbike worn and hard. They raced down the track past Lake Mackenzie, hugging the sandy shoreline, which gave a full view of the cold alpine lake, its dull sage green and navy blue tones, reflecting sky and mountain peak.

If Madison had her way, this would be Eliza's last chance to join the search. Her last chance to guide the search towards where Georgia had seen that figure and maybe, just maybe, find something that'd find the girls, and maybe stop Madison before Wren's life was ruined.

Inflatable orange dinghies bobbed over the waters of the lake, police divers occasionally surfacing. Above was the chopper in the blue sky, darting in and out of view. At least two-thirds of the search party had already relocated to this area, here on the shores of Lake Mackenzie but also all around it. If the motorbike wasn't so loud, she knew she'd hear their cooees and shouts of 'Jasmine! Bree! Cierra!'

She'd instructed Darren to ignore the turnoff for the wallaby trail that led to the hut and instead continue further on the four-wheel-drive track. He explained that because Jasmine and Cierra's packs had been taken, they knew they'd made it *out* of the bush they were now riding into, back up the mountain, but she had insisted.

They came to a stop and Darren switched off the motor. 'Well? This is the place, right?' He untied their hiking packs from the bike, handing Eliza's hers.

They were on a rise in the trail, beside a small grove of twisted white gums, their roots wrapped around large blocks of pale grey dolomite. Aside from this grove, the landscape was largely open: plains of low shrub with rocky points and small lakes. In the distance was the moody-blue haze of Ironstone Mountain. Insects buzzed, crickets chirped.

'You know where we are?' said Darren. He watched her with a stranger's intensity now.

'I think so,' said Eliza.

'I know what happened with Jack last night was . . . difficult. But what's really changed from the last time we tried this?' said Darren. His tone was polite and curious, but his sharp eyes gave away his suspicion.

I shot someone last night. I thought he was a bear-man. I felt that same terror.

'It brought back a lot of feelings,' said Eliza. 'And with that came some patchy memories.' She pointed towards Ironstone Mountain, then drew her fingers back towards a nearby ridge. 'But I'm sure that Georgia thought she saw someone up *there*.'

Perhaps 500 metres distant, a stark sandstone ridge jutted out of the land like the fin of a sailfish. On top of it was a single large white gum, its leaves reaching to the sky. It was so large and out-of-place that Eliza was sure it was the same one.

Darren surveyed the ridge. 'You remember the ridge where Georgia saw the figure?'

'I remember the tree. I remember the fin of rock.'

'There are a lot of trees and ridges around here,' said Darren.

'I remember Ironstone Mountain in the distance. I remember we'd not long passed the trail to Penny Royal Hut. I remember Lake Nameless being somewhere to our east. And I remember that large white gum on a fin of rock, because Georgia claimed whatever she saw was hiding behind it.'

'Then we should've brought more searchers,' said Darren, pulling his satellite phone from his pocket.

Eliza put her hand on his to stop him. 'The less people here, the better: if Georgia truly saw someone, whoever it was has managed to avoid the searchers all this time. That means we'll have to be quiet. Plus . . . I mean, if he's . . . what Georgia saw —'

'This isn't something we can go rogue on, Miss Ellis.'

'That's not what I'm saying,' she said, a hint of exasperation in her voice. 'Look, don't you want to be the one who finds the Hungry Man? For your sister, Rose?'

It was low, and she hated herself for saying it, but it had the desired effect. Darren hesitated, emotions in conflict on his face.

'What could we possibly hope to find up there?' The lines in his face were hard. 'You're putting me in a difficult position.'

'Who knows what we might find,' said Eliza. 'Clues, maybe? Evidence. Answers.'

Darren watched her, suspicion plain on his face. 'Alright. Let's go.'

As they stepped off the track and walked towards the ridge, Eliza heard Tom's voice in her head. *Leaving a trail in the Great Western Tiers is an exercise in suicide. Do not attempt it.* He'd given the whole camping group that speech before they left school.

But surely it wouldn't be so bad. This area was a little more open than most, and they had that grove of white gums to orient themselves by.

But she should've known it wouldn't be so easy. What looked like low shrubs from the rise of the trail were in fact bushes that reached up to her shoulders, even over her head in some places. Underneath them, the ground was craggy and uneven and full of inexplicable swampy patches.

'Let's stop here a moment,' said Darren after ten minutes. Even though it was fairly flat land, it was tough hiking. They were among copperleaf snowberry, a plant that was found only in Tasmania. It had dark green, serrated leaves and clusters of little white flowers shaped like urns. It was starkly beautiful, smelling wild and free, flowering and perfect out here in the wild.

'Close your eyes and turn around three times,' said Darren.

'What?' said Eliza.

'I want to show you something.'

Eliza closed her eyes and turned, then opened them when she heard the crash of Darren through the shrub. She leaped back, the sharp leaves drawing a thin line of blood from the back of her hands.

Darren was standing behind her now. 'What are you *doing*?' she said.

'I want you to point back to the trail. I moved so you wouldn't have a reference point. Point back to where we came from.'

Eliza pointed.

Darren shook his head. 'Wrong. Try again.'

Eliza hesitated, then pointed forty-five degrees from her first attempt.

'Wrong again. Now you're dead. Lost in the wilderness. And we're what: ten minutes from the trail?

'Do *you* know where we are?'

'Yes.' He lifted his sleeve to show a waterproof compass strapped to his wrist by a paracord bracelet. 'Because *I* know I can't rely on my own sense of direction, not out here.'

'But do you still know the direction to the ridge?' said Eliza.

'I'm trying to help you understand. Setting out, just the two of us, is stupid. Thinking that there might be something up there on the ridge, after all this time, and the weather we've had, is stupid. Searching out here, when we should be back where we *know* the girls have been, is *stupid*.'

'Why agree to come, if I'm such a stupid little girl?'

'Because, Miss Ellis, you *aren't* a little girl and you *aren't* stupid. Either you know something you're not telling me or you're driven by some emotion that's overriding your better judgement. I'd like to know which one it is.'

'I don't know what you're talking about.'

Darren pushed his sleeve down over the compass. 'Well, we're not moving until you tell me.'

'You can't do that.'

'I want to find these girls more than you could possibly know,' said Darren. 'Until I find out what you're hiding, we're not going back to the trail.'

'Darren . . . listen to me. Just get me to that ridge.'

'Are you even listening to me?'

'Fine.' She pushed past him. 'I'll head there myself.' She ignored the sting of the leaves and the drone of insects.

The copperleaf snowberry abruptly gave way to a small stretch of blueberry flaxlily, offering far better visibility of the ridge. She stomped through it, watching the sandstone ridge and its white gum directly ahead.

She could hear Darren walking behind her. She heard his low chuckle, and it made the hairs on the back of her neck rise. 'You know what's really interesting, Miss Ellis?'

She ignored him, eyes on the ridge.

'A second ago you had no idea which direction you were facing.'

'You're not the only one who knows how to read a compass, *constable*.' She continued to stomp through the scrub covering the ground.

'I'll get to the bottom of it eventually, Miss Ellis,' he said. 'Whatever it is. I always do.'

You won't have to wait that long, she thought to herself, Madison's face appearing in her mind. Con would probably be waiting for her, back in town.

Darren's words returned to her mind: *You're driven by some emotion that's overriding your better judgement.* There was an uncomfortable truth to that.

She thought of the permission slip in her pocket:

I give permission for Eliza Ellis to be strong.
Signed, E. Ellis.

The sandstone ridge was steep and surprisingly craggy, bluff snow-grass covering it like a cramped garden. Up here, on the edge of the ridge-fin, Eliza was especially exposed to the biting cold wind that drowned out all noise: Darren's footsteps behind her, even her own breath. Nothing but the mountain wind.

Eliza stopped, closing her eyes, as the noise blew past her like a train, wrapping her in isolation. Fresh and clear and free. For a moment.

She opened her eyes and wiped away the tears. Up ahead was the giant white gum. Beyond it stretched a heart-stopping view of misty tiers of hills and sombre mountains, thick wilderness.

She walked to the gum and touched it with her hand; it was cold. She looked over it, she studied the ground, pushed back blades of bluff snowgrass to check the soil. She was looking for footprints, scuff marks, scraps of clothing, anything.

There was nothing. No clue to indicate who might have stood here, who had hit her on the head, whose footsteps she'd heard. Just like Darren had said: nothing to see at all.

But she had found it. Darren could direct other searchers to cover this area. She *wasn't* entirely useless.

'Miss Ellis,' said Darren.

She shook him off. 'Cierra!' she shouted into the wind. *'Bree! Jasmine!'* The wind blew her words back in her face. 'Cierra! Bree! Jasmine! *Cierra, where are you?'*

'Miss Ellis, look at the clouds. We need to be getting back —'

'Cierra! CIERRA!' she shrieked.

The wind didn't care. The mountain didn't care.

Her knees weakened, but still she held onto the tree and screamed. 'BREE! JASMINE! *CIERRA!!'*

Where are the girls? Where are the girls? Denni, why couldn't I save you?

Now she fell fully to her knees. The sun grew dim behind a shroud of thick cloud and she saw the rainclouds rolling in. The first thick droplet hit her cheek.

She couldn't scream anymore, couldn't say their names. She wrapped her arms around her knees and, for a moment, completely whited out.

Darren took his raincoat out of his pack and she felt him wrap it around her, his arms warm. Shame and guilt and pain rushed through her, making her feel small and friendless, adrift in a sea of wilderness.

When the rain grew heavier she allowed Darren to pull her to her feet and lead her back to the trail through the mountain plants, numb and wooden.

The return trip seemed to take no time at all, the icy rain leaching all feeling out of her face and hands. Darren kept looking at her with concern, but her ability to care had been snatched by the wind along with her screams.

Madison is going to tell the police.

The motorbike was where they'd left it. Eliza struggled to feel anything when she saw it.

Darren spun her around, facing her. 'Listen, Miss Ellis, I know it's cruel, but you might still be the only way we have to find those girls. You're a good person. It's not your fault they went missing.' She wished he'd stop, but he kept talking. 'You can't give up yet . . . stay with us —'

She looked up into his eyes. She struggled to focus. She looked back down.

He sighed and turned the ignition.

The motorbike roared into life, the sound of the engine blocking out the wind and the rain, warming her, a reminder of technology and civilisation, as they set off, back towards town, away from the wilderness.

All the while, Eliza thought of her niece.

And of what was to come.

CHAPTER 29

MURPHY

The dream was familiar enough by now that he could almost remember he was dreaming.

And he fell slower now, the foggy ground taking longer to reach him.

We're going to find you, Jasmine. We're going to find you.

He expected to see his daughter, waiting for him on the ground, but it wasn't her . . . It was his wife.

Sara stood, face upturned, hair tousled in the wind, laughing as she reached up for him. A lavender dress left her shoulders bare; her teeth flashed white, excitement in her eyes, as he crashed into her.

He jerked awake. He took a few heavy breaths, then rolled onto his side and stared into the darkness.

Later that morning, Murphy stood on the footpath outside his house, reading the profanity that had been marked into his front lawn with weed killer.

An old woman power-walked past: her daily exercise route. She slowed and pointedly looked at the words. She made a noise and glared at Murphy, before power-walking on.

'Well I didn't write it!' he shouted after her.

She just increased her pace.

Across the road were two parked cars: a police car, the cops inside watching Murphy, the second a journalist's, who stood there snapping photos of him. Murphy slowly scratched his balls, looking the man dead in the eye, then stalked back to the front door. He slammed the door shut behind him.

'Don't do any more damage to the bloody house,' muttered Butch, wearing his Blundstone boots to clean up the broken glass scattered across the kitchen floor, the window broken during the night by another brick. It seemed Madison's heartfelt video declaring his innocence hadn't convinced everyone.

Murphy threw himself into the couch. He looked at the TV and turned away. The TV had a hole in the middle of it: that had been Butch's foot.

Apparently last night, after Skinner had left, Butch had come inside to watch the 24-hour coverage, and yeah, he'd still been high on the angel dust, but he'd just become so enraged that he'd kicked in the TV screen. The latest development had surrounded Murphy – *'we don't sell weed to minors'* – and how he seemed to hold power over Madison Mason, enough to make her adamantly declare he had nothing to do with the disappearances.

Madison Mason . . . Murphy would usually never hurt a girl, but he wanted to throttle the little bitch.

His heart lifted. Sara had appeared in his dream. Did that mean she'd heard his prayer? Maybe.

Still, Madison was to blame. She had constructed this plan and *now his Jasmine was missing*. Or maybe she wasn't missing, just didn't want to be found.

Hope and fear mingled within him, making him even edgier. Where would she go? Her backpack presumably had the same gear as the ones at the Hut. So where would she set up camp, where would she think no one else would know to look?

It hit him. *Of course.* The crop.

She wasn't supposed to know where it was, but Murphy had always suspected Jasmine had followed them there, at least once.

He got off the couch and found his brother. 'Let's go check on the crop.'

'Bad idea, lad,' said Butch. 'The cops are watching.'

'Good. Let them. You know we'll lose them in the gully. And we have a right to walk through the bush if we want to.' He couldn't hide the excitement in his voice, but he didn't want to tell Butch the real reason.

'It's just adding fuel to the fire. If they catch you in the bush, they'll think you're off to bury the bodies or something,' said Butch. 'What's gotten into you, lad? Usually it's me wanting to do the risky shit.'

Murphy hadn't told Butch that Jasmine had intended to disappear. It was stupid, but there was always that sibling rivalry when it came to raising Jasmine. He wanted Butch to think he was a good dad, even though his daughter had captured the entire world's attention by . . . It'd come out sooner or later, but if he could find Jasmine today, then maybe it wouldn't be as bad . . .

And well, maybe, he wanted to protect Jasmine's reputation in Butch's eyes. He thought the sun shone out of his niece.

'Let's just go check the crop. I know it sounds stupid but . . . maybe Jasmine is there.'

'It's too risky. We've never been watched this closely.'

'Bro. *Jasmine* could be there.'

Butch threw his hands up and went to get changed.

———

Almost immediately after leaving their property, they were enveloped in scrub. Cool green dogwood and musk, and the *cak-cak-cak-cak* of a native hen. The sounds of the town were lost behind them as the ground rose, rocky and heady.

They climbed. The harsh cries of the native hen mixed with a forlorn-sounding kookaburra, a loner up high in the ghostly white gums. This whole place felt haunted – Murphy had always hated this walk as a kid, whenever Dad had made him hike up here when he was too lazy to check the crop himself. Dad had known how much it scared him, so it was one of his favourite punishments, other than belting the shit out of him.

Butch seemed to read Murphy's thoughts. 'What do you reckon Dad would tell us to do?' he said, voice hushed, subconsciously respectful of the sacred quiet of the bush.

'He'd probably be out here, night and day, looking for her,' said Murphy. 'A beer in one hand and the shotgun in the other.'

His mind flashed to the Glock now stashed in his bedside drawer.

'What about Sara?'

Murphy was silent for a moment. 'Don't know.'

They both bent down to all fours to scale a slope of scree, fingers in the slated rock.

'Wish she was here,' said Butch once they were at the top, upright and getting their breath back.

'Me too,' said Murphy. He wafted a spiderweb out of his way as they pushed through a copse of white gum and dogwood, a wallaby trail. Then: 'I dreamed about her last night.'

'Yeah? She say anything?' said Butch.

'Nothing.' Murphy's feet squelched over rotting gumtree bark, wet and slippery. 'Just smiled.'

'That's a good sign,' said Butch.

'Yeah,' said Murphy.

Another stretch of silence. A brown wren flitted onto a fallen branch, its yellow eye on Murphy.

'You're a strong man, Murph,' said Butch. 'I dunno if I've ever told you that.'

'I'm not,' said Murphy instantly. 'I'm weak as piss.' His voice caught. 'I fell apart after she died – you were there, you saw it. Everything went down the shitter. Lost the landscaping business, the house. I wasn't even there for Jasmine —'

'You have *always* been there for Jaz. Always,' said Butch. 'Don't say that. Every presentation night. Every netball training. Every bloody tantrum. Whenever she needed a chat you dropped everything. You were – shit, I don't know – you were there for her feelings. You're a bloody good dad, Murph.'

'I'm a drug dealer, Butch.'

Butch hesitated. 'Lad . . . it's only weed.'

They pushed through into a glade of myrtle beech – a faerie-land. The singing trickle of a mountain stream wending through the roots and blocks of dolomite, the bright-red fungus of strawberry bracket spreading over the beech trunks. A mountain dragon the size of a beer bottle clung to a rock, its wise, lazy eyes watching the brothers. Ferns tickled the edge of the glade, moving in a mountain-breeze dance.

They stopped. Murphy took breaths, tears threatening again. 'What am I gonna do, Butch? What am I gonna do if she doesn't come back?'

'She *will* come back. You saw Sara. I reckon that means she's sending Jasmine back to you. She can do shit like that. Talk to the Big Fella and bring Jasmine back.' Butch was always full of such certainty.

The itch in his throat was the only warning before the tears came, hot and fast. Butch grabbed his shoulders, hugging him. Murphy clutched his brother's broad back, fingers digging into his singlet, burying his head in Butch's bare shoulder, stinking of sweat and marijuana.

'I'm sorry, I'm sorry, I'm so sorry . . .' sobbed Murphy, apologising to Butch, apologising to Jasmine, apologising to Sara, apologising to God.

'Shhh, it's okay, lad. You're okay . . . We'll find her. I promise, mate. I promise. We'll find her . . .'

The myrtle beech rustled above, as though in consolation. The mountain dragon blinked its lazy eyes and looked away.

Before long they were in a gorge full of twisting King Billy Pine. Murphy's weary mind kept spinning back to the day Jasmine had gone missing. Especially the night before. The amnesia tickled at him – something Skinner told him had come trickling back now. *If I wasn't in the house that night . . . where was I?*

He stopped, but Butch shoved him forward. 'I said, don't *stop*.'

'What?' said Murphy.

Butch grabbed his shirt and dragged him on. 'Didn't you hear a word I said? There's someone following us. *Don't* turn around.'

'Cops?' said Murphy. He wasn't worried. He knew they could lose them.

'No. There's only one of them.'

Murphy nodded. 'The usual, then?'

They came to the head of the gorge and broke off to the right, where they came to a cave, the entrance fringed by ferns and spider-webs and fallen branches. It was a crack in one of the smaller cliffs that held up the escarpment.

Glancing around to check the coast was clear, they ducked inside.

It was dusty, dirty, muddy, secret. Dripping bonnet mushrooms poked out of the olive-green moss near the entrance.

They stepped over discarded beer cans to get to the back of the cave, dodging a family of skinks, running their fingers over their names still engraved in the back wall, and out the back exit.

Doubling back, they crept back up the hill and wriggled under a patch of ferns in the pines, from where they could see the main entrance to the cave. They didn't have to wait long: a weedy little man with a thin beard walked slowly up to the cave, dressed in patchy jeans and a blue woollen jumper.

'That's one of Doble's guys,' whispered Butch.

The man glanced around, then ducked inside the cave.

Butch and Murphy slithered out from their hiding place and each grabbed a heavy pine branch.

'Don't intervene, Murph,' said Butch, his voice full of a hardness Murphy hadn't heard in a long time. 'Let me handle this.'

'Butch?'

'I'm serious. You don't think Doble's the reason people are pinning this on you? Let's not give him anything.' He tightened his grip on the branch. 'It wouldn't surprise me if Doble was the one behind whatever's happened to Jasmine.'

'Butch . . .' said Murphy. He needed to tell Butch the truth about the girls' plan, sooner rather than later.

The weedy man came stumbling back out into the light, looking around, his cap dislodged.

His confusion turned to fear when he saw Murphy and Butch.

'Didn't find what you were looking for?' said Butch.

The man shrank back, raising his hands. 'Easy, fellas. I'm just out on a walk.'

'You were looking for our crop,' Butch said, walking forward. 'Doble sent you.'

The man stumbled back, feet slipping and falling on his backside. 'Don't touch me! He'll get you if you do!'

Butch growled, low in his throat. 'Fuck me, I'm tired of this.' He smacked the branch into his open palm and stood over the man. 'Tell Doble that the next man he sends will end up even worse than you.'

He slammed the branch into the man's face. His nose cracked and blood came pouring out. 'It won't happen again. I swear it,' he squealed, putting his hands to his face to stem the bleeding. 'I'll tell him!'

'That'll be hard with two broken legs.' Butch lifted the branch high over his head, but Murphy held him back.

'Butch,' he warned.

'Stay out of this, Murph.'

The man scrambled to his feet and raced off into the bush, blood on his shirt and running down his arms.

'What's *wrong* with you?' snarled Butch. He shoved Murphy away.

'You were actually going to break his legs.' Murphy stepped back. 'And how was he going to get back down after that? Were you going to carry him?'

Butch swung the branch underhand like a cricket bat. He couldn't bring himself to look at Murphy. 'You go check the crop. I'll stay here in case he comes back with some mates.'

'Butch,' warned Murph.

'Just *go*,' hissed Butch.

So Murphy went. A short distance away, through King Billy Pine so densely packed their corrugated trunks seemed to be kissing, were two massive dolomite boulders, leaning against each other to form a narrow passage. He leaned down to trigger a fishing line strung taut across the opening, then stepped back.

A 4.5 kilo sledgehammer, hidden in the ceiling crack of the two boulders, swung down with a *whoosh*, right where Murphy's chest would've been. He waited for it to still, then picked his way past it and down the short tunnel. He emerged onto a shelf of land about the size of a basketball court, which looked out over the steepest part of the gorge. Many years ago it had been laboriously cleared by Murphy's grandfather, Brandon Murphy Snr. Now the shelf was blocked off by pines and boulders, accessible only by the passage Murphy had walked through.

And here, in secrecy and solitude, a tall forest of marijuana plants reached into the sunlight, whispering in the wind. Dull green like Christmas trees, with the iconic seven-bladed leaves lush and healthy. A mountain stream trickled down and through the dug-out irrigation trenches.

The smell of the plants, the solitude, the sense of purpose and life – usually this place was a sacred escape for Murphy, where all the good things about cannabis seemed epitomised, where it was a symbol of a good life, lazy and under control and with money in the bank.

But not today.

'Jasmine? Are you here?'

Avoiding the bear traps scattered through it, Murphy ran along a row of plants, looking for any sign of Jasmine, her tent, her footprints. He came to the brink of the gorge and rested his hand against the trunk of a tree, peering over the small cliff, down into the dense gorge filled with foliage and fallen trees.

'Jasmine?' he called. 'Jasmine!'

There was no response but the rustling of the marijuana plants and the slow growth of the Tasmanian bush.

He called for a long time.

His only answer was bird call.

Walking back with Butch, Murphy's heart was as heavy as his footsteps. When they got home, Murphy stepped in the back door and kicked off his boots. Then he froze – he'd heard a girl's cough. Someone was in their house.

Murphy motioned to Butch and put a finger to his lips.

'What now . . .?'

Murphy ignored him and crept up to Jasmine's bedroom door. Footsteps creaked on the floorboards inside.

'Jasmine?' croaked Murphy, and opened the door.

A terrified shriek answered as a teenage girl leapt off Jasmine's bed, thin and dark-haired. Jasmine's photo albums lay open on the bed.

'*Carmen?*' Murphy croaked. He knew her from Jasmine's class. She'd come over a few times for sleepovers, and was one of Jasmine's closer friends outside the Fab Four.

The girl swallowed and nodded her head.

'Why are you here?' shouted Murphy.

'A while back . . . Jasmine showed me the spare key,' whimpered Carmen, quailing before Murphy's anger.

'*Why* are you here?' Murphy stepped out of the room, gesturing for her to leave, struggling to force his temper back under control. 'Can you get out of my house, please? You'll only get me in more trouble.'

'That's why I'm here.'

'No.' He walked through the dining room, opening the front door wide. 'You need to leave.'

'Please, Mr Murphy.' Carmen followed him but stopped short of the door. 'I know you didn't take the girls. I know you're not what everyone is saying.'

'I need you to *go!*' He didn't mean to roar the last word and regretted the way it made her squeal and jump back. But he kept his hand on the handle of the open door.

'You heard him,' said Butch, leaning against the doorway. He folded his arms and stood taller.

'No,' said Carmen shakily. 'I have something to tell you . . . I-I know who Cierra was sleeping with . . .'

'Then you need to go tell the police, not me,' said Murphy. 'Please, leave before someone sees you here.'

'The condoms were just . . . just a bit of a joke, I think . . .'

'*Go.*'

'I know you weren't sleeping with Cierra because she . . . well, because . . . *Cierra was sleeping with Miss Ellis!*'

There was a moment of silence. Murphy's hand dropped off the door handle.

Butch slipped where he was leaning against the doorway, swearing loudly.

Murphy's mouth opened and shut. 'That . . . doesn't make any sense. Eliza isn't . . . she's not a . . . is she?'

'Cierra is not straight,' said Carmen firmly. 'Cierra and Miss Ellis were . . .'

'This is bloody perfect,' said Butch. 'We need to go down to the station. You'll tell the detective this, won't you?'

Carmen nodded quickly. 'Yeah. Of course.'

'No,' said Murphy suddenly.

'Sorry?' said Butch.

'We're not telling the cops.'

'Why the fuck not?' shouted Butch.

'Eliza couldn't have taken the girls,' he said. 'She had that blow to the back of the head. She *couldn't* have done it. And I don't believe for a second that she's . . . that she'd —'

'Sleep with another chick?' said Butch.

'Sleep with a *student*,' said Murphy. 'She's a good person. A good teacher.'

'That detective needs to know! And it'll take the heat off you —'

'Exactly!' shouted Murphy above Butch's increasing volume. 'You've seen what they did to me. If this comes out about Eliza, she'll be lynched in the streets —'

'So she fucking should,' shouted Butch. 'And they'll leave you alone!'

'No, Butch . . . This . . . this is my decision to make.' Murphy leaned forward so his face was level with Carmen. 'I need you to promise not to tell anyone else.'

'How the hell is this *your* decision to make?' said Butch. 'This is Carmen's decision!'

'But you don't deserve all this horrible stuff they're saying!' said Carmen.

Murphy's face was unchanged. 'I'll go talk to Miss Ellis. But you're not to tell anyone else. Okay? Promise me.'

Carmen gripped his hands. 'That's not all. Madison wanted me to give you this.'

'Madison sent you over here?' said Murphy, pulling his hands out of hers, feeling suddenly cold.

'She wanted you to know about Miss Ellis —' began Carmen.

'Madison *told* you to tell me?' said Murphy. '*What else has she said?*'

'Just about Miss Ellis, and that she wanted you to have this.' Carmen fished a USB drive out of her pocket.

Murphy took the USB drive but held it away from himself like it was another tiger snake.

'Murph, you *need* to tell the cops,' said Butch.

Murphy glanced at the driveway, then at the USB. *Anything that little witch says is lies and poison. Whatever is on this USB is just something to help her get her way. I won't be part of her game – I don't believe for a second that Eliza slept with Cierra, but I need to go warn her.*

He put the USB in his pocket. 'I'm taking the Hilux and I'm going to speak to Eliza. Carmen, promise me you won't tell anyone else.'

Carmen shrugged. 'I guess. Unless Madison tells me to – Cierra's her sister, after all. But —'

Murphy had already grabbed the Hilux keys off the hook and was walking out the door.

CHAPTER 30

ELIZA

Eliza sat on a stool in Tom and Monica's kitchen, showered and warm. She had a new red headscarf around her temple and her golden hoops in her ears. She was drinking white wine straight out of the bottle and staring out the bay window, watching the wind in a maple tree.

It had been an hour since she'd returned from the mountains. Monica was at Tom's mother's house with Wren. Tom himself was volunteering up at the search around Lake Mackenzie. Sarge the dog was locked in the backyard: she didn't want him getting in the way when the police came.

On the counter were a line of three post-it notes.

I give permission for Eliza Ellis to do what is necessary to protect her niece.
Signed, E. Ellis

I give permission for Eliza Ellis to not lose hope.
Signed, E. Ellis

I give permission for Eliza Ellis to be the strongest version of herself.
Signed, E. Ellis.

She was thinking about the moment Madison had approached her, only weeks ago, with her plan. She'd come into the staff room during lunch, bold and smirking, and in front of all the other teachers she'd asked Eliza to go speak somewhere privately. Then, huddled in the car park, she'd told Eliza that on the camp Madison and Jasmine would stage a fight, and then Eliza would keep the four girls behind after the rest had left.

She left Eliza no choice. 'If you don't, I'll tell everyone the truth about who Cierra was sleeping with . . .'

That's all she'd said, but it was enough for Eliza.

I have permission to not lose hope.

She hadn't been there for Denni. It all came back to that. Denni had been Eliza's treasure, a chance to take what the world had refused to give. Eliza wanted to do for Denni what hadn't been done for her, or for Monica, or for Kiera. But after everything Eliza had done, Denni had still killed herself. Nothing would be good in the world ever again. She'd tried to protect Wren, but she'd failed at that too.

Back in the present, heavy fists thumped on the door.

Alright, here we go.

She left the bottle on the counter and walked to the front door. She opened it and then hastily stepped back as Murphy forced himself inside, his teeth a white grimace in his dark beard.

'Murphy! Wha— Why are you here?' She looked past him, expecting to see a police car, but it was only Butch's Hilux.

Murphy glanced around the room, then turned his eyes on her. Those eyes were sharp and clear, and with the wine and the emotion and the fear, mixed with the breadth of his shoulders and the set of his jaw, Eliza found him suddenly extremely attractive.

He grabbed her arms and pulled her face close to his. She squeaked, and his eyes looked between hers, and then he forced his mouth onto hers. Her own eyes widened, and for a moment she didn't know what to do. Then she bit his lip – hard – and drove her knee up into his groin.

He groaned and lurched away, bending over with his hands between his legs.

She kicked him in the shin and then punched him repeatedly in the shoulders. 'How *dare* you!' She kept hitting him, wondering if she could pummel him out of the door. 'You disgusting, *horrible* —'

'I had to know,' he moaned, still doubled over. 'You never . . . came across as a lesbian.'

'*Excuse me?*' She gripped his hair and pulled his head back so she could look him in the face. She couldn't believe she'd had the *audacity* to be attracted to him moments earlier. 'First, *how dare you?*' She pulled his face closer to hers, finding pain and uncertainty there. 'Second, what *possibly* makes you think my sexuality is any of your business? And third, *you think you can tell someone's sexuality just by kissing them?*' She grabbed his beard now and wrenched his face even closer to hers. 'I could be heterosexual, homosexual, bisexual, *pansexual* – kissing me would tell you *absolutely nothing.*'

He groaned.

'To think that I've been *defending you* . . .'

'That's what Madison is telling everyone.' He held her wrist to keep her from pulling more of his beard out. 'You and Cierra. I never believed it.'

Eliza didn't let go of his beard. 'Exactly what has she told you?'

'She sent Carmen —'

'What did she *say?*'

'That you and Cierra have been sleeping together.'

Eliza looked down into his eyes. She didn't move, didn't say a word. Her hand slipped through his beard and fell to her side.

Of course.

When Madison had come into the room that night, all she'd seen was a scantily clad Cierra and Eliza in her dressing gown. Eliza had assumed Cierra would've explained the truth to her sister later, but in fact . . .

That night Cierra had called Eliza, afraid, because Tom had passed out in her bed. Eliza had pulled herself out of bed in a rush, driven across town, and climbed up the trellis to Cierra's window. The two of them had managed to get the very drunk Tom to the window, where he had dropped down into the thick conifer hedge below. The crash had woken the Masons' dog, Mr Bruiser, who had then brought Madison bursting into Cierra's room. She drew the wrong conclusion, apparently.

Now she faced a choice . . . No, of course she had to come clean about Tom. But what would happen if she did that?

Tom gets blamed for the disappearance, even though he didn't do it. The girls don't get found.

Monica hates me. I lose my sister.

Wren hates me. Her dad loses everything.

I don't care. I don't care! I'm not taking the fall for him!

'It isn't true, is it?' demanded Murphy, standing upright unsteadily, his hand hovering protectively over his groin. 'I haven't told the police. I don't believe it. I told Carmen not to tell anyone, but who knows what Madison will do. This is all part of her publicity stunt, isn't it?'

'Carmen was going to tell the police?'

'Yes.'

'And you stopped her? Why?'

'They'd crucify you,' said Murphy, rubbing his chin beneath his beard. 'They were going to kill me, imagine what they'd do to you.'

More loud knocking came at the door. 'Eliza? Open up, please,' came Con's voice.

Eliza and Murphy turned to the door as one. They stepped closer to each other.

'I didn't tell them, I swear,' whispered Murphy. 'You can run. I'll stall them.'

Eliza laughed, but there was no humour in it. 'Run? Are you serious?'

'Eliza,' called Con. 'We need to talk.'

She walked forward and opened the door.

Con stepped in, his shirtsleeves rolled up. He looked stressed. He was followed by a woman who flashed her badge and ID card at Eliza, identifying her as Detective Melinda Tran.

Con frowned at Murphy. 'What are you doing here?'

'Visiting a friend,' Murphy said. 'What are *you* doing here?'

'Eliza, we need you to come down to the station.'

'What's this about?' she asked.

'Madison's latest video: I'm not sure if it's been uploaded to her channels yet, but she sent it to the police station fifteen minutes ago.' His hands were clenched into fists. 'And also, I think, to every major media outlet. Take a guess, Eliza: what do you think the video is about?'

Shouting sounded outside and then Tom burst into the house, breaking one of the glass panels of the door as he slammed it open. His immense muscular bulk loomed in the entryway, his large jaw muddied as though he'd fallen. His eyes were wide, the guilt and remorse painfully obvious.

'Eliza?' Tom looked between the detectives, lingered on Murphy for a moment, and then to her. 'I just heard. Madison has shared it all over Facebook.'

Eliza felt a surge of relief. Tom was here to confess. He'd take the decision out of her hands.

He took her up in a big hug and turned to the police. 'She's not saying another word until she has her lawyer. Her relationship with Cierra has nothing to do with this.'

Detective Tran turned her dark eyes back on Eliza. 'Miss Ellis, if you please?'

Eliza's relief had deflated in Tom's squeezing arms, but she kept her spine straight.

'Remember Wren, please,' whispered Tom in her ear.

'Don't say a word,' said Murphy into the other.

Eliza walked, tall and proud, down to the waiting patrol car. Ignoring the journalists, she climbed into the back seat, pulling her phone from her pocket. She saw the missed calls and texts from concerned friends and family – Monica and Tom included. She ignored all of them, opening YouTube.

As the car pulled away from her house, the media snapping photos in through the window, Eliza watched Madison's latest video.

Madison sat in her usual spot, in front of her bed. She was wearing the same green jacket as at the hospital: she looked stunning, the perfect mourning internet icon.

'I have something to confess to you all . . . something I was not fully honest about before . . . I know who my sister, Cierra, was having sex with.'

Madison took a deep, shaky breath.

'Cierra is loving. Incredibly loving. She builds relationships faster than anyone else I know. With friends, family . . . teachers.

'I should've known from the start. I mean, Miss Ellis has always been closer to us than any other teacher . . . after her niece died last year – Denni King, you all remember – we became even closer. We'd lost a friend, but she'd lost a family member. I didn't know at the time, but . . . Cierra and Miss Ellis began to comfort each other . . .

'Now, I'm not a homophobe. Cierra is free to love whoever she wants to love . . . but I can't sit back and let people like Jack Michaels and Mr Murphy take the blame when the one who was

sleeping with my sister was Miss Eliza Ellis. And . . . if you needed
any more proof . . . here's Cierra herself.'

The scene cut to another face: identical but in a different part of the
room, different make-up, wearing a violet wig. Eliza knew, though. It
wasn't Cierra, it was just Madison trying to look like Cierra.

'. . . I love her. And I know she loves me. Maybe it won't last, but
isn't this the time to experiment? Miss Ellis makes me feel happier
than I've ever felt . . .' said Cierra/Madison. 'Why should that be
anyone's business but my own?'

Eliza turned her phone off.

How could she fight that? How could she convince people that
Madison was pretending to be Cierra?

And if she did . . . what would happen to Wren? Everything
always came back to her. She felt deeply, deeply exhausted.

Eliza sat at a metal table in one of the station's interview rooms, the
fluoro lights sparking the beginnings of a headache at the back of
her skull. Tom had arranged and paid for a lawyer – an old, thin-
faced woman called Rosalie – who sat beside her, lips pursed.

Detective Melinda Tran sat across from them, taking her jacket
off, eyes dark and foreboding. She was alone.

'Have you had sexual relations with Cierra Mason?' said
Detective Tran, her lips pressed in a hard line.

'I think she needs a moment,' said Rosalie.

'I'm afraid she's had long enough,' said Detective Tran.

'Eliza, dear, you are going to need to answer them – just tell them
the truth,' said Rosalie.

The truth . . .?

You have permission to be strong.

'Yes.' Eliza had to force herself to say it. 'Yes, I have.'

'What? Eliza, did you understand the question?' said Rosalie.

'I think she understood the question perfectly,' said Detective Tran. 'How long has this been going on? Who else knew?'

'I don't know. No one.'

'Did you conspire to have Cierra kidnapped?' said Detective Tran.

'Of course not.'

'Then who do the condoms belong to? The marijuana?'

'The weed is mine. The condoms were from my last fling.'

'With a man?' said Detective Tran.

'Obviously.'

'You identify as bisexual?'

'That is not pertinent,' hissed Rosalie.

'You've had no sexual relations with women before this?' said Tran.

'No – I mean, yes, I have . . .'

'How is this relevant?' demanded Rosalie.

'We are still building a profile for the kidnapper, including sexual appetite. What other women have you slept with, Miss Ellis?'

'I haven't.'

'So Cierra *was* the first girl you had sex with? You lied?' said Detective Tran.

Eliza looked away. It was getting hard to speak. She felt claustrophobic.

I am a good person! she wanted to shriek.

'We need to know,' Tran continued, leaning forward. 'We have three girls still missing, and you're the last adult in contact, and you were sleeping with *at least* one of them. Now that we can see some motive . . . Did you find Bree attractive? Jasmine?' She paused. 'Georgia?'

'Detective, I don't think that's a reasonable line of questioning,' said Rosalie.

'I didn't take the girls,' said Eliza.

'You were the only one with them on that mountain,' said Detective Tran. '*What* was it about Cierra that attracted you?'

'This is *completely* inappropriate,' said Rosalie.

'Well, Miss Ellis?' said Detective Tran. 'No answer?' She tapped her long lacquered fingernails on the table. 'Then the next question is going to be very uncomfortable for you. Remember, this is all being recorded and transcribed, so please be very specific and explicit: what *exactly* did you and the *very underage* Cierra Mason, your student, who trusted you, do during your sexual encounters?'

'This is ridiculous!' cried Rosalie.

Eliza quietly agreed. The questioning was offensive, unnecessarily vulgar.

And then, in a crashing instant, Eliza realised why.

These questions were not trying to draw anything out of her: they were designed only to put her off balance, to make her misspeak, to find flaws in her story.

She doesn't believe me. She doesn't believe I was with Cierra.

She had a brief moment of relief, followed by outrage – *how dare she* – followed by unease.

She glanced up at the camera. This wasn't Detective Tran's idea. She thought of Con's deep blue eyes, back in the hospital room on that first day: his knowing gaze, his attempt to make her uncomfortable, to draw truth out of her.

Con knows I'm covering for Tom.

CHAPTER 31

CON

On the monitor, Con watched Eliza make eye-contact with the camera. *She knows we're on to her,* he thought.

'What do you see, Cornelius?' said Commander Agatha Normandy from her seat beside him. She had arrived from Hobart an hour before and quickly made herself at home. She was a short woman, with a bob of grey hair, and wore a woollen cardigan. She sipped a cup of tea, her lipstick not marking the china.

'She's covering for someone,' said Con. 'My guess is her brother-in-law, Tom North.'

'Melinda is doing well, isn't she?' said Commander Normandy offhand. 'It's an unusual line of questioning, and a rather specific style: almost like she was coached by someone before she went in there.' She turned her eyes on Con and sipped her tea. 'Why is it hard for you to believe Eliza could have been sleeping with Cierra Mason?'

'I don't know, maybe because she can't answer Tran's questions quickly? Maybe because she doesn't seem that upset by the questioning?'

Maybe just because it's too left-field. In a case like this, something has to be normal – the steroid-fuelled gym teacher *has to be more likely to hook up with a student than the orphaned English teacher with the dead niece.*

'Unfortunately we have no proof of that,' said Agatha, as though she could hear his thoughts. 'Besides, your male intuition and the way you've coached Tran both presuppose a particular conclusion. Eliza isn't here to defend a suspicion: she's confessed. Madison made the allegation and Eliza has admitted to sleeping with Cierra,' said Agatha. 'As with Cierra's own video confession, we need to take this seriously, and that means Miss Eliza Ellis has just become suspect number one.'

She inclined her head and turned her tea cup where it stood on the desk.

'However, I agree that . . . it doesn't *feel* right. But that doesn't constitute evidence . . . Unfortunately . . .' She lifted her tea, holding the cup close to her mouth. 'You know, I really don't like that this was all brought about by Madison Mason. If she orchestrated this whole disappearance, any videos she puts out – any information – must have a certain aim. What I would like to know is what she's hoping to achieve by shifting our scrutiny onto Eliza Ellis.'

'Then I should go speak with Madison,' said Con, relishing the thought.

'Not yet. I forbid it,' said Agatha. 'She must be handled very delicately from now on, which you'll leave to me. And I don't want a *whiff* of her planning this whole thing getting out to the public yet. We need that to be handled carefully too.' She put her finished cup of tea on the table. 'And another thing. Carl Lenah still hasn't been found.'

Con shook his head. 'It would be good to tie up the loose end, but we need everyone working where they're most useful. I think we can safely rule him out. From what we can tell, he and his family are just deeply suspicious of police.'

'I agree. If he surfaces before this all blows over, we'll talk to him, but let's not make a big deal of it. If we handle *him* wrong, it only reinforces Madison's narrative.' She glanced at her watch. 'Speaking of which – the commissioner has asked to speak to me about that video of you and Gabriella.'

She patted Con on the shoulder as she left the room.

Con looked back at the screen. Eliza Ellis. 'Why are you protecting him? *Are* you protecting Tom?' he murmured. He tapped the table with his fingertips.

Finally, the first part of the interview was over and Melinda Tran walked out.

Eliza sat alone with her lawyer. Neither of them was speaking. The lawyer had angled herself away from Eliza and was very red in the cheeks.

Eliza stared up at the camera, a tiny frown behind her glasses.

'Good job,' said Con when Tran entered. 'What do you think?'

'I think you're right: she's trying to cover for someone else,' said Tran. 'She's not as good an actress as she thinks she is. What next?'

'Get Detective Coops to bring Murphy in for a chat. He should ask nicely, but without giving Murphy the option of saying no. He was there at the house with Eliza before we arrived: I want to know why.' Con returned his eyes to the screen. 'Meanwhile . . . Monica and Tom North are waiting to see Eliza. I say we let them have a chat, but somewhere they can be overheard. Then, afterward . . . how do you feel about teachers, Tran? I think Mr North needs someone to vent to about his sister-in-law's betrayal.'

'I'll offer him a shoulder to cry on,' said Tran with a wicked smile. 'Let's see if he's a better actor than her.' She left the room, her high heels clicking.

Con watched the monitor a bit longer, studying Eliza, thinking about his plan of attack for when he spoke to her himself.

The door opened and the young Constable Cavanagh stepped in, her face flushed. 'Detective Badenhorst? I have a phone call for you, from . . . Pastor Hugh. Sorry, this is my personal phone. He called my number . . .' She held out her phone to Con. 'You need to hear what he has to say, but . . . keep it in this room. Don't tell anyone else from this station.'

The pastor! He'd completely forgotten. That wasn't a good sign. He took the phone from Cavanagh and, beginning with a profuse apology, listened to what the pastor had to say.

CHAPTER 32

MURPHY

Murphy pounded the steering wheel as he drove home from Eliza's. He ignored the journalists outside his house and ran inside, slamming the door behind him.

'Have you seen it?' said Butch, excited, his laptop open on the table. 'Madison put up a new video —'

'I don't wanna see it,' said Murphy. 'Eliza wasn't sleeping with Cierra and you know it. Let me use the laptop – I'm gonna look at this USB of Madison's, maybe there'll be something on there I can take to Con to help Eliza.'

'We're calling him *Con* now?' said Butch. 'What, are you two mates?'

'Shut up, dickhead.' Murphy shoved the USB drive into the port of Butch's laptop.

The drive held a folder named 'Jasmine's Footage' and a text file entitled 'Read Me First'.

Jasmine's Footage. Murphy's heart began to pound in his head. *Don't get excited. Madison can't be trusted . . .*

He opened the text file and began reading:

Mr Murphy,

*I know you probably hate me, and I understand. I would if
I were you.*

*I promise I don't know where Jasmine is. And I don't
know what happened to Georgia, or why Bree's backpack
was still at the Fisherman's Hut. But if Jasmine's and Cierra's
backpacks are gone, I know that they're safe. I'm sure of it.*

*I think it'd be good for you to understand why Jasmine chose
to be part of this, why she chose to disappear for six months. Why
she played along with my plan. Here's all the footage I have of her.*

If you share this footage with anyone else, I'll end you.

Once you see what's in the folder, you'll realise that I can.

Start with video #1.

Lots of Love,

Madison xoxo

The drive held six numbered MP4 files.

'What is it?' said Butch.

Disappear for six months . . .

'I'll be in my room,' said Murphy, taking the laptop down the
hallway and ignoring Butch's protest.

He made sure the worn door was firmly closed and sat on his
bed, the springs squeaking. He clicked open the first video.

It was Jasmine. She was sitting on Madison's bed. Her make-up
was heavy, her shoulders back, and she had been crying.

Murphy leaned forward, resting a hand on the screen.

'. . . and that's why I got with Jack,' she said. 'He was strong,
and caring, and he made me feel safe. He loves me. For the longest
time I wasn't sure if . . . if I was worthy of love. If I could trust
another man —'

'And why was that, Jasmine?' came Madison's voice from
behind the camera.

Jasmine looked at something above the camera for a moment. She shrugged uncomfortably. 'Well, I guess you could say my father raped my mum, right?' Her lips trembled. 'That's how I was conceived: my father raped my mum.'

The video ended.

Murphy heard a buzzing in his head and the edges of his vision went blurry.

My father raped my mum . . .

'I didn't rape her,' he whispered. 'I've never done anything – I never *would* do anything like that.'

But of course, the thoughts came. *Did I? Did I have consent? Did she . . . did I come on too strong?*

He hadn't. He was sure he hadn't. He was almost 100 per cent sure he hadn't . . . they'd had sex plenty of times . . . of course, Sara had fallen pregnant very young . . .

Did she only marry me because she was scared of me?

And that's when he caught sight of his hunting jacket, the unexplained tear in the arm. He'd been wearing it the night of the angel dust. He'd been wearing it the morning of Jasmine's disappearance. The night he couldn't account for.

If you raped Sara without knowing it . . . what else might you have done without knowing it?

This was a real thought, churning in his mind. And in a way it was the same thought that had been churning ever since he'd found Jasmine was missing – he *didn't* know where he'd been at the time that she disappeared.

But he'd convinced himself that no matter what Skinner said about angel dust, he doubted it could've taken him from his backyard all the way up to the track where she'd been taken, without him even being aware of it. But . . . was it possible there was something dark within him? Something that he didn't even know about? That the drugs had snapped something within him, unleashed some hidden demon?

That's not how drugs work, he thought angrily.

'Murphy?' came Butch's voice from behind the door. 'The cops are here for you.'

Murphy rushed to the door – he hadn't heard sirens or even knocking. 'Have they found something?' he croaked.

Butch shrugged. 'They're in the kitchen.'

Murphy ran down the hall.

Two uniformed policemen and a detective stood there: the detective he'd seen up at the car park the first day of Jasmine's disappearance.

'Who are you?' he asked the detective.

'Detective Stuart Coops. Would you mind coming down the station with us?'

'What's this about?'

'Detective Badenhorst wants a word with you,' said Coops.

'And he couldn't do it here?'

'He's busy. Come on, I'll give you a ride.'

'And if I refuse?' said Murphy, fists curled. He felt the anger starting to rise. His mind kept spinning back to the video, Jasmine's damning confession, that hunting jacket . . .

'I'll still be giving you a ride to the station,' said Coops. 'Come on, mate. This way is much nicer for both of us. Sooner we go, the sooner you can come back.'

Murphy ignored Butch, who was hissing under his breath, trying to get his attention, and walked out the door with Coops and the other policeman.

He pushed his anger down. He'd go see what Con had to say.

I didn't rape your mum, Jasmine.

I know I didn't.

Please come back to me.

Murphy walked up the front steps of the police station with Detective Coops in front of him and the other two policemen behind. Media crowded the steps, shouting questions at him.

'Mr Murphy! Do you have anything to say?'

'Was Eliza Ellis sleeping with Jasmine, too?'

'Were you and Eliza seeing each other?'

'How disgusted are you that a local teacher —'

Inside the station was another crowd of people, some that he recognised from the community. At the sight of him, their phone cameras came out.

Tom North leapt out of a chair and planted himself in front of him. 'Murphy, you have to confess,' he said urgently. 'Admit what you did. Tell them you took the girls —'

'Excuse me, mate.' Detective Coops pushed Tom roughly out of the way, leading Murphy down a long corridor and into the same interview room as before.

Waiting at the table was Con Badenhorst. He took in everything about Murphy in a single glance. 'Take a seat.'

'I'll wait in the office, Con,' said Coops, as he closed the door behind him.

Murphy took a seat, perched on the edge of the chair. 'What's going on?'

'How are you feeling?' said Con. 'After last night, after what happened with Jack?'

'As if you care how I'm feeling. Why have you brought me here? To interrogate me some more?' demanded Murphy. 'My lawyer's gone back to Hobart, but one phone call and Dave will be right back here.'

'I'm not here to interrogate you. I just want your advice. You were there last night,' said Con. 'You heard what Jack said: Madison planned it. You're not on my list of suspects anymore, Murphy.'

Murphy hesitated, studying Con's face. 'So why am I here?'

'Obviously something went wrong with Madison's plan. Georgia is dead, Bree didn't take her backpack from the Fisherman's Hut either, whereas Jasmine and Cierra's bags were missing. That makes me think those two *did* get to the Fisherman's Hut, but maybe someone took them afterwards. But who? And why? Or *are* they just hiding somewhere? Is Bree?'

He shrugged expansively.

'But you were with Eliza today. So can you help me make sense of this new wildcard: the allegation that Eliza was sleeping with Cierra. Do *you* believe it?'

'Not for a second,' said Murphy instantly. Remembering a twinge of pain in his balls from Eliza's knee, he quickly added, 'Not that I know anything about her sexuality. She could be bi, for all I know. And that would be okay! I mean, sleeping with a student is not okay. But, you know, she can sleep with whoever else she wants. But she wouldn't sleep with a student. I don't know what her sexuality is —'

'Okay, okay,' said Con, raising his hand. 'But you were at her house earlier. Why?'

Murphy considered lying, but made a split-second decision to be honest with Con. 'Madison sent someone to tell me she was sleeping with Cierra. I wanted to warn Eliza – I knew she'd get crucified.'

Con studied Murphy. 'Are you aware that Eliza has admitted it?'

'*What?* Bullshit.'

'For what it's worth, I agree. I think she's protecting someone, and it may be whoever's taken the girls. If that someone is not *you*, then I don't know who it is.'

'It's not me,' said Murphy firmly. 'I would never sleep with an underage girl.'

He heard Jasmine's voice in his head: 'My father raped my mum.'

Shut up. No I didn't, he thought back fiercely.

'Everything about this case has changed, Murphy,' said Con, looking away, studying the wall. 'They *planned* to disappear. So I have to ask: do you *really* think Jasmine would willingly cut herself off? Her phone, the internet, all media? Her family?'

Murphy had a brief flash of defensive anger. 'No.' Then he slumped back in his seat with a long sigh. 'Yes. She honestly could. She's stubborn – if she decided she didn't want to hear or read anything, she would make it happen. Once, in Year 7, she threw her phone and laptop in the river because she wanted to go without social media for a month. She went vegan for almost a year just because Butch told her she wouldn't be able to handle it for even a week. She doesn't do things by halves. She takes after her uncle in that way. Is this seriously what you brought me in for?'

'No,' said Con. 'I had a very interesting phone call from Pastor Hugh earlier. He said he had information about Sergeant Doble, but wanted me to come to the church to meet with him. Given what you've told me about the sergeant, I thought you might want to come along.'

'Are you saying you're taking *my* word over another cop's?' said Murphy.

'I'm saying I want you to come with me to church and see what you make of the pastor's information.'

Murphy hesitated, then glanced up at the ceiling. *God, if Jasmine disappearing is just Your sneaky way of getting me back to church, I'm going to be extremely fucking pissed.*

CHAPTER 33

CON

The Limestone Creek Baptist Church sat alone on a rise, a lawn cemetery around the back. There was a brick chapel with stained-glass windows and a steeple, but attached to the side was a more modern, flat building built out of rendered brick.

Con knocked on the glass entrance of that building, peering inside at the carpeted hallway. When no one answered, he pushed the door open and walked in. Murphy trailed behind, eyeing the walls like they were going to fall down.

The plaster walls of the long corridor were lined with posters and framed photos, as well as bumps and scratches. It smelled like a church always smells – of sanctity and paper and food. It instantly took Con back to the church at his Catholic school.

'Hello?' he called. 'Anyone here?'

A door in the hallway opened, and Con expected a good-natured grandmother to emerge, an apron around her waist, inviting him into a kitchen for a cuppa and a chat. Instead a giant bear of a man stepped out, bald with a thick greying beard and grey grizzled eyebrows.

'Bloody hell,' muttered Con, taking a step back before he could stop himself. The man was at least six foot five.

'Detective Badenhorst?' The man reached out a paw to shake Con's hand. 'Peter Hugh. Good of you to make it. Glad to see you've stopped dodging my attempts to make contact.' Con now recognised the pastor from one of the search parties one the day of the disappearance. He was thick in the chest and arms, and wore a blue short-sleeve button-up and jeans, with faded naval tattoos down both arms.

'I promise you it wasn't intentional.'

Hugh's face creased into a smile. 'You know, I believe you. Sometimes timing is Divinely appointed.'

A thin-faced man with grey skin appeared from the same doorway as the pastor. 'There's a detective?' he whined.

'He's not here for you, Wes,' said the pastor over his shoulder. To Con, he said, 'Listen, I'm having a counselling session with a friend. We're just wrapping up. Sorry to keep you waiting, but I'll be with you in a tick.'

'Nah, I'll get going, Pastor Pete,' whined Wes, slinking towards the back door.

'Don't you dare,' growled Hugh. 'Get your arse back in there.' He turned back to Con and Murphy. 'Give me a minute.' He followed Wes into his office and shut the door.

Murphy paced the corridor, running his hand through his beard, up on his toes like he was about to run. Con took a seat on one of the chairs outside the pastor's door, fascinated, picking up the conversation.

'He's a copper,' whined Wes.

'Yeah, mate, but he's not here for you,' said Hugh. 'He's here about the girls.'

'He'll smell it on me.'

'Then don't go kissing him and it'll be fine. Now, when we meet next week, what are you gonna have done?'

Wes mumbled something.

'What was that?' prompted Hugh.

'I'm going to have cut back to just one a day.'

'And?'

'And I'm gonna call you if I feel tempted.'

'I'll hold you to that. Now, are you gonna pray, or am I?'

After a moment, Wes muttered, 'I will, I guess . . .'

'How do you know the pastor?' Con whispered to Murphy.

'This is Limestone Creek,' said Murphy. 'Everyone knows everyone.'

'Liar,' said Con. Murphy didn't respond.

The door to the office opened and both men walked out. 'And no kissing Detective Badenhorst on your way out,' called Hugh loudly.

Wes flinched and scurried to the door.

Hugh winked at Con. 'He's a good man. God's got a big plan for him. Now, gents, please come into my office.'

Inside, posters of motorcycles and mountains covered the walls, the bookcase was overflowing, but the desk was empty save for a laptop and a thermos.

Con took a seat opposite Hugh's desk, his eyes taking in everything at once. Murphy remained standing. On his side of the desk, Hugh steepled his fingers and peered down at them. 'Alright. Let me pray to begin with.' He bowed his head.

Con, nodding, bowed his head.

'Relax, mate, I was joking, just trying to break the ice,' laughed Hugh.

Con shrugged. 'Our father, who art in Heaven, hallowed be thy name . . .' said Con, finishing the Lord's Prayer solemnly.

'Amen,' said Hugh slowly. Con caught his eye, and Hugh raised a thick eyebrow, then closed his eyes. 'Okay then, my turn: Papa God, thanks for today, thanks for bringing Detective Badenhorst here today, and our good friend Murphy. I pray You give Detective

Badenhorst guidance and strength during this investigation, and that You keep him safe from stress and anxiety, compassion fatigue, and anything else that might come with his job, such as post-traumatic stress . . .'

Con glanced up suddenly, but Hugh, eyes closed, kept praying.

'. . . also, Lord, please help us find these girls, help Con find the sick and twisted soul who took them and bring them to justice. Be with those girls, Lord. You love them more than we do; You care about them more than we do. Right now, in this conversation, let Your Holy Spirit guide my words and Con's mind so that he can . . .'

Con's eyes trailed over the spines on the bookshelf, catching on one particular tome: *Stress Disorders*. He saw, for the first time, a framed degree on the wall, in golden tint. *Masters in Counselling and Psychotherapy*.

'And be with Murphy. You love him, Lord. Let him know and feel that. Let him take comfort in You, even in this horribly shitty time. Amen.'

Con was shocked a pastor would swear. Murphy gave an annoyed sort of grunt.

Hugh reached behind his desk, there was the clink of glass, and he pulled out three bottles of ginger beer from what seemed to be a small bar fridge.

'Let me guess,' he said to Con. 'Catholic?'

Con nodded as he accepted a bottle, but left it unopened on the table. 'Catholic school. And my parents.'

'Great,' said Hugh. He studied Con, his eyes like cameras, recording his every move and twitch. Con shifted in his seat. Was this what it felt like when he did this to other people?

'Can you tell me why you wanted me to come here?' he asked. 'You said on the phone you had something important to tell me.'

Hugh drank from his ginger beer. 'Straight to the point, then?' He tapped his chin for a moment, as though collecting his thoughts.

'Well, before we begin, I want you to understand that we have more than just a Sunday service here. We have ministries throughout the week, including a Men's Group, but I also offer one-on-one counselling. Men like Wes come here during the week and we work some stuff out together.'

He gestured towards his degree and accreditation hanging on the wall.

'Now, there's one client I'm seeing at the moment. A man who's . . . quite lost. Usually I am stringent on confidentiality, but in the circumstances I *can* tell you: Sergeant Doble is a client. Since you've brought Murphy along, I suppose you're aware of Sergeant Doble's cannabis trade?'

'So it is true?' said Con. 'And nothing's been done about it?' Murphy snorted in an altogether too-smug kind of way.

'It's a sad rule of life that corrupt police are kept in place by even more corrupt superiors. But it's also a well-known fact in this town that it's the Murphy brothers versus Doble in the cannabis trade. I want you to fully understand the gravity of the alibi I'm about to provide, and that I wouldn't make it up.'

'What are you talking about?' said Con.

'Sergeant Doble didn't take those girls. I know because on the day they went missing he was here, in this room with me, all morning.'

There was silence.

'You called me here to tell me Doble *didn't* take the girls?' clarified Con.

'That's not all, although it's important. I felt that eventually the scrutiny would fall on him, and I feel obliged to make sure you have all the facts first.'

'Doble is getting counselling?' said Murphy, now very interested in the conversation. 'What's troubling his poor little soul?'

'I will honour his confidence, just like I've never told anyone about the subject of all of our sessions together, Murphy.'

Con sensed a trap. 'You tricked me. You could have told me that in perfect confidence on the phone. But you wanted me away from the station.'

Pastor Hugh grimaced. 'Come in, Yani, Detective Pakinga.'

The door opened and in walked a young, timid woman with short black hair. Gabriella trailed behind her, eyes dancing.

Con stood up. 'Gabriella, what are you . . .?'

'I asked him to call you here,' she said. 'I couldn't risk the commander catching me at the station, but she can't have a go at me for running into you at church . . .' She took a seat on the couch, and the young woman sat beside her. 'I didn't think you'd bring Murphy.'

Con sighed. 'Are you *trying* to lose your job?' He turned on Pastor Hugh. 'And what are you doing, playing her games?

'I know Detective Pakinga is no longer on the case. But after seeing her challenging Madison on her livestream, Yani insisted on speaking only to her. And since you were apparently uncontactable . . . Yani is my daughter.'

'It's alright, Yani,' said Gabriella. 'Con is going to hear you out, and we're going to look into it, but Madison will never know you spoke to us.'

'Gabriella —' began Con.

'Do you know something about Jasmine?' interrupted Murphy.

'Yes,' said Yani. 'I do.'

Con sat back down.

Yani's voice trembled as she spoke, looking at the ground. 'Well . . . I'll start from the start. See, we were all in this group chat together.' Yani looked up at Murphy, then at Con, then to her feet. 'It's called . . . the Honcho Dori Club . . .'

'Honcho Dori?' said Con.

Yani opened her mouth but nothing came out.

'Bring up the screenshots,' said Gabriella kindly, 'and I'll explain it.'

Yani nodded, pulling her phone out of her pocket and beginning to scroll.

'Pastor Hugh made contact with me,' said Gabriella. 'Before, Yani was worried that anyone she spoke to would go back to Madison, that she would be targeted. She's been targeted by Madison before, remember? But then she saw me confront Madison.' She looked smugly at Con.

'Targeted how?' said Murphy. 'What was Madison going to do, Yani?'

'The nudes . . .' said Con.

Yani's cheeks went red. She shook her head, glanced at Gabriella, then kept scrolling through her phone.

'The Honcho Dori Club is an online chat group that Madison set up. The messaging app lets the girls use pseudonyms – it was supposed to be an anonymous support group for self-harm,' said Gabriella. 'You know, like cutting?' Yani handed Gabriella the phone, and she handed it on to Con.

'Cutting is a big thing at our school,' said Yani in a small voice.

'Even Jasmine?' said Murphy, voice strained.

'Even Jasmine,' said Yani.

'Self-harm is more common than you'd think,' said Pastor Hugh. He reached out and grabbed his daughter's hand. 'It's not a sign of weakness, it's a sign of distress.'

'Con . . . just . . . be careful, as you read,' said Gabriella, her eyes on his.

Con looked at the first screenshot. The girls had nicknames in the chat, with Yani's messages clear in a different colour. Her nickname was xxDogGodxx.

He swiped through the screenshots and his stomach began to churn.

At first there were messages of support from all the girls, with photos of self-harm injuries – bleeding cuts, on arms or thighs – with captions like: 'Today was so hard. I couldn't help myself . . .'

These prompted messages of love and support from the other members of the chat. 'You're strong, girl. You can do this!' and 'Ouch, that looks deep. Are you okay? Have you put something on it? You should talk to a teacher.'

But over time the pictures grew more graphic, the self-harm more severe, showing photos of wrists and thighs oozing with lines of blood, some videos actually showing the act of self-harm – razor blades, Stanley knives, kitchen knives. The wounds grew deeper and bigger, the words of support fewer. Black humour crept in.

'At least I've got good knife skills now. I'm getting As in Home Economics.'

'I thought of a good one: Just call me Bloodpunzel, because I let down my blood whenever boys get in my hair.'

'Don't even remember doing this one lol. Stings like a bitch.'

Con sat back and looked at the ceiling, feeling faint.

Why is this triggering you? They're not even dead. You're stronger than this.

'Show me,' said Murphy.

'I'm not sure you should —' began Pastor Hugh.

Murphy took the phone off Con, his face turning pale behind his beard as he swiped through the screenshots. 'What the hell is wrong with these girls?' he breathed. 'It looks like a competition . . .' After a long moment, he said, 'Which one of these is Jasmine?'

'MountainLion,' said Yani.

'No . . .' moaned Murphy. He put the phone down on the desk and pressed the heels of his palms to his eyes. 'I can't believe I didn't know.'

'Tell Con why you left the group, Yani,' said Gabriella.

'Because . . . it was because of Denni King,' said Yani. 'We all thought she was getting better, like, her mental health, and then she . . .'

'She was in this group?' said Con, taking the phone back.

'Yes. She was VoodooQueen,' said Yani. 'I wanted to go to the police, I wanted to tell them about how the club might've been part of Denni's suicide, but then Madison found out . . . She has photos of me. Nude photos. She gets them from all the girls before they can join the Honcho Dori Club, as insurance. And then she shared one . . .' Yani's cheeks turned an even more brilliant red.

'Does Madison have something over Jasmine?' asked Murphy.

'The same as the rest of us. Nudes. Secrets.' Her voice grew hurried. 'You can't trust Madison. She'll use anything against you. She kicked me out of the club, she started spreading rumours about me . . . I can't defend myself, because if I do she'll ruin my life . . .' Tears rolled down her cheeks.

'Yani, thank you. You're doing something really brave and it's going to help us a lot,' said Con. 'Gabriella, send me those screen-shots and I'll —'

'No,' said Gabriella.

'Excuse me?'

'Yani doesn't trust anyone else to have them. Only me.' Gabriella sounded apologetic, but Con could see right through it. 'And since I'm not *on the case* anymore . . . I don't have to do what you tell me.'

'You got kicked off the case?' said Murphy.

Con turned to Yani. 'I need you to understand . . . if you don't let us have those screenshots, we can't look into this further.'

Yani glanced at Gabriella, then back to Con. 'I can't risk Madison finding out. I'd rather Detective Pakinga keep them.'

'I've asked her too, detective, but Yani is seventeen and she can make her own choices,' said Pastor Hugh, 'But she's agreed to answer any questions.'

'I need more than that —' began Con.

'I didn't know,' Murphy said suddenly. 'Jasmine never – I had no idea . . .'

'No one's blaming you,' said Pastor Hugh. 'There are plenty of ways to hide self-harm.'

Murphy turned to Con. 'Are you going to take Madison down for this?'

'No,' shouted Yani. 'You can't tell her!'

'But this could be why Jasmine went along with Madison's plan to disappear!'

'The *what*?' said Pastor Hugh. 'They *planned* it?'

'There's something else,' said Gabriella. 'Something important. But you *have* to take this seriously, Con.'

Con knew that tone of voice. His hackles rose.

'Madison has another secret . . .' said Yani. 'She's also . . . a witch.'

'Oh for the love of —' began Con.

'Hear her out,' interrupted Pastor Hugh. 'Don't dismiss everything you don't understand.'

'Madison turned all the girls into frogs and that's why we can't find them, got it,' said Con.

'Shut up, Con,' snapped Gabriella. 'Yani, go ahead.'

Yani swallowed, and when she spoke, her voice trembled. 'M-Madison was trying to s-summon the Hungry Man.'

'This just gets better and better,' said Con.

'Yes, it does, Con,' spat Gabriella, standing up. 'Because Madison knew about a *ritual* to summon the Hungry Man.'

'You actually believe this, don't you?' Con laughed again.

'Madison does!' said Yani, suddenly louder than both of them. 'She's *obsessed* with the Hungry Man. She thinks he's linked to the gateways in the mountains, the portals the Aboriginal people used.'

'This is madness. What the hell is wrong with this town?' shouted Con.

'Easy, detective,' said Pastor Hugh.

'What does the ritual require?' said Murphy, leaning forward. 'Do you know?'

'No, but apparently there's a way to protect yourself. Madison told us the second part to the Hungry Man rhyme. It goes:

'If you see the Hungry Man's face,
he'll never allow you to escape.
If you want to stay awake,
these three things you first must make:
carve a face and blind its eyes,
bind its throat with thread and twine,
and spend a night in the trees alone,
confess your sins, pray to atone,
then hang a girl from a tree to die,
and the Hungry Man will pass you by.'

'I told you, bloody madness,' snarled Con, standing up. 'Let's go, Murphy, we don't need to get wrapped up in this.'

'Con, I think that's why Denni King killed herself,' said Gabriella. 'That's why she arranged for Madison to find her. It was part of the ritual! Remember what Eliza said? Denni was obsessed with the Hungry Man.'

'We all thought she was getting better,' said Yani. 'But she was always protective and caring – it'd make sense if she thought she was protecting her friends by —'

'No. No, I don't want to hear this, Gabriella,' said Con. 'This is real life. There *is* no Hungry Man.'

'Think about what Eliza experienced up there,' said Gabriella, poking Con in the chest. 'The shoes. Dorrie Dossett. The yowie. There's so many weird things about this case, Con, you need to open your mind up.'

'And you believe this too?' said Con, turning to Pastor Hugh.

'I know that there are demonic forces all around us that we don't understand, that would love to trick us into doing terrible things. And I know that Madison is a very twisted girl. Who knows what she's opened herself up to?'

Con looked at Murphy. 'I need to get back to real investigating to find your daughter.' He walked to the door. For a moment he thought Murphy was going to balk, but then he followed Con outside.

'If you don't look into this, I will,' Gabriella shouted after them. 'Stay out of my way!'

Con kept walking, muttering under his breath. Murphy stayed silent as they climbed into the car, and it wasn't until they were driving away that he asked, 'Why did you freak out about that?'

'*What are you talking about?*'

'Didn't know you could lose your cool like that,' said Murphy. 'You don't even realise you're shouting, do you?'

'I'm not . . .' Con took a deep breath. 'I'm not shouting.'

'You lost it in there. Why? It's not completely crazy for this to be part of some stupid teenage delusion about the Hungry Man, is it? I mean, I can see how it would be good for Madison's online thing.'

'It's ridiculous.'

'But why does it upset you that much?' said Murphy.

Con focused on the road. By the time they pulled up at Murphy's house, Con felt the first prickles of shame at his outburst, but the faces of the Jaguar girls wouldn't leave his mind.

'You owe me the truth,' said Murphy. 'Why won't you look into this?'

'Alright!' Con threw up his hands. 'Alright. I worked a case in Sydney . . . a number of girls were tortured to death. It was ritualistic. Everyone in the investigation got wrapped up in all the stupid supernatural shit involved in the rituals, me included, and we missed the obvious evidence and leads that come from good police work.

We missed . . . There were girls we could have saved. I just don't want to make that mistake again.'

'So that's why you lost your shit,' said Murphy.

'I am well and truly in possession of my shit, thank you. I'm saying I have experience with ritual killings, and this feels different!'

'Easy, mate. If you say so. You're the detective,' said Murphy, climbing out of the car.

Con sped off the kerb, driving back to his hotel in silence. The Jaguar girls rolled through his mind and he could see their wounds afresh.

Con walked into his room and stopped cold.

The TV was playing soft chatter, as was his radio, but that was normal: he'd left them on. But the position of his medication bottles was not normal.

He turned and walked out, shutting the door behind him.

By the time he reached the reception desk, he was quivering.

'Yeah?' said the woman behind the counter.

'I'm in room Sassafras 5. I requested a permanent "Do Not Disturb" status, but someone has been in my room.'

'Hang on.' She tapped at her computer. 'Yeah, the alert is still on here. None of our lot would've gone in.'

'Well, someone did.'

'And I said it wouldn't have been anyone on our staff. Did you give your key to anyone?'

Con slammed his hands on the desk. 'Where is the manager?'

'Listen, handsome,' she replied, leaning forward, 'we have enough rooms to clean around here without going into those of blokes who obviously think they're better at it than us.'

He left. The tension in his shoulders and neck was building. He walked back to his room and locked the door behind him.

He looked again – his medication bottles were all facing the wrong direction.

You're losing it, Cornelius, he told himself angrily. *No one has touched your stuff.*

He stripped naked and walked into the shower.

The hot water on his back was soothing, the steam filling the room, the sound of the fan buzzing above him. He put his head against the tiled wall and closed his eyes. It helped him relax a little, but he still couldn't think clearly. His thoughts wouldn't enter their boxes; he couldn't arrange everything into a list.

Georgia's body appeared in his mind. Broken, at the foot of a cliff, a life snuffed out forever.

How? Did you fall? Were you pushed? Did you jump?

He hadn't even thought to ask whether Georgia had been part of the Honcho Dori Club. He'd have to ask Gabriella. She'd make him pay for it, but she'd give him the answer.

I can't let the commander find out Gabriella's still involved.

Maybe Georgia did jump. Maybe the pressure she put on herself to build the museum was too much. If she was in this Honcho Dori Club, she must have struggled with self-harm . . .

Self-harm group. A ritual. Hang a girl from a tree to die. Why is it always a girl who has to die?

Eliza's chilling account came back to him. What Georgia thought she'd seen. Maybe Georgia was chased off the cliff?

The Hungry Man. A man the size of a bear . . .

The Jaguar himself had been a big man.

No. He's dead. It's not him, thought Con. *Big breath; slow release.*

Georgia's body appeared again in his mind. This time, others seemed to be lying alongside hers. Mottled purple faces, swollen limbs, staring eyes, gaping mouths. The Jaguar girls.

Con's stomach lurched. *Get back into your boxes!* He crouched down to his knees, heaving into the plughole.

He beat his head softly against the tiled wall, breathing through his mouth. He had to be strong: it was up to him to find Jasmine, Cierra, Bree.

And Madison was the key to it all.

A ritual . . . a secret club that glorifies self-harm . . . all of this for her YouTube subscribers . . . Denni King's death . . . a witch.

Madison is a witch. She summoned him.

The Hungry Man.

The Jaguar girls appeared again in the shadows of his mind, their eyes open. *Are you sure monsters don't exist?* they seemed to ask. *Are. You. Sure?*

He turned the water off abruptly. He stood there, dripping, the steam dispersing into the fan.

The Jaguar girls peered down at him. Georgia joined them.

You didn't solve it fast enough.

You never solve it fast enough.

He wrapped the towel around his waist and headed to his bed, grabbing his laptop from the desk. The sound of the radio and TV was like a balm on his mind. These days he always needed the sound of human voices in the background. It calmed his anxiety at being alone.

He opened his laptop and started writing down thoughts as they appeared in his mind, trying to force them into boxes:

1. JASMINE MURPHY –
   DAUGHTER OF A DRUG DEALER = RANSOM/
   BLACKMAIL?
2. CIERRA MASON –
   SEXUAL ABUSE = ELIZA ELLIS IS PROTECTING
   SOMEONE
3. GEORGIA LENAH –
   ABORIGINAL HISTORY MUSEUM

4. BREE WILKINS –
PTS???

Jasmine was the most obvious target, as some sort of leverage against Murphy. If Sergeant Doble really was corrupt, Con still couldn't believe he had been allowed so much freedom in the town. He needed to tell the commander – unless he really just didn't understand Tasmania? Just because Doble had an alibi, it didn't mean he didn't have an accomplice who took Jasmine. But to what end would he have done that, really? There had been no demands made of Murphy, no contact at all.

Cierra Mason was also a possible target. Con didn't believe Eliza Ellis had slept with her, but the person she was protecting . . . Con suspected it was Tom North, but he had an alibi too. And why take the other two girls? Why kill Georgia?

This was the question he kept coming back to: why would anyone take three girls and kill one? Did the kidnapper need four girls, or *want* four girls, and something went wrong? Had the kidnapper wanted just one of them, and the others had to be taken out as witnesses? Would *any* of the four girls have done?

He thought again of Carl Lenah. He was still on the run, and with cops like Doble around, no wonder. In an ideal world, he'd throw more resources towards finding him, but they could only do so much. His instincts told him not to waste time on Carl Lenah.

When it came to directing resources, he needed to find out more about Bree. He hadn't even spoken to her parents himself, except briefly on the day of the disappearance, up at the trail. Detective Coops had spoken with her father, Marcus Wilkins, and then also spoke to her mother later. The report hadn't said much, so Con hadn't looked into it any further. He couldn't be everywhere at once, he barely had time to think as it was. He had learned to set limits, otherwise he overreached and made mistakes . . .

But was he missing something? He needed to gather more information about Bree. Did post-traumatic stress come into it? Did she snap and kill Georgia? *No, that's not how mental illness works. People rarely just snap and commit murder, that only happens in movies.*

Was he dodging Bree because he didn't want any uncomfortable questions about post-traumatic stress coming up?

Unless drugs are involved, then people can snap. Are *drugs involved?*

Cannabis was, but anything harder? When he'd first met Murphy, the man had clearly been under the influence of something else. He could see it in his eyes, in his reaction speed, and then in how he lost it and lashed out at the SES worker.

Murphy had mentioned Jack having ice debts. The teacher's assistant definitely needed more attention too, but he was currently in a medically induced coma.

Murphy was in the box for people who weren't suspects. Currently he was the only person in that box.

What about Eliza? Which box should she go in? Surely she wasn't a suspect, but she'd known about Madison's plan and hadn't done anything. Why was she protecting Tom? Was she hiding anything else? He needed to speak with her again.

Bloody hell, there was so much to do! He couldn't be everywhere!

Did one of the girls kill the others and they just hadn't found all the bodies yet? How did the Honcho Dori Club come into it? What about the girls' plan to disappear?

Maybe whoever killed Georgia knew in advance they were going to try and disappear . . . *Lawful Evil*, Madison . . . or it was motivated by something else, even random . . . *Chaotic Evil . . .*

Maybe the Hungry Man really is the most logical answer . . .

He opened a new webpage and typed into the search bar: *1985 Great Western Tiers disappearances.*

He began to read. He couldn't get the stupid rhyme out of his head. That was probably why he kept thinking he saw faces at the window. Those lights out there in the woods were surely just the torches of the search team.

That night, when they came, the nightmares were fierce.

CHAPTER 34

CON

It was morning, and the rain had cleared, but mist clung to the summits of the Tiers.

Con and Commander Agatha Normandy sat across from Madison in a quiet room at the police station, Nelly Mason seated beside her daughter. It was the room usually reserved for difficult meetings with mourning family or for social work sessions. The couches were comfortable, the lighting gentle, a window looked out onto the street and the Tiers beyond.

'I've already told you what I saw,' said Madison. Her face was drawn and her whole body shook: she looked unwell. Even her deep red hair seemed to have lost some of its shine and the make-up didn't hide the bags under her eyes. Her sleeveless green jumpsuit, at least, looked elegant. 'You've already got the bitch: why can't you find my sister?'

Nelly Mason held Madison's hand, her eyes empty as she looked at the floor. Con wondered if she was even aware of where she was.

'I'm sorry, dear, we just need to ask some further questions,' said Agatha.

Madison folded her bare arms, but still kept a hold of her mother's hand. 'What else do you need to know?'

'You told us that you caught Miss Ellis in your sister's room, is that right?' said Agatha. 'Can you run me through the details again?'

Madison folded her arms tighter. 'I already talked about this —'

'I know. But it will help if I hear the details directly from you, in case I have questions.' Agatha smiled.

Madison rolled her eyes. 'We were home alone. Mum and Dad had gone away for the weekend. It was late at night, I was in my room editing videos, and Mr Bruiser started going psycho. He ran towards Cierra's room. She wouldn't open the door, but I thought she might've been in danger so I forced my way in, and that's when I saw Miss Ellis by the open window, in her dressing gown. There were all these empty beer bottles, and it stank of weed. Cierra . . . wasn't wearing much.' Madison's cheeks reddened.

Nelly didn't even twitch.

'What did they do?' said the commander.

'Cierra pushed me back out of the room before I could see anything else. She made me swear to never, ever tell anyone.' Tears now glistened in Madison's eyes. 'So I went back to my room and put my headphones in.'

'Why did you think Cierra might have been in danger?'

Madison shrugged. 'Just did.'

'I need you to be honest with me,' said Agatha. 'Why did you believe there was danger?'

Madison shrugged again.

'Even if you don't think it's important, Madison, you need to tell me.'

'Alright!' Madison looked away. 'Because of who I thought she was seeing. Okay?'

'You knew she was meeting Miss Ellis?'

'No.' Madison's cheeks went red. 'If I'd known that, I would never have . . . She was dating a boy, and before that she had asked me . . .'

'What did she ask you, Madison?'

'She asked if I wanted to join them.' The tears returned in a sudden rush.

Nelly started. She turned to Madison, pulling her close. 'Shh, baby . . . shhh . . .'

'She told me she was seeing someone,' Madison's voice was hoarse and trembling, 'and that both of them really wanted to try a threesome, because we were twins and he was really into that. I said no – of course I said no, it's disgusting. The boy she was dating is an absolute *slut*. His name is Tyler Cabot. You should question *him*. He was at school all day, but I just . . . I thought maybe Tyler was hurting her, but then I walked in and it was *Miss Ellis*. And then the whole twin thing made sense!'

Madison became hysterical, shaking her hands in front of her as though trying to fan her face. Nelly pulled her head closer.

Con was certain Madison's tears were real. For the first time, she had lost control of a situation. That meant she truly did think Eliza was the one in Cierra's room.

'It's alright,' said the commander absently. 'It's okay . . .'

An hour later, Con and Agatha stood outside the interview room, Agatha with a manila folder in her hand.

'Why does this feel wrong?' he muttered.

'You've never had a problem with bending the rules before,' said Agatha.

Con was silent a moment. He'd already told her about Doble, and she hadn't been surprised in the least. It still rankled him, more so now he saw that what he was about to do could, probably, be construed as something akin to entrapment. *I'm nothing like Doble.* 'Why didn't you ever tell me there was this kind of corruption around?'

'Because sometimes, Cornelius, you only see the good in people, and sometimes that's what makes the best detectives – and I sorely need good detectives. Now stop fidgeting.'

'I never fidget,' he said, affronted.

She opened the door and the two of them walked inside.

Eliza Ellis was already waiting – alone, without her lawyer, whom she'd not requested to attend. She'd been kept in remand all night and was now dressed in the clothing her sister had brought in for her. Across the metal table she appeared weak, pale.

Con and Agatha watched Eliza for several minutes. She kept shivering occasionally, but her back was straight.

Suddenly Agatha stood up, so quickly Eliza flinched. Agatha opened the door and shouted, so Eliza could hear, 'Could we have the heaters turned up in here?'

She returned and sat back down. She gave a sad smile. 'Well, I can't say I agree . . .' She took some papers out of the folder and shuffled them. 'But I suppose I understand.'

'I don't know what you mean,' said Eliza.

'I had the most interesting chat with Madison Mason earlier today. She remembers a lot that she initially didn't think was important.'

The commander pretended to read through a typed-up 'report', which she and Con had fabricated just half an hour earlier. It was full of things that Madison definitely did not say. It wasn't illegal, as it wouldn't leave the room: it was just a prop. That's what Con kept telling himself, anyway.

'Madison said Cierra told her that there was a man coming – a *man*, mind you – who wanted to experiment with *twins*.' She glanced up at Eliza. 'She said that she heard a thump, like a heavy body hitting the ground. And that, now that she thought about it, the hedges outside her sister's window *were* much flatter than before. As though someone had jumped out the window. In fact, that's likely the bump that she heard.'

The commander showed Eliza a photograph from the Masons' house, which Con had raced to take just fifteen minutes earlier, with a red circle drawn around the hedge underneath Cierra's window. There did seem to be some damage to the conifer.

'The smell of marijuana and the empty bottles in the room . . . Tell me, what *is* Tom's alcohol tolerance like? Of course, when you add marijuana, you're much more likely to feel . . . unwell. No doubt you saw it firsthand when you rushed to the Masons' house to rescue him. I've also heard you should never drink while on steroids.'

'I don't know what you're talking about,' said Eliza.

'What I *am* surprised by is that he called *you*. Did his wife know about it? I'm guessing it was a fetish of his long before he even met you?' Agatha grimaced. 'I'm not begrudging the man his sexual tastes, but when it comes to underage girls, *especially* his students . . . wait, no . . . *Cierra* called you, didn't she? Not Tom. She called you, the only person she thought might be able to help in that situation. Did she call from her own phone or from Tom's?'

'I want my lawyer.'

'Certainly. You don't have to say anything more until she arrives.'

That was Con's cue.

He tapped at his phone under the desk. Ten seconds later, the timer's alarm began to ring, sounding like his ringtone.

He made a show of pulling out his phone and looking at it, puzzled, then pretended to answer.

'This is Con. What have you got, Tran?' He raised his eyebrows and pitched his voice higher. 'She's *alive*?'

Eliza leaned forward over the table. Con mirrored the action, leaning towards Eliza. He met her eyes, looked away.

'Yes. Where? Any sign of Jasmine?' He let his shoulders slump. 'But Cierra? She'll be able to talk?'

Eliza released a sob. 'Thank God!'

'I'll be there soon, I just need to finish with Eliza . . . Yes, I agree. We'll ask the girl to corroborate.'

Eliza had one hand resting on the table and again he mirrored her pose, not letting his gaze linger too long. Mirrored body language to build subconscious rapport. Drawing her into his web.

'I'll call you back soon.' He pretended to hang up the phone, then blew out a long sigh through his teeth. *'She's alive,'* he whispered, almost to himself.

'Perhaps next time you can take the call *outside* the interview room?' said Agatha, words clipped.

'Where is she? Where did they find her? What about Jasmine?' said Eliza. 'Con, please!'

Con opened his mouth to reply, but Agatha spoke over him, her voice hard. 'No. You've already said enough, Badenhorst. She's still a person of interest.'

Eliza fell back, anguish playing on her face.

Con felt a stab of guilt.

'You know what I think, Miss Ellis? You're taking the fall for Tom,' said Agatha. 'I think you wanted to do the best thing for your sister, her daughter. And I understand that. But I wonder what it is about Tom that makes you want to protect a man like him.'

For the first time, Con saw anger in her face.

'If Cierra is alive,' Agatha said wryly, glancing at Con and his phone, 'then we'll be finding out the truth soon anyway. But in the meantime, we're wasting time and resources investigating *you*. We should be investigating Tom.'

'You know Tom can't have been involved,' said Eliza. 'He was far ahead of our group.'

'Then why lie about his relationship with Cierra?'

Eliza was silent.

'He'll go to jail. Maybe you will, too, if we don't find Jasmine. Once Cierra confirms you were lying, it won't take long until people start wondering why you haven't been more closely examined as a suspect.'

'But Wren will be the one to suffer . . .'

'And how much has Cierra suffered? And it *could* have been Madison, too, that night. It was only a matter of time before Tom had them both, just like he wanted. You *realise* this is sexual abuse, right? Does Monica know?'

'Yes,' Eliza finally forced out. 'She stayed with Wren when I went to get Tom.' Tears rolled down her cheeks. 'Cierra is safe . . . thank God . . .' She began to cry.

Con felt the prickling of guilt all over his body.

When Eliza regained a little composure, Agatha slid one of the pieces of paper across the table – it was a typed confession. Agatha, with Con's input, had included everything. 'You'll sign this, confessing that Tom was the perpetrator,' said Agatha.

Eliza picked up the pen and signed.

An hour later, Con and Agatha sat across from Tom North and his lawyer, a Mrs Barrow.

'Whatever that bitch said about me, it's all lies,' Tom shouted.

Commander Normandy took a long sip from her cup of tea, never taking her eyes off him.

'Shall we discuss the ludicrous charge against my client?' said Mrs Barrow finally.

'Yes,' said Agatha, 'we shall. We have a statement here, from Eliza Ellis.'

'You're basing this on the word of a woman trying to save her own bacon?' said Mrs Barrow. 'Surely you're smarter than that?'

'It won't be long before we have a forensic report showing Mr North's DNA matches that found on the weed and condom wrappers from Cierra's room. Curiously, did you know your client tried to refuse a DNA sample? It had to be taken from him by force.'

'Be that as it may —'

'Be that as it *is*, Mrs Barrow. Mr North, are you going to be honest with us, or will I need to make another cup of tea while you continue playing games?' Her voice was hard. 'There are three missing girls, and a family mourning the loss of another. I would like to put my energy into investigating that. The more you delay me here, the more I suspect you have something to do with it.' She leaned forward. 'Word has already started to spread about you. Our custody may well be the safest place for you right now. If you continue to waste our time, imagine what will happen if that time is the difference between life and death for Cierra?'

'Tom, be careful,' warned Mrs Barrow. 'Once you've said it, you can't take it back.'

Tom grimaced.

And then he confessed everything.

Yes, it had been him in Cierra's room. Yes, they'd been having an affair. Yes, Eliza had been in the room that night, she had helped him out the window and then to the hospital. Yes, they could check the hospital's records. Yes, he knew he was in real trouble. No, no, no, he had nothing to do with their disappearance. No, no, no, there was nothing he wasn't telling them.

Later, when Con was outside to get a break from fluorescent light and some fresh air, he caught sight of Eliza across the car park. Constable Cavanagh was going to drive Eliza back to Monica North's house – likely an awkward place for her to be, considering her testimony against Tom.

When she caught Con's eyes, the look of utter betrayal on her face made him stop. Obviously, she now knew Cierra still hadn't been found.

Con ducked his head, ashamed, and fled back inside.

Did the end justify the means? He wasn't so sure anymore.

CHAPTER 35

ELIZA

When Eliza was dropped off, Monica wasn't home – she was still at the station, where she had tearfully ignored Eliza.

She was so *angry* at Con! She quickly collected her things and drove herself back to her own house. She'd shared that cottage with Denni for most of last year, just the two of them, auntie and niece . . . but really, Eliza had been of a blend of big sister and mother.

She drove up the driveway to her cottage, at the end of a steep block, the long grass brushing the underside of the car. The lawn was overgrown with blackberries and bracken ferns, and a riot of bursting yellow daffodils.

The cottage itself was small, crooked, haphazard on the steep country block, although the previous owners – an elderly couple with a lot of grandchildren – had edged the whole front wall with a large timber deck. The walls were trailed with deep green English ivy that grew wild up to the roof.

Eliza had fallen in love with the entire house at first sight, and had bought it from the elderly couple for a steal. She could barely stand to look at it now; this would be her first night sleeping in the house since Denni's death. The rusting barbecue on the deck, the creak of the rooster weather vane, the broken back fence – every part of it brought back painful memories.

But Eliza had to live here now. She couldn't stay at Monica's.

But it was the truth. I don't need to feel guilty about telling the truth . . .

Tom deserves to take the fall, no one is denying that . . .

She sat in the parked car, smothered by guilt over Wren. What would her niece's life look like now? How long until Monica forgave her?

She pounded the steering wheel in anger.

All because Con lied to me. How could he do that? How could he?

She climbed out of the car and stood in front of the house.

I was tricked. He led me into doing exactly what he wanted. Him and the commander both!

Never again.

A couple of hours later, Eliza lay back in the little bath, full of hot water and lavender oil, holding a glass of wine on the edge of the tub. Gentle music played from her phone while afternoon rain played on the roof, a comforting pitter-patter.

I have permission to be okay.

But she'd forgotten how creepy the house was, creaking and cold. As though Denni's ghost – malevolent, vengeful – haunted the walls.

Then she heard pounding on the front door. She lurched, spilling the wine. The knocking continued.

She climbed out of the bath, wrapping a white bathrobe around her, and crept to the front door. She opened it a crack.

Madison stood there, her hair wet and clinging in the rain, her red lips drawn back in a snarl. 'You witch,' the girl hissed. She shouldered her way forward and forced the door all the way open. She had something in her hand: a small wooden statuette.

'Get out of my house,' said Eliza, rage boiling up.

'I've heard all about your "confession". You're a liar. A *liar*. I know what you really are. *How did you get into my room?*'

'*Your* room? What the hell are you talking about?' spat Eliza.

'This.' Madison held up the statue in her hand. It was a carved figure of a woman, about the size of a carton of milk, rough and messily hewn from light brown sassafras, shards of bone driven where its eyes should be and a rough rope noose around its neck.

Eliza stepped back. 'What is *that*?' she said in disgust.

Madison dropped the statuette on the floor, trembling. 'Don't lie to me – I know you're the one who put this in my room! This is one of Denni's statues! I know you're *lying* about *Cierra*, too!'

'*Denni's* statues?'

'*Why did you help us?* You played along with the fight, you did what I said, but now you're claiming you weren't sleeping with Cierra?' Madison's voice shook, and her eyes kept coming back to the statuette, like iron filings to a magnet. 'You know what I can do to you, so why did you go along with our plan only to mess with me now?'

'Aren't you happy, you little bitch? Everyone's looking at you. Everyone's watching your videos. *Poor little Madison, her sister and her friend are missing. Poor little Madison, her friend Georgia is dead, just like poor Denni.* Good for you, you got what you wanted.'

'*Shut up!*' shrieked Madison. '*You* took the girls! I'm going to tell *everybody!*' Madison looked at the statuette again, whites showing around her eyes. 'Where are they? *Where are they?*'

'Get out of my house. *Get out!*'

'Or what, you'll call the police?' said Madison.

'No. I'll make my own video, telling everyone how you black-mailed me, how you planned for the girls to disappear.'

'You can try,' said Madison, her pale hands clenching and unclenching. 'Don't you realise I'm three steps ahead of every one of you?'

'Then I'll tell everyone about the Kundela Game.'

Madison froze. A beat later she sneered, but it was forced. 'I don't know what you're talking about.'

'I know Denni was playing. If it had anything to do with her death —'

'Stupid *bitch*.' Madison turned and stormed out of the house, slamming the door behind her.

The thud of the door set the timber walls creaking. Denni's ghost, raging.

Eliza fought to regain control of herself. Madison had left behind the statuette. She turned it over in her hands, touching the bone fragments in its eyes, then shuddered. The thing was hideous, and sickly, like the taste of blood in her mouth.

Denni made this . . .

She left it on the little table by the door and walked back to the bathroom, biting her lip. She let the water out of the bath, the drain squealing, and dried herself with trembling hands. She dressed herself and headed back out to the kitchen, tying the red scarf over her forehead.

The statuette filled the room with a slimy menace.

There was another knock on the door.

She straightened her back and wrenched it open, ready for Madison, but it was Detective Gabriella Pakinga. Her eyes were bright, her face flushed.

'I heard you gave up on trying to protect Tom.' She sounded excited. 'And I heard about Con's dirty trick. But I think I'm close to something, and I need your help . . . I'm not sure if you've heard, but I'm not on the case anymore.' She was taking off her denim jacket when her eyes caught on the statuette. The blood drained from her face.

'Madison brought it just before. I don't really —'

'Madison?' Gabriella looked up from the statuette. 'She was here?'

Eliza took Gabriella into the adjacent lounge room and they settled onto a couch, where Eliza recounted the conversation she'd just had with Madison.

'What I don't understand is why the police haven't made it public that Madison planned their disappearance?' said Eliza. 'Doesn't that change the whole case? There are still people searching the bush.'

'Madison thought it was Denni's statue . . .' said Gabriella, lost in her own questions. 'Why would she think that?'

'Denni was good at woodwork. Her mum, Kiera, was good at it too.' Eliza picked up the hideous statuette again. 'But I've never seen anything like this in my life . . . except I think I heard a mention of it . . . Has any of your investigating brought up the Kundela Game?'

'What's the Kundela Game?'

Eliza was silent a moment, and when she spoke her voice was heavy. 'I once overheard Denni talking about it on the phone to Madison. It was some sort of social game . . . a series of dares, one a day, and you had to prove you'd done them. I only really know about it because Denni was suspended for flashing her bra at the principal. It took a long time for her to admit to me it was a dare, and then I put two and two together. When I asked about the Kundela Game, she completely flipped out. She made me swear never to mention it to anyone, especially not Madison.' Eliza's voice grew quiet. 'I think that's around the time she stopped trusting me.'

Gabriella tapped her chin in thought. 'In one of her YouTube videos, Madison had "the word is kundela" written on her sleeping bag . . . Maybe it's just harmless pranks like flashing your underwear, but if it became more than that . . .' She paused. 'Were you aware that Denni was cutting herself?

'I know . . . the coroner's report said Denni had scars . . . What does that have to do with —'

Gabriella looked away, talking to herself again. 'The Honcho Dori Club was a precursor to this Kundela Game. When Madison realised she could get people to do what she wanted, she got a taste for it . . . But who would have put a Hungry Man warding statue in her room?'

'Hungry Man?' Eliza shuddered. 'What does that have to do with it? What's a Honcho Dori?'

'Do you want me to make us coffee first? This might be hard.'

An hour later, Eliza was still scrolling through the screenshots of the Honcho Dori Club group chat on Gabriella's phone. She felt sick.

Gabriella sipped her second cup of coffee, deep in thought.

Eliza was a teacher – she knew how teenagers worked. She could easily read between the lines of the 'messages of support', seeing the hints of approval each time a self-harm wound was sufficiently large:

Wow, u must be in so much pain, ur so strong

Damn bitch, don't blunt the knife lmao, you need to be kind to yourself girl

I wish I was as strong as you sis

And then the messages of slight derision from someone nick-named Honcho if someone's wound wasn't deep enough:

Looks like you are recovering

A band-aid will cover that up

Not much blood on that one. You must have wiped the blood away already, hope it didn't get on your school skirt

Dare you to cut deeper next time. Really feel it.

Both subtly and overtly, Honcho was encouraging self-harm, and the others were following suit.

Honcho had to be Madison's username.

Eliza recognised the photos of Denni's arm, from the freckles and skintone, and then by the photos of a knife that even now was in the kitchen drawer of this house. She was VoodooQueen.

She had yet to decipher the other usernames; she wasn't sure she wanted to. The only consolation was that VoodooQueen's photos became less severe over time, demonstrating a semblance of recovery, even as the other girls' comments seemed to be trying to egg her on.

C'mon, VoodooQueen, anyone would think you weren't feeling anything anymore.

Aren't you strong enough for the Honcho Dori Club, VoodooQueen?

'What does Honcho Dori even mean?' whispered Eliza.

'I googled it,' said Gabriella. 'It was a street in Yokohoma where American sailors went to find prostitutes. They started talking about feeling "hunky-dory". But I think Madison chose it because she's the head honcho. They're all feeling hunky-dory on the outside, but they're hiding all this stuff, and she's in charge.'

Eliza sat the phone down. 'And these little statues . . .?'

'Yani told us the second part of the Hungry Man rhyme. Part of a ritual, for warding off the Hungry Man.' Gabriella repeated the rhyme.

The awful conclusion had already occurred to Eliza. 'So if Denni made this one, as Madison claims, does that mean . . . Denni thinks she saw the Hungry Man?' Eliza put her forehead in her hands. 'Hang a girl from a tree to die.'

'Looking at her photos in the group, it seems she was getting better, and a few people we've talked to said they thought so too. But if you ask me, *any girl* who was involved in the Honcho Dori Club would have a hard time recovering. I don't need to tell you that self-harm can be linked to depression and suicide. That's why this is so serious.' Gabriella's voice softened. 'Sorry, I'm trying to be considerate, but this is all just so left-of-field. I was wondering . . . do you still have Denni's phone?'

'In her room. I haven't been in there since the funeral.'

Gabriella gripped her shoulder. 'I know this is hard. Thank you for helping.'

'What else can I do? Especially now everyone knows I was covering for Tom.'

'Yeah. Not gonna lie, that was a bad move,' said Gabriella.

Together, they headed deeper into the house, to Denni's room.

It was exactly as Eliza had left it. The rickety single bed was still made up, with a purple doona, and the walls were covered in posters of space and indie bands. Drawings of trees hung above the little desk, and they seemed to immediately draw Gabriella's attention.

'Was something here?' she asked Eliza, pointing to an empty spot where the tack marks still showed.

'I took it down. It was a sketch Denni drew of . . . the symbol on the Hanging Tree.'

'The what?' said Gabriella.

'It's carved on the tree out by the mountain track. Kind of a messy capital A.'

'Wait, is it . . .' Gabriella pulled out her phone and swiped through the Honcho Dori screenshots. She held it up for Eliza to see. 'Is it this? The picture they've used for the group chat?'

'I think it's supposed to be a stickman with a noose,' said Eliza. 'This is definitely the same as what's on the tree.'

'The Hanging Tree. Can you tell me about it?'

Eliza licked her lips, hesitating. 'It's where Denni died. And Ted Barclay. I'll show you. It's not that far from the road, really.'

'Eliza, I'm so sorry. You don't have to take me there, I've rented a car – you can just tell me where it is.'

'No, it's okay. I take flowers there for Denni sometimes,' said Eliza. 'And before you ask, that symbol was there before these girls were even born. Legend says it was on the tree even before Ted Barclay.'

She pulled open a drawer in the desk and took out Denni's phone. She plugged it into the charger still attached to the wall and they waited for it to turn on. 'What do you want to see?'

'Her messages with Madison. If Denni was getting better . . . Madison came out with this new rhyme about a Hungry Man ritual *and* she was the first person to find Denni's body . . . maybe she really wanted to cement this new part of the Hungry Man legend.'

'You think Madison talked Denni into killing herself?'

'I just want to see her messages . . .'

Eliza sat down on the bed, feeling faint. 'When Denni died, Madison was desperate to come into this room. She begged me, but it just didn't seem right. It was all still so raw. I found her in here, the morning of the funeral. I chased her out.' Sudden anger came into her voice, and her hands clenched into claws. 'Do you think she was looking for Denni's phone?'

'It's possible,' said Gabriella. The phone had charged up enough to turn on, and she opened Denni's Facebook Messenger app. There were dozens of unread messages to scroll through. 'Ah . . .' She showed Eliza the screen. 'See this message thread? It only says "Facebook User". I think that means the other person has blocked her. That has to be Madison.' She kept scrolling and gave a sad grunt. 'Oh no.'

Eliza took the phone from Gabriella and read the messages:

Facebook User: I'll be right behind you. I'll make sure we find your body before it gets gross xx
Denni King: I can't believe we're actually doing this. I'm starting to feel a bit sad now.
Facebook User: I'll meet you out the front of your house and we'll talk about it. Bring the stuff, I'll help you carry it up there. xx
Denni King: Alright. See u soon xxoxoxoxoxoxoxoxoxxoxoxox

There was a bizarre sound in Eliza's ears. She didn't realise she was crying until she could taste the tears on her lips. And that sound was coming from her, a high keening like a dying bird.

Pitiful.

She would never be pitiful again.

I have permission to be the strongest woman there ever was.

'Eliza . . . I'm so sorry . . .'

I have permission to kill.

'I'm gonna kill her.' Eliza stood and walked to the door.

'No, Eliza – we can get Madison for this. This is *proof*. These messages can be —'

'That won't bring Denni back!' shouted Eliza.

She was almost out the front door, each step a promise of death.

Gabriella dashed in front of her, blocking the door. 'No. Eliza, you can't. If you hurt Madison, you'll get blamed for the other girls, too.'

'*She deserves to die!*'

Eliza tried to push past, but Gabriella knocked her away. 'No, Eliza.'

Eliza raised her fists. 'Move, Gabriella.'

'No.'

Eliza punched, but Gabriella grabbed her wrist and the next moment Eliza was face-first on the ground, Gabriella on top of her. 'Eliza, calm down —'

Now the true emotion came. Gabriella eased off her, but Eliza remained on the ground, thrashing first and then curling into a ball. 'Denni! Denni, no! No, no, no . . .'

Gabriella pulled her up into her arms. 'It's okay. Shhh. It's okay.'

Eliza buried her head into Gabriella's shoulder. 'I'm sorry . . . I'm sorry, I'm sorry, I'm sorry . . .'

CHAPTER 36

MURPHY

Murphy locked his bedroom door and rested Butch's laptop on his knees. He opened the USB drive.

My father raped my mum . . .

Jasmine's words still rolled through his mind.

He played the second video.

Jasmine appeared in front of the camera in Madison's room. It was a recent video: her hair was dyed black, pulled back in a pony-tail. When she spoke, her voice trembled.

'The first time I saw Mum crying, I was eight years old. It would've been after midnight and she was in the bathroom on her knees, her head on the edge of the tub. I remember her smell: like cooking and perfume.

'I asked what was wrong, and she turned to me and smiled. "Nothing, baby. I'm just praying."

'I kneeled down with her and asked if I could pray too. She hugged me close and told me I could, but only for a little bit and then I had to go back to bed. She showed me how to pray to God, and told me that if I asked him to, Jesus would come live in my heart forever. Then I asked her whether Jesus lived in her heart, and she said he still did but she didn't like to think about him too much, because there was someone in her life that she couldn't forgive. She wouldn't tell me who.

'Five years later, when I turned thirteen, she did. It was only a few months after that that she died.'

Jasmine chewed the inside of her cheek.

'But she told me something, that last week. She warned me what would happen if Dad found out, so I promised I'd take care of it. And the only way to make that happen was to do something drastic.

'Dad . . . I need you to know. I'm doing this for the right reasons. You'll see. I promise you'll understand. When I come back, I'll explain everything.'

Murphy felt he was coming apart at the edges.

'For everyone else . . . secrets can destroy you. If you have your Mum and Dad close by, give them a hug. You never know when they might be taken away from you. And if you have a son or a daughter . . . sometimes it's our job to protect *you* . . . or your memory.'

He heard a creak on a floorboard outside his door, saw the shadow of movement under the door.

He leapt up and flung the door open. Butch was creeping back down the corridor.

'You were listening!' shouted Murphy.

Butch flinched. 'I was worried, I was coming to check on you, and then I heard Jasmine's voice. Were those old videos on your phone or something?'

Murphy hadn't shared the videos with him yet. He still hadn't even been able to bring himself to tell Butch that Madison had planned it all. And the longer he waited, the worse it became.

'Why didn't you knock?'

'Honestly . . . I didn't think you wanted me to see you crying again.'

Butch came in and sat on the bed. The two brothers were silent for a few moments.

Then Murphy's phone buzzed. An unknown number was calling him.

'Yeah?' he answered.

'Murphy. It's Constable Cavanagh. Con told me to call you. He thought you might want to . . . look, get online right now. Madison is streaming live, and it's . . . it's massive.'

Murphy opened the laptop and Butch leaned over his shoulder. He opened the MMMMadisonMason page. He began the live-stream from the start.

'I have a confession to make, and I need everyone to listen closely.' Madison sat on her bed in her usual spot. Her mascara had bled, almost too well – artificially well. Her lips were red as blood. She looked straight down the camera.

'I planned it. I planned it all.

'I mean the disappearances. Cierra, Bree, Jasmine . . . our other friend, who can't be named. We all planned it together, but it was my idea. They were always going to go missing on the school camp.

'Yes, I know it was stupid. Yes, I know it was dangerous. But I had a good reason. I'll explain everything in my next video. But the honest-to-God truth is that I have no idea what happened up there. The plan was for the girls to make contact with me when they were safe, but they haven't. Now they really *are* missing.

'I'm not responsible for our friend who can't be named's death. Our plan was for the four of them to leave the trail and meet at Lake Mackenzie, gather the supplies we'd stashed there, and drive to a safe location. I have videos of all of them, speaking before the camp. I'll share them tonight, so you can understand our reasons – their reasons.

'But before that, I want to have a vigil for our friend who can't be named. Everyone who's watching this, everyone who cares: bring your candles, your flowers, and your prayers, and meet me at the school. We'll walk from there to the bottom of the trail and then to the top of the cliff where she fell. Please, no photos of her, and don't say her name, out of respect to her family. And thank you as you continue to search for my sister, and my friends, who I may have lost forever. I promise, I'll apologise personally to each and every one of you.'

Madison broke down. Even Murphy, who was trying to block out the sound of Butch's incredulous cursing beside him, almost felt sorry for Madison in that moment.

Almost.

She was a good actress.

'We'll meet at Limestone Creek District School. I hope you all know while the school has been closed since the disappearance, it's providing free counselling for any students who want it, and will continue to do so for the rest of the week. We'll meet at the school at seven o'clock – that's one hour from now – and make the short walk together,' continued Madison. 'Come and join us, as we light a candle for our friend.

'Love you all.'

Butch exploded. 'She *planned* it? Jasmine *meant* to go missing?'

'Looks like it,' said Murphy woodenly.

'So she might be okay, lad! She might be safe!'

'Except that Georgia is dead.'

'But if Jasmine was close to Georgia, she might be at this vigil tonight!'

Murphy's heart lurched. He hadn't thought about that. Everyone would be there – locals, strangers, media, police – so she would be keeping a low profile, but she *would* want to go for Georgia.

'Look . . . this might sound paranoid, but I don't think we should go together,' said Butch. 'Or at least, I think you should call your new cop buddy, see if he'll take you. That way it's all above board, no one can say you had anything to do with anything.'

Murphy paused, but he couldn't deny the wisdom. 'You're right, bro. I'll call Con.'

CHAPTER 37

CHAPTER 37

ELIZA

Gabriella parked her car on the side of the mountain road, in a gravel pull-off. Invisible in the night was a secret path, known only to a few, that linked up with the trail from the school, a short five minute walk to the Hanging Tree.

'We don't have to do this right now,' said Gabriella.

'No,' said Eliza. 'We do.'

The two women headed into the trees, following the path. Although it was well into the evening, the sky was still just about light, Daylight Savings and the southern extremity of Tasmania keeping the night alight.

Eliza inhaled the cold peat-bark smell of bush, the wet-gravel spice.

All she could think about was Madison Mason.

Madison had convinced the girls to disappear. Madison had convinced Denni to kill herself. Madison had to pay.

'This place is so creepy,' said Gabriella.

'The most haunted forest in Australia, according to MMMMadison,' said Eliza. 'Don't forget to like, comment and subscribe.'

Gabriella stepped a bit closer to her, looking up ahead over the trail that curved through shoulder-high ferns. Eliza led the way, feet crashing through the growth.

A noise growled in the path beside them: a shrieking howl, an unholy beast.

Gabriella screamed, clutching Eliza's arm.

'Just a Tassie devil,' said Eliza. 'We're nearly there.'

'That was a devil?' hissed Gabriella. 'It sounded like . . .'

'How do you think they got their name?'

It didn't take long until they had joined the main trail, which was wider and straighter, red soil and rocks showing the path in the twilight. More Tasmanian devils growled in the night around them, mixing with the sound of insects and the *cussik-cussik* call of a green rosella. Candlebark and swamp peppermint reached over their heads, deeper darkness, a perfect corridor.

Emotion – so many deep and heavy emotions, one after the other for days – had sapped all her energy. But they were close now. She switched on her torch against the building dark. There, just ahead, was the craggy clearing, dotted with fern-like clubmoss, in which that ancient King Billy Pine known as the Hanging Tree stood alone.

'What's that?' said Gabriella suddenly, her voice strained. When Eliza stopped to listen, she could hear voices from behind them.

Through the trees, back down the trail towards the school, in the gloom, were little lights, bobbing through the trees. Eliza's blood chilled, until she heard the music coming from a portable speaker. They weren't ghosts: they were people. A lot of them.

'Another search party?' said Eliza.

'What's with the candles?' said Gabriella. 'Should we wait for them to catch up?'

'Those are cameras.' Fury filled Eliza – how dare people intrude on this moment of mourning and grief. She strode ahead, towards the tree, and Gabriella scrambled to keep up.

The next moment they were beneath the branches of the Hanging Tree. Eliza's shoulders were tense: a great weight of sadness. Her torch beam lit the cut flowers and memorials around the trunk, some of them left by her.

'Oh no,' choked Gabriella.

Eliza's torchlight followed the trunk, until it landed on something hanging from one of the branches.

Eliza screamed.

'Shit, shit, shit,' said Gabriella.

The mass of people with the candles and music and cameras stampeded towards them, drawn by Eliza's scream, until the space around the tree was full of more screaming, and candlelight, and music, and cameras – TV crews and newspaper photographers and YouTubers and Instagram influencers.

'Who is it?'

'She's dead! She's hung herself!'

'It's Bree. Oh God, it's Bree Wilkins.'

'Someone call the cops!'

'They're here! Where are they? Police! Call an ambulance!'

Eliza backed further away, her torch knocked from her fingers.

'*What's that thing? Is it tied to her wrist?*'

'*It's a wooden statue.*'

'*It's voodoo! It's voodoo!*'

'Everyone! Police! Don't touch anything!' Con Badenhorst's voice boomed as he stepped through the crowd.

Gabriella let go of Eliza, running to him.

Suddenly Murphy appeared in front of Eliza. 'Don't look at her, Eliza. Look at me.' He put his big hands on either side of her face to drag her eyes away from Bree's body.

'Why are all these people here?' Eliza struggled to focus her vision.

'Madison's vigil. Weren't you with us?'

'Madison is here?' Eliza spun around. 'Where?'

It was chaos. People swarming around the clearing, voices mingling, screams and sobs. Children and adults, teenagers and the elderly, locals and strangers, people everywhere, everywhere, *everywhere*.

'Where are you, Madison?' screamed Eliza, her voice lost in the cacophony. 'Are you happy? Are you *happy*?'

But Madison was nowhere to be seen.

CHAPTER 38

CON

It was a long night up at the Hanging Tree.

Con watched as the forensics team went to work, the clearing lit up by their floodlights, casting everything into high relief and drawing biting insects to the scene. And always, the devils howled in the night.

Finally, Bree's body was lowered out of the tree. He had vomited twice already, back in the trees where nobody could see, but he still shook uncontrollably.

Pull it together, Cornelius, he told himself, digging his nails into his palms to force the images of the Jaguar girls out of his head. *There's nothing you could've done.*

He asked to inspect the wooden statue that had been tied to her wrist before Forensics bagged it. The statue had baling twine in a noose around its neck and chips of bone that had been hammered into its eyes. They hadn't tested it yet, but everyone felt sure they were animal bones. Forensics continued to do their job, their team leader speaking to the recently arrived commander and Melinda Tran.

'It was part of that ritual Yani told us about,' said Murphy, crouching next to Con at the edge of the clearing. 'Blind its eyes, hang a girl from a tree to die.'

Con didn't reply. He suspected Gabriella wanted to tell him the same thing – she'd been calling his phone on repeat ever since he'd dismissed her. Finding her in the crowd at the tree had been a blow – she was one of the few people who understood what seeing Bree's body would do to him, triggered in him. It was always worse when someone knew. He'd avoided her and she had eventually left, presumably to take Eliza home, with the teacher in a serious state.

Gabriella was calling again. He knew, deep down, he should answer. But *not* with another dead girl lying on a tarp, hidden from view by a tent. Not with so many of the vigil walkers still hovering at the edges of the police tape, watching with curiosity and eager cameras. Not with the commander so close, able to overhear.

Even when he wasn't looking at the body, his mind's eye saw the bloated corpse of Bree Wilkins, her lank blonde hair such a stark contrast to her purple face. She had been dead for days.

This was not a ritual killing. There was nothing I could've done. She killed herself. She simply killed herself.

Except, how has no one found her until now? That body is old.

Agatha finished talking to Forensics and walked over to Con.

'Cornelius,' she said, 'why are you shaking?'

'It's cold,' he said.

'Then why are you sweating?' She shone her torch in his face. 'Good Lord, man.'

He raised his arm to shade his eyes and she grabbed his hand, her fingers pressed around his wrist. She pulled him closer.

'Go back to the Inn, Cornelius,' she said firmly. 'Everything can wait until tomorrow.'

'But —' he began.

'Do *not* argue with me.'

'I don't —'

'*Go*,' she snapped. 'Before I have one of the other officers take you home. You,' she pointed at Murphy. 'You came with him?'

Murphy rose to his feet and nodded warily.

'Cornelius, give him your keys: he can drive you back. There shouldn't be any civilians this side of the tape.'

Con straightened. 'I'm fine, commander —'

'We'll talk about this later. *Go*.'

'Commander, Gabriella was here tonight, with the vigil. She said she had something important to tell me, about the statue. Maybe you should speak with her.'

'Gabriella Pakinga is not a part of this investigation anymore,' said Agatha. 'Anything she has to tell me can come through the appropriate channels.'

Con hesitated, glancing back towards Bree's body, then turned towards the trail.

Suddenly Agatha caught his arm and spun him around to face her. With surprising strength she nudged his foot outward, putting him off balance. 'Are you having bad flashbacks?' she asked fiercely, directly into his face.

Con, keeping hold of her to regain his stance, nodded, then grew angry, both at himself and at her dirty trick – she had dislodged the truth by physically throwing him off balance, forcing him to lean on her.

He pulled himself away from her grip. 'No,' he said, too late.

'Get a good night's rest, Badenhorst,' said the commander, the ferocity leaving her as fast as it had come. She sounded as tired as Con felt. 'I'm sorry for not taking better care of you.'

Con walked off down the path, ignoring the questions of the civilians still watching, the media who swarmed towards him. Murphy walked alongside him, big loping steps, glowering at anyone who approached.

'I'm fine,' said Con.

'I didn't say anything,' said Murphy.

'What do you make of this?'

'If Bree's killed herself, that makes it more likely the other girls are safe too, right? It means Bree was never taken.'

'She looks like she's been dead for days. And her bag was still at the Fisherman's Hut,' said Con. 'But what are the odds that Madison would organise a massive vigil that just happened to walk past the place where Bree was hanging?'

'Madison knows where Jasmine is. I'm sure of it.' There was almost a bounce in Murphy's step. 'How long until we know how long Bree's been hanging there for?'

'At least an hour to get her to the hospital for the autopsy,' said Con. 'If they do it tonight.'

'Can we go ask Madison about it?' said Murphy.

'Tomorrow? Definitely.'

'Can I come?' said Murphy.

'Probably not,' said Con.

Murphy nodded, as though he'd expected that answer. Their footsteps crunched through the red soil and stone, Tasmanian devils in the bush around them, a masked owl watching from the branch of an ancient pencil pine.

And still, Con struggled to get his shaking under control.

It's normal: you're only human. It's the shock of finding Bree. You tried hard to find her, to save her, and yet she killed herself. Sudden weariness. What's even the point?

Murphy said, 'I need to tell you something.'

'What is it?' said Con.

Murphy explained the USB drive Madison had given him via Carmen. He said he'd only had time to watch two of the videos Jasmine had made, and was very sparse on the details of what they contained.

'Can I see them?' said Con.

'They're a bit private . . . maybe once I've finished them all . . .'

'I need to see them, Murphy. Two girls dead. Two girls missing. One of them your daughter.'

'Piss off.' Murphy rose himself up to his fullest height, but after a moment he deflated, sighed. 'I mean, maybe. But not yet.'

Con thought about pushing him, but he just didn't have the energy for more conflict. He'd do it tomorrow.

That made him feel ashamed. He was the worst detective in the world. All he wanted to do was to get back to his room at the Inn: better yet, back to his house in Launceston. Even better again, back to Sydney, his mates, a city he understood, a state that wasn't wild Tasmania. His mum and dad.

By now they had reached the school car park, and were heading towards the BMW. Another wave of exhaustion rolled through him and he tripped on a stone.

Murphy grabbed his shoulder, steadying him. 'Want me to drive, mate?'

Con glared at him. 'I'm bloody fine.'

Murphy shrugged, still keeping hold of his shoulder, and flashing the car keys he'd just lifted from Con's pocket. 'Your boss lady told me I should drive, and honestly, I'm more scared of her than I am of you.'

Con thought about fighting. Then he just nodded and let Murphy help him back to the car.

CHAPTER 39

MURPHY

Con fell asleep the moment Murphy started the BMW. He drove back to his own house, the detective occasionally shifting in his sleep.

When they arrived, Murphy saw that Butch's Hilux wasn't in the drive. He roused Con from his nap. There was a feral glint in his eyes before he oriented himself to where he was. 'Thanks for waking me,' he said, back to hiding the hint of pain that had briefly been on display.

Murphy felt a sudden protectiveness. 'Do you want to crash here? You can have my bed, I'll sleep in Jasmine's.'

'No, it's okay. But I appreciate the offer.'

As they parted, Con clasped Murphy's hand and gripped his shoulder.

Inside, Murphy stopped by the fridge to grab a six-pack of beer. He sat on his bed, back against the headboard, and opened the laptop.

He cracked open a bottle and drank as he played the third video.

Jasmine was in Madison's room again, a different day. She picked at the hem of her sleeve.

'I was thirteen when I discovered that my dad is not my biological father.'

Murphy choked on his beer, spitting it over the screen.

'It's Dad's brother, Butch. He raped my mum. That was how I came to be.'

'No,' said Murphy aloud. He leaned forward.

'Mum told me the whole story. She was dating my dad, but then she and Butch got drunk. He came on to her, she couldn't stop him . . . nine months later, there I was. They had the DNA test not long after.

'So Butch knows, but Mum made me swear never to tell Dad. My real dad, Jordan Murphy. She didn't want him thinking less of her, or less of Butch . . . or less of me . . .'

The video ended.

That was it, the entire file.

Murphy clicked on the next video, his finger trembling. He couldn't even feel the rage yet, but it was coming from a distance, like the rumble of the railroad when a train is coming.

Jasmine's make-up was done more sharply this time, eyeliner and thick foundation and red lipstick. This video began even worse.

'Dad . . . if you're seeing this, then you know. Uncle Butch is my biological father.' She took a deep breath. 'And that means you also know me and the others planned to disappear. I know it's hard for you to believe this, but I'm doing this for us. For you and me.

'Now that I've taken this step, what I need you to do is . . .

'Move out of Butch's house. Cut all ties with him, including that horrible job, and move far away from Limestone Creek. Far, far away. Go to Port Douglas, like you always talk about.

'Once you've done that . . . once you've cut Butch out of our lives . . . I might just meet you there.'

The video ended.

Murphy was barely aware of himself as he left his room. The Glock was in his hands. Where had it even come from? Had he had it with him all day? Wasn't it beside his bed?

The anger had arrived, but it wasn't burning.

It was cold, hard, and lonely.

Butch.

Butch had raped his wife.

Butch was Jasmine's biological dad.

He thought of him in his singlet and shorts, his goofy grin. Cuddling Jasmine, doting on her, a good uncle.

A criminal. A rapist. How many times have I left him alone with my daughter?

Butch knew. He knew all along.

So did Sara.

Jasmine never let on. She'd never mentioned anything to Murphy. She'd never treated Butch as anything but an uncle, and Murphy had never even been jealous.

Butch is the reason Jasmine ran away. Jasmine wants Murphy to have nothing to do with him. My father raped my mum.

The white noise hit him. Burning ice. The fury like a locomotive, in his face, his teeth, his stomach – uncontrollable rage.

He thought of Bree's body. How easily that could have been Jasmine, swinging there.

Get rid of Butch and Jasmine will come back.

He held the Glock in one hand and another bottle of beer in the other.

Where was Butch? He'd have to track him down.

What else did Jasmine ask him to do? 'Move out of Butch's house. Cut all ties with him, including that horrible job, and move far away from Limestone Creek.'

Yes, he'd move out of the house. That could be done right now. Already he'd punched several holes in the walls. He wasn't aware of doing it, but there were holes there now and his knuckles were bleeding.

'. . . including that horrible job.'

He kicked the back door open and stopped by the shed. Tucking the Glock into the back of his jeans, he picked up a headtorch, a cigarette lighter, and the can of petrol for the lawnmower. Where did the beer go? He must have drunk it.

Murphy's feet seemed to know the path without effort, crunching through the bush and over rocks, even in the darkness. The bushland welcomed him, the damp and the deep smell of wilderness. He felt no fear, the beam of the torch lighting his way. A wallaby thumped off into the trees nearby, a possum scurried up a tree – his torchlight caught its eyes, reflected like tiny yellow lanterns in its ancient face.

He arrived at the two dolomite boulders leaning against each other. He triggered the fishing-line. The sledgehammer swung down. He walked past it, into the small forest of marijuana plants. They towered over him, casting wild skinny shadows in the torchlight, whispering in the darkness.

Avoiding the bear-traps, he doused each plant with petrol. He knew the fire wouldn't spread – all the rain the last few days had dampened the bush, the King Billy Pines too ancient and tough – but the marijuana crop would be no more.

Moving back to the tunnel between the boulders, he picked a leaf and lit it with the cigarette lighter. It caught easily. He dropped it at the base of the closest plant. It caught with a *whoof*.

He watched the flames spread, mixing with the pine needles and marijuana.

He headed home, so drunk on rage that time was malleable. One moment he was walking away from the blaze, the next he was at the house.

But Butch still wasn't home yet. Murphy would have to find him, instead.

CHAPTER 40

CON

Con stood in the steaming shower. The shaking had stopped, but the fatigue was still there. The faces of the Jaguar girls rolled across his mind, now joined by Georgia's broken body and Bree's bruised face.

He needed sleep.

He had to focus on Georgia and Bree.

Option 1: Bree killed Georgia and/or the other girls, then killed herself out of remorse.

Option 2: Someone killed Bree and hung her up to look like a suicide.

Option 3: Bree killed herself, believing it would protect the others from the Hungry Man.

Option 4: Madison had convinced both Bree and Georgia to kill themselves, and this has all been part of some sick, insane plot.

He thought back to the Honcho Dori Club. He thought back to Denni King. He thought back to the wooden statue tied to Bree's wrist.

Chaotic Evil: the Hungry Man. Chaotic Evil: Madison Mason. Was there a difference?

There was banging on his hotel room door. He walked out of the shower, wrapped a towel around his waist, and opened the door.

Gabriella came stumbling in, arm raised in mid-knock. 'Con, you toolbag, why don't you answer your calls?'

'Gabby, I'm —'

'Madison killed Denni King,' she said in a rush. 'I saw the messages. On her phone. Madison convinced Denni to kill herself.'

'*What?*'

'Do I have your attention now, Cornelius?'

'I'm listening,' he said.

She refused to come further into the room and started bouncing on her toes as she spoke. 'They were both part of something called the Kundela Game, a series of dares. Remember when we saw 'kundela is the word' on Madison's sleeping bag? It has something to do with that. *And,* Denni was a woodcarver. And this,' she held out the wooden statue that had been tied to Bree's wrists, 'Madison found in her room!'

'How do you have that?' said Con, taking it from her. 'This is evidence. It should be with Forensics.'

'It's not the one from Bree's body. Madison brought *this* to Eliza's house today. She accused her of putting it in her room, but Eliza had never seen one before.'

Eliza Ellis appeared at the door. 'Can I come in now?'

Con swore, clutching his towel. He grabbed his clothes off the floor and fled into the bathroom to change. When he came out in a white button-up, grey slacks and bare feet, the two women were sitting on his bed.

Eliza studied Con, expectant.

'Look, Eliza, I'm sorry for lying about Cierra being found,' he said.

'I don't forgive you. It was a cheap trick.'

'No worse than covering for Tom,' shot back Con. He sat in the chair by the desk.

'That's in the past now,' said Gabriella. 'We need to work together. I think Jasmine Murphy is still alive, and she's in Limestone Creek. If Denni made these statues as protection, who else would have them but her friends? I'm sure it was Jasmine – she must have put it in Madison's room.'

'Wouldn't it make more sense for it to be Bree?'

'Only Jasmine or Georgia would have the foresight to go against Madison,' said Eliza. 'Given what Madison has on all of the girls – the nude photos, her influence with her YouTube channel – it would be a way to mess with her head. Madison's all about the head games and power, right? Why not gaslight her? Disappear, using Madison's own plot, but then pretend to go really missing, pretend the Hungry Man really did take them. Make Madison admit everything to her followers, put all her guilt on display.

'Jasmine has always had a keen sense of justice – you should see her arguing with me whenever I give her or any of her friends detention. She'll make a good lawyer one day,' said Eliza.

'But why would Bree have one of the statues?' said Con. 'I don't accept the idea that all four of those girls believed in the Hungry Man.'

'You're not from around here, Con,' said Eliza. 'You don't understand what it's like, living in the shadow of these mountains, the 1985 disappearances.'

'Yes, thank you, Eliza. I am by now *keenly* aware that I am not Tasmanian, nor do I live in Limestone Creek. Although I'd bet I'm having a pretty authentic experience . . .'

Con's phone buzzed. It was Murphy calling. He answered instantly.

'I'm out the front of the Inn. I need to talk to you.' Something seemed wrong – Murphy's voice was too flat. 'I brought Madison's USB drive.'

'What's happened?' said Con.

'Come let me in the side door. I'll show you.'

'Eliza and Gabriella are here.'

'I don't care, let me in.'

'Murphy's outside,' said Con to the room. 'Eliza, can you go find the side door and let him in? I don't think he wants to be seen.'

'Okay,' said Eliza, still full of energy following their conversation – she jogged out of the room.

The moment she was gone, Con hissed at Gabriella, 'Why the hell is *she* here?'

'Because she's a part of this,' Gabriella snapped back. 'You keep forgetting how *strange* this case is. *Remember* how Eliza was found? What Georgia saw?'

'What she *thought* she saw! This isn't the time to start bringing pet civilians into the investigation.'

'Pet civilians? Then why is *Jordan Murphy* rocking up at your hotel in the middle of the night?' demanded Gabriella.

'Because he has actual evidence.'

'And this statue *isn't*? It's the same as the one tied to Bree's wrist!'

'It tells us nothing. If you hadn't handled it, we might've been able to dust for a print.'

She poked him hard in the chest. 'Don't you dare, Badenhorst. Madison and Eliza had both already touched it. Don't you dare: I'm just as much a detective as you are. Don't take your testosterone out on me.'

'Is this a bad time?' said Eliza wryly from the doorway.

Murphy stood beside her, his face haggard and pale. The smell of spilled beer and a strange foresty smell came into the room with him.

Con reached for his laptop. 'Show us, Murphy.'

'Show us what?' said Gabriella.

'It's a USB drive Madison gave to me. She and Jasmine made these videos . . .' Murphy handed the USB to Con. 'Butch raped her mum . . . Sara . . . my wife. Butch is her real father.'

'Butch?' said Eliza, horrified. 'He raped *Sara*?'

'*What?*' said Gabriella.

'And now I don't know where he's gone . . .' said Murphy, voice flat. 'But I came here because otherwise I'll kill him.'

'Good for you, Murphy,' murmured Gabriella.

'She's still your daughter, mate, no matter what,' said Con firmly. He put the USB drive into the port. It opened to show the six video files. 'Have you watched them all?'

Murphy nodded once, then hesitated. 'Well, actually . . . no. Not the last two.'

'Let's start from the top, then,' said Con.

The others crowded around as they watched the videos.

By the time the fourth video ended, with Jasmine asking Murphy to cut Butch out of his life, Murphy's eyes were wet, his teeth bared in his beard. Every breath seemed to physically hurt him. 'I think Butch took the girls,' he said. 'He knew where the Fisherman's Hut was: we're the ones who showed it to Jack in the first place. I think he knew Jasmine was going to tell me what he did to Sara, and so he killed her to keep her quiet.'

'Murphy . . . I don't think that's likely,' said Gabriella. 'Butch has had plenty of times to hurt Jasmine if he wanted to. Besides, you both have an alibi.'

'No,' said Murphy. 'We don't. I don't know where I was when the girls went missing: I was high on angel dust.'

Gabriella's eyebrows flew up. She turned to Con and mouthed, '*What the fuck?*'

Con shook his head. 'Butch was there when Constable Cavanagh came to your house to get you: I know, I read the report, and then talked to her about it myself.' Gabriella tried to catch his eye again, but Con put his hand up. 'I don't believe Murphy did it, Gab.' Con clicked on the next video.

Jasmine spoke to the camera.

'If you're watching this, it's been six months. No, we weren't taken by the Hungry Man. We left of our own accord. And these are our reasons why.'

The video cut to Georgia, sitting on the same bed. She sat up proud, her glasses catching the light. 'People say that teenage girls are helpless.'

The video shifted to Bree, long blonde hair and blotchy face. 'That we are weak.'

Cierra, with a blue wig. 'That we're nothing but a pretty face.'

Back to Jasmine. 'Everyone assumes that if four girls go missing, they must have been taken. They couldn't possibly have left for their own reasons.'

Bree: 'Isn't it strange that a whole community will come to the rescue when a girl is missing, but when she's right in front of you, crying out for help, no one gives a damn?'

Cierra: 'So we disappeared. Because we chose to.'

Georgia: 'My whole heritage is ignored, and no one gave a damn about my museum. Now that people think I'm dead, my vision is alive. That's what it means to be a teenage girl.'

'She didn't intend to die,' said Gabriella softly.

Jasmine: 'When my mum died, my dad went a bit crazy: depressed, anxious. He lost his job, our house. People avoided me in the street because they didn't know what to say. My dad turned to his criminal brother for help, because everyone else abandoned us. I had to move into the house of a drug dealer. I watched my dad, once happy doing landscaping like he loved, become one too, just to provide for us. Now that I'm missing, you've all rallied around him again. Why is it that a missing girl is so much sadder than a dead wife? Why did no one in this town reach out to him when they saw him struggle to keep his job, struggle to help me?'

'Fair to say Jasmine got that one wrong,' said Con.

Murphy snorted.

Jasmine: 'But where were all of you when my uncle raped my mum?'

Cierra: 'Where were you when a teacher seduced me, snuck into my room to sleep with me, then said no one would ever believe me? I was too scared to do anything. I didn't want anyone else getting hurt.'

Georgia: 'Where were you all – so in love with justice – when I tried to honour the First Peoples of this place?'

Bree: 'Where were you when I tried to tell you that my best friend, Denni, was going to kill herself? Where were you when the same thoughts came into my head?'

Cierra: *'Down in the towns, they hide and wait. Up in our bedrooms, they hide and kill.'*

Georgia: *'The world's hungry men, who treat girls like strays. Who'll silence their cries and make them obey.'*

Bree: *'Don't believe what the adults say: we teenage girls can find a way.'*

Jasmine: *'Join the movement and disappear, and see what they do when we are not here.'*

The video cut to Madison, on her bed, with the four girls on either side of her.

'Teenage girls of the world: join the movement. Pack a bag, take a tent, and go missing for a week. Make the people in your life appreciate you, get them to see you for who you are. This is the Hungry Man movement. #HungryManMovement, #JusticeForTeenageGirls. #TheKundelaGame.'

The video ended.

None of them knew what to say. It was like the aftermath of a bomb.

'There's one more video,' said Con eventually.

'What Bree said about Denni,' said Eliza, struggling to get the words out. 'No one . . . I had no idea Denni was suicidal. Who did Bree tell?'

'I think I need a moment,' said Gabriella.

Murphy leaned over them all and clicked play.

It was Jasmine, in a light blue Billabong jacket and hiking tights. She was in a different bedroom, much less lush than Madison's; Con assumed it was her own.

Murphy moaned. Jasmine was dressed in the same clothes she'd been wearing in that video Madison had posted the school bus, the first day of the camp. This must have been what she was wearing the last time Murphy saw her.

'Hi, Dad.' She smiled, but she had been crying. 'I asked Madison to give this to you six months after we go missing. I'm sorry it's not sooner, but I couldn't risk you ruining what I'm trying to do here. I'm sure you've watched the other videos, but always remember you're still my dad. Mum made me swear never to tell you, but . . .' She began crying. 'I confronted Butch, and he had the balls to tell me that Mum came on to *him*. He said that she gave consent, that she wanted it. Both of us know Mum would never do that.

'He couldn't even apologise! So this is how I'm getting back at him. I want the whole world to know what he did. To understand what Mum had to suffer through in silence. And I want you, Dad, to leave Limestone Creek. Get out of his house, get far away from Butch, and get a job somewhere else. I'm going to stay away for a year – yeah, I'm dedicated now to a full year – and then I'll come find you: I'll send a postcard to the Limestone Creek Police Station for you, with the time and place to meet me. I'm planning on being near Port Douglas, so, if you want to make things easier for both of us . . . find a house up there! Find a job. Start a new life. Get away from Butch, and weed, and Limestone Creek.

'This is the most important thing I'll ever do: we have to try and make a difference, while we have Madison's channel. Don't worry about a thing – I'll see you in six more months, I promise: one year to the day since we disappeared. If it helps, just imagine me sitting on a tropical beach!' She winked. In the video, Murphy's voice came from the other side of Jasmine's bedroom door. 'I'm just making an Instagram story, Dad! I'll be out in a sec. Love you!' She looked down at the camera, winked again, then kissed the lens.

The video ended.

Everyone looked at Murphy. A suite of emotions played out on his face, pain and hope and anger and sorrow. To see his daughter so optimistic, so full of the belief it was all going to work out exactly as she'd planned, to have her lay it all out so honestly . . . Con couldn't imagine the pain in Murphy's heart right then.

Finally, Gabriella said, 'And yet, something went wrong.'

'Don't say that,' growled Murphy.

'Madison is to blame,' said Eliza.

'We'll talk to Madison. Tomorrow,' said Con firmly. 'Right now, we all need to sleep as much as we can. It's the middle of the night, and we need to be thinking clearly tomorrow.' He looked at his watch. 'Today.'

'Alright. Eliza, you can stay in my room if you want,' said Gabriella.

But Eliza was now paying attention to Murphy. He was still looking at the last frame of Jasmine's video on the computer screen.

'Don't worry about him: he can stay here. I'll sleep on the floor,' said Con. He moved to the wardrobe and pulled out the spare pillows and blankets.

'We'll see you boys soon, then. We'll be back here at nine sharp,' said Gabriella, and she and Eliza left the room.

Murphy wordlessly took the pillows and blankets out of Con's hands, spreading them out on the floor. He climbed under the covers.

'How . . . how are you feeling?' said Con.

'Like I need a drink.'

'Feel free,' said Con, gesturing at the bar fridge.

Murphy pulled out all the bottles, eventually settling on wine straight from the miniature bottle. He handed another to Con.

Con hesitated, then took a drink too.

The men drank in silence. Murphy lay back on top of the covers, an open bottle beside him, and soon was alternating between snoring and turning fitfully.

Con took his medication, flicked off the lights, stripped out of his clothes, and climbed into bed. When he finally fell asleep, he dreamed of the Jaguar girls.

CHAPTER 41

CON

Con's phone buzzed at eight. It was the commander calling.

'We're going to the Wilkins farm. Meet me in the lobby in fifteen,' she said, hanging up before Con could speak.

Con glanced across at Murphy on the carpet, still asleep. Con tiptoed into the shower, running over the events of the previous day.

Teenage girls are maniacs was his conclusion.

Murphy was still sleeping when Con left, taking the laptop and USB drive. Agatha would surely want to see for herself.

She was waiting for him in the lobby, tapping her foot, and together they walked to his car. Con gave her a quick summary of the videos, then passed her the laptop to watch them while he drove. But before he could start the car, she handed him a two-page typed summary of the findings from Bree's autopsy and the forensic examination of her clothes and possessions.

'Horse chestnuts in the tread of her boots, concrete dust in her clothes . . .' he said. 'Do we know anywhere that's under construction? And horse chestnuts . . . I'm sure I've seen them somewhere . . .'

'We'll ask her parents,' said Agatha.

It took them ten minutes to reach the entrance of the Wilkins' farm, a long tree-lined driveway, by which point Agatha had finished the videos.

'Oakdale,' read Con, as they passed a wooden sign. Just beyond the trees, cows dotted the paddocks of a massive farm that reached right to the bushland of the Tiers.

'Do you think Butch Murphy had anything to do with the girls going missing?' said Agatha.

'I don't think so,' said Con. 'But at this point, who knows?' They crossed a stone bridge over a creek and came to the house itself. 'Bloody hell. It's like a palace.'

The three-storey Wilkins manor was square and white, with balconies and columns, and a modern art installation of metal flowers and a water feature on the front wall. The building was sleek, stylish, the household of a rich family: Con remembered reading, early on, that the Wilkins' beef farm was extremely successful. At least seven cars were parked in the expansive driveway.

'All of the family, come to support them, I imagine,' said Agatha.

He parked the BMW and they walked to the front entrance, Agatha bringing both Con's laptop and a black leather folio. Barking sounded from up ahead and two shaggy border collies appeared, their tails wagging.

Con grinned, and crouched.

The mansion's door swung open. 'Millie, Max! No!' shouted a thin, athletic-looking woman – Bree's mother, Isabel Wilkins. 'Oh, it's you lot, is it?'

'It's alright, ma'am.' Con pushed the dogs away from his face as they started licking his mouth.

'Well? Why are you here?' said Isabel. 'It's a bit late, isn't it? Bree is dead.'

'The forensics report has come in overnight,' said Agatha. 'I'd like to discuss it with you and your husband.'

'Will it bring her back?' snapped Isabel, as she tossed her hair back and walked inside.

Con and the commander followed.

'I'm guessing she doesn't like police?' said Con.

'My guess is she's angry and isn't sure who to blame. In her defence, it's remarkable that Bree managed to evade police and all the search efforts, to the point where she could hang herself on that tree. She has good reason to assume we weren't doing our jobs properly.'

Isabel waited for them at the end of the timber-lined corridor, in the massive dining room, where no fewer than thirteen people were eating a breakfast of bacon and eggs. She squeezed the shoulders of a burly dark-haired man sitting at the table, dressed in a dirty hi-vis farming shirt and ragged jeans. Con recognised him as Marcus Wilkins – he had seen him up at the car park on the day the girls went missing. His eyes were ringed by shadows and he wiped his sleeve across a chin dark with stubble before making to stand.

'No, please stay seated, Mr Wilkins. Could we have the room, please?' said Agatha to everyone else, midway through their breakfast.

'I'll not have you ordering my family about,' said Isabel shrilly.

Marcus waved his hand. 'It's alright, guys. It'll be about Bree.' His voice broke on her name.

The other people in the room left, muttering among themselves, until only Isabel and Marcus remained.

'Sorry about the mess,' said Marcus. He extended a callused hand to Con. 'Marcus Wilkins. I haven't met you yet, but I understand you've been leading the investigation.'

'You've volunteered for the SES search, Mr Wilkins?'

'For all the good it did,' he muttered.

Isabel rubbed his shoulders. 'He doesn't stop. As soon as he finishes work, he heads out there onto the mountains. He's back long after dark, and then up before the sun to see to the cattle.' She pierced Con with her gaze. 'You can't expect him to keep going up there. Our daughter is dead!'

Marcus reached up to pat Isabel's hand absently. 'Forgive Isabel. She knows you aren't truly to blame.'

Isabel sniffed.

'What brings you here?' said Marcus.

'We have early forensics,' said Agatha. 'Bree passed away three days ago, the cause of death a broken neck from hanging. It would've been quick and painless.'

Isabel sat down. '*Days* ago?'

'How could she have been there that long?' said Marcus.

'We're not sure yet,' said Agatha. 'What we do know is that the same rope that killed her is the one she was hanging from. How everyone missed her hanging there for days . . .'

'It's impossible,' said Marcus. 'I know people were there. I walked that path myself – I walked the entire trail from the school to the Trapper's Hut. I even saw people at the Hanging Tree, bringing flowers. Bree was not there three days ago.'

'So someone killed her?' said Isabel, hands to her mouth.

'We don't know that,' said Agatha. 'Her stomach was full of fruit, chocolate, potato chips, dried meats. Nothing like what was found in Georgia's stomach, nor did they eat it during the camp, as far as we know. If Bree did kill herself, she found somewhere to stay between disappearing from the path and the moment she died . . . and that's why we wanted to speak to you. Do you know anywhere Bree might have gone that has horse chestnut trees?'

'What are those?' said Isabel, turning to her husband.

'I didn't think they were edible,' said Marcus.

'No,' said Agatha. 'We found traces of them on her shoes.' She pulled a photo out of her folio and laid it flat. It showed a horse chestnut. Con *knew* he'd seen some, and recently, but where?

'We called them conkers when we were boys,' said Marcus, picking up the page. 'You play a game where you knock each other's until they break, but we always just pegged them at each other across the footy ground.' He looked up, right as Con remembered.

'At the school,' said Con.

Marcus nodded. 'There's a big row of them, right along the main driveway.'

'Are they building anywhere at the school?' said Con, remembering the concrete dust in Bree's clothes.

'Yes . . . half of the Home Economics block is being renovated,' said Marcus. 'Bree *loved* Home Ec.'

'Thank you, Mr Wilkins,' said Agatha.

'No one will be there today,' said Isabel, 'the students are staying home. Most of them would've been there . . . last night . . .' She took a deep, shuddering breath. 'Did Madison really *plan* all of this?' she finished in a whisper. 'Bree *hated* Madison.'

'I think it might be best to show you some footage we've recently recovered,' said Agatha. 'It's confronting, I'll warn you, but it may shed some light on your daughter's headspace.'

'Just ask, why don't you?' said Isabel.

'Ask what, Mrs Wilkins?' said the commander.

'Why she killed herself. Why we didn't get her more help. Ask us why she didn't think she could come to *us*, but instead chose to —'

'We believe there may be more to it, Mrs Wilkins,' interrupted Con. 'If you could just watch this video . . .'

Agatha set the laptop down and played the video that featured all five of the girls.

Isabel and Marcus leaned in, Marcus even touching the screen when Bree appeared, as they watched the four girls explaining their reasons.

The door swung open. 'Oh,' said a new woman, clearly a relative of Isabel's by the look of her. 'You've already seen it?' She pointed at the screen.

'What do you mean?' said Agatha.

'What do *you* mean?' said the woman in a haughty tone. 'The new video Madison Mason just uploaded.'

'It's on her YouTube?' Isabel stood up. 'I'm going to kill that little bitch.'

'Con,' said the commander, as Marcus rose to hold Isabel back. 'I'll deal with this. Call Detective Tran and get her to meet you at the school together with the forensics team. When you're done, come back to the station. It's time we brought Madison in for questioning again.'

Con parked near the school office. Melinda Tran was already there, but the forensics team were still running some final tests on the evidence from the Hanging Tree.

'What's our approach?' said Tran. 'No one's even here.'

'The office staff are. They're expecting us,' said Con. 'We have a lot of CCTV footage to look through.'

Together, they walked into the school lobby. The woman behind the desk smiled sadly at them. 'Hello, detectives,' she said, her nose blocked, eyes red from crying. 'I'm Lois. Come through.' She opened a door into the office. 'You can set up here. I've already fired up the system for you on both computers.'

With both Con and Melinda trawling through the footage of the external cameras, it wasn't long until they found Bree, in a dark hoodie, leaving through one of the doors of the Home Ec building.

'Lois?' called Con, his voice rising.

She came over and leaned down to check the monitor. She gasped. 'That's her.'

'Where is this? What's she been doing?' he said.

'It used to be the laundry,' Lois said. 'But it's closed off for renovations at the moment. There's no power in there or anything.'

'Tran, look: she's carrying rope,' said Con. 'And the time stamp: 3 am, three days ago.'

Tran gave a sad sigh. 'Lois, can you take us down there?'

'Certainly,' she replied.

She set off at a brisk pace and the detectives followed, but unless there was clear urgency, they would have to wait for the forensics team before they could enter a possible crime scene. Tran called them, informing them of the development, and they promised to come directly to the scene.

Con, Melinda, and Lois stood waiting outside the laundry door. It had begun to drizzle. The footage of Bree sneaking out with a coil of rope over her shoulder played over and over in Con's mind. It would be someone else's job, now, to look through the footage and find the moment she arrived at the school, but he imagined it would be the same night the girls went missing.

A clever place to hide, he thought. *With all the rain that night, it would've been easy to slip in here unnoticed, and she would have known the school would be closed after their disappearance.*

Finally Forensics arrived and Lois unlocked the door. With rubber gloves, serious voices, cameras flashing and recording, they walked inside.

Immediately they found the space where Bree had been staying. It was a small tiled room just off the laundry, Lois explaining that the freezers for the cooking classes had been kept here before the renovations began. There was a doorway into a small toilet, which was still connected to the plumbing, and the floor was covered in a blankets, pillows and junk food wrappers. The full *Deltora Quest* series lined one of the walls, and paints and markers lay in a neat pile in the corner.

But what drew everyone's eyes was what was written on the walls. On one wall:

The Hungry Man is real the Hungry Man is real the Hungry Man is real the Hungry Man is real the Hungry Man is real the Hungry Man is real the Hungry Man is real the Hungry Man is real the Hungry Man is real the Hungry Man is real

On the second wall:

I'm sorry Hungry Man I'll never tell anyone what I saw please don't take me please don't take me please don't take me please don't take me

On the third wall:

Hang a girl on a tree to die, and the Hungry Man will pass you by. I'm sorry Denni. We should have believed you.

On the fourth wall:

She was right.
He took them into the caves.
And their bones will feed him.

Two hours later, Con walked into the interview room at the station. Madison was alone, having refused a lawyer and even the support of her mother, who was instead waiting in the room next door.

Agatha wasn't there, either: she was giving a press conference. Con was supposed to wait for her to finish before he spoke
to Madison. This was a formal interview of a minor, he needed to
wait for a second police officer, at the very least. Preferably a social
worker would be there too, as she'd refused her parent's presence,
but Madison said she wouldn't speak a word to anyone but Agatha
and Con. It definitely would not go well for him if he began this
interview by himself.

Con took a seat. Madison watched him, hands folded on the
table. On the back of her arms he spotted scars from self-harm, pale
lines. He'd never noticed them before. Her eyes burned like a zealot,
a smirk tugging at her red lips. 'What's on your mind, detective?'

Anger rushed through him. 'How did you know Bree was hanging there?' he said.

'Whatever do you mean, detective?' said Madison.

'You arranged for hundreds of people to see her. Just like you did
with Denni. Why?' said Con.

'Well, I'm not admitting to anything at all, but theoretically,
if you killed yourself, wouldn't *you* want hundreds of people to see
you? To finally *feel* for you?' she said. 'Footage of Bree is all over the
internet now. No one will ever forget.'

'How did you know she was there?'

'Don't you understand, detective? My subscriber count is now
eighteen *million,*' she said.

'And the other girls? Cierra and Jasmine? *Georgia?*'

She watched him. No response: just a tiny lick of her lips.

'You need to tell me the truth,' he said.

'I am telling the truth,' Madison said.

'How did you know that Bree was there?' said Con again. 'She
died three days ago.'

A flicker of doubt on Madison's face. 'What are you talking about?
She died moments before we got there. Her blood was still warm.'

'I can show you the reports. How did you know she was there? Did you tell her to do it, like you told Denni?'

'*You're lying*. It wasn't three days since she'd died.'

'Did you tell her that it was the only way to stop the Hungry Man?'

'*Badenhorst!*' snapped the commander. He hadn't even heard the door open. 'Outside. *Now!*'

He stepped into the hallway with her, shaking.

'Go back to the Inn, Cornelius,' she said, her voice so icy it could have frosted the window.

'Two girls are still out there!'

'Stop, Cornelius,' she hissed. 'If you leave your hotel – and believe me, I will know – I'll take you off the case.'

Their exchange had drawn a crowd in the corridor, including Doble.

Con turned to walk away, but Agatha said, '*Wait.* Give me your phone.'

'What?'

'Give me your phone, Badenhorst, or I *am* taking you off the case. I'll not have you contacting Gabriella or Murphy or whoever else you'll manipulate into doing your investigating for you.'

He threw his phone at her feet, then pushed through the crowd and ducked into a bathroom.

Standing in front of the mirror, he willed himself to calm down. He hadn't been so angry in a long time.

'Hello, detective,' said Sergeant Doble, walking in behind him. He was in uniform, and his basset-hound face was alive with malice.

'What do you want?'

'Heard you were investigating me,' he said.

'Not yet,' said Con.

'You don't look too good, mate. I've heard post-traumatic stress can be a real bitch. I bet even those medications aren't enough. I mean, you've got a real cocktail going there.'

Con's hands clamped over the edges of the sink. 'You were in my room.'

'I wasn't in your room,' said Doble. 'But one of the cleaners is a client of mine, if you know what I mean. I had him have a look, once you started investigating my little enterprise, just to get a little insurance. Nice job with the curtains: does it help with the nightmares?'

Con turned on him, his hands balled into fists.

'The funny thing is, PTS isn't listed in your personnel file. I wonder what the commissioner would say about the lead detective on the most important kidnapping cases of the decade being mentally unstable. I mean, it wouldn't just be bad for you, but also your commanding officer.'

Con stepped forward. Doble didn't sense the danger.

'Here's what you're gonna do, Badenhorst. You're gonna tell whoever you need to that I am *clean,* or I'll tell the media and you and Normandy will never work in law enforcement again.'

'The first thing I'm going to do is find the missing girls,' said Con. 'Then, after that, I'm going to bring you down. And, if you're lucky, I won't let Murphy have a piece of you.'

Doble swung his fist at Con's face, but Con was ready, dropping Doble to the ground with an Aikido throw. Doble landed on his back, groaning.

He staggered to his feet, cheeks red. 'You just assaulted me, detective,' he growled.

'You're the reason people hate cops,' he said. 'You're worse than a grub.' He walked out of the room.

He didn't need the commander. He had at least three allies to help him get to the bottom of this: Gabriella, Eliza and Murphy.

CHAPTER 42

MURPHY

This time, Murphy knew what the dream was trying to tell him. Sara stood below, looking up at him. Her ginger hair caught the wind, her lavender dress billowing.

We're going to find you, Jasmine. I know it.

Sara smiled as he crashed down on top of her.

Murphy jerked awake. He was fully clothed, tangled in the blankets on the floor of Con's hotel room. Someone was pounding on the door. The clock read 9.04 am and the detective was nowhere to be seen.

Before he stood up, he checked the Glock was still in his belt.

He opened the door, and Gabriella walked in. 'Where's Con?'

'Dunno,' said Murphy.

'What time did he leave?'

He shrugged again. 'I only just woke up. Where's Eliza?'

'I called a taxi to take her home. She needs time to grieve – she cried nearly all night, though she tried to hide it.' She peered into his face. 'How are you feeling, after Jasmine's videos?'

'Like I still want to kill Butch.'

She nodded. 'You want help finding him?'

He looked at her in surprise.

'I have a feeling Con will contact *you* before he contacts me, and I need to talk to him.' She walked out of the room, calling over her shoulder, 'Besides, who else is going to help you? Of course, if you *actually* try and kill Butch, fair warning, I'll have to intervene. Remember how that worked out for you last time?'

CHAPTER 43

ELIZA

The taxi pulled up at the bottom of her drive and Eliza climbed out. Once the taxi pulled away, she put her arms around herself and walked up the drive towards her little crooked cottage.

The front door slammed open and Butch appeared in her doorway, wearing only a singlet and shorts. He had a bottle of her wine in his hand and was swaying slightly. 'Eliza,' he called, voice slurred.

She saw now his black Toyota Hilux parked behind an apple tree.

'Butch?' said Eliza. 'What are you . . .? How did you get inside?'

'I nee' your help.' He teetered on the sill, then grabbed the door-frame.

'Butch . . .' Eliza felt panicky. 'Murphy saw . . . He knows you're Jasmine's biological father.'

'I know. Heard through his bedroom door – Madison gave him videos . . . Can you still help me? You said you would help me.'

Eliza stepped closer. 'What do you need, Butch?'

CHAPTER 44

MURPHY

Gabriella pulled up outside Butch's house. There was still no sign of his Hilux.

Murphy pushed through the front door, Gabriella close behind.

'Butch!' called Murphy.

Gabriella wandered down the hall, looking around, and a moment later, she shouted, 'Murphy!'

He sprinted down the hall and found her in Jasmine's room.

Hanging by baling twine from Jasmine's light globe was a wooden statue, bone fragments hammered into its eyes.

He felt sick.

'When was the last time you were in this room?' said Gabriella.

'A couple days ago? I don't know.'

'We need to check the rest of the house,' she said, running out of the room.

Murphy didn't move. He couldn't take his eyes off the statue.

'Murphy!' shouted Gabriella. 'In here.'

He followed her voice, into Butch's room.

On Butch's bed were clothes – jeans and tights and crop tops and bras – torn apart and covered in blood. Sitting in the middle of it all was another wooden sculpture with a noose and bones in its eyes.

Written on the wall in blood were the words:

3 down
1 to go

'I have to call Con,' said Gabriella, voice shaking.

Murphy backed against the wall, looking between the clothes and the writing.

He'd been angry, so angry, but he still couldn't . . . it couldn't be Butch . . .

Part of him had wanted it to be Butch, part of him hadn't. *It couldn't be . . .*

'Commander Normandy? Why do you have Con's phone? What's happened to him?' said Gabriella. She stepped out of the room.

Murphy's own phone buzzed. It was Eliza calling.

'Murphy, are you alone?' she said.

'Eliza —' began Murphy.

'I need you to promise me something,' she interrupted. 'Meet me at my house. Tell no one.'

'What's going on?'

'Butch is here . . . Can you talk to him and —'

'Eliza, listen to me.' He looked up at the words on the wall. 'Butch is not safe. You need to get out of the house, get away from him.'

'Why? What's happened?'

'You need to leave right now.'

'Should I call the cops? What's going on?'

'No,' he said. He touched the gun in his belt. 'Don't tell a soul.'

'Alright. I'll just . . . go over to Monica's?'

'Yeah,' he said. 'I'll see to Butch.'

He walked out to the kitchen. Gabriella was pacing the hallway, talking to the commander, demanding she send someone over.

Her car keys were on the bench. Murphy took them and walked out the door.

CHAPTER 45

CON

Con stood in his hotel room shower, eyes shut, letting the water roll over his back.

Breathe in . . . and out.

Madison was the one who had started all this, and she *knew* Bree was hanging there, somehow. The Hanging Tree . . .

He opened his eyes.

Marcus Wilkins, Bree's father, had said that he'd seen mourners at the Hanging Tree. Had they missed Bree's body, standing that close? It seemed unlikely.

He left the shower, drying himself. He wanted to call Marcus Wilkins, then remembered the commander had his phone.

He checked the drawer beneath the hotel room's phone and found a phone directory. *MN & IC WILKINS, 'OAKDALE'.*

He called them. A young voice answered.

'Hi, this is Detective Badenhorst. I need to speak with Marcus.'

'Give me a sec . . .'

A moment later, Marcus was on the other end. 'Detective? Is everything okay?'

'You said you saw mourners by the Hanging Tree,' said Con without preamble. 'Did you see who they were?'

'Well, there was only one person, and I didn't want to pry while they were paying their respects.'

'But who was it?'

'Well, I can't be sure, I only saw the back of her head, but I think it was Eliza Ellis?'

CHAPTER 46

MURPHY

Murphy screeched to a halt outside Eliza's house. He left Gabriella's car running and ran towards the front door.

He could hear Eliza's screams for help from deep in the house.

He threw the door open. *'Eliza! Where are you?'*

He followed her screams and burst into a bedroom, taking in everything at once.

Butch lay naked on the bed, handcuffed to the headboard and his ankles tied to the end with baling twine. He was gagged by a sock in his mouth and a tea towel tied around his face, his chest and face bruised in mottled angry purple, blood pouring from a smashed nose and a cut above his eye.

When Butch saw Murphy he strained against the cuffs, trying to lift himself off the bed.

Eliza didn't look much better: her clothes were ripped, exposing her underwear, her face was bruised, her head scarf gone and the wound on her forehead revealed. She held high a cricket bat and almost collected Murphy with it as she turned. 'Murphy!' She dropped the bat and she threw herself into his arms. 'He tried to handcuff me to the bed, but I knocked him out —'

Butch pulled against the cuffs, his shouting muffled by the gag.

'He confessed everything!' said Eliza. 'He took the girls – he's killed Cierra and Jasmine! He confessed!'

Heat flooded Murphy.

He pulled the gun from his belt.

'Kill him, Murphy,' screamed Eliza, pulling on his arm.

Murphy looked into his brother's eyes. His vision blurred at the edges. He felt Eliza's hands on his, dragging his arms up, aiming the gun at Butch's chest.

Butch looked deep into his brother's eyes, full of tears and terror, deep piercing blue eyes . . . the same shade of cut-glass that Jasmine had inherited.

Jasmine had Butch's eyes, not Murphy's. Because Butch was her father.

Memories, emotions, images of Butch with Jasmine. Hugging her, caring for her, supporting her through her grief, supporting Murphy in his fatherhood.

Butch loved Jasmine. He'd never kill her.

Eliza's fingers closed over the trigger.

'No,' shouted Murphy, trying to wrench his hands out of hers. With a loud *blam*, the gun kicked in his hands.

The sound of the shot in the small room was explosive, and Murphy staggered. He saw a hole had appeared in the wall. Then something hard whacked into the side of his head.

Pain and rainbows – the world spun. He fell to his knees.

Eliza stood over him, cricket bat in her hands. She swung it again but this time Murphy saw it coming, catching the blow on his meaty forearms. He was still holding the gun. He fired a warning shot into the ceiling. Another explosive sound. 'Eliza! What are you doing?'

Eliza screamed and ran from the room. 'Help! *Help!*'

Murphy pulled himself to his feet, feeling the side of his head where she'd hit him. It was swollen and bloody. A surge of nausea rolled through him.

Butch screamed into his gag and Murphy took it from his mouth.

'She's a maniac, bro. She attacked me —' Butch shouted. 'I didn't do anything to her, mate, I swear.'

'Where's Jasmine?'

'What? I have no idea! I would have told you if I did!'

'Then why the *hell* are you here?' he shouted, pointing the gun at him.

'Easy, lad!'

'*Answer me!*' It took physical energy not to let the anger pull the trigger – his forehead was wet with sweat.

'Because Eliza knew!'

'Knew what?' demanded Murphy.

'About me and Sara, what we . . . did together. She knew that . . . she knew that Jasmine is my kid!'

'What you did *together*? You *raped* her!'

'I didn't! Mate, I swear to you. Sara was the one who came to me! And Jasmine knew —'

Murphy pressed the gun against Butch's head.

'Alright. Easy, mate, easy.' Butch pushed himself upright as best he could, as far away from the gun as possible. 'Listen to me. Will you just fucking listen?'

Murphy didn't reply. His chest heaved.

Butch spoke quickly. 'Last year, Jasmine went to Eliza. She told her what Sara had told her before she died: that I was her real dad, okay, but I *didn't* rape her, alright? Sara wanted it. She *wanted* it.' He talked faster as Murphy's arm twitched. 'And if you kill me, you'll never know the truth, alright, so will you put that fucking thing down?'

'Why would Jasmine go to *Eliza*?'

'Because she wanted to get me charged, Murph! Because she trusts Eliza and wanted her help to throw me in jail! Eliza called me after, because she knows me better than that, she didn't just take Jasmine's word for it. I showed Eliza the letter . . .' Butch's eyes lit up. 'There's a letter! At home, an honest-to-God letter from Sara, admitting what she and I did. A letter to you! I wanted to give it to you, I really did —'

'Then why didn't you?'

'Easy, lad, easy . . . Jasmine didn't want me to. After I showed it to her, she begged me not to. I thought you deserved to know, but Jasmine said it would destroy you, that it would ruin your memory of Sara. Jasmine wanted me to say I'd forced myself onto Sara. She really wants Sara's memory to be perfect. I don't think you know how important that is to her.'

'Sara *was* perfect,' growled Murphy.

'You know me, mate. You *know* I wouldn't do that, bro' said Butch. 'Surely you know that. Even Eliza said she'd vouch for me, if Jasmine went to the cops or anyone. I've got the letter! Take me home and I'll show you the bloody letter . . . I wish I could tell you we were drunk, or stoned, but . . . I don't even remember where you were . . . it just . . . happened. In that moment, Sara wanted it to happen . . . and so did I!'

Murphy couldn't grasp what he was hearing, it both touched him and missed him. He felt so alone. He realised, distantly, that this feeling was what Jasmine wanted to protect him from . . .

'After that . . . Nothing ever happened again, I *promise* you,' said Butch. 'Sara told Jasmine the truth, but she didn't want to believe it. Jasmine's convinced I raped Sara. I suppose it's easier for her to . . . I showed her the letter, but she . . .'

Murphy began yelling, at first just noise, pure anger and anguish and pain. Then he heard his own words: *'Don't you say her name!'* His gun was pointed at Butch's head.

'You know me, brother. You know me!'

'Drop the gun, Murphy.' Con stood at the door, his pistol trained on Murphy. 'Easy.'

Murphy turned to Con, his gun still raised, still shouting. '*Don't say her name!*'

Con took a step forward. 'I won't ask you again, Murphy. Put the gun down.'

'Just do it!'

Con held his eyes.

Murphy's gun began to wobble. '*Just shoot me!*'

Slowly, Con lowered his gun. 'No, mate.' His hands raised in surrender, he came within reach of Murphy.

Murphy held onto the Glock as tightly as he could but his whole arm was trembling now, he could barely see through the tears. 'Don't you come near me, mate. Don't you dare come *fucking* near me!'

Con gently took the gun from Murphy's hands. 'It's okay, mate.'

'It's not okay! *It's not okay!*'

Murphy slumped forward and Con wrapped him in a big bear hug. 'It's not your fault,' said Con, sadness in his voice. 'It's not your fault.'

'*Then why did she leave?*'

Murphy didn't know which one he meant: Sara or Jasmine.

They stood there for a while, Murphy gradually calming, pulling himself out of Con's arms, ashamed.

'Could you un-cuff me, do you think, detective?' said Butch in a small voice. 'I think my ribs are broken . . .'

'What happened here?' said Con. He still had a careful, concerned eye on Murphy.

'Eliza attacked me,' said Butch.

'Where is she now?' Con said. 'Those look like police cuffs.' He rummaged in his belt for the keys and tossed them to Murphy. 'Eliza can't get away.'

Murphy looked at the keys, then at Butch.

'Don't you leave me here,' whimpered Butch. 'Don't you dare.'

Murphy unlocked the cuffs, then put the keys in his pocket. He picked up the Glock from the floor and stuck it in his belt.

He walked out and didn't look back.

CHAPTER 47

ELIZA

Eliza pulled up in front of Monica's house, the tall poplar trees outside casting barely a shadow in the noonday sun. She'd thrown off her torn clothes as she left the cottage and grabbed a floral dress from the laundry – the one with the deep pouch pocket. There she had the second pair of handcuffs she'd stolen from Gabriella's room that morning.

A yellow post-it note was stuck under the sun visor:

I give Eliza Ellis permission to do whatever it takes.

She pulled it off and scrunched it up in her hand, then walked up the side of Monica's house to the back door. She took the spare key from under a peace lily pot plant and crept inside.

The sound of the news coverage came from the TV in the lounge, abuzz and ablaze with commentary on Madison's latest video and the discovery of Bree Wilkins' body.

Monica would be the one watching it, for any news of Tom, but she wouldn't have let her daughter watch it with her. So Eliza slowly walked up the stairs, to Wren's room.

It was the perfect little girl's room: princess wallpaper and a four-poster bed. Wren lay on glittery pink carpet in a little red dress, playing on her iPad.

Her face brightened when she saw Eliza. 'Aunt Leesy!' She threw herself into Eliza's arms.

Eliza's resolve wavered. She tightened her grip on the permission slip. *I can do whatever it takes.*

She began to cry: real tears, not fake ones, for the first time in a long time.

'Aunt Leesy? It's okay.' Wren put her hand on Eliza's cheek.

Eliza shoved the permission slip into her pocket and took hold of Wren's little forearm with both hands.

Eliza felt sick. She was shaking.

But she had to do this.

Eliza smiled through her tears and snapped Wren's little forearm – both radius and ulna.

Instant agony. Wren screamed, and screamed and screamed.

Pounding footsteps up the stairs and Monica appeared at the door, cheeks puffy, terror in her red face. 'Wren!' she shrieked.

Sarge raced up behind her, the big dog adding his booming barks to the mix.

'I'm sorry, I snuck in to see her, and she wanted to show me a trick on her bed – she's broken her arm!' shouted Eliza.

'*Wren!*'

'Quick, Monica – take my car, get to the hospital, call an ambulance to meet you on the way. Now! Hurry!'

Eliza knew how to respond to children feeling strong emotion – short instructions, direct tone of voice – and Monica, already exhausted from Tom's arrest, was in shock, fearing for her child, in pain. She did exactly as Eliza said without question.

Eliza helped Monica carry Wren, intentionally jostling the little girl's arm. She fainted, overwhelmed by the pain.

She helped Monica strap Wren's limp body into the back seat, then Monica was driving away and Eliza was alone, save for Sarge barking at her.

She dragged the dog through the house by the collar and locked him outside. His booming barks and whimpers could be heard all through the house.

Shaking, remembering the feeling of Wren's little arm snapping in her hands – *I'm so sorry, Wren* – she used the kitchen scissors to cut her hair in the bathroom mirror to roughly the same length as Monica's, sweeping up the hair and dumping it in the bin. She took the cheese grater and raked some lines down her cheek and forehead. She winced at the sharp pain, the hot blood trickling down her face, but she'd successfully disguised the forehead wound she'd sustained up in the mountain.

Now she slipped her glasses off and put them in the pocket of her dress.

She looked more like Monica than herself, now. Or at least, enough to fool anyone who came to the house. The sight of blood would go a long way to keeping them from thinking rationally, and they'd hopefully jump to the conclusion Eliza wanted them to.

She took a tea towel and tied it around her mouth, then used a zip tie from under the sink to bind her wrists together, using her teeth to pull it tight with some difficulty around the loose gag.

She walked to the front door, her vision blurry without her glasses. She pushed over the entrance stand, including the glass vase of purple tulips on top, and laid herself down in the puddle of water and petals.

Before long she heard a car pull up outside.

CHAPTER 48

CON

Con searched the little crooked cottage, but Eliza was nowhere. Her car wasn't outside either.

Murphy appeared next to him, the side of his head bleeding down into his beard. 'She's gone.'

'We need to talk to Monica,' said Con, leading the way to his car. 'I can't think of anyone else who would know what's going on with Eliza.'

'Why did you come here?' said Murphy, as Con started the car and pulled out.

'Bree's dad thought he saw Eliza at the Hanging Tree days ago – on the morning we now believe Bree died.'

'You think Eliza's involved?'

'She handcuffed Butch to a bed and hit you with a cricket bat,' said Con. 'Obviously she's involved.'

They drove through the centre of Limestone Creek to Monica's house. There were people everywhere: walking their dogs, chatting over low fences, actual lemonade stands set up by kids capitalising on the carnival of people who had flocked to the town these past few days. Spring had drawn out the red waratahs, riots of yellow daffodils and multicoloured tulips in the garden beds. TV crews from all over the world were interviewing people on street corners. It was like a sick festival.

Con felt he was the only one who could put a stop to it. He had to find Eliza. He had to solve this puzzle.

Finally they reached Monica's house, and before Con could even pull the handbrake Murphy stepped out of the BMW and headed towards the front door.

'Wait, Murphy,' said Con, running to catch up. He could hear Sarge's great, booming barks.

Murphy didn't knock, he just pushed the door open. 'Monica? Are you in here?' he roared.

'You can't just walk into someone's house,' said Con. Then he froze.

A glass vase lay shattered on the tiles, tulips in a puddle of water, and Monica on the floor in the middle of it all. Her hands were bound in front of her with a cable tie and her mouth gagged with a tea towel. Her face was bleeding and her amber eyes were wide and wild.

'Monica!' shouted Con, falling to his knees beside her and unknotting the gag. Her bound wrists were already bruising and her arms scraped against the shards of the vase.

'She's taken Wren!' she screamed the moment he had the gag out.

'Easy,' said Con. 'Murphy, grab a knife from the kitchen.'

'Eliza came here and attacked me,' said Monica. 'She took Wren. She said they have a boat waiting for them in Launceston!'

Murphy returned with the knife and broke the cable ties.

Monica was lapsing into hysterics: it was hard to make out her words. 'Eliza ... Tom and Eliza ... Eliza can't have kids, so wanted Wren and now she's ... gone.' She rose shakily to her feet, grasping at the hooks on the wall where the keys hung, searching for balance. She held her stomach and vomited onto the tiles.

'Murphy, give me your phone,' said Con. He typed in a number and a moment later the commander answered. As quickly as he could, he explained everything that had transpired since he had called Marcus Wilkins. 'We believe Eliza may be headed towards Launceston with Wren.'

'I'll make the calls,' said Agatha. 'You stay there. I'll call you right back on this number. *Don't think this gets you off the hook for disobeying my direct order.*'

She ended the call and Con relayed the information to both Murphy and Monica. 'Do you need us to take you to hospital?' said Con.

'No, it's fine,' said Monica shakily. She touched her face, grimacing at the pain. 'I . . . I think I should just stay here. I have a friend who's a doctor. I'll call her around.'

'Okay, great idea,' said Con. He put his concern about Monica into the box labelled People Who I Don't Need To Worry About Right Now and focused his mental energy on the immediate issue: Eliza had kidnapped her niece and was fleeing.

Monica lurched, again holding her stomach. 'I'll go lie down in my room and call her.' She wandered off upstairs, shivering.

Outside, Sarge kept barking, working himself into a frenzy.

'I need a drink,' said Murphy. 'Do you want a drink?'

Without waiting for Con's answer, he walked into the kitchen and began rummaging around. Murphy took a bottle of whisky off a high shelf and poured himself a glass.

'You can't just —' said Con.

'I think I've earned it, mate.' Murphy pawed through their freezer, pulling out a tray of ice cubes. He dropped some into his glass, then pressed the tray against the side of his head.

'Did you know Eliza couldn't have kids?' said Con.

'No,' said Murphy. 'But that would explain it, right? Why she took Jasmine and Cierra.'

'How the hell does that explain anything?' said Con.

'I dunno,' said Murphy in a tired voice. 'I'm just trying to make sense of it, mate. She was really attached to Denni. Maybe she's trying to replace Denni?' He drank his whisky. 'Either way, I'm believing she took Jasmine and we're about to find her.'

Murphy's phone rang in Con's hand. The commander was calling. Con put it on speaker.

'Well, we've sent the word out,' said Agatha. 'We've got everyone from Limestone Creek to Launceston out on the roads. From the sounds of your timeline, she can't have gone far.'

'Good,' said Con.

'There's something else you should know,' said the commander. 'This probably isn't the best time to tell you, but I don't want you to hear it from one of the other officers.' She sighed. 'I've had a call from the commissioner. He asked whether I felt you were fit for service.'

'Why would he ask that?'

'Oh, I don't know, maybe because you punched Sergeant Doble?'

'Doble? I didn't punch him. I just . . . put him on the ground.'

Murphy shot Con a look of surprise. 'You punched that prick?'

Con waved him off.

'Con . . . why did you continue today, after I made it very clear you needed to take a break?'

'Because I got new information – Eliza was at the Hanging Tree the day Bree killed herself!'

She sighed. 'You've left me with no choice.'

'What?'

'I need you off the case.'

'Right now? When we're *just* about to find Eliza?'

'Yes, Badenhorst, right now. You have the satisfaction of knowing you've solved it, but neither of us is getting into deeper trouble than we're already in. I should've taken you off the case days ago . . . Don't deny your PTS symptoms have been getting in the way.'

'What you're saying is I've done all the hard work but will get none of the recognition?'

'Physically assaulting Sergeant Doble, Badenhorst?' she said.

'He tried to punch *me*! I didn't even hurt him.'

'Listen . . . post-traumatic stress is nothing to laugh at —'

'I do *not* have PTS,' Con shouted. He ended the call.

'You punched Doble?' asked Murphy again, sounding impressed. He poured a whisky for Con and slid it across the counter.

It smelled like exactly what Con needed. He watched it for a moment, then took it. 'It's fine, they'll find Eliza,' he said, taking a sip. 'We'll get answers. We'll save the girls. That's *all* that matters.'

Outside, Sarge kept barking.

CHAPTER 49

ELIZA

Leaving Con and Murphy in the kitchen, Eliza headed towards the upstairs bathroom and locked the door behind her. Her rough new haircut tickled the back of her neck.

She put her glasses back on and allowed her bloody reflection a brief smile.

Next she took down the first-aid kit, dabbing cream on her cuts and then covering them with plastic plasters. She wiped the remaining blood from her face and applied some of Monica's gold lipstick, gold eyeshadow. Then she put in some big gold hoop earrings.

Tom's car key was already safely stowed in her dress pocket: she'd taken it off the hook when she'd vomited. It was time to go for a drive. She had time to go over what happened, and to plan her next steps. *Permission to do whatever it takes.*

Finally, she'd had some good luck.

She hadn't expected to find Butch at her house that morning, although of course she was on his side – she had never believed Jasmine's lies about him raping Sara. Jasmine was a two-faced, double-crossing, murderous bitch.

Butch had been begging for help, but he'd been so drunk he hadn't even remembered the letter from Sara, even though he was the one who'd told Eliza about it, years ago. When she offered to retrieve it from his house, since he was obviously too drunk to drive, he took her up on the offer immediately.

And so she'd driven to Butch's house. She'd killed one of their cats, the fat black-and-white one, and spread its blood and guts all over Butch's bed. Then she'd written the message on the wall – *3 down, 1 to go* – and cut up some of Jasmine's clothes, ending it all with her tribute to Denni: one of her Hungry Man warding statues. She had several of them hidden in the spare tyre compartment of her car.

When she got back to her house, it was easy to trick the drunken Butch into lying down on her bed, handcuff him with Gabriella's handcuffs, tie up his feet and gag him, cut all his clothes off, and then hit him a few times with the cricket bat for effect.

Her hope was that Murphy would burst through the door and, in shock and unable to regulate the overwhelming emotion, kill Butch. With Butch out of the picture, unable to defend himself, it'd be all the easier for the cops to suspect him of taking the girls.

If it came to the worst, she'd thought she could probably kill both brothers – make it look like a murder–suicide.

But it hadn't worked. Murphy hadn't killed Butch, and she hadn't been able to take him out with the cricket bat. That had made her angry. Now she'd had to resort to her next plan. Poor little Wren.

She left the bathroom and headed to Monica and Tom's room, putting on one of Monica's dresses, a sleeveless long white summer dress with prints of blue and pink butterflies – the only one that had pockets. She transferred her permission slip, the handcuffs and Tom's keys.

Her armour; her inventory. It was time to go to war. Her final plan.

Giving herself a once-over in the full-length mirror, even spraying some of Monica's perfume on her wrists, she took her glasses off and walked downstairs and out the back door.

Sarge stopped barking when he saw her. Whimpering, he licked her fingers.

She patted him, then walked down the side path, through the gate, and out to Tom's Landcruiser.

Putting her glasses back on, the drive to Madison's house went by in full technicolour glory. Spring flowers and birds, the afternoon sky a brilliant blue. Helicopters overhead, police cars in the streets, media everywhere. The population of Limestone Creek had doubled overnight. There were SALE flags everywhere, pennants hanging from trees, MISSING posters of all four girls, the disrespect of Georgia's face still being on display apparently lost on those who had put them up.

This is all for you, Denni.

She pulled up at Madison's house. The last time Eliza had come here had been two days ago, after being released from custody. Before going home she'd climbed into the Masons' house through Cierra's window – the same way Tom always had, thanks to the broken latch on Cierra's window – and left one of Denni's dolls in Madison's room.

She took her glasses off once again and left the Landcruiser running. She pounded on the front door, working herself up into a flurry, letting the tears flow.

A moment later, Madison answered the door. She was wearing her school uniform – she must have been filming a video.

She had her iPhone in her hand, brandished like a sword. Her weapon.

Her weapon, against Eliza's new armour.

'Uh . . . Eliza?' Madison said, thrown off balance by Eliza's transformation.

'It's me, Monica . . .' Eliza said hurriedly. 'Eliza is in the hospital. Butch *attacked* her.'

Madison swayed, holding the door. 'So it's true?' she whispered. 'Butch took the girls?'

'Yes, and I think I know where they might be. I need someone they trust: will you come with me?' Eliza spoke in a hurry. 'Please, before it's too late – you're the only one who can help me. Quick, come with me.' Again, she used her teacher's voice, direct short commands.

Madison hesitated, then nodded. 'I'll grab my jacket.'

'We don't have time!' Eliza turned and ran to the four-wheel drive. 'Quickly!'

As Eliza knew she would, Madison followed, a few steps behind, climbing up into the passenger seat. 'What happened to your face?' she said.

She took a shaky breath. 'Butch is . . . scary when he's angry.'

'Oh my God,' said Madison. Her face was flushed. Her phone was in her hand, but she didn't call the police.

Of course Madison wants to be there before anyone else, she wants to film the whole thing, thought Eliza.

It was hard to drive without her glasses. She squinted from the effort. She was so close to the end! The end of everything she'd set out to do.

'Did Butch say anything about Bree?' said Madison.

'I don't think so,' said Eliza.

'Detective Badenhorst said Bree had been dead for three days when we found her, but . . .'

'But what?' said Eliza.

'She texted me, yesterday morning. She was about to do it. She was really going to kill herself. She told me what time she'd do it and everything! So I could organise the vigil.'

'You've been in contact with the girls?'

'Not really . . . Georgia was the one who had the phone. We all agreed she'd be the one who'd use it most wisely, the only one who wouldn't get cold feet. When they found her body, I assumed the phone had been lost . . . but they must have switched the phone, because Bree texted me with it yesterday morning . . .' She stomped her shoe in the footwell. 'I don't know where Jasmine and Cierra are.'

Eliza's hands on the steering wheel were starting to ache from how tight she held them there. Suddenly all she could think about was killing Jasmine's cat. Who knew cat blood could be so warm?

And why had she done it? It was stupid. The police would know it was cat's blood. If anything, it'd direct suspicion *away* from Butch.

She was making mistakes. Like a stupid little girl. Making mistakes.

Soon. Soon it would all be over. Justice. And strength. Both would be hers.

Warm blood, and the feeling of Wren's arm breaking in her hands. *I have permission to do what it takes!*

The Landcruiser bumped along over the haunted bridge and through the outskirts of Limestone Creek, until oak trees and poplars gave way to the white gums and candlebarks and paddocks full of bracken fern, and above it all the stepped outline of the hazy blue Great Western Tiers. All of them were up there. Projection Bluff, Liffey Bluff, Drys Bluff, Billopp Bluff . . .

Eliza pulled off the main road and onto the bumpy four-wheel-drive track of a forestry road. She slowed right down, driving to the conditions, and rolled down the windows – the *cussik-cussik* of green rosellas, the harsh cry of a cockatoo.

'Do you know where you're going, Monica?' said Madison, as the Landcruiser pitched from side to side. Doubt had crept into her voice.

'I know exactly where . . .' said Eliza. 'Tom showed me. Butch wouldn't have had any difficulty getting Jasmine to follow him.' She said it firmly, allowing no argument.

The gradient grew steeper, in a series of undulations through rocky soil and red dirt. Eliza pulled over at a rocky outcrop – a clearing in the canopy – that offered a view of Limestone Creek.

'I think this might be close. Can you help me?' Without waiting for Madison's reply, she climbed out of the ute and then up into the tray. 'Come up and help me.'

'What is it?' said Madison, climbing out of the car. 'Is *this* where they are?'

Madison screamed as a wombat, heavy and broad, snuffled off into the undergrowth of ferns and grasses. Then she laughed at herself, shakily smoothing out the skirt of her school dress.

Eliza stood upright on the tray of the Landcruiser, her white dress billowing in the breeze, weighed down by the contents of her pocket. 'Come up here.'

Madison followed, reaching out for Eliza's hand for help.

Eliza allowed Madison one final view of Limestone Creek. Her little kingdom, and the chaos she had caused. She could hear the helicopters, the hum of traffic, thumping music from the paddock beside the community hall.

Madison looked out over the town, her deep red hair catching the wind, her shoulders rising and falling with excited breath.

'Can you see that?' Eliza said softly, leaning over the cab of the Landcruiser, pointing into the bush some distance away. Her other hand was in the pocket of Monica's dress, on the cold metal of the handcuffs.

Madison shuffled to stand beside her. 'What is it? All I see is the bush.'

'Maybe if you lean forward . . . put your hands here,' said Eliza, pointing at the black steel of the cab guard.

Madison put her hands where Eliza wanted them and Eliza moved quickly, slamming Madison's head down on top of the cab, bloodying her nose, dazing her. Quick as a snake, she cuffed Madison's wrist to the cab guard.

Madison groaned, tried to feel her nose, then realised her wrist was cuffed. She tried to yank away, but the cuffs shackled her to the cab guard. 'What are you doing?' she screamed.

Eliza pulled Madison's phone from the pocket of her school dress and stepped back, out of reach. She weighed the phone in her hand, before taking a photo of Madison.

Madison's eyes widened, blood dripping out of her nose. '*You* took them, Monica?'

Eliza took her glasses out of her pocket and slid them onto her nose. Now she could see Madison in sharper focus: the terror, the blood running from her nose, the panicked breathing.

'Eliza! *You're Eliza!*'

'Where are Jasmine and Cierra?' said Eliza. 'You know where they are.'

'*I don't! I don't!*'

'Doesn't matter. You'll tell me soon.'

Eliza jumped off the tray of the Landcruiser, climbed back into the driver's seat. She turned on the ignition.

She drove higher into the mountains, Madison handcuffed to the tray, pounding on the cab with her other hand, screaming for Eliza to let her go.

If a helicopter flew overhead now, they might see the white Landcruiser, through gaps in the eucalypt canopy. And the school-girl thrashing and trying to break free of the handcuffs in the tray. But the whole search party was still focused on Lake Mackenzie.

Only Eliza could hear Madison's screams. She smiled as she drove towards the bluffs.

CHAPTER 50

CON

'Monica's done a runner,' said Murphy, returning to the kitchen. 'I had a look, and she's taken Tom's four-wheel drive.'

'Can't say I blame her,' said Con. 'She's probably gone to join the search for Wren. Don't worry, I called Gabby and she'll —'

There was pounding on the front door.

'Speak of the Kiwi.'

Gabriella marched in, chest swollen in outrage. She pointed a furious finger at Murphy. 'You! Dickhead! Steal my car again and I'll kill you!'

'Alright, Gab,' said Con. 'Listen —'

'Don't you start!' she said, turning her finger on Con. 'You're only inviting me back into the club now you're off the case too. Don't think I don't know!'

Murphy stood at the window. 'Sorry to interrupt your couple's quarrel, but there's a kid messing around with your car, Con . . .'

Con swore and ran out the door, Murphy and Gabriella close behind.

'He's jumped over that fence,' said Murphy, pointing.

'Just leave it,' said Con. 'We have other things to worry about.'

'Look what he's scratched into your car . . . Kundela . . .'

'The Kundela Game!' Gabriella crouched down, running her finger over the scratches. 'This is the same as on my car . . . *K-U-N* . . .' She swore. 'It was Georgia's brother, Carl Lenah.'

'What's the Kundela Game?' said Murphy.

'We need to find out,' said Gabriella. She ran for the fence. 'Catch him!'

Cursing, Con ran out onto the street, sprinting along the footpath, trying to cut off the fleeing vandal.

It was Gabriella who caught Carl Lenah, two blocks away, behind a green bus stop shelter. Con and Murphy quickly caught up.

Carl was a short but stocky lad, face as angry as a thunderstorm. He was wearing thongs, which had allowed Gabriella to catch up to him. She pushed him up against the wall of the bus shelter.

'Stay away from me, pigs,' said Carl.

'He's drunk,' said Gabriella. 'You can smell it on him.'

'I'm not drunk. Piss *off*.' He struggled against her.

She pushed his shoulders harder against the wall. 'Tell us about the Kundela Game.'

'Piss off,' said Carl.

'We need your help, Carl,' said Con.

'I'm not telling you shit.'

'Hold him still, Gabriella,' said Murphy. He squared up to Carl. 'Listen to me, kid. My daughter is missing. She's dead for all I know. What does the Kundela Game have to do with Madison and Jasmine? Tell me.'

'It has nothing to do with Jasmine,' said Carl.

'So what is it to Madison?' said Murphy. He pulled the Glock from the back of his belt and pressed it up against Carl's chin. 'Tell me everything.'

'Hey, hey, hey!' shouted Gabriella.

'What the hell, Murphy,' said Con. He couldn't believe he'd been so careless that he hadn't taken the gun from Murphy after the situation at Eliza's house.

'I have nothing else to lose,' said Murphy without emotion. He peered into Carl's eyes, who had gone still. 'I don't mind going to jail for killing anyone who gets between Jasmine and me.' He pressed the gun harder against Carl's chin.

Murphy's bluffing, Con realised, and he put out a hand to stop Gabriella from disarming him.

Carl hesitated. 'It was . . . it was Bree who told me about it . . . me and her were a bit of a thing.'

'You were dating?' said Gabriella.

'Shh,' said Con, 'let him finish.'

'Don't shoosh me, Con. You're not in charge anymore,' snapped Gabriella. 'Relationships are important.'

'Bree said Madison had some kind of . . . I dunno, freaky spiritual shit going on', said Carl. 'Madison reckoned she'd found a spirit guide, "Kundela", who could show her the way through portals on what she called the Sacred Cliff. The girls started having these weird nightmares and all that. Bree and Denni both came to me. Because I'm Aboriginal they thought I'd know what was going on – but my sister wouldn't have a bar of it. It's all bullshit, obviously. There's the kundela bones, but not bloody portals: there's nothing Aboriginal in it. At all. But they must have got in my head, because I started getting the nightmares too. I was so pissed off, because this stupid white girl was using *our* history for her psych hippie shit . . .'

'And then?' said Murphy.

'Madison said Kundela asked her to start the game. There's this website she made. You put in your details and you send . . . you have to send Madison a nude, and then you get your first dare. They start off simple – going the night without sleep, burning a hundred-dollar note – and then they start getting bigger, like shoplifting, or . . . burning bigger stuff.' He snuck a glance down at Murphy's gun.

Con could feel the tingle of new connections, new theories. 'Keep talking, Carl.'

'My latest dare was to scratch "KUNDELA" into a cop car and take a photo. But then they said it had to be one of your cars: Badenhorst or Pakinga. Madison sends the tasks, but she reckons she's getting them from Kundela – which is *all bullshit* – but when she starts "channelling Kundela" her voice changes and everything. And this Kundela tells us on the other side of the portal we'll be kings and queens. But before that afterlife, you have to keep proving your worth.'

'You know it's bullshit, but you're doing it anyway?' said Murphy.

Carl bared his teeth. Murphy clamped the pressure point at the top of his trapezius – as always, shock and adrenaline were the best truth serum. Carl stammered, 'Madison's blackmailing me. The day they went missing, up on the trail, I was the one who knocked out Miss Ellis – that was the dare Madison had given me. Now she's making me keep playing, else she'll expose me.'

'*You're* the one who hit Eliza?' said Gabriella.

'Madison made me! She's an animal. She's got all those girls wrapped around her finger. Denni was convinced: she finished all ninety-nine of the tasks Kundela gave her, and then she killed herself on the mountain. Because that's the way to get through the portal: the hundredth task. I bet that's why Bree killed herself. I didn't know what my sister was doing, but there's no way that's —'

A police car pulled up beside them, the siren giving a short *whoop*.

Murphy kept his gun against Carl's chin. 'Did Jasmine play the game?'

'No. Bree said Jasmine didn't know anything about it,' said Carl.

Constable Cavanagh stepped out of the police car and Murphy pulled the gun away from Carl's chin, although he kept a hold of him.

'Con? Gabriella?' said Cavanagh. 'Someone reported a confrontation here. They found your Eliza – she was at the hospital with Wren. Except it was *Monica,* not Eliza. She was just driving Eliza's car.'

'That's impossible, Monica was with us,' said Con, turning to Murphy. He saw the realisation dawn in Murphy's face, just as it occurred to him. 'We're idiots.'

Murphy loosened his grip and Carl scrambled away, sprinting off down the road.

'We let her *go*,' said Murphy.

'That's not all,' said Cavanagh. 'Someone saw Eliza and Madison in Tom's Landcruiser, headed up to the Tiers. When they heard the report of people chasing Eliza, they called it in.'

Something occurred to Con. 'Could Eliza know more about the Kundela Game than she told us?'

'If she knows the Kundela Game is the reason Denni killed herself . . .' said Gabriella.

'Then she blames Madison for Denni's death,' said Con.

'Where would she be taking Madison?' said Gabriella.

'The cliff from the video,' said Con, while at the same time, Murphy said, 'These so-called Sacred Cliffs.'

'How do we find those?' said Con.

'Jack Michaels will know,' said Gabriella, pulling out her phone.

'Jack Michaels?' said Con, a prickle of guilt. 'I forgot all about him.'

'Well, he's awake and recovering,' said Gabriella waspishly. 'Luckily I remember all the important witnesses. This is why you need a partner who's a detective, not a drug dealer.'

'Your civilian pet was Eliza, so I don't think you can talk,' said Con.

'Drop us off at Eliza's house – I need my car,' said Gabriella to Cavanagh, climbing into the squad car.

Con held out his hand to Murphy. 'We're gonna need that gun, Murphy. I can't have you walking around with it.'

'Who do you think I'm gonna shoot: Madison or Eliza?'

Con kept his hand out.

Murphy handed the Glock over.

'Cavanagh, when you get back to the station, bag this as evidence but . . . keep Murphy's name out of it.'

They all climbed into Cavanagh's Stinger, Gabriella calling the hospital to speak to Jack while the sirens blared.

CHAPTER 51

ELIZA

Eliza slowly brought the Landcruiser to a stop. Ahead of them, through gaps in the trees and out over the high cliff, were the ancient Tasmanian mountains, clouded, the deep blue of eucalyptus mist. They were on a downward slope of red dirt and jagged rocks that led right to the cliff's edge. Eliza pulled the handbrake and switched the engine off.

Madison beat on the top of the cab, screaming. To Eliza, it was a beautiful sound.

The edge of the cliff was perhaps 20 metres away.

Eliza climbed out of the Landcruiser.

'Please, Miss Ellis,' said Madison, her make-up ruined by tears and sweat. 'Please . . .'

Eliza found a thick branch fallen from a snow gum, covered in leaf litter. When Eliza lifted the branch, Madison started shouting, 'No, no, no, no!', but Eliza only dug it in deep right in front of the rear wheel.

She opened the back door and retrieved Tom's hunting rifle from beneath a blanket on the back seat. She slung it around her shoulder and moved around to the front door of the cab, reaching inside to release the handbrake.

She locked the doors and then walked to the edge of the cliff.

'Please! Miss Ellis, *please*!'

The mountains. The breeze. The bush and rocks and bluffs. The blue sky and pearl clouds. A wedge-tailed eagle wheeling on the wind.

Eliza threw two sets of keys over the edge of the cliff, the handcuff keys and the Landcruiser keys.

'Please . . . Oh, God, help me!' screamed Madison.

Eliza walked back behind the Landcruiser, the slope setting her above Madison, and sat on a rock at the side of the road. She rested the rifle across her lap.

For a short time she watched Madison sobbing, pleading. Then she said, 'I'd like to leave this town. There're too many memories here.'

'Miss Ellis . . .'

'Let me tell you the best memory. It was my big sister Kiera arriving with Denni. I knew. The moment I saw Denni, I knew. I *wanted* her – as a child. I wanted to save her, nurture her, give her what I never had. Limestone Creek was supposed to be a fresh start for Denni. A *new life*.' Eliza looked Madison in the eye. 'And then she met you.'

'Miss Ellis, please —'

'Before Denni came . . . I didn't feel lost, exactly,' Eliza said, her throat bone dry, 'but I felt like nothing I did mattered. No legacy. A dry womb. I had only my students, my work. But Denni – Denni was a treasure.

'You took her under your wing, and I thought, "this is perfect": Madison Mason, the most popular girl in school, the leader of the pack, taking an interest in my Denni. You, Jasmine, Georgia, Cierra, Bree. Good friends, the perfect gang. It was like a cloud had lifted – I can't imagine what Denni went through under Kiera's care. Nothing good.'

Madison clung to the cab guard, wretched. 'Please . . .'

'But then the clouds came back. She was depressed, angry, emotional, distant. It crept in slowly, along with her new obsession: the Hungry Man. That was when your subscribers boomed. Denni loved telling me all about it, your ghost-tour videos. I'm not sure why, but that's when Tom started to take an interest in her.

'You didn't just know about Tom's interest in Denni, you wanted her to go for it: you *encouraged* her. I know, because Bree told me. She told me many things, once Denni died . . . after you murdered her.'

'*You* texted me,' said Madison suddenly, gasping. 'On Georgia's phone. You took that phone off Georgia and pretended to be Bree. *You* pushed Georgia off the cliff?'

Eliza was silent. She held onto the gun.

'*You killed Georgia!*' She yanked at the handcuffs, then began kicking the cab guard.

'I wanted all of you dead. Eventually.'

'*What else have you done?*' She tried to chew at the links in the chain.

'You isolated Denni. All of you. Spread rumours. Made her feel worthless. Made her think that all she was good for . . . was to die. To leave this world behind.'

Madison slumped to her knees in the tray of the Landcruiser. 'Please . . .' she whimpered.

Eliza stood up and pushed against the ute with her foot. She felt the resistance of the branch against the tyre, the only thing holding the car in place on the gentle slope. She saw the terror in Madison's eyes, and it went some way towards soothing her. Denni had suffered for months at Madison's hands. It was only right that she suffer too. Eliza wanted her to know not just what awaited her but why this was happening. That it was Eliza who was the one doing it; she was in control, like she always had been.

'You killed Denni,' she said simply.

'I didn't,' wailed Madison. 'She told me she saw him! She saw the Hungry Man! She killed herself because of the ritual!'

'And you invented the ritual.'

'I didn't! Kundela told me! He told me about the ritual!'

The girl really should have chosen a better lie.

Eliza pushed on the ute again, harder. The branch creaked. 'You know, Bree and Denni were closer than you realised. Everything you told Denni, Denni told Bree.'

'Yes, Denni was convinced she met the Hungry Man, one night in the bush, and barely escaped with her life. You convinced Denni that the Hungry Man would never stop hunting her, that killing herself was the only way to escape. *If you see the Hungry Man's face, he'll never allow you to escape.*

'Bree told me she was going to be your second victim – that you'd arranged for her to kill herself, too. I didn't want her getting cold feet once they found Georgia's body – she would realise what I'd done – so I spoke to her and simply brought forward the day . . .' She sighed. 'If only Georgia hadn't been the one you gave the phone to, I might not have had to . . . but Bree's death needed to work right. She told me all about your plan . . . you'd kept her intentions secret from the other girls: she would die on the Hanging Tree on the third day of the disappearances, like some anti-Christ, for all to see her pain and to cement the mythology you were creating . . . to bring you even more followers.

'I arrived at the Hanging Tree just in time to watch her do it, you know.' She scowled, waving a hand beside her ear, swatting away the discomfort that memory brought. 'Once she died, I had to climb up after her. I dragged her body higher, using the rope to hide her in a crook of the tree, up high where no one would see. It wasn't time, yet, for everyone to see her: I didn't want to draw attention to myself by taking it further than you had planned, especially if the police realised she'd been using my key to hide in the school.'

Madison's face was a sheen of sweat, stark with the horror of understanding what Eliza was truly capable of.

'She'd already written a message on the wall at the school, so I wrote some more to throw them off further. A few days later, the day they released me from custody, I went home to get Denni's Hungry Man warding dolls – the statues *you'd* made her carve – and I took one to your house, another to Bree's body. And then I texted you, pretending that Bree had taken the phone instead of Georgia. Letting you know the deed had been done.'

Silence. Madison quaked, weeping, and looked off over Eliza's head and into the distance in vain hope of rescue. Her eyes widened briefly, and then she brought them back down to meet Eliza's. She could hardly believe it: there was new fire in the girl's eyes. She straightened, brushing dirt off her school dress.

'I didn't kill anyone,' said Madison. 'You hear me? Denni killed *herself*, you stupid bitch. Denni was messed up: she was always going to kill herself. She wanted to kill herself the moment she got to Limestone Creek. You should be thanking me for keeping her alive as long as I did. She finally decided she couldn't do it anymore and I helped her find peace. I helped her find purpose.'

Eliza dug her fingernails into the stock of the rifle. Madison lifted her chin in defiance. 'My online presence is the greatest tool anyone from this nowhere town is ever gonna have: the amount of good I can do is more than you could even understand. Denni was already dead, you just refused to accept it. But *you* . . . you killed Georgia. In cold blood. You're the real murderer.'

Eliza stood close now, resting her foot on the tailgate of the Landcruiser.

'And Jasmine and Cierra? Did you kill them too?' said Madison.

'Don't act dumb. You're in contact with them, somehow. And now you're going to tell me where they are, or I'm going to kill you.'

'Go to hell, Miss Ellis.' She put her head back and screamed. 'Just shoot her already!'

What?

Eliza spun.

There, in the middle of the track, stood Con, Gabriella and Murphy.

Con's pistol was aimed at her.

Eliza swung the rifle up and shot at them. It went wide.

The trio split into three directions.

Eliza turned and pushed the Landcruiser with all her strength, a savage grimace on her face as she caught Madison's eyes.

The branch gave way and Madison screamed as the vehicle rolled towards the cliff.

CHAPTER 52

MURPHY

Con had huddled behind a snow gum, ready to return Eliza's gunfire.

Gabriella hid behind another: she didn't even have a weapon.

Eliza ran towards a ridge where the gums grew thicker, carrying the rifle across her chest, her white dress billowing.

Murphy sprinted towards the girl in the Landcruiser, slowly rolling towards the cliff. He reached it less than ten metres from the edge, slapping his hands on the tailgate. He heaved, digging his heels into the rocky ground, but it was no good. The Landcruiser pulled him forward, boots slipping.

He yelled, forearms bulging, shoulders burning.

Con appeared beside him, adding his strength to Murphy's. The Landcruiser slowed but didn't stop, the sound of their sliding feet mixing with crunching tyres and Madison's screams.

Behind them: gunfire. Con must have given Gabriella his Glock.

'Madison, is the door locked?' shouted Con.

'Yes!' screamed Madison.

'We've got to chock the tyres!' shouted Murphy. There was no way to fight the momentum of the Landcruiser.

'With what? No time!' shouted Con. 'Madison, you need to break your thumb and pull your hand out of the cuff!'

'It's too tight!' screamed Madison. 'Oh, Jesus, help me! *Help me!*'

Con was red from the strain, patting at his pocket with one hand while he pulled with the other. 'Where are my handcuff keys!'

And Murphy remembered. Con didn't have keys to the handcuffs because *Murphy* had them. He'd used them that morning to release Butch from Eliza's bed.

The cliff was approaching. Beyond it, the fog and the mountains, swollen clouds and a perfect pastel blue sky.

They had maybe five metres.

Sara.

He remembered the dream. It had been warning of this the whole time . . . This was the moment of his death.

No time to think, then. Bite the bullet and go for it.

'Hold it steady, mate,' Murphy said. He pulled himself up onto the tray of the vehicle.

'What are you *doing*?' shouted Con. The Landcruiser lurched forward without Murphy's strength.

Time slowed down.

He pulled the little key out of his pocket. He pushed it into the cuff attached to Madison's wrist.

Madison clung to him. 'I'm sorry, I'm sorry, I'm sorry.' She was no longer the larger-than-life mastermind: just a terrified teenage girl.

Murphy turned the key in the cuffs and they sprang open. He cradled her like a baby.

You're out of time.

The Landcruiser tilted, front wheels over the edge. Con's shout was drowned out by the roar of metal scraping the cliff edge.

Murphy heaved Madison off the back of the tilting tray, throwing her like a haybale, and she grasped onto the very edge of the cliff, one leg dangerously over the precipice until she scrambled all the way up.

The back tyres of the Landcruiser met the brink of the cliff.

Murphy was ready.

This was it.

He was going to see Sara again.

Already the wind of the cliff whipped his plaid shirt, his beard, his tear-filled eyes. Just like he had dreamed.

The tray tipped further.

'Jump, Murphy!' Con's voice broke through his trance. He reached across the back of the tray, raised up on his toes. 'Jump!'

Murphy ran to the tailgate and jumped towards him.

Time froze.

Wind all around him.

Sky above.

Sharp rocks way below.

The cliffside.

Adrenaline.

The dream.

Madison.

Jasmine.

He hung suspended, afloat, pitching forward – *this is it, Murph* – and then Con's sweaty palm grabbed his wrist.

And time sped back up.

Con heaved and Murphy's whole body slammed against the cliff face, his feet dangling free, the wind knocked out of him.

Con was dragged forward, flat on the ground, his chest digging into the rocks at the edge. He looked down at Murphy, teeth gritted, wind ripping at his hair.

Murphy's feet scrabbled against the cliff. He couldn't find purchase. Their sweaty hands were starting to slip. Murphy gripped Con's forearm with his other hand. Con slid forward another inch.

'My weight is gonna pull you over,' shouted Murphy. 'You have to let me go.'

'Shove your heroics up your arse!'

'You have to find Jasmine.' Murphy slowly took his hand off Con's forearm.

'You absolute cockhead!' Con reached down with his other hand and gripped Murphy's shirt. *'Don't let go!'* Murphy let go of him, but Con held tighter. 'Don't you bloody dare!'

A strange, detached peace had swollen in Murphy's chest.

And then Madison was there, hair blowing in the wind, her arms reaching down and pulling on Murphy's shirt. 'This is not what Jasmine wants. Jasmine needs *you*!'

Murphy's peace grew tattered at the edges, a ripped white flag. The terror of the drop began to fill him. A long fall and a painful end. Never seeing Jasmine again.

Sara wouldn't ask me to do that, would she?

He scrabbled for purchase again, grabbing Con's arms, suddenly hooking his boot over a small rocky spike that hadn't been there before.

Wind and sky, rock and death. Lichen, a feather caught in a spiderweb.

'Push, Murphy!' shouted Con.

'I am bloody pushing!' shouted Murphy.

His hand landed on another rock, he found more purchase for his boots, and with Con and Madison's help he scrambled until his forearms were over the edge. His fingers dug into the earth, his strength pulling him up to his armpits.

The wind; the bluffs; the laugh of a kookaburra.

Gunfire in the distance.

Con grabbed one arm, Madison the other, and Murphy slid forward, grazing his belly on the sharp rocks.

He rolled the last little way on his side, away from the fall, pressed down into the ground. Gravity was his comfort again, the red dirt home.

The wind blew past his ear. He looked up.

Con lay on his back, his scraped and bloody arms over his eyes, chest rising and falling rapidly. Madison was in a ball beside them, bawling, blood running from her nose, bruises down her arms, her black school shoes broken at the strap.

Silence.

Then fury from Con, sitting up. 'You gave up! We're *this close* to finding Jasmine and *you were giving up*?'

'I dreamed about falling from a cliff,' said Murphy. 'Over and over. I thought it was my time to die.'

'That's the thing about dreams, mate,' said Con, panting, slumping back onto the ground. 'They're not bloody *real*.'

CHAPTER 53

CON

Con let himself have a minute more to relive the terror of all three of them almost dying. Then he pulled himself upright.

Gabriella and Eliza were nowhere to be seen, but the earlier gunshot had come from deep in the trees.

Murphy was on his feet, standing over Madison. 'Where is Jasmine?' He looked fierce, blood in his beard, his clothes torn and filthy.

'I don't know . . .' said Madison. 'But Miss Ellis didn't know, either. I think that means she's safe.'

'You have to find her!'

'I c-can't. We have to wait for her to contact us.'

Con came over and kneeled by the girl. 'What about Cierra? Are they together?' said Con.

'They're supposed to be,' said Madison. She trembled, and whispered, 'I want my mum.'

Con looked towards the trees. 'Okay, Madison. You're okay.' She clung to him, weak on her knees, and he helped her to her feet. 'We'll get you away from here.'

They walked up the dirt track, back to where they'd parked the car. Con had called the commander on the drive there, the moment Gabriella had received the directions from Jack Michaels, and he knew she would be waiting for an update.

The screen on Murphy's phone was cracked, but it still worked.

'Con! Are you okay?' said Agatha.

He gave her a brief rundown, adding, 'I don't know where Gabriella and Eliza are, but they're both armed. We've heard gunshots. We need the chopper here *now*. How far away is back-up?'

'Doble's thrown a massive spanner in the works. He's used all his crooked buddies here to run interference: saying you're unhinged, that I'm out of my depth. I've finally managed to get things moving, but the squad cars have only just left. Once I regain the situation, he is *finished*. What kind of state is Madison in?'

'She'll survive.'

'Be kind to her, Cornelius,' said Agatha, hearing his tone. 'She's still just a child.'

He looked over at Madison walking alongside him, staring straight ahead. She was clearly in shock from the trauma. Despite everything, she had helped to pull Murphy off the edge of the cliff, had probably saved his life.

Just a child. What a world we live in now, that a child with a camera can cause all of this carnage.

'I assume I'm back on this case now?'

'Don't be smart with me, detective, it doesn't suit you. Wait for back-up.'

'Okay.'

The commander sighed expansively. 'Cornelius, I know you're not really listening and are likely going to go and give back-up to Gabriella the moment I hang up. Please make sure Madison is safe first, and get Murphy to stay put too. We can't afford any more civilian casualties in all of this.'

'Yes, ma'am.'

'I'll be in touch.'

Con hung up the phone and handed it back to Murphy. Madison had gone quiet, retreating into herself.

Gunshots in the trees. Shouting.

Con and Murphy were running back down the track instantly, but Con stopped in his tracks. He couldn't leave Madison behind, but with Eliza about, nowhere was safe for her, not even the car.

'Come with us: you can't stay here alone!'

Madison had gone pale – she didn't look well – but she nodded, racing up beside him, and the two of them ran into the bush after Murphy.

Immediately they were enveloped by cider gums, their sap filling the air with a scent like honey, their leaves casting mottled shadows on the undergrowth of ferns and fallen branches.

Deeper in the trees, a scream of pain.

Con ran beyond Murphy, dodging branches and massive dolomite rocks. They were now in a grove of gnarled, ancient pencil pines. The buzzing of flies filled the air. The Great Western Tiers, an impenetrable maze of trees, scrub and stone.

Con's partner was in there somewhere, with a murderer.

'Gabby!' shouted Con. He set off into the bush in the direction he thought the cry had come from, Madison and Murphy following close behind.

'*Gabby!*'

'Con!' Gabriella sounded distant. He beat his way towards the sound of her voice, his shirt getting caught and tearing on branches.

Gabriella burst out of the trees ahead. Her face was covered in scrapes, her hair a mess of cobwebs and pine needles. 'I think I hit Eliza in the shoulder,' she said, panting, eyes bright. 'I winged her, but then she lost me. She's somewhere that way.' Gabriella pointed in the direction she had come from. 'I need your help, before she disappears for good.'

'We can't take Madison into a firefight,' said Con.

'Okay, you stay with her, then,' said Murphy, sprinting off in the direction Gabriella had pointed.

'You don't even have a gun, idiot!' said Gabriella, chasing after him.

Within seconds Con lost sight of the two of them in the trees, before he could even say a word.

He looked across at Madison, frustrated to be the one burdened with her. 'Let's head back to the trail and wait for the squad cars.'

Madison looked up at him, a glimmer of boldness back in her eyes. 'And which way is that, detective?'

Con looked around him – an instant thrill of panic. He had no idea. He didn't even have Murphy's phone.

There were no markers anywhere, just endless ancient pencil pines, keeping watch.

CHAPTER 54

MURPHY

Murphy and Gabriella crashed through scrub and over fallen logs, startling wallabies into the undergrowth, each thump from their jumps bringing terror: was it Eliza's rifle? Something else?

'Stay close to me,' said Gabriella, her forehead bleeding from a long scrape. 'She's desperate now.'

'You sound like you're enjoying this,' said Murphy.

'It's the end of the chase. Of course I am. Plus, if I catch Eliza, I'll be able to hold it over the commander and the whole department for the rest of my life. *They kicked me off the case.*' She glanced across at Murphy. 'But I need to do it without anyone else getting hurt. Seriously, stay behind me.'

'I don't care if she shoots me. Hell, I'll be bait. Just find Jasmine.'

'Don't give me that horseshit. Jasmine needs you alive, she needs her dad.'

Murphy grunted.

'Is your head in the right place for this?' said Gabriella. 'What if Eliza tells us Jasmine is already dead?'

'Then I'll kill her.'

'You know I can't let —' began Gabriella, but Murphy had abruptly stopped. She slowed down. 'What's the problem?'

'Eliza's been shot . . .' he said slowly. 'For all she knows she's dying.' He looked back. 'All she cares about right now is killing the person responsible for Denni's death. She's gonna go back for Madison.'

The blood drained from Gabriella's face. She looked down at her Glock. 'Con's unarmed.'

CHAPTER 55

CON

Con bounced on the balls of his feet, looking in the direction Gabriella and Murphy had gone. He was terrified for them, feeling useless, lost among the pines, no idea how to reach the path. He usually had an excellent sense of direction, but this bush was labyrinthine.

Madison lay down on a fallen tree, her arm over her eyes.

Con heard the crack of a twig right behind him and then the butt of a rifle crashed into his head.

He fell to his knees, but fought to stay upright.

He turned, vision blurry, to see Eliza standing over him, her white dress bloody and torn. The rifle was trained on Con's chest, held in the crook of her elbow, even as her other arm hung limp at her side, blood dripping from her fingers.

A strange anxiety filled him. The anxiety of impending, inevitable death.

But still, Con crawled towards Madison, who looked at Eliza in horror.

'Come here, Madison,' said Con, voice shaking.

'Don't move, either of you,' said Eliza.

He clawed his way forward, the world lurching in a swirl. He reached out a hand and Madison helped him to his feet, her terrified gaze never leaving Eliza.

'I don't want to kill you, Con,' said Eliza. 'Just her.'

'Eliza, listen to me,' Con called, throwing his voice as far as he could, letting it echo through the trees. His head pounded from the effort.

'There's no point shouting. Madison will be dead long before they find us.'

'I won't beg anymore . . .' Madison clutched Con's side. 'Now everyone will know it was you.'

'And you'll be dead,' said Eliza.

Con pushed Madison behind himself, sucking in shallow, nauseating breaths.

'You have every right to be angry,' said Con. 'Every right to blame Madison.'

'Shut up, Con,' said Eliza. 'I know you're stalling.'

'She's the monster who convinced Denni to kill herself.'

'And Bree,' said Eliza. Her grip on the rifle wavered as she stepped closer.

'It's not your fault,' he said. 'I feel it too. The guilt.'

'What are you talking about?' She was close enough now that he could see her chalky white face, her bloodless lips.

'There was a case in Sydney. A man led a group . . . they tortured and killed young girls. It was my job to save them, but I was too late. I was *too late*.' He stepped towards her, losing his balance, but Madison grabbed his waist from behind, supporting him.

'What are you playing at, Con?' she said, the rifle now aimed at his head.

'More guilt now . . . If I found you sooner, I could have saved Madison.' He stepped closer again.

'It's not your fault,' said Eliza. 'It's *hers*.'

'I wasn't good enough. I was too late. I'm the reason they're dead.'

Eliza breathed heavily. 'Stop stalling and *move*, Con!'

'Every word is true.' He was close enough now. He pressed his forehead against the muzzle of the rifle. 'It's okay to feel guilty. It's all okay.' He screwed his eyes shut, fighting the wave of dizziness. 'But it's not your fault,' he whispered.

He felt the rifle trembling in her arm.

Then it steadied.

'I won't let you talk me out of this. I've come too far.'

She struck his face with the barrel of the rifle. Hard. His nose broke and blood flooded his mouth, but he remained standing. With the last of his strength he turned and embraced Madison, smothering her body with his. 'I'm so sorry,' he whispered in her ear. His blood ran onto her schooldress.

'I don't want you holding her when she dies, Con,' called Eliza. 'I want her to die *alone*.'

His vision turned black at the edges. 'Don't do this, Eliza.'

'Fine. Then you'll both die.'

The sound of the shot cracked through the trees, stirring a nest of flame robins into the air.

'No!' shouted Con. Madison whimpered below him.

But no pain came. He could feel Madison's heart pounding in her chest.

He turned, bleary eyed. Eliza had fallen to her knees. A ray of sunlight fell through the canopy, lighting up her face. Blood ran out of her chest, a red flower blooming on the front of her dress. The rifle lay on the ground beside her in the pine needles.

Eliza slumped to the side, resting her head against the trunk of a pencil pine. The bell-like song of a green rosella filled the quiet grove.

Her amber eyes remained on Con's even as life left them.

'Con?' came Gabriella's voice from far, far away. 'Con!'

'Madison?' he said.

'I'm okay. She didn't hurt me. Your head is bleeding, Mr Badenhorst.'

He closed his eyes, a distant thrum mixing with the rushing sound in his own head. The darkness came fast.

When he woke up, he was lying in the back of a squad car. Constable Darren Cahil was driving, tears rolling down his cheeks, and Murphy was in the front seat. Con's head was in Gabriella's lap, a cold pack wrapped around his head.

'Rest, Con,' she whispered. 'It's over.'

CHAPTER 56

CON

Con, Murphy and Gabriella sat in the interview room of the Limestone Creek Police Station: the nice one with couches and magazines and a window that looked out over the Tiers. Gabriella was wrapped in a silver shock blanket. Murphy had his head in his hands. Con sat against the wall, a bucket between his legs for the vomit that came with his concussion.

Commander Normandy returned to the room. She sat down, her voice soft and slow. 'You've all done very well. *Very* well. You've saved Madison's life. You've stopped a killer. This community is grateful, your country is proud of you, and your daughter will be proud of you, Murphy, once we find her.'

Murphy didn't reply. Con sensed that, to him, this was no victory at all. Jasmine was still missing, Cierra was still missing. Bree was dead, Georgia was dead, and their killer had been brought to ill justice, before all their questions could be answered.

Con allowed himself to not feel the same despair. He put Jasmine and Cierra into another box. He didn't have any energy left to think about them, and that was okay.

He had done a lot today. They had stopped a killer. They had saved a girl's life.

This time, he hadn't been too late.

It was time for a little rest.

'I need to go finish discussions with the commissioner,' said Agatha. 'There are a few things she needs to sort out, based off everything you've told us. Someone still has to address the media. Until then, it might be best if you all stay in here. Con, I really think you should let the paramedics take a look at you —'

'I'm fine,' he muttered.

'Don't be an idiot.' She stood up. 'But, again – good job.'

Gabriella stood up the moment the commander left the room. 'If the commissioner is here, I'm going to give him a piece of my mind about Doble. And if the media happens to overhear, so be it.'

'You'll lose your job,' said Con.

'I saved two lives today! *After* they kicked me off the case. I think I'm good, and Agatha will support me.' She held up her blanket. 'Besides, I'm in shock. I don't even know what I'm saying.' She swept out of the room, the silver blanket trailing behind her like a cape.

'How are you doing, mate?' said Con softly.

'I can't spend another night in this town,' said Murphy, eyes on the floor in front of him. 'On this island. I'm leaving – on a plane, on the boat, I don't care. Tonight.'

'To Queensland?' said Con. 'Port Douglas?'

'Jasmine knew that's what I always wanted; buy a shack in Port Douglas and spend all day gardening and fishing. I joked about it often enough.' He looked up. 'I've got enough money saved up.'

'Drug money,' said Con.

'Yeah, well, it's getting me out of it. And away from Butch.' He gave the barest grim smile. 'I'm doing exactly what Jasmine wanted.'

'How do you feel about that?' said Con.

'Extremely pissed off. And I'll be telling her so when she comes back.'

'We'll find her,' said Con. 'I'll make sure of it.' His vision rolled and for a brief moment he thought it was going dark again. He stood shakily. 'You know, I think I am gonna go find that paramedic . . .' He took a step and stumbled against the wall.

Murphy was there instantly, slinging Con's arm over his shoulder. 'Here, mate, let me help you,' he said. 'Lean on me.'

CHAPTER 57

MURPHY
One year later

Murphy sat in a café on the foreshore of Port Douglas.

It was ten-thirty in the morning. The weather was balmy, the air like a drunk mate. The ocean – in perfect view, just over the edge of the open-air deck – was mottled blue, perfect little waves rolling in. Salt in the air. His hair still damp from his morning swim. The rustle of lush palm leaves, a frangipani scent from nearby, the laughter from the pair of women at a nearby table eating yoghurt and sipping kombucha.

Murphy wore a singlet, shorts and thongs. His beard was cropped close to his face, which was creased and sunburnt. He had lost a lot of weight since Tasmania: he wasn't skinny, but he was leaner, fitter.

A cappuccino stood on the table. No food; he was too nervous for food. He'd have preferred a beer, but . . . he just wanted to be careful. On today, of all days. He *had* smoked a cheeky joint that morning. Perhaps some things never changed.

Con sat beside him: he'd flown in yesterday. He wore a singlet too. He was sipping his latte, holding the glass too tightly.

Both were silent. Nervous.

The pair had stayed in touch all year, and Con had come to visit Murphy twice before; they considered themselves close mates now, bonded by trauma. Murphy himself had been back to Tasmania a few times, to visit Butch and others, including the Masons, to share their grief, exchange clues and theories. Each time he had stayed at Con's Launceston house.

Not that he had a problem with Butch, not anymore. He just didn't want it to get back to Jasmine.

A year into Con's investigation and still nothing from Jasmine or Cierra. No sign at all, up in the mountains or elsewhere.

Except for today.

Perhaps.

In Murphy's hand was a postcard from Jasmine that had arrived at the Limestone Creek Police Station one week ago. Con had brought it with him, and this was the time and place she'd specified to meet. 'Can't wait to see you,' she'd written.

Con had tried to keep Murphy's expectations in check – it seemed the card came from an online service and its delivery had been scheduled over a year ago. It proved nothing, and yet hope was alive in Murphy's chest, like a bee in a jar. A hope Murphy hadn't allowed himself for a long time.

Jasmine, missing for a year, to the day . . .

He'd almost invited Butch, too, but he didn't. Just in case. He didn't want Jasmine to see him and back away.

It had taken most of the year, but Murphy had smoothed things over with his brother. He had seen Sara's letter, and he believed Butch – Sara had been the one to come to him, that night Jasmine was conceived.

It was a strange thing, to fall a little bit out of love with your dead wife.

He supposed this was exactly what Jasmine had been trying to prevent. Jasmine with her little plans, her little schemes. The agony she had caused him.

Murphy hoped, from the bottom of his soul, that if Jasmine arrived today, she had grown up *a lot*. Because it would take serious maturity for her to handle the decade-long grounding he was going to give her.

'What's the time?' said Murphy. He had turned his phone off: he didn't want any messages from anyone.

'Ten thirty-five,' said Con.

'Okay,' said Murphy gruffly. 'Talk about something. Please.'

'Umm . . .' said Con. 'What's your coffee like?'

'It's good. Next question.'

'Penelope seems nice.'

'Yeah,' said Murphy, with a small smile. 'She's better than I deserve. More patient than Sara ever was. Just as stubborn, though.'

Penelope was a teacher at the local primary school. Their relationship had been rocky at the start – Murphy's grief and anger had got in the way every time something challenged them. She'd forced him to get counselling, which hadn't helped, so then she'd forced him to join a men's group, which *was* helping. She'd also started coming to church with him, as a show of support to the changes Murphy was trying to make. It wasn't a perfect relationship, none ever was, but it was starting to bloom. She'd even taken the day off work in support, but respected his request to go meet Jasmine alone.

'Have you heard much from Pastor Hugh?' said Murphy.

'Yeah, a bit,' said Con. 'Shoots me a message every now and again when he's in my area. I reckon you hear more from him than me: he's really proud of you, did you know that?' said Con. 'How was church yesterday? Get anything good out of it?'

'Well, I zoned out a bit, kept thinking about today. But there's some good people there, and they took me out for lunch. At the start it was only because . . .' He hesitated. 'I promised God if he brought back Jasmine, I'd go to church, so I've been going to church . . . you know, out of faith.' Murphy squeezed his mug. 'But I'll probably keep going. Even if she doesn't show up today.'

He glanced up at the clouds in the azure sky. Murphy had prayed for this day often enough, so God better bloody well be listening in right now.

'I'm glad that it's working for you, mate,' said Con.

'It is,' said Murphy, then softly, 'What will I do if she doesn't come?'

'Don't think about that. Tell me about work.'

Murphy gave a wry grin. 'I don't know why I ever stopped doing landscaping. I'm the bloody best there's ever been. There's a bloke that sub-contracts for me, but the last job he did, the owner refuses to have him around anymore because his work's not as good as mine. I mean, it's a compliment, but it makes my life difficult. Not that I'm worried about money.'

Con was well aware that he received a lot of financial support from Butch, but what Con didn't know was that Butch was still in the drug game and making more than ever. It helped that Doble had been removed from the force, but bizarrely he had teamed up with Madison Mason. She had dropped out of school on her YouTuber wage, but was also earning money from selling Butch's weed on the dark web. They marketed it as The Hungry Man's Bush Bud.

Madison was at least doing a lot of other stuff with her channel now – raising money for better causes.

Murphy, while not happy about the whole situation, still took the extra income Butch sent his way. He wanted to prepare the perfect house for Jasmine's return, the perfect life, and he now had a two-storey house right on the beach, with wide open windows and a rocky path to the sand, a pool, a home cinema, the cleanest kitchen, outdoor swings, a rooftop bar, and three cats – Gus the Muss, Mickey Mouse, and Meredith.

Plus the best landscaped garden in all of Port Douglas.

All it was missing was Jasmine.

And, after Jasmine returned, maybe an engagement ring on Penelope's finger.

Con had run out of conversation topics. Together they watched the waves. The chink of cutlery came from nearby tables, the smell of coffee and roasted meat and eggs, birdsong and insects and murmurs and laughter and a sudden, balmy breeze.

'Dad?' came a tremulous girl's voice.

For a split second, it was like Murphy was hanging from that cliff again.

The table crashed to the ground, cups and cutlery flying, coffee spilling everywhere, as Murphy lurched to his feet.

It was Jasmine. She stood on the deck, a few steps away.

He had one moment to take her in.

She had long ginger dreadlocks, a tanned and freckled face with her piercing blue eyes, a vibrant green dress with a pattern of tropical leaves and flamingos. She wore a canvas shoulder bag, cheap sunglasses on her head.

And then Murphy had crossed the empty space and crushed her into his chest.

She was alive.

She was gloriously, undeniably alive.

He felt her warmth, smelled the scent of her, sunscreen and shampoo, her fragility, the sound of her happy sobs as she nestled against him, back where she belonged, safe and safe and safe.

He made soothing sounds, tasting his own salty tears as they rolled through his beard and into his mouth.

'You're hurting me,' she chuckled, voice thick with tears. She pulled away.

He held her at arm's length and studied her intently, seeing his own hands shaking. The lightness in her eyes, clear of teenage awkwardness, clear of even that shadow of grief that had haunted her since Sara's death. The fullness in her face. Healthy and happier than he'd ever seen, at peace.

His anger was still pushed down for the moment, for putting him through so much, for the audacity of being alive and not telling him *for a whole year*. His heart was soaring, the sight of her was so bright it almost hurt.

Behind him, Con swore softly, over and over.

'Jasmine —' croaked Murphy.

'How bad was the worry?' she cut him off. 'Was it bad? I didn't think about it at the time, but now I realise . . . it was too late, though. I had to see it through!' Her blue eyes flashed with fervour. 'It was important, Dad.'

She twisted her arm, to show him the tattooed text down the outside edge of her forearm: *Permission to do what it takes.*

The bottom fell out of Murphy's stomach. He knew that phrase now, after everything Con had found out about Eliza.

'Do you like it?' said Jasmine. 'It's something Miss Ellis taught us. I can't wait to see her. If anyone from school actually wants to see me.'

She doesn't know, realised Murphy, but it was a distant thought.

Jasmine was alive, and healthy, and here with him.

That was the single most important fact of his entire existence, the fulcrum of his reality.

Jasmine is here.

The whole café had dropped to a buzz, eyeing the table Murphy had flipped, watching him and Jasmine.

The waitress had come, a scowl on her face, but Con was speaking to her quickly, showing her his police ID, gesturing at Murphy and Jasmine. Together the waitress and Con righted the table and re-set it.

'Dad?' said Jasmine, reaching out for his cheek, tenderly brushing the tear that fell from his eye. 'I can see it in your face. You've aged. You were worried. Worried *sick*. Look how much weight you've lost. I dunno, I didn't think you'd worry about me that much . . . or I didn't want to think. I guess you saw my videos?'

'Maybe we should sit?' said Jasmine with a chuckle, taking Murphy's hands and holding them tightly.

So grown up now.

'If it's any consolation, I had the most incredible year ever.' She sighed happily and took a seat. 'I can't wait to tell you all the things I've done. And a complete media fast – I feel *cleansed*, Dad! When I have kids, I'm home-schooling them and not letting them near any kind of screen or newspaper.'

'Where . . . where have you been?' croaked Murphy, perched on the edge of his seat. 'You haven't seen *anything* about . . . you didn't check the news?'

'No. Nothing. I just . . . and I didn't want to ruin it all. I knew once I saw the fallout . . . plus I was sure that Cierra, Bree and Georgia would chicken out. Was it bad when they came back? How did Jack take it? I didn't treat him that nice, we didn't stick to the plan we told him . . . I was pretty nasty to him, but when I found out he stole your seeds, I admit I wanted to get a little revenge. I was such a *child*!'

Murphy saw the guilt in her eyes, the excitement, a grounded-ness that had never been there before. She'd always seemed like a bird about to take flight, but now she was a woman.

How am I supposed to tell her? he thought suddenly. *How do I tell her that Georgia and Bree are dead, and Cierra is still missing? And that Eliza died in front of my eyes . . .*

His mouth was dry. She'd been gone a whole year and found this peaceful version of herself. How was he going to break the news to her? How would he support her, once she realised how horribly wrong the whole thing had gone? Her year of finding herself would become her trauma.

'I want to hear everything now, before I tell you my story,' said Jasmine, clapping her hands, forcing happiness, seeing the state Murphy was in. 'Did Georgia get her museum? Did Cierra start her *own* YouTube channel?'

Jasmine is here, and everything is okay.

'Have you moved here permanently? You didn't happen to bring Moaning Myrtle, did you? I miss her.'

Murphy glanced at Con, who was still watching the two of them, but the policeman just shrugged.

Murphy smiled back at Jasmine and shook his head, tears again rolling down his cheeks.

And then he began to laugh, big booming laughs that brought the café to another standstill.

No, your cat was killed by your teacher, who was a murderer, and who would've killed you if she had the chance.

But it's okay. You're here. Nothing else matters.

I have three cats waiting for you at home. I can't wait for you to see . . .

'You are *here*.' His laughter turned to happy sobbing, and he crushed her in another hug.

'I missed you, Dad.'

He'd enjoy this moment for a while longer – he'd let Jasmine enjoy it a while longer – before he told her.

Everything is okay.

EPILOGUE

BUTCH

Butch had a strange feeling he was finally on to a good one.

His footsteps scrunched over the fallen bark as he followed a wallaby trail through bush dense with mountain needlebush and spicy mountain pepper berry. It was nearing dusk – he'd been out here longer than intended – but he was drunk enough that he didn't care.

It was a year since Murphy had burned their old crop to the ground. It hadn't taken long for Butch to replant that crop and, without Doble on his tail, he'd managed to plant several more small fields, dotted all over the escarpment.

With Madison's help selling the product online, he'd needed them, too. Butch was becoming more successful by the day, struggling to keep up with demand for The Hungry Man's Bush Bud.

He was sending a large percentage of his income to Murphy, so why did he still feel so guilty?

He'd been drinking since Murphy had sent that simple text around lunchtime:

She's here. She's alive.

Butch couldn't handle the emotions. Did Jasmine want to see him? Were they going to talk about the fact he was her biological father? Were they going to talk about Sara . . .?

So he'd come out here to scout for another good location. He'd already had a few forays out into this part of the escarpment, hoping to find a good location for a new crop. Barely a kilometre from his house, he'd found an animal trail leading into dense bush that seemed utterly remote.

He came into a clearing in the white gums. A crag of rock loomed out of the trees ahead, one he was sure he'd never seen before. That was good. Rocky spires *that* big nearly always meant caves, which could be entrances to hidden groves.

He walked faster, but then his heart sank.

A piece of litter, nestled in a tangle of scrub. So, people had been here before.

He picked it up. It was insect-bitten paper, wrinkled from moisture, but it was covered in handwriting in blue pen.

The damage was such that most was illegible, but a few lines were not:

and it won't matter anyway if he doesn't. She said that if we don't last the whole time, we can still

Butch let it fall. It was a letter of some sort, not just your average rubbish. He suspected someone had camped around here.

Disappointed, but curiosity piqued, he continued.

Another piece of paper. This one was entirely damaged – water had turned it to flaky pulp. It was under a mountain needlebush.

The next piece he found, a few metres further, was in better condition:

I hate that stupid bitch so much. She told him what I said.
Now he won't even look at me in Homegroup. I swear I'm
gonna get her back. I don't care how I do it

He stopped reading and let it fall. A fragment from a diary entry. A schoolgirl's diary.

His heart beat faster.

The next piece of paper he found was only five metres away from the base of the crag of rock – the rock which, he realised now, was much bigger than he'd first thought.

The paper had been torn in half:

keep it with me so I could keep a record of the time,
maybe they'll turn it into a book, or a movie, or something.
Imagine if it was a movie. Holy shit. Who would they cast
to play me?

This one had a stain in the corner. A round drop. Dark brown.

And then he saw the dirty blue wig, kicked around to the other side of the same bush.

White noise buzzed through his head.

He looked back the way he'd come.

The thought came to him from a distance, like it was someone else's: *She was leaving a trail . . .*

He walked slowly now, approaching the base of the rock. It was as though his ears were ringing, the pressure against his eardrums growing the closer he got. But the rock wasn't even like the local dolomite. It was no rock he'd ever seen, massive and out of place, dropped out of the sky.

At its base was a dark hollow of stones.

The entrance to a cave.

Beside the cave were a pair of hiking shoes, laces neatly tied.

In the entrance of the cave, something else. He picked it up, feeling sick.

It was a rough stick figure, made from a twisting branch snapped into shape. Shards of rock were driven into where the eyes would be. Around its neck was a cord like a noose. It was made of deep red hair.

Butch dropped it like a hot iron.

Breathing heavily, he looked all around. And there, high up, pressed into a crack in the rock, protected from the rain by an overhang, was a folded piece of paper.

He had to stretch to his fullest height to pluck the page from the rock.

He didn't want to touch it.

He didn't want to read it.

But he unfolded it. It was stained with the same dark brown marks.

All it said was:

> *HELP ME GOD*
> *HE IS REAL*
> *I AM SORRY*

ACKNOWLEDGEMENTS

Thank you to my personal trinity: Haylee, Ali and Jojo.

Haylee Nash, my agent. Feels like I'm well on my way to my dreams coming true, and it's all because of you.

Ali Watts, my publisher. For being the James Bond, Mother Teresa, Danny Ocean and Oprah Winfrey behind this book. Thanks for the fairytale.

Johannes Jakob, my editor. Because of your craft, consolation, collaboration and coaching, you've made the editing journey incredible from start to finish.

To the Holy Trinity. As always, as onwards. JC, Big G, Holy G.

Dan Anstey, for giving me the advice that got my head back in the game: 'Concentrate on pursuing the talent that got you there. That's why people like you, and that's what'll keep you focused, successful and give you a sense of purpose. That's what it's about.'

Jack, my secret police contact, for your advice, experience, and teaching me about search and rescues in the Tiers.

Diana Cohen, for my first job with at-risk youth, for teaching me the effects and chaos of trauma, and for not firing me when that kid nearly cut his finger off with a chisel.

Shovel, my tattooist, for allegedly teaching me about bush cannabis and allegedly teaching me how to grow and sell it, during those long chats under the needle.

Constable Cooper, for answering my questions about Tasmania Police and detectives, and for helping me out when those women tried to break into my car 'because they thought it was theirs'.

Kevin Young, owner of the local, for taking the time to read and give feedback on the manuscript, and then calling to let me know that you'd sent it through to Deb McGowan at PRH for her thoughts. I'll never forgot that moment when I said, 'I don't know who Deb is,' and you replied, 'Yes you do, she was in your mother's wedding'.

Deb McGowan, PRH's Tasmanian sales rep, for being a champion for this book. Thanks for all the support and encouragement, even without the family connection (still spins me out that you were Mum's bridesmaid).

Rebecca Thomson, my first ever proofreader, who went above and beyond as the perfect reader, reviewer, critic and encourager.

Jaime Collins, of the Nash Agency, who helped me crack the psychology of suspense and took this book to the next level.

All my proofreaders, great and small, I'm so grateful for all your support and time for *The Bluffs*. You are numerous and multi-faceted, and I hope you know that there are little pieces of all of you in this novel.

The Penguin Random House Australia team, who privileged me with much support, above and beyond. I take none of you for granted and honour every one of you. It's good to be alive and to be part of this PRH tribe.

And lastly, to my family. For the love and care that has allowed me to flourish, for never doubting I'd get here, and for not being surprised now that I have.

Also by Kyle Perry

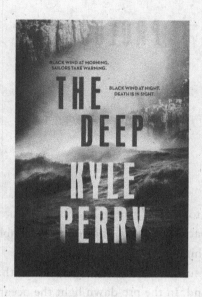

If you encounter the Black Wind while out there at sea, all you can do is race back to shore. There's no predicting it, no sailing it, no living with it. And if you're a Dempsey, it can play tricks on your mind . . .

From the bestselling breakout author of *The Bluffs* comes a heart-stopping new thriller set on the rugged coast of Tasmania about modern-day pirates, family bonds and betrayals, and the hidden dangers that lurk in the deep. Read on for a sample.

PROLOGUE

Pirates Bay, Tasmania

The boy gasped for breath, hair in his mouth, before the next wave slammed him back against the bottom. He tumbled, the fizz of bubbles around him.

Back to the surface. Another desperate breath. Stinging eyes searching for land. In the pre-dawn light the ocean was a roiling grey, the dark gumtrees so close . . .

Knocked under by another wave, bull kelp tangling around his limbs. He clung to it as the current sucked him away from shore. His hands were so cold he couldn't grip the kelp, but he wrapped slick loops of it around his wrists, adrenaline and fear giving him strength.

The water receded in a rush of whitewash and for a moment his head and torso were above the water.

'Help!' he called, voice raw.

A crash and he was under again. He held his breath, wrists locked in the kelp, until the rushing water had passed.

Above the sound of the wind and the waves, a dog barked.

The boy pulled himself forward. He could feel sand beneath his feet.

When the next wave came he let it carry him forward in the swirl of sand and silt. He spun, over and over. Arms tangled in kelp. Forehead scraping rock.

The water pulled away, but he rolled until he found a crevice in the coarse rocks on the shore. He gasped for salty air, the sound of breaking waves close by. He wasn't out of danger yet. He dragged himself forward, grazing skin, all strength gone from his legs, the wind cold against his bare back.

A German shepherd splashed into the rockpool beside him, barked, nudged its nose under his arm.

The boy dug bleeding fingers into the rock as the waves surged over him again, the dog yelping.

Rough hands seized him under his armpits and picked him up.

'I've got him!' the man shouted. 'Here, he's still breathing!'

The dog shook its fur and licked the boy's bleeding shins, its barks mixing with human voices. They were crowding him now, carrying him off the rocks, onto the sandy beach. The man laid him on his back, putting an ear to his chest.

The boy opened his eyes, crusted with silt and sand.

'He's alive,' said a woman. 'Thank God, he's alive.'

She was right in his face and he pulled away, coughing, scrabbling on hands and knees, backing himself against the panting dog. The stink of wet fur and seaweed.

Still these people crowded around him. 'Easy, mate, easy,' said the man.

The boy's grazes stung, his body ached. He shivered from the cold, his heart pounded. He needed to *run* . . .

The sight of the woman holding out a towel broke through his panic, and a new thought reached the surface of his mind.

These people have come to rescue you.

You need their help.

He forced his struggling breaths to slow.

'Thank you,' he croaked. His throat and nose burned raw from the salt water.

Then he turned and buried his face in the dog's fur. 'Thanks, Zeus,' he whispered to his dog. 'You did it.'

'Bloody hell. Look at his tattoos,' said the man.

The boy knew he was a desperate sight. Short, thin, shaggy blond hair. Covered in kelp and sand. He wore only a pair of board-shorts, the cuts and puckered scars all over his skin rising from goosebumped flesh.

'No, it can't be . . .' gasped the woman. 'After *seven years*?'

Tattooed across his scrawny shoulder blade, which dripped icy sea water, jagged words read:

THIS IS FOREST DEMPSEY
BE CAREFUL WHAT YOU WISH FOR

CHAPTER 1

AHAB

Ahab Stark burst out of the bay with a gulping breath, speargun in his hand, an underwater torch dangling from his wrist. He pulled his diving mask down to his neck, coughing. Cold water matted his grizzled beard, the salt water stinging ice-blue eyes long since used to its bite. He bared his teeth in a grin; he'd pushed that dive a little too far.

The sky still had a dusting of dawn stars – no clouds in sight – but under the surface of the water he had heard the vibration of the drone and felt the cross-current. It was easy to feel it here, around the isolated reefs that spired out of the bay, and he had seen a school of Australian salmon flee to deeper water.

The Black Wind was on its way.

He floated in the dangerous silence that preceded it. Of course, the ocean is never quiet, but to Ahab this was true silence. Natural sounds, constant movement around him, waiting with bated breath. He looked up at the lightening sky, content.

'I'll take my time,' he told it.

Eventually, when the cold and the wind had seeped deeper into his blood, he kicked his matte-black fins, swimming over to his anchored rigid inflatable boat. He climbed up the ladder, naked skin dripping water. His fishing haul was in the catch bag attached to his waist – enough king flathead to offer a fish-of-the-day special at his pub. He dropped his mask and snorkel, speargun and torch, slid off his fins.

His diving partner, Ned, was floating on the other side of the boat. Ned wore a ripple-patterned wetsuit – even in the middle of summer, the younger man found the water too cold. 'Fish have disappeared, Ahab,' he called. 'Reckon it's coming? Black Wind?'

'On its way,' Ahab called back.

Ned hurriedly climbed into the boat himself, shivering as he peeled his wetsuit off his lanky frame. A boat was like a footy change room – no one cared if you were naked. Ned dried his mullet and checked it in his phone camera before he towelled the rest of himself dry.

'Let's get out of here,' said Ahab, once they were both dressed.

'Look,' said Ned, zipping up his thick coat. 'Another boat.'

It was visible – just – through the peaking waves.

'They'll be right,' said Ahab. 'They'll see the signs.'

He glanced at the sky – still clear of clouds save for some high horsetail wisps, which caught the first blush of the sunrise. The truth was, there weren't any signs, yet. Sometimes the Black Wind came with little warning. And there were always out-of-towners on these waters.

Ahab let out a sigh. 'Better have a look.'

He fired up the engine and they headed towards the other boat, slicing through a sea of dark interlocking waves, tinges of the pink sunrise now catching in the liquid peaks.

As they drew closer, Ahab identified the other boat, and he backed off the throttle. It was the abalone motherboat, the *Absconder*, a 60-foot Westcoaster, with a flybridge and live abalone tanks, and a crane on the rear deck. It belonged to the head of Dempsey Abalone – Davey Dempsey, his cousin.

Ahab tied his RIB to the side of the *Absconder*.

'I'll stay here?' said Ned.

'Get ready to leave in a hurry,' Ahab said softly, as he pulled himself up through the dive door and planted his feet on the deck.

Davey stood at the stern with his second-in-charge, Chips, and spun at the sound of someone coming aboard his vessel. He cut an impressive figure – a dark-haired, muscular man, in a business shirt but with his sleeves rolled back to show his distinctive tribal tattoo sleeves. He had a rugged face that was, as Ahab had heard Ned sulkily describe it, 'unfairly good-looking'.

He smiled wryly at Ahab's entrance. 'Alright, cuz. Come right aboard.'

Chips wore warm hi-vis, for comfort not style, her sandy hair in a long ponytail under a blue baseball cap. She gave Ahab a deferential nod. A long time ago, when she'd dropped out of high school, Ahab had been the one who'd given her work, then put her name forward for the Business.

She had never forgotten it. Ahab wished he could take it back.

'To what do we owe the pleasure?' said Davey, leaning back on the rail. He was wary of Ahab, with good reason, but tried to hide it.

'Black Wind is on the way,' said Ahab.

Davey grimaced. 'How long 'til it hits?'

'An hour. Maybe two.'

Davey sucked his teeth, then turned and looked out over the water from the bow. Ahab followed his eyes. The aluminium tiller-steer boats were just in view. 'An hour . . .'

Abalone fishing was a strange business. It required divers, who were down there under the water now, to hunt for what were technically sea snails. The thick inner layer of their spiral shells was a source of iridescent, colourful mother-of-pearl, but it was their flesh that was the prize – delicious raw or cooked, it sold like gold in Asia. Tasmania supplied about 25 per cent of the world's yearly abalone harvest.

On those smaller boats all around the *Absconder* were deck-hands, staying above wherever the diver was fishing below. The divers prised abalone from the rocks and sent them to the surface in catch bags, on shot lines with underwater parachutes filled with air from the divers' regulators.

Catch bags full of abalone, but other things too, as Ahab well knew . . . things that were left out here, for Davey to pick up, bring back to shore, and sell on, right under the nose of the law.

'It'll still be there later,' said Ahab.

'Always plenty in the sea,' agreed Davey. 'But we've got a quota. Business stops for no one. I'll signal the divers later.'

'You really want to risk it?' said Ahab.

Davey straightened. 'Don't forget who you're talking to.'

'I know exactly who I'm talking to.'

Chips shuffled her feet. She glanced between the two men, uneasy.

Davey laughed, breaking the tension. 'Don't worry, Chips. We respect the elders that have gone before.'

He might really have intended to be respectful, but all it did was wrench Ahab's chest. There was no way to change the past . . .

Ahab gave a wordless salute as farewell and climbed back down to his boat. Ned turned the wheel, pushed down the throttle, and set them towards Shacktown.

One of these days, he would have to tell the police about the Business. But could he really do it? Ruin Davey's life, Chips's life, the lives of countless others . . .?

But what about the lives *they* ruined?

Angrily, he pushed the thought aside. As he'd done so many times before.

He couldn't do anything – not yet. As much as it goaded him, sometimes to the edge of insanity, Ahab was a man of his word.

But his self-control had its limits. One day he would find a reason to break his promise.

As they neared the sea cliffs, mist from Devils Kitchen caught the pink dawn like smoke. Devils Kitchen: a huge, deep trench in the cliffs of Pirates Bay, where the water and wind had eroded a chasm, forming a dangerous swirl of waves and fury, turning the swells of the Great Southern Ocean into a boiling cauldron. It was gigantic, magnificent, and dangerous as hell. But that wasn't where it got its name – early European settlers in the area had seen this mist rising and claimed it was the Devil, boiling his meat pot.

Now the buildings of Shacktown came into view, spreading across the wooded hills to the stark cliffs, spilling right down to the beaches. Ahab surveyed it all from his boat, the beach mansions and the holiday shacks and all those in between, waiting in the she-oaks and banksias and sands.

As they rounded the point, heading towards the huge maze of wooden piers that made up the marina, they saw red-and-blue pin-pricks of ambulance lights and police cars, far in the distance, down on the northern beach.

'What's gone on there?' called Ned over the sound of the engine.

'We'll find out soon enough,' said Ahab.

Shacktown residents were notorious gossips, and even this early the marina was stirring.

Ned eased them into their berth, and Ahab left him to moor the boat, jumping onto the slick timber pier, catch bag in hand.

He approached a huddle of fishermen who were talking among themselves, dressed in thick waterproof gear.

'Ho!' called Ahab. 'A no-go today, boys! Black Wind's on its way . . .'

'Ahab!' said one of the men, as the others broke apart. 'Have you heard?'

'What's happened?'

'They found Forest. *Forest Dempsey!*'

Ahab dropped the catch bag.

The fishermen edged away from the look in his eyes.

CHAPTER 2

MACKEREL

Sucking on his vape, Mackerel Dempsey stood far away from the entrance to Shacktown Police Station, as was polite. The grape flavour of the vapour filled his mouth and burned his throat, tasting like Nerds lollies. The cloud hovered in front of him before slowly dissipating in the faintly menacing breeze. The station had been renovated to seem friendly and inviting, etchings of seabirds swirling along the windows to make tourists feel safe.

An early-morning tour bus rumbled by, a red double-decker, the top open to the elements. It was full of wide-brimmed hats and cameras. A sunburned woman waved at Mack, cheerful. The side of the bus read: SEE TASMANIA? SEA TASMANIA

He waved back and took another puff. He always put off entering the cop station as long as he could.

A narrow isthmus of land, Eaglehawk Neck was 50 kilometres east of Hobart and halfway down the Tasman Peninsula. Swamping that land, engulfing it like umbrellas on a crowded beach, was Shacktown. The area offered stunning views, unique geology, the tallest sea cliffs in Australia and some of the largest sea caves ever explored – and plenty that were unexplored. There were green parks and white beaches, shops and cafés, danger and folklore. Shacktown had something for everyone. Worth the drive.

The Shacktown locals were a large part of the appeal, their attitude towards tourists one of fondness. They opened their homes as Airbnbs without qualms, invited strangers on the beach back to the cafés for lunch, forced travellers to sign their guestbooks, or, if they didn't have them handy, gave out their address and insisted on postcards from their next destination or a Facebook friend request.

But underneath it all, unseen by most, was the influence of the Dempsey criminal dynasty. And Mackerel, its outcast. Crooked nose, tattoos. Large enough to be intimidating yet for some reason always the butt of people's jokes. His father had once said it just oozed out of him – like he was asking to be bullied.

The automatic door to the police station opened and an old man in a ripped puffer jacket and stained trackpants walked out. He nodded to Mackerel, wandering over for a chat, already lighting his cigarette. 'Hey, Mack. How's the day looking?'

They saw each other every day – every damn day. They had the same daily sign-in conditions and they both chose to get it over with first thing in the morning. The old man stank of body odour, was always drunk, and no one ever stopped to chat with him – which was why Mackerel always went out of his way to do so.

'Looking good, I reckon!' said Mack. 'Just heading out on the boat. First day's work I've been able to land in a while. How about you?'

'Sorry to break it to you, mate, but I heard in there that the Black Wind is on its way.'

'No . . .'

Mackerel couldn't afford another day without the meagre income he made from the only fisherman in town – his best mate – who still gave him work.

'Just go home and get high,' advised the old man, stretching his back. 'Weird feeling in the station today. I think some kinda shit's gone down. Hope you weren't involved, mate.' He took another puff and walked off with a lazy wave, the smoke caught in the breeze.

Out on the ocean, that breeze would soon become a droning wind. The Black Wind. Mackerel had been caught out in the Black Wind once, and it still gave him chills to remember it. It twisted and pulled at the waves like a cyclone. The rage of it, the chaos, the feeling that death was just a bee's dick away and there was nothing you could do but hold on and pray . . .

Mackerel flicked the vape off – five quick taps of the trigger – and slipped it into his pocket. As he stepped into the foyer of Shacktown Police Station, his mind turned and turned. Subconsciously he made slight adjustments to his stance and walk, trying to appear as non-threatening as possible. He had a fresh face and big blue eyes, and he'd been told he had a nice smile. A bit goofy, a bit endearing. These days, he needed every shred of endearing he could manage.

Even in the station, he had to keep on his toes. It was common knowledge that Mackerel had been run out of town five years ago – for very good reason – and should never have returned. But only those with ties to the local underworld knew what this 'very good reason' was . . .

'Morning, Constable Linda . . .'

'Yeah, morning, Mack,' said Linda. She pulled out the bail sign-in registry, jotted down his name, the time and date, and spun the book around for him to sign. There was a briskness to it, and his heart sank. That usually meant it'd be an interrogation day.

How's your health and temper?

How's the job hunt going? How's the psychologist going? Who have you been seeing? What have you been doing? Anything illegal? C'mon, Mackerel, tell me the truth . . . What have you been doing?

Anything you want to tell me now before I find out later?

This daily sign-in was a constant reminder of everything he'd lost. His dignity, the respect of everyone he knew, the ability to ever be more than twelve hours away from Shacktown, even just being able to work his old job. All Tasmanian fishermen have to be of good character and be a fit and proper person, so when he went to prison he'd lost his FLAD – Fishing Licence (Abalone Dive). That meant he couldn't even dive for a living, the one thing he was good at.

Linda glanced up from the work she was doing on her computer, confused to still see Mack there. 'I'm sure you have places to be?'

She seemed distracted. He noticed now the absence of other officers. Where were they all?

'Yes, ma'am.' Mackerel turned and walked out as quickly as possible.

No interrogation today!

That was a good sign.

Yet instantly his mind was back to his upcoming court case. His rehabilitation. What he could do to fix things.

I could go to church . . . No, too transparent. Maybe a religious girlfriend? That'd look good.

While prison loomed? Who'd possibly have a relationship with someone like that?

Someone looking to save a lost cause, that's who.

He felt a pang of fear. If he went back to prison – which was the most likely outcome of his upcoming sentencing – he'd be alone again. He didn't want to be alone again.

These were the unhappy thoughts in his head as he limped to the chemist, the gulls cawing overhead. There was the smell of roasting coffee from a van set up in a little park, and he could hear the shouts of children on the swings there. Sunshine beamed. You'd never know the Black Wind was on its way, except for those rippled clouds blowing in from the horizon.

A couple of local men saw Mack limping past and spat at their feet. This attitude was why no one else in town would give him a job. He tried not to mind. It was just lucky that he could work on Big Mane's boat as a deckie, on the few occasions his best mate actually had the work for him.

'Morning, Mackenzie,' said the pharmacist, the bell jingling as he walked in the door. Fishing lures and glass floats dangled from the ceiling and caught the light. She opened the safe and pulled out his Webster pack, pressing the two pills and a sublingual strip into his hand, which he had to put in his mouth in front of her.

'Want some water today, darling?'

He liked the pharmacist for lots of reasons, but mainly because she was nice to him.

'Not today, thank you, ma'am.'

One antidepressant. One painkiller. One opioid replacement, called Suboxone – he'd become hooked on that, in prison. Well, he had been the one who was dealing it to the others in prison, but still . . .

'How's your day been so far?' he asked.

'It's been good, thank you, Mackenzie. You're not out on the boat today? You heard the weather report?'

'Yes, ma'am. No boat for me.'

'Oh good.' She nodded, a crease of concern between her brows. 'I know how you like to take risks.'

Risks like drug dealing.

Risks like returning to Shacktown even though he'd been warned what would happen if he did.

Risks like getting his hopes up that he might have a normal life one day.

He laughed. 'Not anymore. I've taken enough risks for one lifetime. They didn't pay off.'

And he meant it.

He hoped it came across like he meant it.

He smiled, then limped towards the door. Lately the pain in his knee seemed to be getting worse, but the process for getting more painkillers was too much work for someone like him. As it was, he could only have his daily dose at the pharmacy – they had to be kept in a safe, under lock and key and restriction and regulation, and he wasn't allowed to take them home.

'Have a good day, Mackenzie,' called the pharmacist.

'Thank you, ma'am, you too. Let me know if you need me to get anything in for you . . .'

They both laughed. It was a bad joke. A drug dealer joke. That wouldn't look good for him in court.

Once he was outside, he grimaced in pain. Being reformed hurt – the old Mack could've sourced better painkillers by other means.

Don't think about that. Chin up.

He looked again at the sky. Rippled clouds were forming with speed. The faintest drone filled the air, something visceral and haunting that raised the hairs on Mack's neck.

With his morning ritual complete, and nothing to do until his 8 pm curfew, he could head home and get out of the wind. He set out in that direction, ducking around a gaggle of tourists in big sun hats who were crowding the entrance to the surf shop.

If only he had a job that wasn't dependant on Big Mane and his boat.

A burst of ideas and potential surfaced in his mind. All the jobs he could do if he had money, people working for him.

He slammed the thoughts down. Or tried to. His mind never stopped. Anxiety and post-traumatic stress. Pre-traumatic stress. He was sorry for what he'd done, he was trying to rehabilitate, he didn't want to go back to prison, with all the noise and the politics and the . . .

Focus on the future.

All he wanted in life now was a house of his own, a wife he could love, maybe a pet dog. To be allowed to dive again, bringing in a good honest income. Not driving a third-hand hatchback that was almost as old as he was and struggled to make it up Shacktown's hills. Not dependant on opioids just to get through the day, or painkillers he'd built up a tolerance to.

Who was he kidding? There was no use planning for the future. He couldn't do anything until his court case. Until he, most likely, returned to jail. And then he would have to wait until he was released. Which might be six months, or it might be seven years. It all depended on the mood of the judge on the day, and it's not like anyone in his family was going to put in a good word for him . . .

And the prosecution had already told him they were pushing for as much prison time as possible.

No. *Shut up. Just be happy with what you have.*

There was no one to see him, but he forced a smile onto his face. Bright. Firm. Real.

Endearing. He was Mackerel Dempsey, and he was reformed.

He limped towards Big Mane's house, head held high, even though no one ever looked his way.

League Division Two Towns

	Page	Pubs
Shrewsbury	8 - 9	Three Fishes, Coach and H...
Nottingham	11 -13	Bell, Salutation, Newshou... Fiddle, Globe
Bristol	15 - 17	Ratepayers, Wellington, Cornubia, Kings Head, Brewery Tap, Zerodegrees
Lincoln	18 - 19	Golden Eagle, Sippers, Three Horseshoes
Leyton Orient	20 - 21	Birkbeck Tavern, Churchill Arms Princess Louise,
Darlington	22 - 23	Number Twenty - 2, Quaker Coffee House, Bay Horse
Macclesfield	24 - 25	British Flag, Waters Green Tavern, Sun Inn
Peterborough	26 - 27	Brewery Tap, Charters, Palmerston Arms
Chester	28 - 29	Old Harker s Arms, Ship Victory, Telfords Warehouse
Boston	30 - 31	Coach and Horses, Eagle, Cowbridge House Inn
Oxford	34 - 35	Fox, Far from the Madding Crowd, Railway
Cheltenham	36 - 37	Kemble Brewery, Sudeley Inn, Cotswold
Grimsby	38 - 39	No. 1 Refreshment room, Smugglers Inn, Willies Pub and Brewery
Bury	40 - 41	Dusty Miller, Trackside, Rose and Crown
Rochdale	42 - 43	Cemetery Hotel, Wishing Well, Cask and Feather
Barnet	44 - 45	Head of Steam (Euston), Mitre Inn, Old Red Lion
Northampton	46 - 47	Melbourne Arms, Malt Shovel Tavern, Old Wooden Walls of England
Torquay	48 - 49	Hole in the Wall, Crown and Sceptre, Union
Rushden	50 - 51	Green Dragon, The Griffin, Rushden Historical Transport Society
Mansfield	52 - 53	Bold Forester, Nell Gwyn, Railway Inn
Wrexham	54 - 55	Old Swan Brewery, Albion Vaults Hotel, Crown
Carlisle	56 - 57	Howard Arms, Kings Head, The Crown
Wycombe	58 - 59	Three Horseshoes, Bell, Bird in Hand
Stockport	60 - 61	Arden Arms, Crown Inn, Railway

How to use the pages

Maps

Beware The maps are not to scale

The maps identify streets local to the pubs and best routes to the ground. They also show routes from the main railway station to pubs rather than the grounds. The description on the "shorts" is my summary of, and recommendation for, the real ale scene in the town.

Guide entries

The information is correct on the date of visit but may have changed. I give the beers on tap on the day of my visit. They are written in order of their appearance on the bar. You will have to judge the beer range from that. One would expect that if a winter beer is on when I visit then seasonals will be there when you visit. I do not include the beers that landlords say they have just finished or "will be on to-morrow"

The main bit

I have described the pub as I saw it on the day of my visit. This may have changed. I hope to give a flavour of the pub. In italics are comments made to me via the website / interviews / comment cards etc. The names used are those that they chose to use. If there is no name it is from a person who didn't want to be quoted. I cannot guarantee their accuracy but I include them if they add to my entry in an interesting way.

Owner of the pub. If it is part of a chain I try to give it but most are freehouses. Some abbreviations are used, e.g. W+D for Wolverhampton and Dudley.

G - Guvnor' To save any argument I give the name of either the landlord, / manager / owner of the pub. i.e. whoever the guvnor wanted to be held responsible at the time.

F- Food The pubs describe their own food. if not then I give the time of opening on a Saturday. For evening games then you have to take it to chance as this often varies. No **F** = no food

W - Website I give the website for the pub. I do not guarantee they are working or up to date

S - Smoking policy is described as at the time of my visit.

Photographs

With one exception all photographs were taken by myself and on the day of my visit.

Symbols with the photos.

In each guide I have tried to identify the very best pubs by allocating 11 Championship pub awards. They are indicated by the symbol shown here. There is one such award for the best in each category as indicated in the description. A pub having this award would be good in any town having;-

- a range of excellent ales,
- an interesting selection of ales,
- A friendly, welcoming atmosphere
- recommendations tin real ale guides and web sites and
- a beer policy that encourages the promotion. of real ale

PLUS A specialism in one or more of the award categories.

Award Categories

Within 10 minutes to the ground

The pub is within easy walking distance of the ground, having spaces in a car park or convenient safe parking near the pub.

Pub for food.

Many pubs are specialising in food but this award is for a pub that has something different, perhaps a theme for the food or gearing the menu on the day for footie fans, The food should be reasonably priced and obviously recommended by fans as good quality

Brewery Tap

The pub is an independent brewery tap and show-case its beer with a full range of ales.

Street corner local

This pub has a street corner location or be located in a residential area thus serving local regulars who use the pub during non match days.

Town High Street / Station boozer

The pub that win this award must either be within two minutes walk of the main station or the High Street of the town. It will be welcoming to people who are often unfamiliar to the regulars.

Historic pub

The historic nature can be defined either by the rare pub architecture, historical context or perhaps of beer history value.

Microbrew champion

This pub will normally only serve regional or national microbrews, offering beers that will be something of a surprise to the not so casual beer visitor.

Footie fans pub

The regulars in the pub win this award. They create a welcome to away fans through their general welcome and the way they accept the away fans as lovers of real ale and their team.

Pub with a view

The view might be through the window of the pub or its setting might be in an attractive tourist location.

Community pub

The pub is a place where the Guv'nor encourages local community spirit perhaps by running quiz, darts or footie teams, perhaps they are charity fund raising champions or involved in keeping the village in which they are located alive.

Loads of real ale pub

Not only will the pub have 12 plus real ales always available but the numbers using the pub means the turnaround of ales is constant. You can go in for a couple of hours and try many beers of the type you like while your friends are sampling their different style of craft ale.

The Pub of the year was selected by deciding which pub would fit into the most categories.

Symbols under the photos

sp   sk   jb   pg   d

There are five abbreviations that might appear here. No abbreviation means the pub doesn't have any T.V., music, pub games or good disabled access etc.

c p - car park
sp - street parking
mp - only metre or paid car parking nearby.

tv or sky.

Jb - juke box
bm - background music selected by the pub

pg -pub games like darts pool etc played here

d - disabled access is rated by the landlord as good or excellent.

BWV - Beers when visited

LEAGUE TABLES

The guide is arranged in order of what I think are the best real ale town to the worst. **The best towns have many more real ale guides to those listed here** and the choice of ales ranges from nationals to local microbrews. The most important factor however is that the pubs selected offer a range of drinking locations and are friendly locations for away fans to enjoy without any hassle, The other guides in the Football and real ale guide series are similarly arranged and included are the tables, for the 2004 - 05 season.

Extra towns

I found some great pubs in both Kidderminster and Cambridge. They are now, of course, in the Conference. I thought it would be a shame not to share them with you. Therefore I include two pubs from each town, with fewer details due to space restrictions. Who knows, they both might be back soon.

4

The Football and Real Ale guide 2005 - 06
What's it all about?

The website

www.footballandrealaleguide.co.uk.

The website is a place for you, the reader, to play a part in the process of nominating pubs by telling me interesting things about the people that make them so successful. If you want to be in the guides then the website is there for you to get involved.

I am sure that there are many other great pubs that didn't make the guides this year and with your help we will make future guides both better and more interesting to read.

Hosted by 1and1.com it has details of the work in progress, a beer forum and contact details so that you can get involved in talking real ale and footie whenever you wish. It also includes my Pub of the Week and fun competitions.

The winner of the competition, who wins two away tickets for this season, was GEOFF CLARKE of Wednesbury.

The editor / publisher

WHEN lifelong Bristol Rovers fan Richard Stedman was pondering a change of career, he was asked what were the two great loves of his life. It didn't take him long to come up with the answers -football and beer.

"When I went to see people from the Enterprise Agency, I told them I thought I'd like to run a pub - and they just laughed and told me to forget it. They said to go away and think of the two things I loved most in life and then try to and come up with something involving them both, which is where the idea for the books came from."

"I select what I believe are the best three pubs to visit if, like me, you enjoy tip-top real ale as well as watching your team away from home."

"There will rarely be agreement as to what is the best, so I am spending the next few months visiting all pubs near the grounds and talking to the locals about their experiences of football fans who like to visit a pub, quaff the ales on offer and banter about the game."

He is also looking for feedback from supporters nominating their favourite real ale pubs and can be contacted via his website www.footballandrealaleguide. co.uk.

Chris Swift Bristol Evening Post (Dec. 2004)

What makes a good real ale and football pub?

This guide is compiled with the real ale fan in mind. It is a real ale guide for away footie fans, looking for great ale rather than the company of fellow away fans.

I have tried to get a selection of pubs and locations so that all beer hunter can find something to suit their taste.

For some it is the opportunity to sample local brews. not available in their home town Others look for a location very close to the ground. For some the most important factor is the range of beers, seeking microbrews in particular.

Others seek out the football friendly factors, appreciating a good chat with similar fans in their own pub, often building friendships that last for years.

Whether it is a pub crawl, or a good meal with their pint, in every case it is the people who make a great pub. The Guv'nor is often the key to finding a great welcome and great beer.

Happy hunting

Stedders 2005

Season 2004 - 05 League tables.
Ranking of towns based on number of real ale pubs and their friendliness to away fans

PREMIERSHIP	CHAMPIONSHIP	DIVISION 1	DIVISION 2
Newcastle		Stockport	Shrewsbury
	Sheffield	Peterborough	Nottingham
Norwich	Derby	Sheffield	Bristol
	London	Bristol	Lincoln
London	Nottingham	Swindon	London
	Sunderland	Huddersfield	Darlington
Manchester	Ipswich	Bradford	Macclesfield
	Brighton	Oldham	Cambridge
Liverpool	Reading	Hull	Chester
	Plymouth	Chesterfield	Boston
Bolton	Cardiff	Torquay	Oxford
	Gillingham	Brentford	Kidderminster
Portsmouth	Preston	Port Vale	Cheltenham
	Wolverhampton	Hartlepool	Grimsby
Birmingham	Leicester	Luton	Bury
	Leeds	Milton Keynes	Rochdale
Southampton	Wigan	Bournemouth	Swansea
	Watford	Walsall	Northampton
West Bromwich	Burnley	Doncaster	Southend
	Coventry	Blackpool	Rushden
Blackburn	Crewe	Wrexham	Mansfield
	Stoke	Tranmere	Scunthorpe
Middlesbrough	Rotherham	Barnsley	Yeovil
		Colchester	Wycombe

Stedders Guides Category winners

	Pub	Town
Within 10 minutes to the ground	Wellington	Bristol
Pub for food	Three Horseshoes	High Wycombe
Brewery Tap	Zerodegrees	Bristol
Street corner local	Kemble Tavern	Cheltenham
Town High Street / Station boozer	Waters Green Tavern	Macclesfield
Historic pub	Cemetery Hotel	Rochdale
Microbrew champion	Number Twenty 2	Darlington
Footie fans pub	Rose and Crown	Bury
Pub with a view	Railway (Killay)	Swansea
Community pub	Railway (Wheatley)	Oxford
Loads of real ale pub	Three Fishes	Shrewsbury

Division 2
Pub of the year 2004 - 05

The award goes to the pub which meets most of the criteria above.

CEMETERY HOTEL

ROCHDALE

SOURCES USED TO COMPILE THE GUIDES

A good day out finding real ale before and after the game might involve using these sources. Before I visited each town these are the sources I used to narrow down my search.

Books / guides.

Campaign for Real Ale, Good Beer Guide 2004

Campaign for Real Ale, Good Beer Guide 2005

A.A. The Pub Guide 2004

CAMRA Local pub guides throughout the country.

Rough Guides The Rough Guide to Britain (2002)

Websites

www.thebeerguide.co.uk

www.pub-explore.com

www.beerfestivals.org

www.footballgroundguide.dial.pipex.com

www.camra.org.uk

www.beermad.org.uk

www.beerintheevening.com

www.dafts.co.uk (Darlington F.C.)

www.park-road.u-net.com (London Clarets)

www.theawayend.com

and of course comments on

www.footballandrealaleguide.co.uk

The best of these guides is that produced by Steve Duffy, Ted Blair and their mates at Darlington. It has masses of information on good real ale pubs in the lower divisions. Come on Darlo get into the top divisions so we can all share in some wider detail. Their guide to their home town is included below as an example of their website descriptions.

Real ale
For real ale fans, **Number Twenty 2, 22 Coniscliffe Road** takes some beating. The runner up in the *Darlington CAMRA town pub of the year 2004*, "22's" has an excellent selection of beers and wines, with a pub grub and a separate canteen area during the day. Regular featured beers include Village brewery ales, but others change regularly. Popular with an over 30s crowd at night and nicknamed *Jurassic Park* by those who get squiffy on two Bacardi Breezers. Just one type of lager and no spirits or silly alco-pops. No music, a "fine for charity" for use of mobile phones. Despite or perhaps because of the restrictions, this is a relaxed place for beer and conversation. *Open from 12pm, closed Sundays and Mondays.* Click for map

Voted yet again in 2004 *Darlington CAMRA Pub of the Year* and it's hard to argue. Well worth trying to find this quirky and hospitable bar down an alley-way, **The Quaker Cafe, 2 Mechanics Yard, off High Row, entrance next to Binns** has a small real ale bar downstairs, which now has more regularly changing guest ales - now a choice of 10 hand-pulls, not forgetting the Quaker Ghost Ale regular - the spirits don't just come in bottles at this bar. Also now does bar lunches on Saturday's. *Very football-friendly and open from 11am matchdays.* It recently won a reprieve after being threatened with "refurbishment" into something far less appealing.
"The Quaker Caff" is in the *Good Beer Guide* and in recent months has had a slight refurbishment, with a few more lights and tables for lunches downstairs too. Licencees Steve and Lynda know their beer and there's always a warm welcome for football fans before the game. Click for map

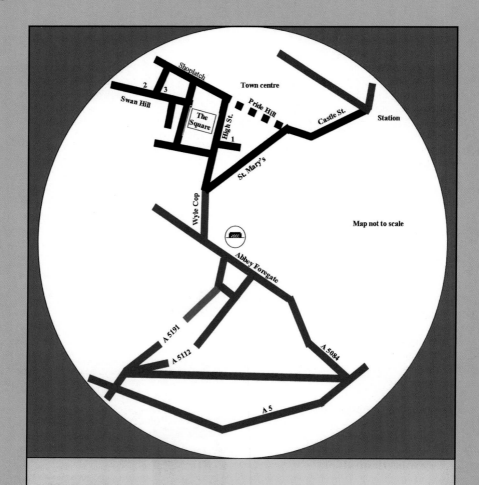

Shrewsbury

Shrewsbury are forever planning to move out of town to no real ale pub country, For this entry I am changing my recommendation. Park up, go into town and wander the historic centre and find ale houses that want you to sample their selections.

Shrewsbury Town

1 Three Fishes Enterprise   **2 Coach and Horses** Freehouse   **3 Admiral Benbow** Freehouse

mp   mp   bm   mp

Fish St Sy1 1UR	Swan Hill SY1 1NF	Swan Hill SY1 1NF
G David Moss	**G** Ross Ireland	**G** Mike Vaughan
F From 12	**F** From 12	**T** 01743 2444423
T 01743 344793	**T** 01743 365661	**S** Separate smoking areas
S No smoking throughout	**S** Separates smoking areas	

BWV 19.11.04 Caledonian **Deuchars IPA**, Timothy Taylor **Landlord**, Downton **Raspberry Wheat**, Fullers **London Pride**

This award winning pub is in an historic street near to Gay Meadow the landlord has created a pub for a wide range of drinkers. This Three Fishes is an instant recommendation whenever I talk to fans about pubs in this town. A small, one bar pub, beautifully kept real ales and with a no smoking policy that is the pub USP. The beams and hanging hops add to the bucolic feel.. The choice of guest ales offer some great surprises and are evidently popular with the regulars. During the day it is quite a tourist and office workers haunt; in the evening the locals take over. The regulars were very keen to give me advice on what makes a good pub and a good pint. *If a beer isn't quite to your liking don't panic another one will be on soon, talk to David and you might even get to choose*. Every time I go there I find something better to tell my friends about, usually related to the dry humour that pervades in every conversation in the pub.

BWV 19.11.04 Salopian **Shropshire Gold**, **Shropshire Icon**, Cheddar **Vale Cider**, Boddingtons **Bitter**, Three Tuns **Toddly Tom**

Two bars and three separate rooms make up this atmospheric ale house. The Coach and Horses champion local brews and have a tradition of welcoming away real ale fans. The pub rotates its guest beers and imported lagers and has the room for groups of varying sizes. The selection leans towards local microbrews but also includes continental lagers and always a real cider. *There are plenty of places to hide away if you fancy a quieter time.* This will be the case on a normal non match day perhaps. The pub will have its fair share of CAMRA members and town beer hunters mixed in with tourists wanting a pub out of the main high street business. On match days get there early to do it justice. The Salopian ales made a great find for me as they are rarely found on my travels. The chat with the bar man and locals set me up for the rest of the day. The Coach and Horses is a top pub in a top town.

BWV 19.11.04 Six Bells **Big Nev's**, **Cloud Nine**, John Roberts **Three Tuns**, Hanby **Bull Rush**, Salopian **Choir Porter**, Greene King **IPA**

Leaving the Coach and Horses and heading downhill you then come across the Admiral Benbow, a complementary pub that has to be sampled. This is a two bar "traditional" pub specialising in local brews finding the smaller brewers and giving them a great outlet in town., It has an over 25's policy that sets it apart and helps to create an atmosphere all of its own, described as *relaxed yet bubbly*. If on a crawl I would start and finish here because the range and quality stands out. On my visit the afternoon office party crowd were ending an all afternoon session. It is a good location for this as they were able to find a back area of the pub totally to their self leaving the regulars and serious ale heads to do the usual supping and chatting in the cosy front bar. It was a great place for both groups to treat the pub as their own. Three great pubs and not a visit to Loggerheads as yet, Shrewsbury just has too much choice.

Frog Island Brewery

Northampton

Fire-bellied Toad	Best Bitter	Natterjack	Shoemaker
5%	3.5 %	4.8%	4.2%

When in the East Midlands the Brewery ales to search for is;-

Frog Island Brewery

The Maltings
Westbridge
St. James Road
Northampton
NN5 5HS

www.frogislandbrewery.co.uk
Contact
Tel. 01604 750754
Fax 01299 270260

Nottingham

1 Bell Inn Hardy and Hanson · **2 Salutation Inn** Enterprise · **3 Newshouse** Tynemill Freehouse

mp   mp sk bm   sp sk bm pg   d

18 Angel Row, Old Market
Square, NG1 6HL
G Brian Rigby
F Full menu / snacks and mains
from 12
T 0115 9475241
S Smoking in bars, Belfry restaurant upstairs is non smoking.
W www.thebell-inn.com

BWV 23.3.05 Hardy and Hanson **Peddlers Pride, Bitter, Olde Trip, William Clarke, Mild.** Burton Bridge **Damson Porter,** Maguire's **Rusty Irish Red, Haus,** Hilden Brewing Co. **Silver.**

I'm not normally keen to try pubs in the main town square but the Bell is a must do experience. The impressive frontage is magnetic, inside the place has a tardis like effect. A passage way separates two small bars that in themselves would make a great town location. Then a back door leads into a much larger hall of a room, all wood panelled and reminding me of a redbrick Junior Common Room. In this room were the serious real ale fans sampling the tail end of their beer festival. Evidence of regular blues music catches the eye for evening entertainment but the most impressive factor was the general air of reflective reverence for a great town pub environment and a rarer range real ales.

Maid Marian Way, NG1 7AA
G Gary Minford
F From 12
T 0115 9589432
S Smoking throughout

BWV 23.3.05 Caledonian **80/-,** Tetley's **Cask,** Everards **Tiger, Bass,** Shepherd Neame **Masterbrew,** Charles Wells **Bombardier,** Brakspear **Special**

Tourists and those outside the town recommend the nearby trip to Jerusalem. Locals and indeed myself prefer the nearby Salutation. The visit showed me why the locals prefer it. At lunchtime groups of women from nearby offices and blokes on shopping trips were sampling real ales and enjoying good food in a pub that has plenty of historic values and is a real pub to boot. The bar on Maid Marian Way is larger and roomier yet has hiding placers for couples and solitary drinkers like myself that day. The entrance from the back street finds a passage and cosy rooms, timber framed and full of the character one comes to expect in Nottingham. While the pub has T.V. and music it is all very discrete, footie is unlikely to be shown whereas Rugby, especially Irish games, are more likely to get a crowd in. The beers are from national chains and are ever changing, no real surprises, just classic choices.

123 Canal St, NG1 7HB
G Bob Fairclough
F Fresh made rolls from 11
T 0115 9502419
S Smoking throughout

BWV 23.3.05 Crouch Vale **Blackwater Mild,** Harvest **Pale,** Beartown **Black Bear,** Hopback **Summer Lightning,** Westons **Old Rosie,** Coach House **Rabbit Punch,** Everards **Perfick.**

The Newshouse is a top pub of the old kind. It has real locals of all professions, ages and interests. It offers a lounge and a bar complete with darts board and bar skittles, Most importantly the ales come from beyond the predictable norm and are in great condition. My visit found teachers, printers and posties among others chatting around the bar over a post work beer. The walls have Forest cuttings and other items of the alleged days of the place being a reading room for the local illiterate. I particularly enjoyed the bar tiles proclaiming the names of regional independent brewers. All in all this is a great town pub in an area with few residents that suggests the nearby station and tram provides the link to home and town party venues. I just had to go back later to play the bar billiards near last orders and get some Black Bear to round off a perfect Friday night with the lads.

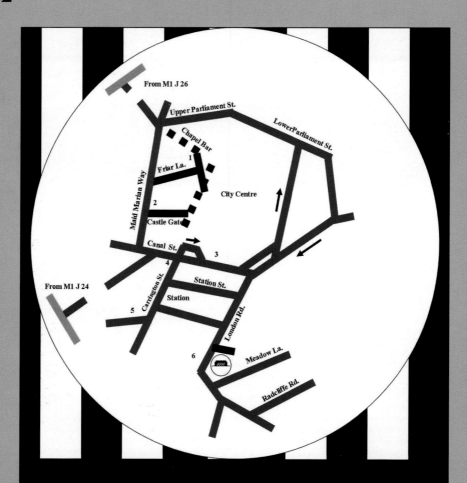

Nottingham

Nottingham is one of the top weekend away towns. The pubs here are numerous, historic and have plenty of alternative styles. The guide has a sample of a much longer list and are unashamedly my preferences from the long list of recommendations. I have chosen them with a north to south pub crawl in mind. Arrive by train as parking here is expensive. The tram is useful, especially on another visit when there is a tram and real ale trek to be undertaken.

4 Fellows, Morton and Clayton En   **5 Vat and Fiddle** Tynemill   **6 Globe** Great Northern Inns

mp   sk   bm   d   mp   tv   bm   pg   mp

54 Canal St. NG1 7EX
G David Willans and Les Howard
F Full menu including hot rolls before the match from 11.30
T 0115 9506795
S No smoking at the bar and non smoking section
W www. fellowsmortonandclayton.co.uk

BWV 23.3.05 Fellows, Morton and Clayton **Fellows, Post Haste,** Castle Eden **Ale,** Fullers **London Pride,** Mallards **Duckling,** Caledonian **Deuchars IPA,** Timothy Taylor **Landlord.**

The FMC is my most recommended Nottingham pub and it is easy to see why. A canal side and town street location, near to the station gives it both tourist and townie appeal. It brews it's own ales, the examples here having interesting variations. The pub itself extends to the canal by means of a conservatory bar and outside tables / patio at various different levels. My visit found a large number of office workers and shoppers mingling with real ale buffs chasing new brews. What struck me was the age of those ale drinkers, the FMC is breeding a younger generation of real ale drinkers. A top pub, one to remember and tell your mates about. This is also the prefect weekend away pub, great on Friday evenings.

12 - 14 Queens Bridge Rd. NG2 1NB
G New management since visit.
F From 12
T 0115 9850611
S Smoking throughout

BWV 23.3.05 Castle Rock **Meadows Gold, Hemlock Bitter, Harvest Pale, Elsie Mo, Painted Lady,** Beartown **Bearcross,** Archers **Golden,** Dark Star **Original,** Crouch Vale **Blackwater Mild.**

The Vat and Fiddle looks out of place in it's town street location. The building is in a style of suburban roadside pubs, complete with being set back from the road. The interior is simply superb, simply laid out, simply a great place to sample great real ale. The pub is the tap room outlet for Castle Rock ales and the range here certainly included rarities that I had yet to sample. Belgian bottles beers and guests add to the range so no wonder my visit found real ale hunters from far and wide essentially making a pilgrimage. The pub was positively buzzing early evening, there were obvious regulars but most appeared to be using the place for the first, but I bet, not the last time before heading off to the nearby station. The Nottingham real ale scene has a great standard bearer in the Vat and Fiddle.

G Pete Odell
F Light snacks from 12
T 0115 9866881
S Smoking throughout

BWV 25.3.05 Archers **Thrust XV,** Wye Valley **Bitter,** Shepherd Neame **Spitfire,** Greene King **IPA**

The Globe was bought by the owner of the MFC four years ago and the renovation is a good one. It occupies an imposing roadside site with views across t'canal and factory to both footie grounds. The main section of bar is light and airy with pine floors and space to chat around large tables. The rear farmhouse style room has settees and a brick surround fire. Pete was as clear as any boss in saying that good footie fans and real ale go together. This is a pub for real ale fans not the Burberry hatted brigade. The locals are friendly and will make you welcome. Any guide site that says otherwise does not know the locals. The beer selection is likely to increase to 6 or 7 on matchdays as both Forest and County fans come here. If you only have time to visit a pub near the ground, this is my recommendation, you will find some alternative ales from unusual sources. Should bouncers be on the door it will be due to the reputation of your non real ale drinking fellow supporters.

1 Ratepayers Arms Freehouse   2 Wellington Arms Bath Ales   3 Cornubia Smiles Pub. Co.

cp   tv   pg   d   cp   d   sp   pg

Filton Leisure Centre, BS34 7 PS
G John Beese
T 01454866697
F From 12

BWV 6.12.04 Otter **Claus**, Butcombe **Bitter**, Charles Wells **Bombardier**, Ind Coope **Burton Ale**, Stonehenge **Great Bustard**.

If you know that Bristol has masses of choice but plenty of associated transport hassles then the Ratepayers offers an interesting alternative. This is a suburban leisure centre bar owned by the local council. In a rare act of enlightened thinking John has been given license to create a real ale bar with a great range of good quality ales. In a typical café / bar style you find a lounge bar that is a really good locals dropping off point. Of course it is frequented by athletic and not so athletic types, the former having played squash, badminton etc, the latter, like me dreaming of past energies and revelling in the real ale. It offers simple food and is welcoming to all ages. The selection of ales specialises in regional microbrews yet has national well-known brands for the less adventurous. Unique as an entry in these guides, it might encourage a local person to take up physical activity, well perhaps not, cribbage or darts while enjoying good ale is enough for me.

Gloucester Rd, BS7 8UR
G Paul Tanner
T 0171 9513022
F Bacon, sausage sandwiches chips cheese + full evening menu
S No smoking at the bar and one no n smoking room.

BWV 12.4.05 Bath **Gem, Spa, Barnstormer**, 3 Rivers **Disreputable**.

My final pub of the 270 or odd visited was purposely selected because I wanted to finish on a pub of real quality. Recently bought by Bath Ales, the "Welly" is well known in Footie and real ale circles for *the quality of its beers and the friendliness of its customers / staff*. The pub is a grand old saloon with palatial Victorian architecture. It is also labelled home only, so it is best to get there early without colours. You will be made welcome. *Its gert lush! (Ian)*. The pub gets very busy on match days, perhaps best so when the "Bris" are "heaving" before a Rugger match. As Grant Buckley says *When you stumble out the door it's a two minute roll down the hill to the ground plus there is top totty behind the bar!* Most will linger longer comforted by the fact that the range of ales and ciders will satisfy most needs and more. This acts as a *good anaesthetic before the dross on the pitch. (Gary K)*

142 Temple St. BS1 6EN
G Julia Richardson
T 0117 9254415
S Smoking throughout

BWV 12.4.05 Otter **Bitter**, Spinning Dog **Mutley Springer**, Palmers **Tally Ho!** Smiles **IPA**, Archers **Bouncing Bunnies**, Cottage **Western Glory**, Bristol Ciderworks **Cider**.

This pub is perfect for weekenders or those returning to the station after the game. The nationally famous Cornubia is not open on Saturday lunchtime. Set back from a side road off Victoria St you have to imagine pre Blitz Bristol to understand its location among the city office blocks and brewery townscape. The Cornubia is a fantastic boozer that has the qualities that I value highly in the best of British ale houses. A simple layout of bar and no frills, an open fire place to toast yourself in winter, a pub front with tables to spill out onto hot summers days. Pickled eggs on the bar, indicators of cerebral pastimes behind it and a fantastic choice of ales. Smiles may have gone as an independent brewer but the Cornubia lives on in spirit and quality. On the Real ale trail, it attracts tickers from the station and office workers at lunchtime. It is Weekend evenings that see it heaving, so get there early.

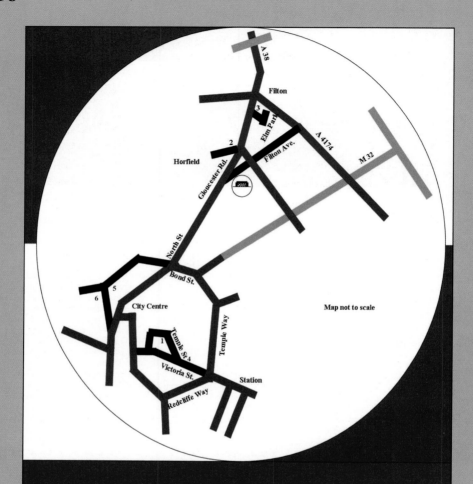

Bristol

There are several really good pubs with real ale in the Hor-field area. Many however, will make a weekend of the stay in Bristol so the Cornobia offers a starting point for an excellent city crawl. What you need is for Rovers to be promoted every year so that the joys of Bristol can be shared around.

Bristol

1 Kings Head Enterprise | 2 Brewery Tap Freehouse | 3 Zerodegrees Freehouse

mp

mp   bm

sp   sky   bm   d

1 Kings Head

Victoria St BS1 6DE
G Jane Wakeham
S Smoking throughout
T 0117 9277860

BWV 12.4.05 Sharps **Cornish Coaster**, **Doom Bar**. Courage **Best, Bass,**

Leaving Temple Meads the first pub you will notice on Victoria St. looks like an antique shop on the outside and, some might say, on the inside as well. It is a great starting (or better, finishing) point to a tour of Bristol. The Kings Head is a low ceiling narrow single bar of National Historic importance. The Courage window is now historic in its own right since the Brewery and the associated aroma has long since gone. The pubs' reputation relies upon the quality and selection of ales, often featuring west country ales.. The place quickly fills up with a great combination of office workers in the day, joined by real ale fans in the afternoon / evening and distant regulars in the evening. Nowhere is far from the bar so it would be difficult not to be noticed here. It is very small and totally friendly. If you are a fan of a bigger club, just check in advance because, due to its convenient location between the station and City Centre, it will sometimes be closed on match days.

2 Brewery Tap

6 - 10 Colston St. BS1 5BD
G Matt Mason
T 0117 9213668
F From 11.30

BWV 12.4.05 Smiles **Heritage, Best, Bristol IPA,** Wickwar Cotswold Way.

Smiles brewing may have joined Courage as being lost to Bristol but the Smiles Company Brewery Tap continues the traditions of this innovative and much loved Bristol beer trend setter. Other local ales will undoubtedly come to take prominence over the months but the comfort and originality of this pub continues to be popular with people of all ages and outlooks. My lunchtime visit found mostly women in the bar; nurses, office meetings, groups of people taking a drink between the town and tourist business. The layout means that you can usually find solitude in one of the back wooden walled rooms or join in more pubby chat at the bar at the front. I like the use of hop sacks on the wall and the general feeling of well planned disorganisation within the rustic furniture. This is a gentle lunchtime pub that gives way to young and old planning nights out in town in the evening. A great pub in a good location and with, one hopes, a bright if now less Smiles dependent future.

3 Zerodegrees

53 Colston Street BS1 5BA
G Stephen Holman
F Pizzas, mussels, pasta, salads and gourmet sausages (Sunday roast)
T 01179252706
S No smoking in restaurant.
W www.zerodegrees.co.uk

BWV 12.4.05 Zerodegrees **Pilsner, Pale Ale, Black Lager, Wheat Ale, Special.**

Have you been to an American style, microbrew, or perhaps, a new German Tavern? Maybe you might have found an architect designed London warehouse serving good ale? The new Zerodegrees has arrived in Bristol and has made an immediate impression on the real ale scene. The sparkling nature of the brewery and its industrial interior make an instant impact. The beer is the ultimate of instant access, direct from the stills to the glass. Add in plasma screens for both big Rugby and Footie matches and you get a wider appeal than merely a trendy bar. The pub has a minimalist look yet still makes me feel like I am welcome as an occasional visitor. After a chat with Martin, the head brewer of German descent, I retired to the balcony in perfect contentment and set off going through the list. Be sure to ask what the special is, it will often surprise, much as the Black lager excites.

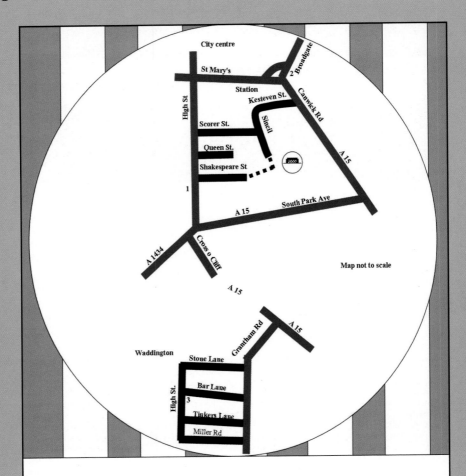

Lincoln

The High Street has the majority of pubs and most will find comfort here but the real ale quarters are divided into two. The brave will climb the hill to see the Cathedral area, the dedicated will use their discretion and seek out these high-lighted gems.

1 Golden Eagle Tynemill

sp   sk   jb

21 High St LN5 8DB
G James Middleton
T 01522 521058
S Smoking throughout

BWV 17.10.04 Everards **Beacon, Bass,** Castle Rock **Harvest Ale,** Batemans **XXXB,** Dent **A Pint of the Ewesual,** O'Kells **Bitter,** Abbeydale **Matins,** Westons **Old Rosie**

The Golden Eagle is one of my favourite pre match pubs. On every occasion over the last ten years or so the pub has had a different story to tell, each involving comfortable chat and real warmth. Two small bars wood paneled and comfortable, describes the architecture. Crowded, bubbly in one bar especially if a lunchtime game is on, quiet, reflective and thoughtful, describes the locals in the smaller front bar. Don't come late on matchday if you want a seat. Loads of Lincoln City memorabilia, programmes etc. are found here and often their will be an affectionate *chat about the plight of Lincoln City and Boston derbies.* My best visit came on the day of the Rugby World Cup final, the post match party was in full swing as I arrived for my afternoon kick off, the Aussies finding solace in a walk to find another pub. If they will drink Fosters what do they expect.

2 Sippers Freehouse

sp   tv   bm

83 Westgate LN5 7HW
G John Gilbert
F From 12 -2
T 01522 527612
S Smoking throughout

BWV 17.10.04 John Smiths **Cask,** Hopback **Summer Lightning,** Timothy Taylor **Landlord,** Danton **Wheat Porter**

With rooms arranged around a central bar, this pub has a feel of a quality tap room. With a regular dark on sale and staff who patently know, as well as love their beer, the pub is rightly popular with locals and visitors alike. John and his wife are well known in real ale circuits and made me feel very welcome as we chatted about how to get this venture going, thanks chaps. The pub has no pretensions to anything other than a great drinking place. The best time to visit is in early evening when Lincoln City fanzine writers, those going for a train and the genuine Imps who know real ale head back into town to mix with away fans. *Perhaps because of its location it has a regular clientele that have made an extra effort to get there. Yet it is so close to the station that it would be the ideal visit on arrival and departure from Lincoln.* Sippers is a top boozer in a town with many good pubs. The difference here is the great welcome you get from the locals.

3 Three Horseshoes Freehouse

cp   tv   jb   pg

Lower High St, Waddington LN5 9RF
G Bob Watton
T 01522 720448
S Smoking throughout

BWV 17.10.04 John Smiths **Cask,** Fullers **London Pride,** Timothy Taylor **Landlord,** Highwood **Tom Woods Bitter,** Warwickshire **Lady Godiva,** Spinning Dog **Mutleys Pit Stop**

This is a proper village pub which has two rooms and a large garden. One bar is long and narrow, laid out to encourage people to talk to each other across the tables. The other is a small snug with T.V. and sporting trophies. The community nature comes to the fore through Bob's support of pub teams and pub games Football, cricket, fishing teams and top notch ale, the locals are in a form of heaven here. The love of Grimsby Town must be a hardship for the landlord, especially since the Imps keep on making the playoffs. It is not a food pub, the locals use the chippie nearby as do the regular riverside ramblers who frequent the pub in summer. It comes recommended as *great for a summer pint in the garden.* I recommend it for the great choice of regional ales and location a few miles from Lincoln yet only ten minutes from the ground by car.

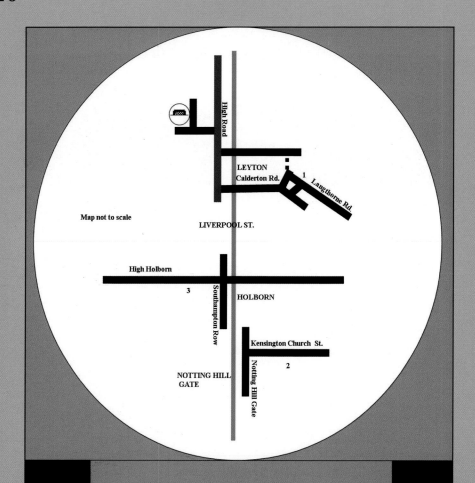

High Road

LEYTON
Calderton Rd.

1 Langthorne Rd

Map not to scale

LIVERPOOL ST.

High Holborn

3

Southampton Row

HOLBORN

Kensington Church St.

2

NOTTING HILL GATE

Notting Hill Gate

Leyton Orient

The M11 route in is notoriously slow so my advice is to get the train and each pub here is easily found from the central line. The Birkbeck is just fantastic, loads of room and far enough away from the ground to not be swamped.

Leyton Orient

1 Birkbeck Tavern Freehouse

2 Churchill Arms Fullers

6 Princess Louise Samuel Smiths

cp   sk   jb   pg

mp   sk   bm

mp

Langthorne Rd. E11 4HL
G Roy Leach
F Various rolls from 12
S Smoking throughout
T 02085392584
S Smoking throughout

119 Kensington Church St. W8 7LN
G Jerry O'Brien
F Thai restaurant from 12
T 020 77274242
S Smoking in the pub only

208 High Holborn WC1V 7BW
G Campbell Mackay
F Sandwiches and ploughman's from 12
T 020 74058816
S Smoking throughout

BWV 25.1.05 Rita's **Special (House Brew)**, Barnsley **Oakwell Bitter**, Skinners **Betty Stogs**, St. Austell **Tinners**

The Birkbeck Tavern is the grand daddy of London lower division pubs. Any supporters of larger teams on a weekend away need to make a tour to find this pub as you are unlikely to play Leyton Orient and have an excuse to visit. Landlord Roy goes the extra mile to make you feel welcome as do the football mad locals. Operating a genuine two day maximum to turn round to a new ale it is popular with the "Pigs Ear" real ale crew and away fans who often phone in advance to check out the brews on offer. They are often surprised but rarely disappointed, over 300 different beers a year have been on offer. *One of my favourite haunts before a game.* It is something very special. The atmosphere on matchdays is just perfect, totally friendly, especially on balmy summers days when the garden comes into its own. In the middle of winter the genuine Leyton warmth comes to warm the cockles.

BWV 6.12.04 Fullers **London Pride, Chiswick, ESB, Jack Frost**

In the heart of café and bistro land the Churchill represents tradition without pretence. The Irish roots come through in the sports themes, particularly Gaelic football and London Irish rugby. The love of real ale is easy to notice within the conversations of its diverse clientele. *The best pint of ESB I have ever tasted* (Overheard in pub - Mike) This is a blooming good pub winning London in Bloom awards. *It is a lovely pub, great beer, really friendly bar staff, (I'm always a sucker for gorgeous, Irish girls!) Its also a great place for a last few pints, as you can leave at around 11 o'clock & still get to Paddington for the last train home. (Nigel C Bristol)* Of note for historians are references to Winny and wartime memorabilia. For TV sports fans the television is more likely to be coveted by Rugby fans rather than those who want their fill of Premiership footie. And then there is the Thai food to sample after a game.

BWV 25.1.05 ,Samuel Smiths **OBB**

Only 1 real ale? But what an ale, and what a place to drink it. There are many pumps, all serving OBB, the eye is also drawn to quality in the bottle cabinets The pub features the full range of Sam Smiths bottled ales and also satisfies the continental beer fan. Most impressive is the price of the ale; no London extortion rates here and no sign of cheap booze cruisers either The bar itself is large and surrounded on all sides by ample comfortable seating. Close to Holborn station it is well worth getting in for a quiet pint before heading North or alternatively making it the place to get over the post match tube experience before heading off to the train home. References to this pub always mention the Victorian toilets, I would rather comment on the ornate mirrors and wall carvings. *I have yet to go in there and not be impressed by the friendliness of the staff and the price of the ale.* A place to meet up with mates as all main line stations being easily accessible.

Darlington

Searching for real ale of any quality is nearly impossible near the Williamson Stadium so the best bet is to indulge in the festival that is Darlington town centre, great pubs and all with different characters. Try Hurworth for quiet pint.

1 Number Twenty-2 Village   2 Quaker Coffee House F   3 Bay Horse

mp   mp   bm   pg   d   cp   tv   bm   pg   d

1 Number Twenty-2

22 Conisliffe Rd, DR3 7RG
G Ralph Wilkinson
F Full lunch menu 12-2 Mon to Sat.
T 01325 354590
S Possible no smoking
W www. numbertwenty2@villagebrewer.co.uk

BWV 21.8.04 Village **Premium Bull White Boar Bitter, Old Raby Ale**, Hambleton **Bitter, Yorkshire Stout**, Skinner **Jingle Knocker**, Castle Rock **Hemlock,** Fullers London Pride, Westons **Stowford Cider**

The "popular ale house and canteen" label doesn't do this place justice. Well planned division of the building means there is demand for both food and top quality ale, often at the same time. *A great pub which never disappoints.* DAFTS.com describes it thus *Popular with an over 30s crowd at night and nicknamed Jurassic Park by those who get squiffy on two Bacardi Breezers. Just one type of lager and no spirits or silly alco-pops. No music, a "fine for charity" for use of mobile phones. Despite or perhaps because of the restrictions, this is a relaxed place for beer and conversation.* Ralph runs a top quality pub that is an example to others of how to get good food and ales to complement without it becoming a gastro den.

2 Quaker Coffee House

2 Mechanics Yard, DL3 7QF
G Steve Metcalf
F Full lunch menu and snacks from 11
W www.quakerhouse.net
T 07845 666643
S Smoking throughout

BWV 21.8.04 Darwin **Ghost Ale**, Shardlow **Whistle Stop,** Cropton **Monkmans Slaughter,** Wychwood **Hobgoblin**, Timothy Taylor **Landlord.**

The Quaker Coffee House is a small wooden floored gem in a small alley off the main square. This is not a quiet coffee house, but during the day it is a good place to find some peace and quiet when out walking the town.. *Don't be put off by the "Café and Bar", it is well worth finding.* It was local CAMRA pub of the year 2003 and has always been a popular venue for visiting football fans. *Mick Hubbard a visiting Aston Villa fans described it in the internet football guide as an Aladdin's Cave of real ales, having nine on tap. It was a fantastic place and also has a separate cafe upstairs.* The excellent website tells much of the life of the pub, a fun place with seriously good choice of real ale tells you much about the character of Steve and his team, Music is live in the evenings, the beer drinking is live every day, *the place rocks,* top banana!

3 Bay Horse

45 The Green, Hurworth, DL2 2AA
G Kevin Melton
F From 12-2, 6- 9.30
T 01325 720663
S Smoking throughout

BWV 21.8.04 Greene King **Old Speckled Hen**, Marstons **Pedigree**, John Smith's **Magnet, Cask**, St Peters **Golden Ale**

The Bay Horse is a quiet, two room locals pub, two miles south of the real ale bereft ground. It is laid out in English traditional style. It has a plain public bar and carpeted lounge that splits into two allowing for food and comfortable supping to co exist. It looks and feels lived in and part of long established local community. Kevin is trying to widen the beer range and build up a real ale fan base, give him your support if you can An. *attractive Inn situated in an equally charming village by the river Tees (CAMRA 2004),* the Bay Horse was my first pub to review way back in September I found it very easy to get in to conversation with the local characters as I returned the next day for a pre match pint in the bar later in the year. The village in itself is well worth a visit, good for a stroll after a long drive North and with plenty of local history that the locals are well prepared to share with you.

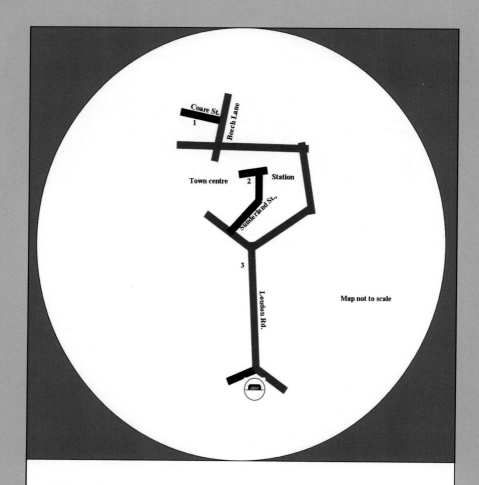

Macclesfield

Macclesfield has so many pubs that one wonders if there will be a lot fewer in years to come. Of the many to choose from the ones shown here represent the best for a drink and walk before the game or in the case of the Flag a pub to retire to before heading home.

Macclesfield

1 British Flag Robinsons 2 Waters Green Tavern 3 The Sun Inn Pyramid

sp sky bm pg d	mp	sp pg

42 Coare St, SK11 1DW
G Lloyd Roberts
T 01625 428118
S Smoking throughout
BWV 26.2.05 Robinsons **Unicorn, Hatters Mild.**

The British Flag doesn't open before the game so it's entry here should tell you just how good it is. If you have the time after a game make a beeline to Coare St where you are guaranteed great ale and a typically Northern, warm and friendly welcome. It is a street terrace local with four small rooms that might all be described as snugs. One is devoted to Pool and a T.V. the others you will find occupied by groups of locals continuing conversations that have lasted from the previous evening. Lloyd will probably arrive at the same time having been to watch the game himself. This is a sports oriented community pub that includes a golf society among the usual darts and crib teams. In November the seasonal Robin is added to the excellent routine Robinsons ales. I was lucky enough to have a bed and breakfast room booked at the end of the street so I was able to sample the pub at it's very best as the locals returned for an evenings revelries to a time long after the game had finished. In a town of many good pubs the British Flag is a top local.

96 Waters Green SK11 6LH
O G Brian McDermott
F From 12
T 01625422653
S Smoking throughout

BWV 26.2.02 There is always a selection of guest ales that include beers like those from Oakham, Pictish and Abbeydale. Some were available on my visit.

You are guaranteed a quality selection of rarer ales as Brian is proud of finding ales that reflect his taste for microbrews. My pre match lunchtime visit was typical as groups of home and away fans entered into pessimistic conversations as to the whole Macclesfield Town experience. On my return nothing had changed other than the people were different and the coal fire was being recharged ready for the evening customers. This is a top pub that relies on the assurance that you will get something different from when you last visited. Highly recommended is the home prepared, fresh food that leaves an impression that, as with the beer, it is the wholesomeness that counts. *It's got real chips!* Come here, mind your language and join in the love of what is good in this type of British pub. It has won numerous CAMRA awards. The secrets of the ale list needs to be discovered.

45 Mill Lane SK11 7NN
G Rita Evans
T 01625 614530
S Smoking throughout

BWV 26.2.05 Wychwood **Hobgoblin**, Camerons **Strongarm.**

Something had happened here because my visit found a long list of beers that had recently finished so its popularity must be justified. Rita assures me the regulars are augmented by 2 or 3 guests and the pub turns around ten or so different ales a week. The pub is very handy, being on the main drag from the town to the ground, that includes the excellent Railway further up the hill. The two bars of this traditional style street fronted pub are very different. The right hand bar has pool and darts to distract the customer. The left hand bar is the retreat for those who are less active and value comfortable seating and access to the next ale. It has a popularity among quiz teams and the itinerant CAMRA guided tickers who find it welcoming and basically charming, ala Rita's personality. One hopes a recent period of frequent Guv'nor changes is at and end and the locals, who love this pub can get a roadside local with a reputation to match the quality of the ale choice. It already has great people who create a vibrant atmosphere.

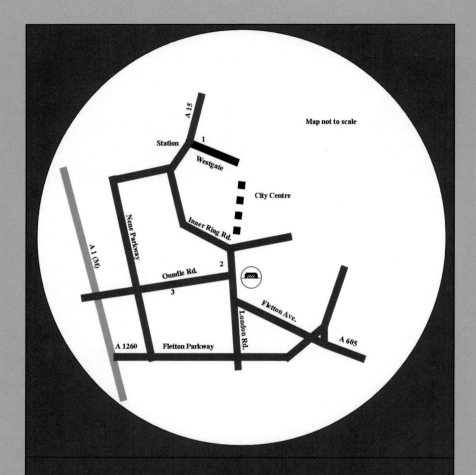

Peterborough

Why is it that the best towns for real ale have teams that gravitate towards relegation or the lower divisions? If this theory was to reach its full truth then Posh would be hosting conference football because this is a premiership real ale town. My guide will cause debate because there are many others that might be included, that is the love of real ale hunting. There is something for everyone within this selection.

1 Brewery Tap Freehouse

2 Charters Freehouse

3 Palmerston Arms Batemans

sp tv bm d

sp bm

cp tv nm d

80 Westgate, PE1 2AA
G Paul Hock
T 01733 358500
F Thai food all day on Saturdays.
S Large no smoking areas.

BWV Oakham **JHB, White Dwarf, Kaleidoscope, Bishops Farewell** Bass, Elgoods **Black Dog**, Butcombe **Gold,** Lee **Ice Breaker**, Ossett **Pale Gold,** Cottage **Huntingdon 800**.

The pub was created as a large and architecturally splendid bar and brewery. in 1998. *It is home to the Oakham brewery who brew world class real ales (You only have to count the number of awards around the walls)* (Pete of Ilford) The beer list is impressive as is the fact that you can see the beer making through large plate glass windows. It has many recommendations to this guide. As Bob the taxi says, *when visitors arrive at the station and ask for real ale pubs the Brewery tap immediately comes to mind.* Brewery tours are available by prior arrangement. For *Hartlepool fans the monkey is alive and well, living here,* come and have a look. Stuart assured me that the range of professionals, students and real ale heads continues throughout the day. I would love to see this place as the music kicks in or when the later night sessions are in full flow. I know it will be good.

Town Bridge PE1 1DG
G Paul Hook
F Snack and lunchtime menu before, oriental food
T 01733 315700
S Restaurant non smoking, separate smoking / non smoking areas in bar

BWV Oakham **JHB,** Oakham **Gravity, Kaleidoscope, Bishops Farewell, White Dwarf** Titanic **Drop Anchor,** Hopback **Summer Lightning,** RCH **Pitchfork,** Newby Wyke **Black Squall,** Elgoods **Black Dog, Bass.**

This Dutch grain barge is both an oriental restaurant (top floor) and a top ale house (below deck) The Leendart R was built in 1907 but became a permanent ale house in 1991. Since then it's reputation has reached legendary stratus among those seeking something just a little different. Don't think for a minute that this is a gimmicky place. The bar is large enough to compete with any land based house. The floor might slope from shore to bar but the ales are consistently high quality As Colin Smith of Norwich says it has *great beer, food, staff and beer garden.* Blues music sets the tone on evenings when live bands are in situ. The pub is likely to have a predomination of Posh fans who follow the no headgear rule. *It is under the bridge!*

82 Oundle Rd, PE2 7PA
G David McLennan
T 01733 565865
S Smoking throughout

BWV York **Yorkshire Terrier**, Batemans **Hooker**, **XXXB**, Nethergate **Suffolk County**, Wooden Hand **Cornish Mutiny**, Newby Wyke **Kingston Topaz**, Nethergate **Hares Breadth,** Hop Back **Summer Lightning,** Titanic **Black Ice,** Batemans **Spring Breeze.**

Bob the Taxi also suggested I shouldn't miss the Palmerston Arms, how right he was. This is one of those rare treasures that I am reluctant to advertise for purely selfish reasons. Where else can a village local deliver 10 real ales under a regional ale flag, all by gravity direct from the cellar? What is more the beers rotate at regular intervals so your visit will find rare Batemans seasonals as well as regional master brews. The pub itself is small and cosy, as you would find in your favourite country village. Posh pictures are of real interest in both bar and lounge as are real ale literature and awards. It advertises itself as a permanent mini real ale festival and this is true. Also check out the Whisky choices. I would love to join the friendly locals Palmy army, if only they had a shirt in my size.

Map not to scale

Ring Road

Raymond St.

Canal St. 2

Hoole Rd

Station

Sealand Rd.

City Rd

3

City centre

Bumpers La.

1

Canal Side

Chester

Chester is one of those tourist towns that has a thriving resident community that support real ale in the face of the keg assault. The town centre pubs have appeal for tourists but this selection follows an alternative route along the newly renovated canal from the station. There are several other CAMRA recommended pubs nearby to add detours to the walk.

Chester

1 Old Harkers Arms B + P 2 Ship Victory Freehouse 3 Telford's Warehouse F

mp	tv	bm		d	mp	sk	bm	pg	
							cp		bm	pg

1 Old Harkers Arms

1 Russell St. CH3 5ALL
G John Thomas
F An extensive pub menu from 12
T 01244 3444525
S Separate smoking areas
W www.harkers arms chester.co.uk

BWV 27.2.05 Wye Valley **Butty Bach**, Castle Rock **Harvest Pale** Ale, **Bass,** Cains **IPA,** Weetwood **Best,** Hartleys **Cumbrian Way,** Baltic Fleet **Weiss, Wapping**, Abbeydale **Devotion.**

Brunning and Price own a small number of good real ale pubs and if this is typical they are meeting the needs of the people who read this guide, big time. This is a large converted warehouse alongside the Canal near the station. I would describe it as a "thirtysomethings" style of ale house, top quality ales and a selection that includes some national and local beers. One room is your favourite second hand bookshop, the other a farmhouse kitchen complete with kitchen tables and families (not full of children when I visited) discussing the inadequacies of student grants as they eat a typical meal that parents and children agree fits the bill. This is a great meeting point for those who want to go on later into town.. For me, it is the place to start the canal side real ale crawl.

2 Ship Victory

47 George St. CH1 3EQ
G Joe Gildea
T 01244 376453
S Smoking throughout

BWV 27.2.05 Archers **Bitter,** Tetley's **Cask.**

In contrast to the other two pubs the Ship Victory is all that is good in a small, proper community ale house. It is indeed "a small pub with a big heart." *Nothing is too much trouble (Ruth of Dustin)* A single bar it is bedecked with numerous pots. Evidence is everywhere of the good causes that Joe supports with an unrivalled zeal. This is a true footie lovers pub. The home of *Man City fans (Chester Branch)* whose flag travels all over the country proclaiming the name of the pub (Joe) Also it is the sponsor of "Los rojos de Chester" (Reds of Chester) at Liverpool games. It is the only Ship Victory in the country, hosts folk nights and on my visit there was a busy karaoke night in full and glorious flow. Joe *takes great pains to keep his beer perfect, he looks after his football supporters, I love the atmosphere when I'm watching my team play (Carol of Chester)* This pub, and its fun, was one of the highlights of my year long research. As Tony says *they welcome strangers like long lost brothers and sisters.* Cheers Joe.

3 Telford's Warehouse

Tower Wharf
G Jeremy Horrill
F Seasonal menu of hearty meals to suit all tastes ranging from traditional to Thai from 12
T 01244 390090
S Ground floor smoking, 1st floor restaurant non smoking
W www.telfordwarehouse.com

BWV 27.2.05 Wheetwood **Eastgate,** Thwaites **Original,** Timothy Taylor **Landlord,** Rudgate **Ruby Mild.**

And so back down to the canal to find a younger ale house geared up for top quality music and quality micro hunting. Busy with a mix of office workers, canal walkers, tourists and Chester dwellers who enjoy its ambience the Warehouse is a rare mix. It is "cool" pub, designed as a redevelopment in a farmhouse style on three levels the lower space has an international reputation for good live music. I preferred the middle levels of the barn, all settees and views across the canal basin. *Spot the Ena Sharples photo above the "T.V."* When American micro brew houses design their pubs this is the mould from which they are cast. Those with children were encouraged to use the upstairs restaurant area. The pub marks the end of the mini crawl and is a place to linger a little longer. before the haul out to the ground.

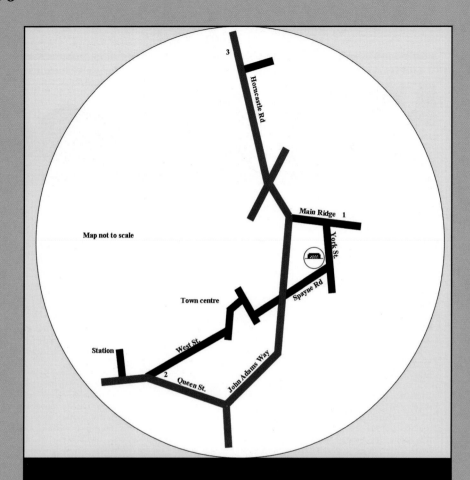

Boston

Many of the pubs serve Batemans and if you are lucky a guest ale. The two recommended pubs are quite close and mean you will have to resist the Batemans temptation. All three are very much geared up to Football and you can't really go wrong. In a rare exception I also add the club pub at the ground.

1 Coach and Horses _{Batemans}   2 Eagle Tynemill Freehouse   3 Cowbridge House Inn

sp   pg   mp   tv   jb   pg   cp   tv   bm   d

86 Main Ridge
G Chris Pogson
T 01205 364478
S Smoking throughout

BWV 17.10.04 Batemans **XXXB, XB**

This is a small one roomed bar with beer garden large enough (not) for an impromptu five a side between fans. This pub is totally sports mad and very friendly. It gets very crowded on match days and on others the locals will always talk about sports and real ale. *My visits have always coincided with ongoing cribbage sessions, games of pool or general chat between rival fans at the bar.* This year being a good case in point, the beer was excellent the home colours prevalent yet the group of visiting fans were positively encouraged to come back later in the day as they left for the game. Chris is a great relaxed landlord who knows the value of making the customer know that the beer is what makes the place better than the rest. Don't expect to get a seat if you don't get here early.

144 West St
G Andrew Rudolf
F Rolls etc from 11
W www.tynemill.co.uk
T 01205 361116
S Smoking throughout

BWV 17.10.04 Timothy Taylor **Landlord,** Nethergate **Monks Habit**, **Augustinian,** Wadworths **6X,** Banks' **Best**

The Eagle is the first pub you will find as you arrive by train. It is a two bar traditional boozer with extra function room and pool area. Tiled floors and bench seats give the feel of no nonsense quality. The big screens attract the Saturday lunchtime fans who want to get their premiership fix before watching the Division Two version of the beautiful game. The recommendations for this pub are numerous and fulsome. As a classic Tynemill house it has a good range of ales and a policy that encourages the promotion of independent breweries. My visit was too short, the friends who stayed longer raved about the good atmosphere, fun and friendship they made in their time before the game.

Horncastle Rd, Cowbridge
G Derek Dawson
F Always (Restaurant)
T 01205 362597
S Separate smoking areas

BWV 17.10.04 Archers **Lydham Manor**, Mansfield **Cask Ale,** Theakstons **Mild,** John Smiths **Cask,** Greene King **Old Speckled Hen**

The Cowbridge is a large pub and restaurant but definitely not in the style of newer versions. Go into the smaller bar to admire the football memorabilia and join in the footie banter. This pub has loads of character and is well loved by locals and landlord alike. Derek will make you very welcome and will be going to the game himself. Of interest to me were the tales on the wall of his son being stranded midatlantic, quite an experience that ended well, thank goodness. My second visit later in the year found similar friendship and different guest ales to complement the national bitters and mild. The food came highly recommended by those in town who use the pub to continue their searches for good ale.

Boston United F.C.

A rare treat in Boston is that what was the supporters club on the corner of the ground now is a pub and yippee it serves real ale. It was busy both before and after the game. It is very friendly. large and serving good footie food, this is a model that all clubs should follow.

THE COMPETITION FOR

I would like to thank the 400 or so people who contributed to the guides by completing the post cards given to them by landlords in the pubs.

The aim was to give the writing a more personalised set of descriptions by asking people who know the pubs best to comment on the good points that make their locals so good.

to visit both this year and next. It also confirmed my view that the beauty of finding good real ale is that the country has many real ale outlets that are as yet given their true worth of advertising. Some of the entries did not serve real ale put are still great footie pubs.

The comments were many and varied and some unfortunately unprint-

Geoff Clarke, (left) the winner of the competition pictured with "Pat" Patel, the landlord of the Old Crown in West Bromwich (right) and the owner of the Malvern Brewery on a recent trip organised by Pat. We wish Pat a full recovery from his recent illness and look forward to Geoff enjoying his two tickets to an away game next season.

Many comments were used in the guide and they can be seen it italics in many entries. Wherever possible I have tried to give the name that the contributor wished to use. If the person wished to remain anonymous the quotation remains without a name rather than as anon.

I also asked the entrants to nominate their best away footie fan pub in the country. This was a very interesting exercise which threw up many pubs for me

able. Without doubt those places that returned cards ended up with a more interesting entry that reflected the humour found in those pubs. The vast majority of comments were a great help in giving me their true flavour beyond that which can be made in my short visits.

From the entries I selected eleven finalists. These cards were the most interesting, funny or informative. The finalists are listed opposite

My personal favourite was from

CONTRIBUTORS TO THE GUIDE

Dawn of West Bromwich who said the Wheatsheaf is handy for the baggies matches as it's *between the Doctors surgery and the church*. I am writing this just as the Baggies have survived for another year. Someone certainly prayed a lot this afternoon.

The draw was held in a London pub on the night of a Conference play off semi final. Pictured here are Clarkie, Tim, Kelly and Graham, surveying the finalists before selecting a winner. The finalists were selected as the most interesting entered, the winner was a random selection from that list.

FINALISTS

Geoff Clarke	Wednesbury
Mike Stevens,	Dudley,
Gary S	Barnsley
Phil Passingham	Market Harborough
Dawn	West Bromwich
Nicola S	Barnsley
Mark	London
Jean Downey	Sunderland
Steve	Luton
David Cuff	Brighton
Dave Knight	Brighton

Geoff's entry for the Old Crown (West Bromwich) said *Not only is it a baggies base we also have Villa, Blues, Wolves and Walsall supporters and the rapport is fantastic - almost as good as the real ale (Always varying in type but never in quality). The best value food in Sandwell and by far the most accommodating host and hostess.*

He also recommended the Black Eagle in Hockley as a Walsall fan.

Good luck if you enter next years competition. I look forward to your entries.

Stedders 2005

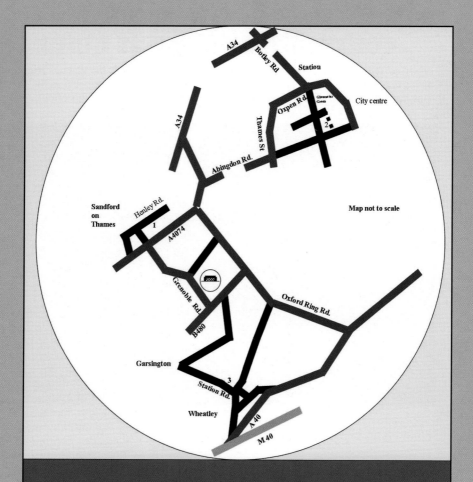

Oxford

A pub can be found if you walk a mile in any direction. The car park barn can be very busy so the best bet are to park(!) in town and find something very different around Gloucester Green. If not then Wheatley offers variety and something special.

Oxford United

1 Fox Greene King | **2 Far from the Madding Crowd F** | **3 Railway (Wheatley)**

sp   tv   pg | mp   d | cp   sk   bm   pg   d

Fox:

25 Henley Rd Sandford on Thames OX4 4YN
G Nigel Rolston
T 01865 7778003
S Smoking throughout

BWV 2.11.04 Greene King **IPA**, Highwood **Tom Wood Bomber County**

This is the quintessential village pub of your youth. Two bars, one very basic at the front that contrasts with the cosy back bar, family room Set on a roadside green / lay by this is a village local that relies on weekend trade to justify a wider range of ale. The village also is home to the pub that many other fans find by turning the "wrong way" when trying to find the Kassam., Oxford fans from afar meet here which must be as good a recommendation as one could have. *This friendly pub was in the guide for 15 consecutive years (CAMRA 2005)* The guide also comments on the refurbishment or lack of it. On my visit I commented on the apparent state of temporary decoration and was informed that *that's how it is and always is.* So it's bare plaster board walls in the bar and stone walls in the back bar. This is a great place for a quiet lunchtime pint, paper to read, walk to plan, or game to watch. It is not big enough for bus loads, leave that to the pub in the club car park.

Far from the Madding Crowd:

10 -12 Friars Entry OX1 2BY
G Charles Eld
F From 12
T 01865 240900
S Separate smoking areas

BWV 2.11.04 Archers Crystal Clear, Great Western **Revival Cider**

You must experience the mix of students, vicars, theatre types and city locals. No music, no alcopops and no bouncers all add to the feeling of relaxation in this alley behind Debenhams. Conversation turns to the arts rather than football but enjoy! It is described to me as a *magnet for town and gown.* At weekends the range of beers increases but the quality remains as good as ever. The pub itself is surprisingly large for a back lane location. *It is also quite modern looking, but that is an attraction rather than something to put off the serious fan of his beer.* I have made three visits this year at different times, (it is fairly close to my home) and every time the bar management and staff have been more than helpful in indulging a ticker like myself. Charles, the landlord, is less enthusiastic about his pub being the home for footie fans, being blissfully unaware that it has been well known for years by the people who will buy this guide. He, like we, do not like that image.

Railway:

24 Station Rd Wheatley OX33 1ST
G Peter Lafford
F From 12
W www.railwaywheatley.co.uk
T 01865 874810
S Separate smoking areas

BWV 2.11.04 Fullers **London Pride**, ESB, Mr. Harry

The pub that meet the need for good food, a rural location and an easy back route to the ground that misses the main queues. My midweek visit was so good I returned later in the day, after visiting equally brilliant Oxford pubs in between. This pub is large yet intimate enough for good conversation. The railway theme prevails with platform signs and train pictures as well as garden furniture off the rails. and it will be especially good in summer where the garden comes into full use. The landlord also puts himself in the centre of the community with his involvement in local issues. All this and excellent Fullers, yes Ray, it was ESB as first choice. My new years resolution is to stop off here on the way home from a game. *Fullers Pub of the Year in 2003* it also has a late licence and has gained some popularity for the party and music scene that develops as the pub becomes popular beyond the village boundaries.

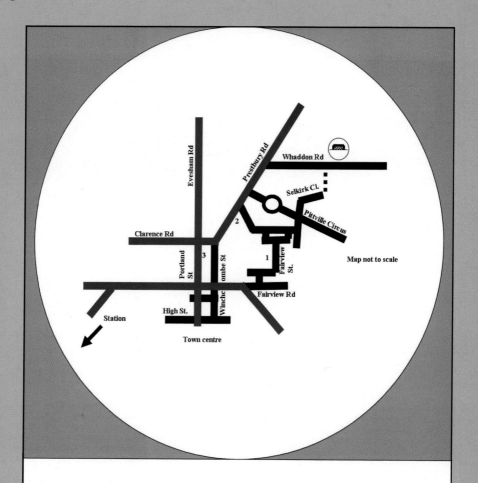

Cheltenham

Cheltenham pubs require a good map and plenty of discretion. From the remote station to the ground, parking is difficult but the hunt is well rewarded. The pubs included here are people friendly and avoid the anti-footie snobbery found in some other great town pubs.

1 Kemble Brewery Inn   2 Sudeley Inn Enterprise   3 Cotswold Wadworth

sp   tv   sp   tv   bm   pg   mp   tv   bm   pg

Column 1 — Kemble Brewery Inn

27 Fairview St. GL52 2JN
G Eileen Melia
F From 1.
T 01242 243446
S Smoking throughout

BWV 29.12.04 Wye Valley **Hereford,** Brakspear **O Be Joyful**, Smiles **Bristol IPA,** Whittington's **Cat's Whiskers,** Greene King **IPA,** Timothy Taylor **Landlord**

Kemble is a Gloucestershire village famous for plane spotting rather than the brewery that used to produce cider for the ex landlord. Very crowded on match days this is a traditional community pub that sets the standard for Cheltenham. Eileen, the landlady looks after regulars and new friends really well in a pub that *is like your grannies front room with piano and T.V. to boot.* The pub has a beer garden for summer games and always has two beers different to the high quality IPA and Timmy Taylors. *This pub always wins awards for being simply the best.* Every visit has found people newly discovering the Kemble and wondering why every back street pub near a ground can't be as good as this. The food is simple pub grub, the atmosphere is positively bubbly, the chances of getting a seat minimal unless you get there early. Never mind, stand by the piano and talk ale.

Column 2 — Sudeley Inn

25 Prestbury Rd GL52 2PN
G Gary Hyett
T 01242 510697
S Separate smoking areas

BWV 29.12.04 Timothy Taylor **Landlord,** Castle Eden **Ale,** Goff's **Jouster**

The Sudeley is the archetypal "potential" pub, the three rooms are off a central bar. Gary caters for a wide range of locals, workers and event visitors. He has created a sporting bias with local teams, pub games and a generally welcoming feel. *Look out for cider from the bin and the pub dog.* It deserves your custom because i*t is rare in Cheltenham to find a real pub with real values of good service* to the regulars and non locals alike. I really enjoyed going in the public bar of traditional design and atmosphere. The locals chat is often related to Horse racing rather than the Robins, well their league status is somewhat shorter than the festival. I can imagine this pub being very popular during the Cheltenham week so to when the pub gets its regulars into party mode. It is a short walk to the ground so I would park up near the ground and walk back for a long leisurely pint, with food taken from nearby chippies or at the ground. The welcome is good, the company just fine.

Column 3 — Cotswold

17 Portland St GL52 2NZ
G John and Clare Freeman
F From 12.30
T 01242 525510
S Smoking throughout
W www.pubs2000.com/cotswoldhotel_index.htm

BWV 29.12.04 Wadworth **6X, Old Timer, Henry's IPA**

This pub is on the up. One for the younger ale drinker it offers something very different to the traditional real ale house. *Good simple food in a grungy atmosphere or quality music in the cellar bar it is a refreshing change to the Cheltenham norm.* My visit included a tour of the downstairs bar where it isn't difficult to imagine the attraction of this place to those who like their music loud, live and lively. I was also tempted by the apparently well priced and good quality pub grub. As A Stinton of Cheltenham says *It is a friendly, open pub where you can always find a good atmosphere. Compared to the majority of the pubs in the town it certainly shines out as the most relaxed and enjoyable.* This was my experience as some pubs, that I will not name, not only declined to discuss the footie and real ale phenomena but were unusually arrogant in their opinion that they had no need to publicise their qualities. I will not then.

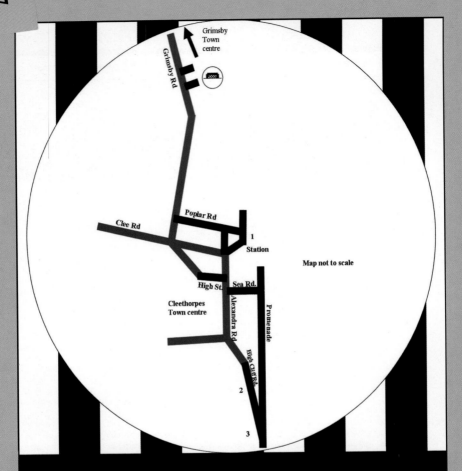

Grimsby

Cleethorpes has pushed its real ale to the sea front, and the southern end of it at that. Around the town the big pubs will cater for the indiscriminate so head for the station and pier and enjoy some quirky locations and styles.

1 No 1 Refreshment Room F **2 Smugglers Inn** Marstons **3 Willys Pub and Brewery**

mp tv bm pg d sp tv jb sp d

Station Approach DN35 8AX
G Colin Coleman
F From 12 to 3
T 01472 691707
S Smoking throughout

BWV 16.10.04 Everards **Tiger,** Highwood **Tom Woods, Bomber County, Tom Wood Dark Mild,** Bateman's **Combine Harvest**

This converted station waiting room usually serves six or seven real ales in an light spacious two room pub. It should not be confused though often is with the Number Two refreshment room further along the platform. You could always get double refreshment but I preferred the larger size of this version. The obvious railway theme is complemented by saucy postcards, pool table and views of the platform. The pub is a town locals pub whose landlord goes to great lengths to find variety in addition to the owners Highwood ales and the choice of beers usually includes a mild. My two visits on different days were equally pleasant especially the post match pint where a programme could be quietly read or conversation struck up with similar footie fans heading away from town or back to the seafront hotels. The lounge is rather more genteel than the larger public bar where the fun is to be found.

12-14 High Cliff Road DN35 8RQ
G Pat Hallam
F From 12 to 8.30
T 01472 200866
S Separate smoking areas

BWV 16.10.04 Marstons **Old Empire, Wicked Witch,** Banks' **Bitter, Bass,** Shepherd Neame **Bishops Finger,** Gales **Mild,** Courage **Directors,** Jennings **Cocker Hoop**

This is a large low ceilinged pub that is more spacious than immediately thought. You enter down some steps to find several wooden screened drinking areas off a central bar. It feels and looks a bit like a cellar bar but then metamorphosis's into a typical farmhouse style carpet and lounge pub. I visited both before and after the game and the staff certainly encourage football fans with TV's in every nook and cranny. All ages and types of pub users are catered for by careful subdivision into different drinking areas. So it was that a group of away fans took up a place in the central area before the game, no problems at all just good humour and even beers served with the sparkler removed for southern tastes. Post match it was the locals who reveled in a good win without any ritual humour, more an interest in the next beer to become available.

17 High Cliff Road DN 35 8RQ
G Bill Parkinson
F From 12 to 3
T 01472 602147
S Smoking throughout

BWV 16.10.04 Bateman's **XB,** Willys **Last Resort,** Cottage **Flying Duck,** Filstow **Objections**

Willy's has been a long standing favourite of mine and a visit to Cleethorpes isn't complete without a visit to the bar to see how the place keeps up its reputation for real ale innovation. White painted walls and tiled floors with industrial pipe work give this a café / brewery tap room feel. This is obviously enhanced by seeing the brewery in situ and knowing the ale is top dog while the restaurant is also important. *They also do reasonable value food, and you can see the brewery. The pub has won a string of local CAMRA awards, including pub of the decade!* Willy's is always busy with a varied clientele. On the lunchtime visit it drew people from miles away, after the match I encountered the early evening couples setting out for a night in town by visiting this ale house for some quality conversation over a beer. If on your first visit then brave the sea breezes to get here and talk of beer as much as life in this unique, trend modifying, pub.

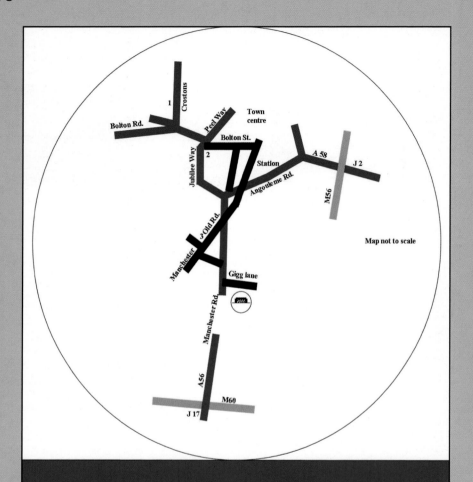

Bury

The Bury Social club and two nearby pubs absorb most who visit Gigg lane as away fans. In the town the locals have a choice of many micro's to choose from so my advice is park up and travel away into town getting a taxi from Dusty's to the game.

Bury

1 Dusty Miller Moorhouses **2 Trackside** Freehouse **3 Rose and Crown**

| sp | tv | bm | pg | | cp | | bm | | d | | sp | sk | bm | pg |

Dusty Miller

87 Crostons Rd BL8 1AL
G Graeme Jones
F From 12
T 0161 7641124
S Smoking throughout

BWV 16.12.04 Moorhouses **Reinbeers Revenge, Black Panther (Cat), Premium Bitter, Pendle Witches Brew**

Graeme has great plans for this Moorhouse tied pub. This two bar pub has extended to a covered outside area and increasingly needs more space as the locals learn of Graeme's quality ales. Here seasonals rotate around the regular bitter from Moorhouses. *Reward yourself and cross that busy road, the prices alone will make it worthwhile.* The pub has a good mix of bar and lounge style rooms, the clientele is also a good mix of real ale fans and lucky locals. The car parking issue is best solved by using the industrial estate on the road opposite. The best solution however is to park in town or near the Rose and Crown and make this part of a circular pub crawl. You will love the ales on offer here, the dark ales are particularly fine and a rare treat for this southern softie. I returned again later in the day to have a great time chatting with Graeme and the locals, the friendliness of the welcome lasting long on a very wet night.

Trackside

East Lancs. Railway Bolton St BL 9 0EY
G Chris Egan
F From 10
W www.elr.co.uk
T 0161 764 6461
S Smoking throughout

BWV 16.12.04 Northumberland **Cunning Cucumber, Santa Secret,** 3 Rivers **GMT,** York **Black Bess Stout**, Poachers **Shy Tack**, Castle Rock **Holly**, Poachers **Trembling Rabbit,** Thatchers **Cheddar Valley, Cider** Broadoak **Perry**

This station café has become a popular stop off for rail enthusiasts visiting the East Lancs. Steam Railway. Between December 2002 and Dec 2004 974 different ales have been sold, mostly at times when the ELR runs steam special events. *A haunt for local ale fans and families in the day. Check out the website to see if you can combine a stream train ride with a trip to Gigg Lane.* There are always loads of rarer ales on offer and I found on my early evening visited a very dedicated group of locals in earnest discussion with the landlady over the ales and their varying merits. This was a cue for a brewery delivery, lashings of rain and a kind lift to the next pub. Bury residents certainly gave me a fine welcome and kindness.

Rose and Crown

36 Manchester Old Rd BL9 0TR
G Ken Sumner
W www.theroseandcrownbury.co.uk
T 0161 7646234
S Smoking throughout

BWV 16.12.04 Caledonian **Deuchars IPA** Wadsworths **6X** Fullers **London Pride** Brains **Bitter** Greene King **Old Speckled Hen** Jennings **Cumberland Ale**

The lift found me at the best of a great threesome of pubs. You will not have tasted Deuchars as fine as here, and the locals drink masses of it. This pub has been internally reconstructed and the pubs renaissance continues at a pace due to Kens enthusiasm for quality and variety of ales. A really friendly place. *Look out for "Shakers Corner." They don't bite, but they do expect to have their space before a game.* The pub is a bit of a surprise being much larger than you originally think. Well furnished it also offers plenty of space for bar fly chat. Well over an hour was spent with Ken and a great hour it was. On my recent return visit my only disappointment was that my fellow away fans were so few I spent most of my time chatting with the locals, watching a lunchtime game and appearing to be "Billy no mates." I left, my mates arrived and a good time was had by all.

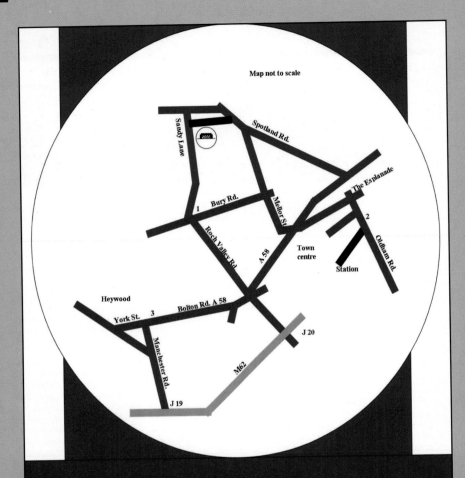

Map not to scale

Sandy Lane

Spotland Rd.

Bury Rd.

Mellor St.

The Esplanade

1

2

Roch Valley Rd.

A 58

Oldham Rd.

Town centre

Station

Heywood

York St.   3   Bolton Rd. A 58

Manchester Rd.

J 20

M62

J 19

Rochdale

There are pubs and a good supporters club near the ground but it would be criminal not to try out those suggested here. Rochdale also has others, like the Merry Monk and Last Orders, but my choice is based on the most recommendations.

1 Cemetery Hotel Punch	2 Wishing Well Freehouse	3 Cask and Feather

| sp | sk | | sp | tv | | pg | sp | tv | jb | pg | d |

---

470 Bury Rd OL11 5EU
G Mark Porter
F From 12 (Sandwiches)
T 01706 645635
S Separate smoking rooms

BWV 16.12.04 Black Sheep **Bitter**, Cottage **Merry Hound,** Adnams **Fisherman**, John Smiths **Cask**

You will find seven beers at the weekend in this classic quirky building. Mark has maintained this pubs excellent reputation for quality ale in comfortable surroundings I visited the Cemetery on Friday as well as on a match day and this pub always has the effect of making me doubt that I really want to go to the game. *Why not just stay here in the warm?* The company is great and there is something in the back of my mind that says "try another beer." *Then to top it all the post match drink coincided with the visit of a local brass band to set up a carol singing session.* Ah! How football used to be. I should have followed my instinct and stayed in the pub, yeh right. On my second visit of the year I was visiting another town but the pull of this pub is such that I was drawn again to the cosy warmth the pub and its locals give you. It wins my Divisional award being close to the ground, an uphill walk but meeting most other criteria that make a great pub.

---

89 York St Heywood OL10 4NN
G Michael Huck
T 01706 620923
S Smoking throughout

BWV 16.12.04 Moorhouses **Pride of Pendle,** Timothy Taylor **Landlord,** Phoenix **Wigwam, Arizona,** Black Sheep **Bitter,** Boddingtons **Cask,** Thwaites **Liberation**

The pub for those who do want to go into Rochdale / Bury / Manchester / Oldham etc. The locals support many sides and disappear at appropriate times only to return after the match. This pub is just brilliant, go on go there. It can get very crowded but an early lunchtime visit will be well rewarded. Stone plastered walls and beams are a surprise when you enter. Its look from the outside doesn't tell you how good it is inside. Chat to the cellarman, he is proud of the beer and will tell you about it. (That's Ron) Better still sample it and ask yourself how popular this place would be if it were located in a big city. But then it might lose some of its village local charm. The locals are truly local, the chat genuinely Lancastrian and the humour distinctively Northern. This Southerner was made to feel totally at ease as they purred with pride over this quality pub. Cheers chaps, see you again next year.

---

1 Oldham Rd OL10 4NN
G Tony Hutchinson
F From 11.30
T 01706 711476
S Smoking throughout

BWV 16.12.04 Mc Guinness **Best Bitter, Feather Pluckers Mild, Tommy Todds Porter, Bull Brow.**

The Cask and Feather is a large single bar pub between the station and town. It has an attractive no frills style, that both locals and visitors like. The real draw, however, is the McGuinness ale list and the friendly staff. They don't need other guest ales as the range meets most tastes. *The other great attraction is that the home brewed McGuiness comes at prices that we Southerners can only dream of.* My non match day visit found the bar staff willing to chat about the town and the real ale scene, some simple food to accompany a good pint that was new to my palate and on to the next pub. When returning with fellow fans the order of the day was to beat *Denis Law* at pool, not the real one of course, sample some different ales and then get a taxi out to the Cemetery. It has the advantage of being in town and close to the station with other good pubs nearby. The pub itself would be in my guide in any town, it is very good.

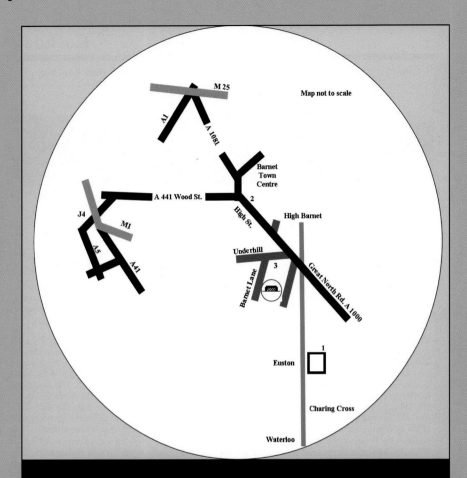

Barnet

Barnet are back in the league and for the moment still at Underhill. For the only time in any of the guides my recommendation for the town includes a pub that the police designate as away fans only. Do they know something about real ale in this part of the world that the rest of the country doesn't. As it is so handy for the motorways I have included just one central London pub. High Barnet is at the end of the Northern Line.

Barnet

1 Head of Steam F	2.Mitre Inn Spirit	3 Old Red Lion McMullens

mp sk	cp sk	cp tv bm pg d

1 Eversholt St, NW1 2 DN
G Dave O 'Sullivan
F From 12
T 020 73833359
S No smoking in upstairs area
W www.theheadofsteam.co.uk

BWV 6.12.04 Banks' **Original**, Dark Star **Porter, Special Edition,** Caledonian **Santa's Little Helper,** Black Sheep **Bitter**, Westons **Vintage Cider**

A station pub as they used to be? No, not cold and draughty, but with railway signs, carriage seating, friendly, helpful staff and a feeling that it's O.K. to miss the train, because who wants to rush anyway? The Head of Steam name is spreading but this version still leads the way in creating a real ale club virtually on the station concourse. There are usually up to nine ever changing real ales When planning my journeys home it has always been a place to factor in to travel times, i.e. wherever you are leave time for the HOS before getting the train from Euston. It has one large bar that is creatively split into separate areas and levels. The TVs are very discrete I particularly like to find space in what looks like a mini railway carriage complete with no smoking signs and, bench seats so close to each other you can read the paper of your fellow commuter.

58 High St. EN5 5SJ
G Paul Hodder
F Pub grub that includes 2 for £6.99 deals
T 020 8449 6532
S Separate smoking areas

BWV 17.5.05 Tetleys **Cask,** Adnams **Bitter, Broadside,** Oakham **Bishops Farewell**

Ye Olde Mitre Inn is the name on the wall and in a beautiful pub window. No surprises then that the pub is a traditional ale house but with a modern attitude to Sports, T.V. and quality beers. There are always two guest ales that rotate, often bringing weekend surprises to savour. It is heartening to hear that real ale outsells lager and to see the playoffs advertised as being on the big screen. The pub also has some character in the design being beamed and partitioned in solid wood. The pub extends backwards to the carpeted lounge and has tables in the car park for the busiest of days. It will be busy on lunchtimes with regulars who know the qualities of good ale and friendly conversation with away fans. On quieter days I would relax in the front bar where light streams into the cosier wooden floored bar. where the wall should perhaps proclaims *God bless the reader who comes to Barnet without drinking in the Mitre .*

Underhill, Great North Rd, EN5 2BB
G Michael Poumos
F Pies and sandwiches 12 - 3 on matchdays
T 020 84493735
S No smoking at the bar or in restaurant

BWV 17.5.05 Mc Mullens **A.K, Country Bitter**

McMullens pubs are either back street boozers or, as in this case, modern farmhouse style community locals. The pub has two separate bars, the smaller one with dart board being the evening snug and likely to be closed on match days. The larger lounge is separated to create a non smoking area. There has been a pub here since 1899 and the locals certainly have a great pub to call their local, Michael is Burnley fan and it was very pleasant to chat over our similar woes related to *where's the money gone?* The rest of my lunchtime visit involved amusing myself as a group of teachers came in to discuss their woes associated with 4B PHSE or the like. On match days there will not be any home fans, the pub becomes home from home to the travelling beer drinker It is a good choice for this, not least because the local ale will be something unusual for all but the those from Watford. .

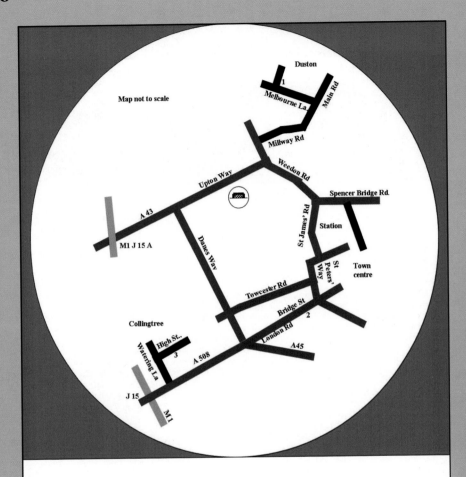

Northampton

Sixfields is over a mile from the town centre within a retail park. The Freehouse Hungry Horse caters for home fans, away fans will need to search further a field. I would seek out Frog Island beers in the town rather than endure the out of town experience

1 Melbourne Arms Enterprise
2 Malt Shovel Tavern F
3 Old Wooden Walls of England

cp tv bm pg   sp   sp tv   pg

Melbourne Lane, Duston NN5 6HS
G Ken Morris
F From 12 (Rolls etc)
T 01604 752837
S Smoking throughout

BWV 16.11.04 Courage **Directors**, **Best**, Fullers **London Pride**

There are three regular beers on offer in this village pub. It has the feel of a locals pub with pool table and sports team trophies. The low beams and stone walls help to give a warm feeling as does the chat with local fans. *Parking is an issue everywhere in Northampton so it might be a good idea to finish up here and walk down to the ground.* My visit found the regulars settling in for the afternoon T.V. racing session. A good hour later the numbers hadn't changed, neither had the number of winners, none. They told me the usual thing on a Saturday was to walk through the local estate to the ground thus avoiding the congestion of warehouse shoppers mixing in with the lack of traffic control at the ground. This is a typical Northamptonshire pub in a village that has managed to keep some of its identity as the town has grown around it. Ken was very tolerant of my intrusion to the normal lunchtime activities, cheers Ken.

121 Bridge St NN1 1QF
G Norman Tetzlaff - Murrell
F From 11.30
W maltsholveltavern.com
T 01604 234212
S Smoking throughout

BWV 16.11.04 Old Slug **Porter,** Tetley's **Bitter** Banks' **Bitter,** Frog Island **Natterjack,** Blindmans **Siberia,** Golden Hill, **Exmoor Wildcat,** Westcroft **Cider**

The Malt Shovel is more recommended by Rugby rather than footie fans. *If the Saints are at home it gets very crowded.* One would be led to think that they have this as a second home away from Franklin's Gardens. It is a large wood and brick one bar tavern with a widely known reputation for quality ales. The owners love of real ale comes through in the beer memorabilia. This is a rightly popular haunt for ale travelers, myself included, who have often caught the train to Northampton with this pub as the Holy Grail. *You even get a "scratch and sniff" experience from the brewery opposite.* It was East Midlands Pub of the year 2004, has regular blues nights and something I recall with affection, it offers Gales Country wines for a different experience. You will be made welcome, no doubt you have been here before.

25 High St CollingtreeNN4 0NE
G Louise Thompson
F From 12
T 01604 764082
S Smoking throughout

BWV 16.11.04 Marstons **Pedigree,** Hook Norton **Old Hooky,** Camerons **Strong Arm,** Banks' **Bitter**

This pub is also a long standing destination of our Milton Keynes based real ale researches. Our charabanc trips would arrive here early doors as it always had a good welcome. Nothing has changed even though the Guv'nors may have. *Two small bars make for a real Northamptonshire village pub just off J15 of the M1.* Cosy and warm, one area is set aside for food but the ever changing guest beers attract real ale fans as well as foodies. Beer mats adorn the beams of this classic village pub. The pub name conjures up images of bygone strengths and long may the traditional ales be served by Louise in this great pub. My early morning visit found fires being stoked for the regular lunchtime trade. Many visitors to the town do not know of Collingtree, hidden by brash golf courses and hotels. If you don't fancy the hassle of a stroll around the town centre then this country pub is a real alternative here

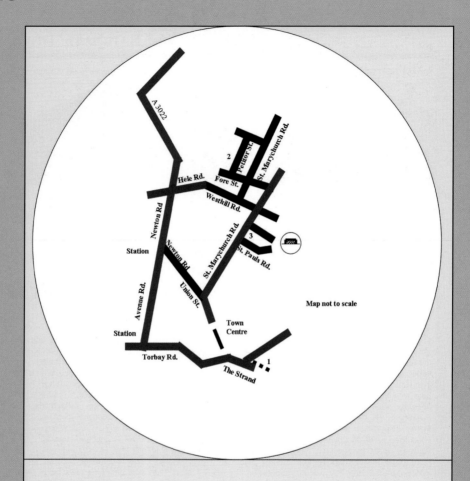

Torquay

Torquay is just about keeping hold of some real ale culture. The town centre does have some good pubs and near the ground the suburbs of St. Marychurch and Babbacombe will be interesting to those who like to find a pub after a walk. The town is my favourite weekend seaside break town because it offers a bit of everything and this includes its pubs.

Torquay

1 Hole in the Wall Unique 2 Crown and Sceptre Ent 3 Union Courage

mp tv bm	sp tv	sp tv jb pg

6 Park Lane, TQ1 5AU
G David Jones
F From 12
T 01803 298020
S Smoking throughout

2 Pettitor Rd, TQ1 4QA
G Roy Wheeler
F From 12
T 01803 328290
S Separate smoking areas

127 St. Marychurch Rd, TQ1 3HW
G Geoff and Sue Brett
F Home cooked bar snacks
T 01803 328290
S One non smoking bar

BWV 10.2.05, Sharps **Doom Bar**, Shepherd Neame **Spitfire,** Charles Wells **Bombardier,** Greene King **IPA, Abbot,** Courage **Best.**

This is the quintessential back alley nook and cranny pub and wonderfully popular without being too touristy. It is reputedly Torquays oldest pub (16th Century) it has pebbled floors, dark paneled walls yet modern attitudes to food and beer, all making it a great pub for a wide range of customers. My visit was good as the locals soon welcomed me into their conversation of Torquay life and beer appreciation. It is *a place that when you find it you resolve to visit again the next day, you get a perfect welcome and good food as well as ale.* I also enjoyed the obvious setting of standards with the *mind your language* notice, quite right too. This is really the only *must not miss* real ale pub in Torquay town centre. Torquay may have been relegated but at least it opens up the possibility of more glorious away day weekends for me and my new found mates on the Riviera, the HITW being a focal point.

BWV 10.2.05 Greene King **Old Speckled Hen**, **Abbot**, Courage **Best,** Theakstons **Old Peculier,** Youngs **Special,** Courage **Directors, Macotten.**

It was very rare on my travels to find a pub quite so welcoming and easy going. As *Roger O'Gorman* says it is due to *the landlord and the people and also the beer is fantastic.* Home of the Torquay Folk Club this village street local comes highly recommended by fans and ale heads from near and far. Stone walls, open fires, great pub banter of which the boss, Roy is often the butt of the joke. But beware, he gives as good as he gets. *He looks like Ken Bates and scares people like Alex Ferguson (Gareth of Torquay). He has mellowed since 1983.* Some locals are quite glad that *away supporters can't find it (Ian Bradbury)* and who can blame them, this pub is excellent, homely and well worth of being protected. And then there is the great choice of national ales with strengths that cover the full range. Top pub, top guvnor, top locals, a top time was had on my longer than expected visit.

BWV 10.2.05 Courage **Best,**

What only one real ale? Yep but good Courage Best, really, honest. This is a great old fashioned honest pub with easy access to local food and the ground around the corner. Courage Best takes me back to my very early drinking days and Geoff would have been well in the know about what makes it good to serve at times. There are occasional guests but my visit was great because the place was buzzing on a wet Thursday night as the lounge became a skittles alley. The bar is draped with away team pennants, Geoff is a true loyal fan of his club (*Simply the best*, not Torquay) and welcomes all in the true spirit of footie. He talks with pride of the Torquay players, past and present who have used the pub and has equal fondness of the visiting away fans who know how to behave when a guest in someone else's local. It is a great find being literally at the end of the street to the ground but in true visitor style don't expect the local police to let you get in their for a quickie just before the match. It is a really friendly place.

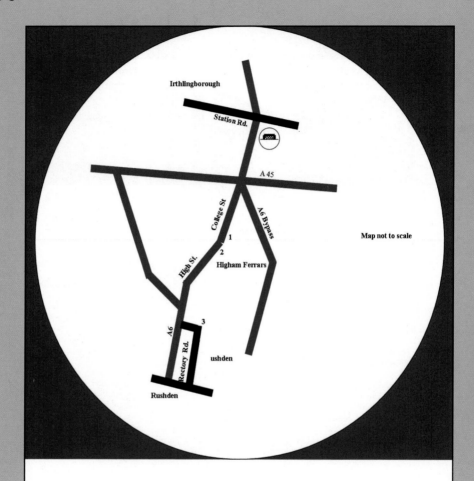

Rushden

The police will herd fans to the village of Irthlingborough. Escape if you can and head to Higham Ferrars or Rushden town centre where there are three gems. There is no station so wherever you go and the distances will be longer than normal, but worth it.

Rushden

1 Green Dragon Freehouse 2 The Griffin Freehouse 4 Rushden Historical Transport Society

cp   tv   bm   pg   d   sp   d   sp   d

4 College St Higham Ferrars
G Joy Ormond
F Snacks from 12 to 2
T 01933 312088
S Smoking throughout

BWV 10.10.2004 Greene King **Abbot, IPA, Old Speckled Hen,** Young's **Special**, Ridleys **Witchfinder,** Westons **Cider,** Westons **Old Rosie**

This is an old coach house with stone walls, beams and wooden floors, a quiet country pub in the High Street next to the town church. It does attract all ages, yet has no juke box or obvious attractions to "yoof" culture. It is also a venue for live music, quite a mix for a village pub. Given that Irthlingborough is rather desperately short of real ale and that the ground is in the middle of open fields Higham Ferrars becomes the nearest choice of town with some selection nearby. *This is a hotel so I might use it for an evening match, especially as there is no railway station.* My lunchtime visit found the Sunday lunchtime regulars arriving with tales of local events the night before to share, it appears the Green Dragon is the centre of village gossip, as a good pub should be. The beers rotate on a regular basis so the casual visitor gets a choice of national and regional ales.

High St Higham Ferrars
G Ray and Lynn Gilbert
F Restaurant
T 01933 312612
S Separate smoking areas

BWV 10.10.2004 Greene King **Abbot**, Everards **Tiger**, Adnams **Broadside**

Ray and Lynn have a stone walled gem furnished with plush leather seating arranged in rooms off a central bar. The relaxed atmosphere of a good restaurant is achieved without the loss of being a real pub. *Most fans will probably not have the time to give the restaurant its true worth.* It has a reputation with plaudits such as *the best place to eat in the county.* This is not a pub for large groups as it will be busy with foodies and there isn't masses of standing room. It is, however a pub that you will remember for it's of hospitality. Ray is quick to make you welcome as a valued guest and selects his ale with the beer drinker in mind, i.e. having a range of strengths.. This is the ultimate take your Mother in Law pub, you would be able to make a good impression and get top quality food at the same time while you indulged in quality ale not from the immediate local area. You also have the Green Dragon next door should she want another beer!

Station Approach Rushden
NN10 0AW
G T' committee
W www.rhts.co.uk
T 01933 318988
S Smoking on platform

BWV 10.10.2004 Fullers **London Pride**, Archers **Village**, Newby Wyke **Summer Session,** Wye Valley **Autumn Delight,** Church End **IPA**, Springhead **Roaring Meg.**

Many away fans arrive in Rushden town, drive the inner ring roads and leave most disappointed at the lack of real ale. All is not lost, let the masses go, keep it quiet and ask for the old station. A long time favourite of mine, this is a barely converted platform waiting room, gas lit, with a real fire and home of active rail historians and renovators. *I am not into railways but this is heavenly.* You will though have a very long wait for a train. Enjoy the warmth in the cosy bar, they will ask for an entry fee as it is a members club, but you won't want to leave. It was CAMRA joint winner of club of the year 2000 and East Midlands winner 2002 *"Our commitment to real ale and our determination to provide a wide range of beers in tip top condition have made the club a huge success. We're very proud of what we've done at Rushden." Simon Bishop*

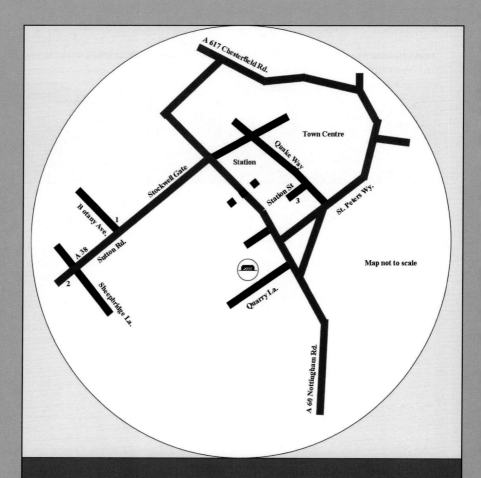

Mansfield

There are many pubs offering keg versions of what were, local ales and classic real ale places are quickly finding themselves to be the exception to this towns norm. You will need to allow time to walk to the ground if you want the best. Nothing is munch of a hurry here, including the train from Nottingham, the timetable being as erratic as the real ale scene.

Mansfield

1 Bold Forester Greene King   2 Nell Gwyn Freehouse   3 Railway Inn Batemans

cp   sk   bm   pg   d   sp   mp   tv   bm   pg   d

1 Bold Forester

Botany Avenue, NG18 5NF
G Neal Earl
F From 12
T 01623 623970
S Separate smoking areas

BWV 24.3.05 Greene King **Abbot, IPA, Old Speckled Hen**, Castle Eden **Ale**, Boddingtons **Bitter**, Gales **Frostie**, Robinsons **England's Champion, Bass**, Brakspear **Ploughman's**, Skinners **Best**, Harviestoun **Belgian White**.

This is a large modern purpose built roadside pub with it's own car park on the main drag into town from the west. It may well be the future of Greene King new builds and the beauty of the pub is found in the choice of ales and the attempt, rather successful, to make it into a real pub rather than an eatery. I does this through good decoration, lots of separate rooms off the large main bar and staff and cellarman who know what makes a good ale. There are usually half a dozen guest ales on top to the Greene King staples, this in itself being unusual in similar pubs in the G.K. homeland. The pub has a small area set aside for pool and the TV's are not intrusive. All in all it is a good compromise on trends for families and the serious real ale drinker. In Mansfield folklore it is <u>the</u> place for real ale.

2 Nell Gwyn

117 Sutton Rd, NG18 5EX
G Gordon Berry
F Sat Rolls from 12
T 01623 659850
S Smoking throughout

BWV 24.3.05 Sarah Hughes **Surprise**, Timothy Taylor **Landlord**.

In contrast to the pub on the other side of the road the Nell Gwyn offers Shangri-la to locals and visitors alike. The pub looks and feels like an Edwardian three bed semi detached house. It is homely to the extreme, On entering at the Seven o'clock opening time I was immediately made to feel like a long lost relative. The locals are the definition of locals. Regular beers were ordered, old conversations struck up and the place got into a routine of gentle banter and genuine warm friendship. The pub is comfortable enough to have professional women arrive unaccompanied and join in the fun without any macho hassle. There are no regular ales, just two continually changing pumps. Having walked the hilly streets of Mansfield searching for these entries I had certainly "Dunroamin" and with great reluctance I made my farewells and resolved to return again soon. This is a top notch friendly pub I would love to be able to call it home.

3 Railway Inn

9 Station St, NG18 1EF
G Pearl Hughes
F Good traditional pub grub from 11.
T 01623 623086
S Non smoking room for eating, the rest is smoking.

BWV 24.3.05 Batemans **XB, Hooker, Spring Breeze**.

Conveniently located between the station and the town centre the Railway offers the best outlet for real ale in town. They describe themselves as *a homely little boozer serving good ale and food (B Harrison, Mansfield)* The pub has three separate rooms, the smallest near the door set aside as no smoking. I preferred to settle nearer the bar where benches around the wall make for good conversation. What stands out on my visit to Batemans pubs is the obvious commitment to the community functions of the town local. As Pete Kowalenko says it is a *good, not spoilt, old fashioned pub*. It is somewhat ironic, therefore, that the pub is under threat of redevelopment into office space. This must not happen, Mansfield has precious few good pubs let alone real ale houses. Make an effort on your way to the ground and help to ensure the Railway continues to offer a quality service to the locals of Mansfield.

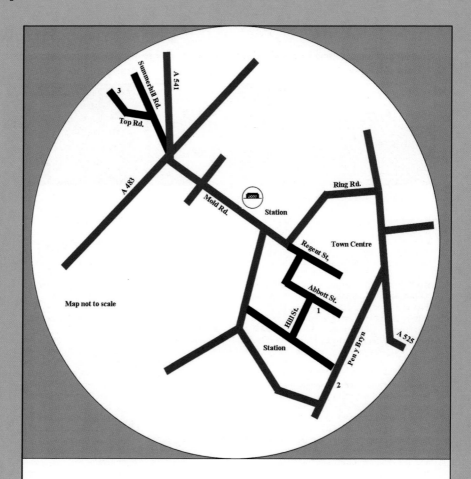

Wrexham

Wrexham's was once one of my favourite beer and footie towns but with every visit the choice has shrunk, so much so that even the once proud Turf, underneath the main stand, is now smooth flow and lager only. I would be sorely tempted to stop off in Chester or Shrewsbury en route. The pubs here are good but the town itself is ripe for an enterprising investor to show the light.

1 Old Swan Brewery Hydes   2 Albion Vaults Hotel   3 Crown, Summerhill Hydes

sp	bm	sp	tv	bm	pg	cp	tv	pg

6 Abbott St. LL11 1TA
G Dave Salisbury
F From 12
T 01978 313139
S Smoking throughout

BWV 27.2.05 Hydes **Bitter,** Old Swan **Brewery Ale.**

This newly acquired Hydes pub is something of a find that will get better over time. It is a long narrow coach house style bar with small corners hidden away from the main standing area. Each is comfortably arranged with sofas and a few tables which all suggests the expectation is for large numbers of evening standing drinkers. It would make a great pub for the start of a crawl around town. It has a certain appeal for the middle aged trendy drinker but has some memory jerkers, like my Welsh Grannies' sideboard as a bar counter and the books piled under the sofa legs. It has Good beer and is a pleasant place to meet good friends making this a good place for Wrexham town centre. Real ale is becoming scarcer here and what remains is often lost to other priorities such as food and / or tourist attraction. My visit was good for a quiet pint, I expect it will be far busier on a match day. I suspect its true value will be on those long hot summer evenings when the outside courtyard is in use.

1 Pen-y-Bryn, LL13 7HU
G Caroline Jones
T 01978 364969
S Smoking throughout

BWV 27.2.05 Lees **Bitter.**

This is a lively, friendly party pub with a landlady's son who is Footie mad. It is not necessarily a youngsters place, the party being related to the traditional themes, St. Patrick's / David's Day etc. Consisting of two large rooms, one with pool and darts, the other the more traditional lounge, making this hotel bar a real pub in the old school style. Because it is a commercial hotel the welcome is good for those less familiar to the locals and the customers are guaranteed to include non locals. It will be busy on matchdays with the locals and CAMRA folk heading off to the Racecourse after a bit of friendly banter. I would consider making the hotel a cheap place to stay if travelling long distances. As it lies just outside the town centre it is easily accessible yet quieter than a High Street location. The perfect footie day sometimes involves a group of lads getting into some serious pool or darts as part of the lunchtime session. The Albion fits the bill. On a normal weekend it will also offer a wider range of Lees ales than on my midweek visit.

Top Rd,, Summerhill. LL11 4SR
G Noel Croot
T 01978 755788
F Hot bar snacks
S Smoking throughout

BWV 27.2.05 Hydes **Bitter,**

I would love to see this pub on a hot summer day. Located a towns length in the opposite direction to town from the ground it is a village pub with an urban feel. My visit found three very distinctive areas, all to enjoy. One bar had the more mature regulars in full flow, continuing the sort of conversations that last for days. The second bar had youngsters playing pool, the third is apparently the evening room, i.e. a lounge more popular at night. What the pub and the garden share is great views across the valley and the many villages within it. *A great village local where you just know you would find someone as a good drinking companion. This would include taking in the regular Hydes Craft beers found here.* It also includes a massive number of guest ales served over the years. As with the other pubs in this section, the number of ales increases at the weekend and includes seasonal ales from national brewers. I will return in the summer and enjoy the garden perhaps before or after a long walk.

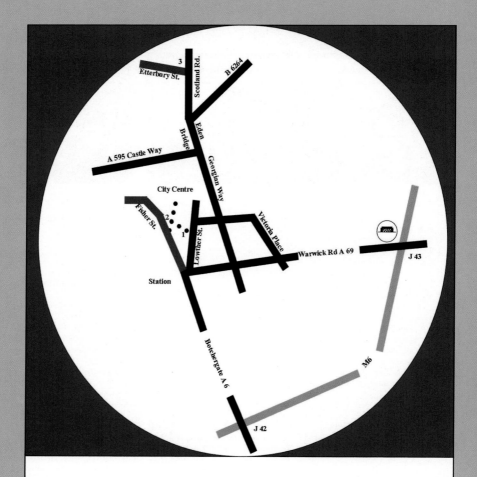

Carlisle

The floods of the conference year have had a long lasting effect. The favourite of mine is the Carlisle Rugby Club yet alas it was still yet to reopen. So this guide selects from the very few alternatives in the City. You have choice of historic, sports mad or aspirational in this guide. Given the distances involved this is very much a train or weekend destination.

Carlisle

1 Howard Arms Avebury   2 Kings Head S + N   3 The Crown Spirit

mp   sk   jb   d   mp   tv   jb   pg   mp   tv   jb   pg   d

107 Lowther St CA3 8ED
G Harry Ross
F Bar lunches 12 - 2
T 01228 532926
S No smoking at the bar

BWV 18.5 05 Theakstons **Best, XB**

Graham, Lawrence and Ian, doing the whistle stop tour from Newcastle pointed me in the direction of this pub from the Cumberland Arms. It has connections with long gone theatre opposite and by a quirk of fate the unearthed ornate tiled frontage now helps to guarantee its historical importance. As a real ale pub Harry runs a rarity, a great town centre pub with character, and a locals boozer The pub started with, and keeps, its original cosiness. The extensions to the rear have only created more small rooms and an outside patio equally compact in size. The locals were fantastic, old boys talked of the season to come, walkers staggering in off Hadrian's wall to sup thirst quenching ale, even a ladies circle could be heard discussing which pub to meet in next week. It was busy on my lunchtime visit and very friendly. It is Harry's 21st birthday as landlord here and the pub is obviously well loved. It appeared to be very much a gentlepersons club, refined, yet a place to enjoy.

Fisher St. CA3 8RF
G Mike Vose
F Traditional pub food from 12
T 01228 533797
S Separate non smoking areas

BWV 18.5.05 Yates **Bitter,** The Old Mill **Bullion**

Mike is a Cumbrian Gooner who has a passion for liberating the locals from smooth land to real ale. As such the Kings Head is the only pub in the town centre to offer genuine local ales, i.e. Yates, and a guest that is ever changing. The Kings Head is smack bang in tourist and shopper land yet has a real locals following. The regulars were gathered around the bar talking of last weekends triumphs in Stoke, often bemoaning the lack of quality real ale there. The pub is a carpeted, timber roofed tavern that extends deep to the rear where the best sitting and chatting space is found.. And so it was that I found my final pub of the year, several weeks later than planned. Matt and the locals were great company, as is the case whenever you come in this pub. They shared tales of away fans and pubs in the Conference and dreams of beer hunting this season, good times!. The renaissance of Carlisle town centre real ale, I predict, will start here. As it grows give Mike your support, you know it makes sense.

23 Scotland Rd, Stanwix CA3 9HS
G Paul White
F Good value meals and sandwiches from 12
T 01228 512789
S Separate smoking areas and no smoking at the bar.

BWV 18.5 05 Theakstons **Best,** Wadworth **Summersault**

The Crown is a large street corner pub on the way north out of the town. It is a good local that supports a pub team. Not loads of real ale but enough to subtly point them away from the smooth stuff. Paul is a Carlisle season ticket holder and appreciates that the locals like their sport. The T.V. screen was tuned to afternoon racing, I left as the pub favourite missed out on a punters reward. It is 75% non smoking, yet large enough for those who wished to play pool, drink ale and do normal pubby activities. Designed in the wood panelled library style it suits the younger as well as more mature, drinker, so too the those seeking food. Apparently the local CAMRA crew have been sighted and one would think it would make a good addition to their guide. A taxi or 15 minute walk from the ground and town, the Crown offers an alternative to suit both ale heads and your mate who hasn't yet seen the light.

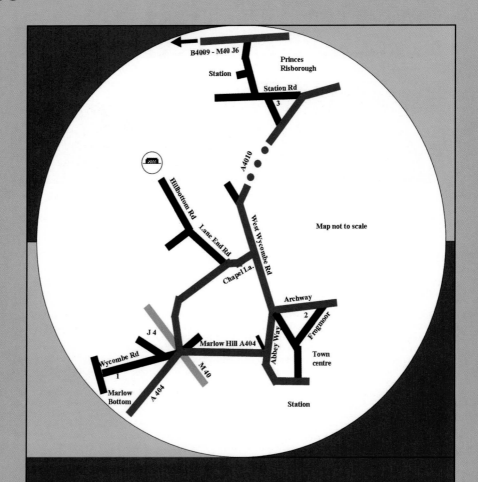

High Wycombe

The Causeway is miles from anywhere let alone the nearest pub. The area is also notable for superb village ale houses and High Wycombe doesn't really try to compete. The Bell in Town is the exception and the Horseshoes sets a high country standard.

1 Three Horseshoes Fr

cp   bm

Burroughs Grove Hill, Marlow Bottom SL7 3RA
G Nigel Douglas
F Extensive lunch and evening menu's from 12
T 01628 483109
S Unknown

BWV 2.11.04 Rebellion **Mutiny, Storm, Smuggler, IPA, Mild .**

The Three Horseshoes is a great pub which is quickly building a reputation for top quality food and ale (both locally produced). It has a brick and beam theme to complement a flagstone floor and fire making this large pub more welcoming. It is what many imagine a Wycombe pub should be like, if only! Denise of Marlow says its great *because the Rebellion brewery is only 500 yards down the hill* and the choice is fantastic (*real ale for every occasion (MRJ of High Wycombe))* Six of their beers are always available. *If playing in Wycombe and the weather is warm then I would live in this pub garden.* In winter this is the place to graze and chill out before negotiating the Causeway traffic. This pub has recently won the local CAMRA award for best pub and this is quite an achievement given the quality of rural competition in the surrounding Chiltern villages. Get there early!

2 Bell Fullers

cp   bm

Frogmoor, High Wycombe HP13 5DQ
G Ben Bloor
F From 12
T 01494 452733
S Separate smoking areas

BWV 2.11.04 Fullers **London Pride**

Low wooden ceilings, walls and floors, along with comfortable seating are found in this refurbished town centre pub. It is a haven of spotless tranquility among the nearby chain pubs. Expect the chat to be of Wasps as well as Chairboys. *A great place to go for a beer - easily my favourite pub in Wycombe.* The town centre is probably the biggest disappointment in this guide. The Bell is, however, a pub that would be of merit in any town and should not be compared with its near neighbours. I spent a very pleasant hour or so chatting with the manager and locals about the demise of what once was a great town for local ales. They reassured me that all is not lost and on match days you will be made welcome as you make the journey from station to the taxi ranks needed to get to the ground., If coming by car use the Sainsbury's car park nearby rather than squeeze into the few pub spaces. It does of course have wonderful Fullers ales, consistently well served.

3 Bird in Hand Greene King-

sp tv bm pg d

Station Rd Princes Risborough
G New landlord arriving soon
F A variety of pub grub and pizzas from 12
T 01844 345602
S Smoking throughout

BWV 2.11.04 Greene King **IPA, Abbot Ale, 1799**

This is a small and friendly one bar pub. The chat here is never ending with a strong sports leaning, rugby leading the way on Saturdays. The quality of the beer sets it apart from the rest. On sunny days use the garden perhaps counting the garden gnomes and recognizing the local characters. In mid winter watch the locals playing darts, cribbage or just giving Colin a hard time. *You might even get to meet the author of this guide relaxing after a day of real ale hunting.* Of course you will but not on a match day as I will be researching for next years guides. The location makes it easy to get to the ground, a ten minute drive away My visit is given here but it is my local and as such you can probably guess why I like it so much. Good friends, plenty of things going on, bar staff who know you and make new time visitors welcome, good consistent ale, and good craic are the hallmarks of pubs I hope are found throughout this guide.

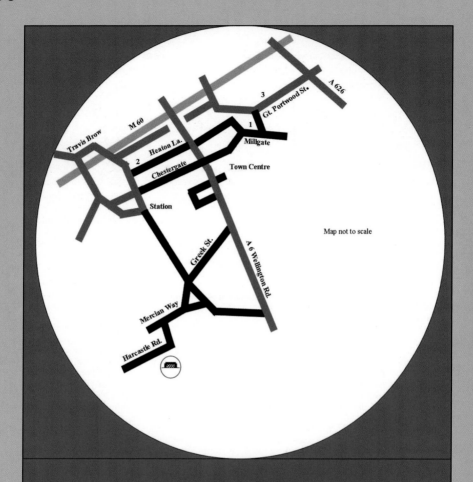

Stockport

Stockport is the real ale capital of the Greater Manchester area. From nationally known pubs to small back street locals there is variety enough to suit all demands. Some do not open during the day so my trip picks out three in walking distance of the station. Don't forget there are many others here but these are ones that should not be missed. The best bet is to come back year after year, book it into your ale hunting diaries.

Stockport

1 Arden Arms Robinsons

sp   tv   bm   pg   d

23 Millgate SK1 2LX
G Joe Quinn and Steve King
F High quality pub lunches from 12
S One no smoking snug room.
T 0161 480 2185

BWV 11.3.05 Robinsons **Unicorn, Hatters Mild, Double Hop, Enigma.**

The Arden Arms was runner up in the CAMRA national pub of the year. This is a place of real ale and good pub dreams. Joe and Steve have created an ambience that is popular to all ages and as importantly both sexes. Rarely do pubs in this guide find young women chatting in comfort over a pint as parents talk of the important facts of life, i.e. the merits of Robinsons seasonal ales. Everything in the Arden says understated class. The freshly cooked food trade, dominates lunchtime activity while in the evenings it is real ale fans from a wide area. There are several different snugs each with a distinctive feel. The Millgate room, for example, has chandeliers and a large mirror to complement the art work on the walls. Non smokers get the privilege of walking through the bar to a leather furnished snug / office. I would walk miles to this pub, next summer I will return to sample the summer brew in the courtyard.

2 Crown Inn Portfolio

sp   tv

154 Heaton La. SK4 1AR
G Jeanette Mascord
S Separate smoking areas
T 0161 4290459

BWV 11.3.05 Pictish **Mild, Porter,** E + S **Shot in the Dark,** Bank Top **Volunteer,** Port O'Call, Crown Inn **Best,** Ramsbottom **Provident, Tomfoolery,** Storm **Silk of Amnesia,** Wilkins **Dry Cider, Black Sheep Best,** Phoenix **White Monk.**

This pub predates the arches under whose shadow it falls (1745 V 1875). It is a gem of a pub with an atmosphere of gentle good craic. It has several small parlours, one of which is designated as non smoking. There was a great temptation to attempt to become a member of the Gallon club achievable with a different beer each time. Those who do (Sampling 8 ales over 4%) are entered on to the roll of honour. More curious was the Knitting pattern challenge: next time perhaps. More traditional pastimes might include a game of guess the tipple played as the many newcomers sample the first ale from the impressive list of regional independent breweries. A great pub that will be revisited by most who find it for the first time. When I go again I will make sure I have enough time and a place to stay nearby so the beer list gets due justice.

3 Railway Porters

sp   pg

Avenue St, SK1 2BZ
G David Porter
F Quality pub grub (Real chips)
S Smoking throughout
T 0161 4296062

BWV 11.3.05 Slaters **Premium,** Skipton **Copper Dragon Black Gold,** Blackpool and Barnsley **March Hare,** Porters **Bitter, Dark Mild, Rossendale Ale, Railway Sleeper, Floral Dance.**

I chose a great time to visit this quality ale house. The Friday guests were available and the range of Porter brews was in its full glory. Understandably, the pub was very busy. It was early Friday evening, the average age was particularly younger than most houses of this type and the young were setting into the real stuff with encouraging relish. There is an impressive list of European beers on the boards but the local ales certainly held their own. The place had a delightful mix of people; posties enjoying a jar on their way home from work; courting couples and regulars who talked beer, footie and all things blokey. The occasional real ale ticker came, sampled a few and moved on, down the line that is. All of this and a bubbly murmur that one finds in top ale houses. It is a pub that is very difficult to leave, the same can be said for Stockport as a whole.

Fancy writing for a Stedders Guide?
Or
Writing descriptions of real ale pubs?
Maybe
Getting paid for visiting pubs and talking real ale?
Does this
Sound too good to be true?

There are several ways that you can be involved in Stedders Guides.

Yes you can;-

- Complete a card in a pub to comment on a pub, 400 people did so for this years guides.
- Contribute by commenting on www.footballandrealaleguide.co.uk
- Email me at Richard@footballandrealaleguide.co.uk

But

The real fun is to be paid to join the team.

So

I am looking to create a small team of part time contributors for the football and real ale guide 2006 -07 and in the future similar guides for Rugby / Cricket and Real ale guides in the Stedders Guide format.

You must be:-

- a real ale fan
- have knowledge of the needs of away fans when they visit a new town.
- able and willing to travel independently to parts of the country at times other than when following football to chat to landlords and local people.
- have good I.T. skills and be contactable via email and telephone.
- able to work to strict deadlines.
- willing to share the fun of footie and real ale in you writing and conversation.

If this is you and you can organise your other commitments to get involved then why not apply for a job working with me on next years guides.

Any post will be on a part time basis and will include either expenses or a bursary related to the number of entries and sales of future guides.

The posts would suit someone who has the time to work outside of their full time occupation.

OR

Perhaps you are seeking a change in life direction that involves having time to manage your own work /leisure time.

IN OCTOBER 2005 I WILL BE ADVERTISING FOR TEAM MEMBERS

Application forms will be available from September 2005.

GET IN EARLY,

CONTACT ME TO DISCUSS THE JOBS AND POSSIBLE RENUMERATION at

r.stedman1@btinternet.com

or

01844 343931

It takes all sorts to campaign for real ale

Join **CAMRA Today...**

Just fill in the form below and send, with a cheque (payable to CAMRA ltd) or for Three Months Free membership (for those renewing or joining by Direct Debit) complete the Direct Debit Form. All forms should be addressed to membership secretary, CAMRA, 230 Hatfield Road, St Albans, Herts, AL1 4LW. Alternatively you can join online at www.camra.org.uk. Rates for single membership are £18 and joint £21. Concession rates are available on request.

Title   Surname   Forename(s)   Date of Birth

P'tner Surname   Forename(s)   Date of Birth

Address   Postcode

Tel. no.(s)

I wish to join the Campaign for Real Ale, and agree to abide by the Memorandum and Articles of Association.

I enclose a cheque for........... Signed.. Date ....

Applications will be processed within 21 days